Robert Goddard was bo[...] History at Cambridge. Hi[...] was an instant bestseller. Since then his books have captivated readers worldwide with their edge-of-the-seat pace and their labyrinthine plotting. The first Harry Barnett novel, *Into the Blue*, was winner of the first WHSmith Thumping Good Read Award and was dramatized for TV, starring John Thaw. His thriller *Long Time Coming* won an Edgar in the Mystery Writers of America awards. *The Ways of the World* is the first part in Robert Goddard's extraordinary *The Wide World* trilogy set in the years after the First World War and featuring James 'Max' Maxted.

To discover more about Robert and his books, visit his website at www.robertgoddardbooks.co.uk and join the conversation at RobertGoddardBooks.

www.**transworldbooks**.co.uk

ROBERT GODDARD

WHERE WILL HE TAKE YOU NEXT?

1720

SEA CHANGE What are the contents of a mysterious package that could spark a revolution in England?

1880

PAINTING THE DARKNESS
The arrival in London of a stranger claiming to be a man long thought dead uncovers dark family secrets.

1910

PAST CARING Why did cabinet minister Edwin Strafford resign at the height of his career and retreat into obscurity on the island of Madeira?

IN PALE BATTALIONS Loss, greed and deception during the First World War – and a murder left unsolved for more than half a century.

TAKE NO FAREWELL A murder trial forces Geoffrey Staddon to return to the Herefordshire country house that launched his architectural career – and to the dark secret it holds.

1920

1930

CLOSED CIRCLE On board a grand cruise liner, a pair of chancers are plunged deep into a dark conspiracy.

1960

DYING TO TELL What happened in Somerset in the summer of 1963 that holds the key to a devastating secret?

FAULT LINE A father dead in his fume-filled car. His young son alive in the boot. Not your average suicide . . .

1970

LONG TIME COMING For thirty-six years they thought he was dead. They were wrong.

1980

INTO THE BLUE   When a guest goes missing from his friend's villa on the island of Rhodes, Harry Barnett becomes prime suspect and must find her if he is to prove himself innocent.

HAND IN GLOVE   What long-buried secret connects the murder of a dead poet's elderly sister with the Spanish Civil War?

BEYOND RECALL   Dark family secrets are unlocked when a man seeks the truth behind the suicide in Truro of a childhood friend.

SIGHT UNSEEN   A trail of dangerous deceits connects eighteenth century political writer Junius with the abduction of a child at Avebury more than two hundred years later.

1990

BORROWED TIME   A chance meeting. A brutal murder. How far will one man go to gain justice?

OUT OF THE SUN   Harry Barnett must unravel a web of conspiracies if he is to save the son he never knew he had.

CAUGHT IN THE LIGHT
A photographer is drawn into a complex web of deception and revenge following an encounter with a beautiful woman in Vienna.

SET IN STONE   A house steeped in a history of murder and treason exerts an eerie and potentially fatal influence over its present inhabitants.

DAYS WITHOUT NUMBER Five Cornish siblings are dragged into a deadly conflict with an unseen enemy as they confront their family's mysterious past.

PLAY TO THE END   An estranged husband becomes caught up in a dangerous tangle of family rivalries and murderous intentions while appearing in a play in Brighton.

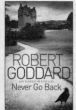

NEVER GO BACK   A group of ex-RAF comrades, Harry Barnett among them, uncover an extraordinary secret during a reunion in Scotland, which puts them all in mortal danger.

NAME TO A FACE   When an ancient ring is stolen in Penzance, a centuries old mystery begins to unravel.

FOUND WANTING   What connects a dying man's grandfather with the tragic fate of the Russian Royal Family, murdered ninety years earlier?

BLOOD COUNT   There's no such thing as easy money, as surgeon Edward Hammond is about to find out.

THE WAYS OF THE WORLD

Robert Goddard

CORGI BOOKS

TRANSWORLD PUBLISHERS
61–63 Uxbridge Road, London W5 5SA
A Random House Group Company
www.transworldbooks.co.uk

THE WAYS OF THE WORLD
A CORGI BOOK: 9780552167055(B format)
9780552170437(A format)

First published in Great Britain
in 2013 by Bantam Press
an imprint of Transworld Publishers
Corgi edition published 2014

Addresses for Random House Group Ltd companies outside the UK
can be found at: www.randomhouse.co.uk
The Random House Group Ltd Reg. No. 954009

The Random House Group Limited supports the Forest Stewardship
Council® (FSC®), the leading international forest-certification organisation.
Our books carrying the FSC label are printed on FSC®-certified paper.
FSC is the only forest-certification scheme supported by the leading
environmental organisations, including Greenpeace. Our paper
procurement policy can be found at
www.randomhouse.co.uk/environment

Typeset in 11/13.5pt Giovanni Book by Falcon Oast Graphic Art Ltd.
Printed and bound in Great Britain by Clays Ltd, St Ives plc

2 4 6 8 10 9 7 5 3 1

THE WAYS OF THE WORLD

SPRING, 1919

THEY COULD IGNORE THE TELEPHONE. THAT WAS ONE OF the unwritten clauses of the Armistice. No telephone would have rung unanswered for long at the squadron base in France where their paths had first crossed in the summer of 1915. But they were not in France. And the war was over. So there they stood, side by side, aware of the importunate ringing in the unattended office in the corner of the hangar, but unmoved by it, lulled by the scent of oil and varnish and the fluttering of a pigeon in the rafters and the vernal brightness of the light flooding in around them.

It was a silvery late-morning light that gleamed on the fuselages of an array of aircraft that had never strained through dives or loops in combat, or been strafed by enemy fire, because they had been constructed just as the war was ending and were now as redundant, for all their elegance and cunning of design, as the pair of youthful Royal Flying Corps veterans who were admiring them.

Even at a glance the two men would have struck an observer as dissimilar, so dissimilar that probably only the war could account for their ease in each other's company. The taller and slimmer of them was James

15

Maxted, former lieutenant, known to all but his family as Max. He had a good-looking face that held a promise of rugged handsomeness in middle age, boyishly flopping fair hair, pale-blue eyes and an ironic tilt to his mouth that hinted at cynicism. His companion, a shorter, bulkier figure, was Sam Twentyman, former sergeant. Max had served in the RFC as a pilot and known Sam as the most reliable and resourceful of the engineers who kept his plane in the air. Sam was five years older than Max, but looked younger, despite some greying of his curly brown hair, thanks to his round, rosy-cheeked face and general air of terrier-like eagerness.

'You're sure Bristols are the ones to go for?' Max asked, arching a sceptical eyebrow. 'Some of the lads who flew them said they preferred the Sopwiths.'

'They did at first, sir,' Sam replied. He still addressed Max as an NCO would an officer and showed no sign of breaking the habit. 'But after all the modifications we made the Bristol was the best two-seater by a long chalk. You were out of circulation by then, of course.'

By 'out of circulation' Sam meant held for the duration in a prisoner of war camp in Silesia. Max smiled at the euphemism and stepped close enough to the nearest plane to run an appreciative hand over the burnished wood of its propeller vanes.

'Well, you're the boss, Sam.'

Now it was Sam's turn to smile. They were spending Max's money, not his. He had no illusions about who would be calling the tune in their future enterprise. 'Will the budget stretch to a couple of SE5s, then? Beautiful machines, they are. Ten quid the pair. A real bargain.'

'Is that what Miller said?' Max nodded towards a

scurrying, overalled figure who had just entered the hangar by a side-door and was heading towards the still-ringing telephone in the office. He wore an irritated frown on his thin, oil-smudged face. 'The air-worthiness certificates will treble that price, remember.'

'You're right. They will. But . . .'

'But?' Max turned and gazed at Sam expectantly.

'Our customers will want to fly solo eventually.'

'If I teach them well enough?'

Sam grinned. 'You're a natural, sir. You gave quite a few of the Hun a flying lesson, as I remember.'

The telephone had stopped ringing. Miller had finally answered it. In the welcome silence Max recalled the intoxicating pleasure of his first flight, a joy-ride from this very aerodrome eight years before, in the summer of 1911. Was it only eight years? It seemed longer, so very much longer, in so very many ways. Cambridge. Farnborough Flying School. The Western Front: those crazy days of scouting above the trenches, nerves stretched as taut as the rigging of his plane, ending in a crash behind enemy lines he had been lucky to survive – doubly so, given the rapidly declining life expectancy of pilots as the war advanced. Then eighteen months of tedium and privation in the POW camp. And now, here he was, back at Hendon, birthplace of his passion for flying, about to acquire a training squadron of his own at a knock-down price.

'Miller would let you take one of the SE5s for a spin,' Sam continued, 'if that's what you need to make your mind up.'

'I'm sure he would. And I'm sure you reckon it *would* make my mind up.'

'They're sweet as honey, sir.'

'And we deserve some honey, don't we, Sam, you and I?' Max clapped his friend on the shoulder and was suddenly overtaken by a surge of optimism about their joint venture. He planned to call the flying school Surrey Wings. He had the perfect partner in Sam. He had the site, courtesy of his father. And soon, after a little horse-trading with Miller, he would have the planes. Flying was the future. For the first time in years, the sky was wide and blue and full of promise.

'*Mr Maxted.*'

'What?' Max emerged from his fleeting reverie to find Miller looking towards him from the doorway of the office. 'What is it?'

'This call's for you.'

'For me? Impossible. No one knows I'm here.'

'Well, evidently your mother knows. And she wants to speak to you. She says it's urgent.'

'My mother? Confound it all.' Max glanced at Sam and shrugged helplessly, then hurried towards the office.

In the twenty seconds or so it took him to reach the telephone, Max concluded that the only way his mother could have tracked him to Hendon Aerodrome was first to have telephoned the flat. Saturday was one of Mrs Harrison's cleaning mornings. He had mentioned his destination to her on his way out. She must still have been there when Lady Maxted rang. But as explanations went it did not go far. Lady Maxted was of a generation that scarcely made habitual use of the telephone. Off-hand he could not recall her ever calling him before.

He grasped the receiver. 'Mother?'

'James?' No telephone line could drain from her voice the querulousness that always seemed to attach itself to her pronunciation of his name.

'Yes. I'm here.'

'I think you should come home at once.' By home she meant Gresscombe Place, the house in Surrey where Max had spent a sizeable portion of his childhood and youth without ever quite thinking of it as home. 'There's been . . . an accident.'

'What sort of accident?' Max felt the mildest tug of anxiety, but nothing more. Surviving the aerial war in France had inured him to most of the calamities of everyday existence. Whatever his mother might be about to say, it surely did not represent a turning point in his life.

But such moments come when fate decrees. And this was such a moment. 'It's your father, James,' said Lady Maxted. 'He's been killed, I'm afraid.'

MAX USED TO TELL ANY FRIENDS WHO ASKED ABOUT HIS father that they could know him as well as he did simply by studying his entry in the Foreign Office List. He was only half-joking.

MAXTED, Sir Henry, 2nd Baronet, born 1853. Educated Eton and Trinity College, Cambridge. Clerkship in the Foreign Office, 1875. Assistant Private Secretary to Lord Granville, 1880–82. 3rd Secretary, Vienna, 1882–86. Vice-Consul, Budapest, 1886–89. 2nd Secretary, Tokyo, 1889–91. Home attachment, London, 1891–92. 2nd Secretary, Constantinople, 1892–96. 1st Secretary, later Chargé d'Affaires, Rio de Janeiro, 1896–1910. (Succeeded as 2nd Baronet, 1897.) Consular Counsellor, St Petersburg (later Petrograd) 1910–18.

That was as much as the latest edition revealed. There was no mention of Sir Henry's father, Sir Charles Maxted, a diplomat in his own right as well as a noted Assyriologist, who had earned the baronetcy his son inherited through his negotiation of the route of the Odessa–Tehran telegraph in the 1860s. Nor was his marriage to Winifred Clissold, the future Lady Maxted, alluded to. Their eldest son, Ashley, was born in 1882, Max's senior by nine years. Max was born in Tokyo, during the last posting on which his mother accompanied his father. She professed a dread of Turkish sanitation and sent her husband off to Constantinople alone. The threat of yellow fever precluded her joining him in Rio de Janeiro and by then the pattern was set. Lady Maxted led a contented life in Surrey with little thought (as far as Max could tell) for Sir Henry's activities a continent or half a world away.

So it was that Max knew his father merely as an occasional visitor during periods of leave, which often coincided with his school or university terms, thereby limiting their contact to a stilted conversation in an Eton or Cambridge tea-room. Sir Henry struck the young Max as a gruff, stiff, emotionally restrained man, the archetypal diplomat in that sense, who conversed with his son about as freely as he might with an official of a foreign government. But perhaps he was too gruff and stiff for his own good. Rio de Janeiro was far from the diplomatic high road and St Petersburg was no place for him to spend the concluding years of his career. Lady Maxted sometimes referred to him 'losing his way', though precisely how he had done so she never specified.

Retirement was bound to reunite Sir Henry and Lady Maxted in due and problematical course. It came while the Great War was in its final months and Max was still a prisoner of the Germans. But by the time he was repatriated, in January 1919, Sir Henry was abroad on government business again. The British delegation to the Paris Peace Conference required the services of expert advisers in numerous fields. Sir Henry was asked to be one of them. He departed with what Lady Maxted later described as 'alacrity'.

Who, in the circumstances, could blame him? Paris, even in the aftermath of the war to end all wars, was still Paris. He was hardly to know that death lay in wait for him there.

After a hurried explanation, Max left Sam to stall Miller as best he could and set off for Surrey.

He and his mother had never enjoyed the warmest of relationships. There were reasons for that they had never spoken of and probably never would. He was not her idea of what a son should be. Nor was she his idea of a good mother. Still, Sir Henry's sudden death was an event which even Max acknowledged as a family emergency. His place, now if hardly ever, was at home. So, home he went.

The journey took longer than he would have wished, involving a forced march to Hendon station, a train to St Pancras, a hectic crossing of London by Tube and another train from Waterloo to Epsom. The Tube he particularly loathed. The horror of confinement he carried with him from the camp meant his nerves were tested whenever he descended into the Underground's malodorous depths. The services were busy that day, reminding him how uncomfortable he now was amidst any mass of humanity.

He was, of course, unduly familiar with death in numerous forms and disguises, thanks to the swathe it had cut through his squadron in France. But there were many men of his age carrying gruesome memories with them into the genteel peacetime world. He would have claimed no distinction on that account. He had fully expected to die himself. The expectation had aged him, he suspected. He was young, in the veritable prime of his life. But he did not always feel so.

Yet the depression that had claimed some had never touched him. 'You're a tough 'un and no mistake,' Sam had once said to him, in the wake of a particularly heavy day of losses, when Max had been keener to discuss minor adjustments to the gun-mounting on his plane than mourn the comrades he had seen shot down in flames. But toughness was not quite it. Max knew that to allow himself to care would be fatal. 'This is all just a joke we can't quite see the funny side of, Twentyman,' he had replied. And he had believed it. That was why he had laughed the afternoon his luck had run out behind German lines and, with a failed engine and a jammed gun, he had gone down like a falling leaf spiralling through the Flanders sky.

But his luck had not quite run out, not to the last morsel. The shots that had stopped his engine had missed his fuel tank by a matter of inches. And the ground was flat and soft enough to make some kind of a landing. He had emerged, to his own astonishment, in one piece.

And that astonishment stayed with him to this day, as an unsmiling light-heartedness, a blithe disregard for how others expected him to lead his life. It meant the news of his father's death, though surprising, had not shocked him. He was not indifferent to such things, but he was well accustomed to them.

His mother had supplied little in the way of concrete information. Sir Henry had died in a fall from a roof, apparently. It was, Lady Maxted had emphasized, an accident. 'A tragic and dreadful accident.' How she could be sure of that she did not say and Max had known better than to ask. He would attempt to elicit more details when he reached Gresscombe. His brother would be there. He might be in possession of the facts. When it came to facts, Ashley could generally be relied upon. *Sir* Ashley, as he was now, of course. Max was going to find it hard to think of him as such, but he supposed he would grow used to it. Ashley himself would relish the status of the baronetcy, though perhaps not as much as his wife. Lydia had the prize for which Max suspected she had married his brother – and many years earlier than she could have expected. She would be mourning her father-in-law, but with secret satisfaction.

All in all, Sir Henry Maxted's passing was unlikely to prompt an outpouring of grief among his relatives. For the last twenty years and more he had been largely absent from their lives. He attributed this, in one of his typically lofty phrases, to 'the exigencies of the service', and Lady Maxted never suggested it was otherwise. To Max, however, it seemed an arrangement that suited both parties to the marriage. How Sir Henry filled the waking hours not given over to the tireless and patriotic pursuit of British interests in foreign parts Max could only imagine. As for his mother, good works, Surrey society and occasional forays to London appeared to content her, though Max had cause to believe that had not always been the case, if indeed it was now.

Sir Henry's death raised a delicate issue, however, one which Max turned over uneasily in his mind as the train

24

steamed slowly through the countryside south of Wimbledon. He had not yet told Ashley of the agreement he had reached with their father and he doubted if Sir Henry had either, since there would surely have been some reaction to the news from his brother. The question now – the devilishly tricky question – was whether Ashley would honour the agreement, as the new owner of the Gresscombe estate. If not, Max's plans for the future, along with Sam's, would go badly awry. He had not mentioned this disturbing possibility to Sam. It had not actually occurred to him until after he had left Hendon. Without the land his father had promised him, there could be no flying school. And the land was now in his brother's gift.

'Damn it all to hell, Pa,' Max murmured under his breath as he gazed out through the window of the train. 'Why'd you have to go and die on me?'

SIR CHARLES MAXTED, MAX'S GRANDFATHER, BOUGHT THE Gresscombe estate following an early retirement from the diplomatic service funded by his prudent investments in mining and railway stock. The estate had suffered from decades of neglect. But Sir Charles had a keen eye for a bargain. He re-tenanted Gresscombe Farm and demolished the tumbledown Georgian manor house to make way for an Arts and Craft mansion of his own commissioning. Gresscombe Place was a red-brick house of multiple gables and parapeted bays, with high windows to admit as much light as possible in a vain attempt to recreate the dazzling brilliance of Mesopotamia, where he had served as consul for fifteen years. An abundance of Middle Eastern rugs and beaten copper were nods in the same direction, overwhelmed since his death by the more cluttered and heavier-curtained tastes of his daughter-in-law.

Max barely remembered his grandfather. He was only six when the old man died. Sir Charles's greatest claim to fame was to have assisted Henry Rawlinson, his predecessor as consul in Baghdad, in his pioneering translation of cuneiform script. Max's father was named in honour of Rawlinson and Sir Charles pursued his interest in Sumero-Babylonian languages to the end of his days.

Haskins, the chauffeur, had been sent to meet Max at Epsom station. He was a taciturn fellow at the best of times and Max knew better than to seek his views on what he described, uncontroversially, as 'a bad business'. He would doubtless have said the same, in the same neutral tone, if Max had been killed in the war. He was more sentimental about the internal combustion engine than the crazed doings of humankind.

Accordingly, there was nothing in the way of idle conversation to distract Max as they passed the flat quartet of fields west of the town where he planned to open his flying school. Sir Henry had agreed to their use for the purpose with disarming readiness. 'Gladly, my boy,' had been his exact words. But gladness was likely to be in short supply now at Gresscombe Place.

And so it proved. The family had gathered to discuss the sad news from France. None of the early-spring sunshine penetrated to the drawing-room where they were assembled: Lady Maxted, the Dowager Lady Maxted as she now was, with Ashley and Lydia, as well as Uncle George, Lady Maxted's brother. There was a notable dearth of tears, though Max would not have expected his mother to be prostrated by grief, even if she felt it. She was rigidly self-controlled at all times. She considered any display of emotion to be an admission of weakness. And she was not weak. Nor was her daughter-in-law. Lydia was a woman of hard features and firm opinions, who spoke to her husband, her children and indeed her brother-in-law in the same tone she used to instruct her several dogs and horses.

Ashley was predictably subdued in the presence of the two women who dominated his life. He was shorter and bulkier than Max, with darker hair, a puffier face and a ruddier complexion. A knee mangled in a hunting accident ten years before had left him with a slight limp that had spared him frontline service in the war. Somehow he had acquired a captaincy by sitting behind a desk in Aldershot for the duration. He never referred to the contrast with Max's aerial derring-do and nor did Max, but that did not mean either of them was heedless of it.

George Clissold had arrived hotfoot from an undemanding half-day in the City, where he was something (probably superfluous) in marine insurance. He was, as usual, not entirely sober, but sobriety had never suited him. Lady Maxted claimed to rely on him for advice in financial matters. For his part, Max would have relied on him for nothing beyond the recommendation of a good malt whisky. But he was a genial and unobjectionable presence. And he did at least raise a smile at his nephew's arrival.

'Bit of a facer, what, James my lad?' he said in his rumbling voice as he clasped Max's hand.

'A terrible shock, Uncle, yes.' He turned to Lady Maxted. 'How are you, Mother?'

'It is a fearful blow, James,' she responded. 'But we must bear it.'

'That's the spirit, old girl,' said George.

Tea was served. Lydia plied Max with an unsought account of how bravely little Hetty had taken the news of her grandfather's death and the arrangement she had made for Giles's housemaster to inform him of the sad event. Max knew convention demanded that he display some interest in the welfare of his brother's children, but he felt even less able than usual to express any. Besides, Lydia was clearly only filling in until the maid left them to it.

'I shall tell you what Mr Fradgley from the embassy in Paris told me, James,' said Lady Maxted as soon as privacy was restored. 'Heaven knows, it leaves much unexplained, but I do implore you all to guard against unwarranted speculation.' She paused to let her request, which was more in the way of an instruction, sink in. There was already an implication that they should be guarding her good name as well as her late husband's. 'Some time last night, Henry fell from the roof of an apartment building in Montparnasse. Precisely when this occurred is unclear. No one seems to have seen him fall – that is, no one has yet come forward to say they did. He was found . . . in the early hours of the morning . . . by a group of people leaving a . . . well, some place of amusement. According to Mr Fradgley, there can be no doubt the fall killed him instantly, which is a blessing, I suppose. Mr Fradgley had already spoken to the police. They were satisfied the fall had been . . . accidental.'

Max assumed he was not alone in wondering how the police could be so swiftly satisfied on such a point. In the circumstances, suicide was surely a possibility, although not a likely one in his opinion. Sir Henry was hardly the self-destructive type and had been in notably good spirits when Max had visited him in Paris two weeks before. There was, of course, a third possibility. But he was not about to mention it. Still, there was one obvious question he reckoned he could risk asking. 'How can the police know Pa fell from the roof rather than a window on one of the upper floors, Mother?'

'I don't know, James. There must be . . . evidence pointing to that.'

'But Mr Fradgley didn't say what the evidence was.'

'I'm sure the poor man didn't want to burden your mother with the particulars,' said Lydia.

'But he was definite this occurred in . . . Montparnasse?'

'Are you familiar with the area?' Lydia asked sharply, as if unfamiliarity with Montparnasse would somehow disqualify Max from querying the point.

'No, I'm not. But . . . his hotel was off the Champs-Elysées. That's a long way from Montparnasse.'

'Is it?'

'You know he was always very keen on astronomy,' said George. 'That'll be what got him up there. Someone offered him the use of their roof to admire the night sky. It was the equinox, wasn't it?'

Into Max's mind came a memory of his father instructing him in the distribution of the constellations one clear summer night around the turn of the century, when his home leave had briefly intersected with Max's school holiday. Sir Henry had given him a cardboard-mounted chart of the heavens – a planisphere – as a late birthday present and shown him how to identify Perseus and Orion and the Great Bear. On the reverse was a chart of the southern sky, the one Sir Henry saw from his residence in Rio. Max had looked long and often at it after

Sir Henry's departure, imagining what it was like to be so far away that even the stars were different.

'Please, George,' said his mother, her words cutting through the memory. 'This is exactly the sort of futile supposition I wish to avoid.' She allowed herself a sigh of exasperation. 'And it is why I want you and Ashley to go to Paris as soon as possible, James, to clarify the circumstances of your father's death and to arrange for his body to be brought home for a funeral here in Surrey at the earliest opportunity.'

'Really?'

'I can't see why we both need to go,' said Ashley in his first contribution to the discussion. 'I can perfectly well deal with . . . whatever needs dealing with.'

'You must both go,' said Lady Maxted, in a tone Max recognized as brooking no contradiction. 'It is only fitting that his two sons should accompany him . . . on his final return to these shores.'

'Well . . .'

'You will do this for your father, won't you, James?' His mother stared expectantly at him.

'Of course, Mother.' He glanced at Ashley, who was frowning dubiously. The arrangement evidently did not suit him, nor in all likelihood Lydia, which was something to commend it from Max's point of view. 'Of course I'll go.'

After tea, Ashley suggested Max accompany him to his study, so that they might consult *Bradshaw* and plan their journey. Max suspected he also wanted a word alone with him, out of their mother's – and his wife's – earshot.

Certainly planning the journey did not occupy them for long. 'We can have Haskins run us up to town first thing in the morning and catch the eleven o'clock train from Victoria. Where did you stay when you went over?'

'The Mazarin. Pa booked it for me. He said it was one of the few places not overrun by delegates to the peace conference.'

'Conveniently located?'

'I should say. Halfway between the Arc de Triomphe and the Eiffel Tower.'

'We'll cable them, then. We shan't need to stay for more than a couple of days.'

'You don't think so?'

'You heard Mother. Sort out the paperwork and ship Pa home p.d.q. That's what she wants. So, that's what she must have.'

'But we don't know what we'll find out when we get there, Ashley.'

Ashley hurrumphed at that and subsided into the chair behind his desk. Above him hung, as it always had, a large framed map of Mesopotamia circa 1850. The study had originally been their grandfather's and was furnished much as he had left it. The clay jar on the desk that served as a pencil-pot could easily have been thousands of years old, chanced upon in one of the places marked on the map. Max had been angling for a transfer to the Mesopotamian Front in the months before he was shot down. He had dreamt of flying over the sun-baked remains of the ancient civilization whose language his grandfather had helped to translate. But a dream was all it had been.

Ashley flicked open the silver cigarette-box that stood beside the pencil-pot, took out a cigarette, tamped it on the blotter and lit up. Max sat down and lit one for himself. A short interlude of fraternal understanding elapsed as smoke curled into the air between them. Then Ashley said, 'Unless you credit Uncle George's hare-brained idea about star-gazing, it's hard to imagine anything reputable lying behind this . . . accident.'

'What are you suggesting?'

'You saw Pa more recently than I did. How would you describe his . . . state of mind?'

'Cheerful. Optimistic. Rather more so than I'd have expected.'

'Retirement didn't suit him, you know. He prowled round here like a caged lion. He greeted the summons to join our delegation in Paris as a gift from the gods. "I'm back in the saddle," he said to me.'

'He said the government wanted someone with knowledge of Brazilian politics to advise them on how to respond to Brazil's claims at the peace conference. Something to do with confiscated German ships and impounded cargoes of coffee.'

'Coffee? Small beer, more like. I can't believe his expertise has been in high demand. And given that, he's probably not been kept very busy . . .'

'Yes?'

'An accident pure and simple's highly unlikely, James. You know that as well as I do. And suicide's out of the question, I think we can agree. Montparnasse is a long way from the Champs-Elysées, as you yourself pointed out. I believe it has a somewhat . . . dissolute reputation.'

Max shrugged. 'I bow to your superior knowledge.'

'Well, it's full of artists, isn't it?'

'I believe so.'

'There you are, then. Models *au naturel*. Drugs. Drink. Debauchery of all kinds.'

'I'm sure that's a—'

'The point is, Pa probably started mixing in circles he shouldn't have and ended up dead. How exactly, we may never know. And perhaps we *needn't* know. If the French police are happy to write it off as an accident, there's no sense our raising a stink, is there?'

'Well, Mother wouldn't want us to, it's true.'

'She certainly wouldn't.' Ashley regarded Max studiously through a slowly exhaled plume of smoke. 'We're of one mind on this, are we?'

'I won't do anything that risks . . . embarrassing our family, if that's what you mean.'

'Good.'

'Though—'

'Why did you go and see him, by the way?'

'Pa?'

'Yes. Why did you go and see him?'

Max was damned if he would pretend this was anything but a strange question, even though it was not quite as strange as he meant to imply. 'I hadn't seen him in nearly five years, Ashley. Even by our standards, that's a long gap.'

'You'll have noticed how his time in Russia aged him.'

'He *was* five years older. Like me. I dare say I'm not as twinkle-eyed and clear-browed as I was in 1914. Actually, I thought he was . . . surprisingly invigorated.'

'And receptive?'

'If you like.'

'You had no other reason for going, then? No . . . proposal to put to him?'

So, now they had come to it. Sir Henry had promised he would write to Ashley, telling him of his agreement to let Max open his flying school on part of the estate. Max had expected to hear from Ashley once he had received the letter. He had heard nothing. Until now. 'Did he write to you?'

'Yes.' Ashley opened the desk drawer and pulled out a letter, still in its envelope. The stamp was French and Max recognized the handwriting as his father's. 'A flying school, eh? Well, well. That's your plan for the future, is it, James?'

'Pa liked the sound of it.'

'I doubt Barratt will.'

Barratt was the tenant at Gresscombe Farm. According to Sir Henry, he had no legal right to object and Max had confidently assumed that was true.

'He doesn't seem to be making much use of the fields.'

'Appearances can be deceptive in farming, as you'd know if you'd ever taken an interest in the estate. I've had to manage the place in Pa's absence. You may be surprised to learn it doesn't run itself.'

'Are you going to let me open the flying school, Ashley?' The moment had come to pose the question directly.

'Do you really think you can make a success of it?'

'Certainly.'

'These are straitened times. Who's going to have money to throw away on flying lessons?'

'People who see the commercial potential in becoming a pilot and consequently *won't* be throwing their money away.'

'And what is the commercial potential? No, no.' Ashley held up his hand. 'We can save this for the trip. Make a good enough case, James, and, who knows, I might let you go ahead.'

'I was hoping you'd honour Pa's agreement.'

'I'd like to, obviously.' Ashley smiled, but his smile in fact made nothing obvious. 'I have to consider the financial security of the estate as a whole. I wasn't going to mention it, but Lydia's expecting another child. And there'll be no easy money for anyone while the nation pays off its war debts. Pa may not have thought this through properly.' His smile broadened. 'I owe it to the family to be sure that I do.'

WINIFRED, THE DOWAGER LADY MAXTED, HAD ANNOUNCED that she would rest before dinner. She had retired to her room, where she lay on her bed and contemplated the slow advance of twilight through the half-curtained windows.

Sir Henry's retirement from the diplomatic service had hung over her head for a decade or more as an unwelcome but unavoidable end to a long separation both had found increasingly congenial. Strictly speaking, she could not be sure Sir Henry had found it congenial, but he had never given her cause to doubt it. She assumed and rather hoped he had found some discreet companionship along the way. She bore him no ill will. And certainly she would not have wished him dead in this sudden, strange and possibly scandalous manner. A fall from a roof in Paris, indeed. She shook her head at the tragic inappropriateness of it all. This was not how Sir Henry Maxted should have ended his days – though, to be sure, precisely how he had ended them she did not know.

She thought for a moment of how close they had been at the loving outset of their marriage, of the lengths she had been prepared to go to to ensure his happiness and to protect his good name. Tears came into her eyes for the first time since she had heard of his death. 'My poor dear Henry,' she murmured. 'Who would have predicted this?'

There came a knock at the door. She dabbed her eyes with her handkerchief and was instantly composed. 'Come in,' she called. She did not sit up, for she knew who her visitor was. And he would take her as he found her. He always had.

'You wanted a word, Win,' said George Clissold, stepping quietly into the room. There was something in his tone and bearing that was fractionally different from the buffoonish uncle he had presented himself as in the drawing-room. 'Is this a good time? If you really do need to rest . . .'

'Sit down and tell me how I'm placed.'

George conveyed an armchair to the foot of the bed and eased himself into it. The evening light fell obliquely on his silvery hair and handsome man-of-the-world features and Winifred smiled affectionately at him.

'Why did you never marry, George?'

'Who'd have had me?'

'There were quite a few who were willing, as I recall.'

'But I always played fair by letting them glimpse the depraved core of my being before I popped the question. That generally settled it.'

'What nonsense you do talk.'

'Yes. I'm known for it. And nonsense is what I may have been talking when I said I thought I'd seen Henry last week. I was probably mistaken. Chance resemblances are common enough. He was out of sight before I could get a proper look at him.'

'It was Henry you saw.'

'A few days ago you were sceptical, to say the least. What's changed your mind?'

'A letter from the curator of the county museum.'

'What has he to do with it?'

'Some years ago – many years ago, in fact – Henry's father presented to the museum a small collection of what the curator tells me are Sumerian cylinder-seals. I've never actually seen them. I'm not even sure they've been on display recently. He didn't say.'

'And you don't visit the museum often.'

'No. Nor had Henry ever interested himself in the seals, as far as I know. Until last week. They were only on loan, it seems, albeit indefinitely extended. But last week, on the very day you thought you saw him in Lombard Street, he went to the museum and reclaimed them.'

'Did he, now?'

'Yes. The curator wasn't there. He wrote to me asking for an address where he could contact Henry, in order to ascertain whether their removal was permanent. He mentioned that the seals are probably . . . quite valuable.'

'Really?'

'It's clear to me Henry told no one he was in England because he didn't want to have to explain the purpose of his visit. What could have taken him to Lombard Street, George?'

'His bank.'

'Money, in other words.'

George shrugged. 'Probably.'

'And I think we can assume he didn't want the

Sumerian cylinder-seals to decorate his hotel room in Paris.'

'I admit it sounds as though he was . . . raising funds.'

'I don't care about ancient Mesopotamian knick-knackery. But I do care about this house and the estate. Ashley has his children to consider. Lydia's expecting again, you know.'

'You always said she was good breeding stock.'

'I'm sure I never said anything so indelicate.'

'Perhaps I said it, then.'

'My concern is that if Henry was so desperate for cash that he resorted to pillaging the county museum, might he have mortgaged the estate?'

'We'll know soon enough if he did. Once the boys return from Paris with a death certificate, we can make the necessary enquiries.'

'And learn the worst.'

'Mortgages aren't agreed and paid overnight, old girl. Even if he was in London to negotiate one, it's highly unlikely the capital will have been released yet.'

'Let's hope not.' Winifred sighed. 'What can he have got himself mixed up in, George?'

'It may be better for you never to know.'

'Papa was so pleased when I told him Henry would be asking for my hand in marriage. "You can't go wrong with a Foreign Office wallah, Winifred," he said. And I believed him. I believed him absolutely.'

'Why wouldn't you? Henry always seemed such a fine fellow.'

'He was. In his way.'

'Brigham's in Paris, isn't he?'

Winifred propped herself up and frowned at her

brother. 'Half the Foreign Office is in Paris. What are you implying?'

'Nothing. But if he crosses Ashley's and James's path . . .'

'There's no reason why he should. He may write to me, of course, offering his condolences. I'm sure many people will write to me. Henry was well liked wherever he went.'

'Are you sure Ashley *and* James is a good idea? They always tend to rub each other up the wrong way.'

'It's time they learnt to cooperate. I don't want their . . . temperamental differences . . . to fester into some kind of feud.'

'An admirable sentiment, I'm sure.'

'But a foolish one, in your opinion?'

'Not at all. You know them better than I do. They're *your* sons.'

'Hah!' Winfred laid her head back on the pillow. 'Only someone with no children could suppose that having them means you understand them. You never do, George, believe me, you never do. Ashley and James are grown men, and Henry was their father. They must do their best for him. And I must let them.'

MAX TOOK A SIP OF WHISKY AND REPLACED THE GLASS ON the chair beside his towel, then lay back in the bath and let the heat of the water ease some of the stresses and anxieties of the day. He had returned from Germany ten weeks before – ten weeks that sometimes felt much longer than that and sometimes much less – determined to live his life henceforth on his own terms. Being alive at all was so outrageous a piece of good fortune that he had no intention of squandering his existence on dull pursuits and workaday routine.

So much for intentions. They did not trump circumstances. The flying school was such a good idea. He did not want to abandon it. He knew Sam was pinning his hopes of liberation from the family bakery business on it. He was pinning a good many hopes on it himself. And the last thing he wanted to do was to let Sam down. But could he trust himself to dance obediently to Ashley's tune in order to pursue it?

Everything had seemed so much simpler a fortnight ago. He had travelled to Paris, wondering how his father would react to his request. His memories of their meeting were confused by a growing suspicion that he had overlooked abundant evidence that all was not well in his father's world, so preoccupied was he with the question of the flying school. To be sure, Sir Henry had been cheery and welcoming. But in retrospect his exuberance had been unnatural. He too had been pre-occupied, happy to let Max do whatever he wanted with a portion of the Gresscombe estate, perhaps because he was caught up in matters which made the fate of four fields west of Epsom seem as distant as it was insignificant.

But what might those matters have been? And did they have any bearing on Sir Henry's death? Max took another sip of whisky, rested his neck against the rim of the bath and tried to force his brain to reconstruct the details of their final encounter in search of the answers.

The journey from London to Paris was supposed to take seven hours, but there were delays all along the line in France and Max's train eventually pulled into the Gare du Nord three hours late. He went straight to the hotel Sir Henry had booked for him, the Mazarin, in Rue Coligny. There was a note waiting for him there on Hotel Majestic writing paper.

5.iii.19

Dear boy,
Welcome to Paris. I am so sorry about this, but I
have to cancel our luncheon engagement for
tomorrow. I am not my own master during this
damned conference. But dine with me instead.
The Ritz at eight. It will be a grand evening.
Affectionately,
Your father

There they were again, Max, supposed: those famous exigencies of the service. The peace conference was important. No one who had fought in the war could doubt that. It was a re-ordering of the world map – the creation of new countries and boundaries intended to heal the old divisions. It was the shaping of a future that would be safe for all to live in.

Still, his father's postponement of their reunion seemed odd, not to say unfeeling. As he unpacked, Max decided he would not simply wait for their dinner date at the Ritz. The Majestic was only a shortish walk away. Armed with directions from the concierge, he set off into the Paris evening. His hopes for a touch of spring were misplaced.

A fellow looking remarkably unlike a Parisian hotel doorman was guarding the entrance to the Majestic. He was, in fact, as he swiftly revealed, a Scotland Yard detective. No chances were being taken with security at the headquarters of the British delegation. Without a pass, or someone to vouch for him, Max was not going to gain admittance.

He was escorted as far as the reception desk, however. But Sir Henry Maxted was out. 'He generally leaves very early and returns very late,' the clerk informed him, discouragingly. The clerk, like the policeman, was English. 'I've been imported from the Grand in Birmingham, sir,' he explained, noting Max's puzzlement. 'The gentlemen from the Foreign Office wouldn't be happy with French staff. They want people they can rely on. So, here we all are.'

'Would you tell Sir Henry when he gets in that his son called to see him?'

'Certainly, but I wouldn't like to say when that might be, if you know what I mean.'

Max was far from sure he did know what the man meant, but he left it at that. He felt a sudden desire for life, colour and entertainment. He hopped into a cab and named the Folies Bergères as his destination.

Max rose late the following morning and treated himself to a gentle day. He walked down to the Seine and crossed to the Quai d'Orsay, briefly joining the small band of onlookers outside the French Foreign Ministry, hoping for a glimpse of someone notable – Lloyd George, perhaps, or President Wilson – coming or going. But those who came and went were anonymous functionaries to a man. He returned to the Right Bank and wandered east, noting the captured German cannons in the Place de la Concorde and the enormous bomb crater in the Tuileries rose garden. There were refugees everywhere from the war zones and disabled ex-servicemen begging at street corners. He rewarded them with cigarettes, which he suspected were more valuable than the sous and centimes in his pockets. The war was over. But in Paris it could not be said to have ended. It was settling around him: the dust of a vast upheaval falling slowly to earth.

The Ritz was as glittering an oasis of opulence as Max had hoped. There were no doorkeepers from Scotland Yard to be braved. It was open house for those with money and fine clothes, many of whom were laughing and flirting over cocktails in the bar. It was there that Max waited for his father, after leaving word for him with the maître d' of the restaurant. To Max's no very great surprise, Sir Henry was late.

'Dear boy,' were Sir Henry's first words to his son, before astonishing him with a hug. Stiff handshakes had been their usual greeting, but Sir Henry was in an expansive, expressive mood. He looked older than when they had last met because he was. His dress and appearance were those of a senior civil servant of a bygone era: bow-tied, starch-collared, frock-coated and Edwardianly bewhiskered. But that, Max instantly sensed, was not the whole story. There was a sparkle in his pale-blue eyes, a warmth to his smile and something Max could only have described as a bounce in his bearing. He was not as stout as he had been either. He looked like a man with plenty on his mind, but uplifted because of it.

Champagne was ordered and Max soon found himself infected with some of his father's unwonted good cheer. They moved into the restaurant and were plied with fine food and wine by waiters gliding to and fro beneath glistening chandeliers. Max was persuaded to describe a few of his more hair-raising exploits with the RFC and to recount some of his experiences as a prisoner of war. Sir Henry could hardly be said to have had a quiet war himself. From his post at the British Embassy in St Petersburg, he had had a ringside seat during the upheavals of the Russian revolution. 'They were dangerous days, my boy. I could easily have got in the way of a Bolshevik bullet if my luck had been out. Fortunately, the Ambassador took pity on the older members of staff and took us with him when he was evacuated. The people we left behind had a very rough time of it, I can tell you.'

And what of his activities in Paris, which were evidently keeping him so busy? Officially, he explained, he was there to give advice to the leaders of the British delegation, as and when required, about the demands and expectations of the Brazilian delegation in respect of German merchant ships held in Brazilian ports and cargoes of Brazilian coffee the Germans had never paid for. 'It shouldn't matter a damn to LG.' (Sir Henry referred to the Prime Minister so casually Max assumed they were on familiar terms.) 'But our American cousins want to be seen to be doing their continental neighbours a few favours, so we have to be on our guard. And fourteen years in Rio de Janeiro made me the closest to an expert the FO could find. Most of the time, though, I just make myself useful. And when that fails I try to enjoy myself. I always wanted a posting to the Paris embassy, but I never got it. This is the next best thing.'

It was over Tokay and crêpes Suzette that Max finally unveiled his plans for a post-war career as a flying instructor. By then he was optimistic that his father would give him the use of the land he needed at Gresscombe. And his optimism was not misplaced. 'You shall have it, James, you shall indeed. I'll write to Ashley and have him tell Barratt to grub up whatever miserable crop he's planted and make way for you. It's the least I can do – the least *he* can do – after what you flyers endured in the service of your country.'

The discussion could hardly have gone better. And in the circumstances it seemed fitting to return to the bar after their meal to toast Max's airborne future with the Ritz's finest cognac. It was there that the evening took a faintly puzzling turn, when a man detached himself from a party in the farthest corner of the room and came across to greet Sir Henry as a close, if not necessarily cordial, acquaintance.

He was tall, lean and slightly crooked in his posture, immaculately dressed and groomed, but with rugged features bordering on rough and a scar, partially concealed by a pencil moustache, that distorted his left nostril. He had dark, wary eyes and a fine head of grey-flecked hair. He was not the sort of man it was easy to place at a glance, either as to nationality or profession, although, as soon as he spoke, it was obvious he was an American.

'Good to see you, Henry,' he drawled. 'Who's your young friend?'

'My son, James. James, this is Travis Ireton.'

Max rose to shake Ireton's hand. His grip was firm and cool, his gaze likewise. Max had the disquieting impression that he was being treated to swift but skilful scrutiny.

'Are you with the US delegation, Mr Ireton?'

'Sometimes. With but not of, that is. More often neither. I'm here in a freelance capacity. And you?'

'Visiting my father.'

'Ah, you'll be the pilot. Henry's mentioned you. Congratulations.'

'For what?'

'Surviving. Not many did, did they?'

'I was lucky.'

'Aren't we all? To be here in Paris, having a swell time of it, while gatherings of old men in smoke-filled committee-rooms decide the fate of the world.'

'If you take a look at Travis's passport, you'll see he

records his occupation as cynic,' Sir Henry remarked affably. 'Who are you with, Travis?'

'Rumanians.' Ireton glanced back over his shoulder. 'I'd better not leave them too long. Patience isn't one of their strengths.' Max glanced in the same direction and saw several dramatically moustachioed men glaring towards him. 'But we need to talk, Henry, you and I. You've been . . . elusive . . . recently.'

'Elusive? No, no, merely busy, I assure you.'

'But busy with what? That's the question. There are quite a few people who—' Ireton cut himself off with a strange little half-smile of self-reproval. 'We do need to talk.'

. 'Then we will.' Sir Henry grinned. 'Those Rumanians are looking restive, Travis.'

'Good of you to point that out to me, Henry. Excuse me, will you?'

As soon as Ireton was safely back on the far side of the room, Max sat down and asked his father, 'Who's he, exactly?'

'He's a man who talks to everybody and tells them nothing,' Sir Henry replied. 'He's never been inside one of those smoke-filled committee-rooms he referred to. But he knows what's said in them. Often word for word.'

'How does he manage that?'

'By persuading people like me to be indiscreet.'

'You'd never be indiscreet, Pa. It's against your nature.'

'I'll accept that as a compliment, my boy. You're right, I'm glad to say. I'm impervious to the wiles of Travis Ireton. But he never gives up, even when he should. And now . . . I think this may be the moment for me to give up, before I have one cognac too many.'

They walked back to their hotels together along the Champs-Élysées. Sir Henry puffed at a cigar and listened with occasional nods of encouragement as Max expounded his case for the air as the universal medium of transport in the future. 'Roads and railways are old hat, Pa. One day you'll be able to fly across the Atlantic – or round the world – as a fare-paying passenger. The war did aircraft design a big favour.'

'I'm glad it achieved something, James. And that you may benefit from it.'

'It'll happen, Pa. Believe me.'

'I'm sure it will. I wonder if I'll live to see any of it come to pass, though.'

'I should jolly well hope so. Why don't you take a maiden flight with me once we have the flying school ready?'

'I should like that.'

'Consider yourself booked in.'

Sir Henry pulled up and turned to his son with a smile. 'Capital, my boy.' He clapped Max on the shoulder. 'Capital.'

They parted at the door of the Majestic. Sir Henry did not look back as he went in. And it did not cross Max's mind even as a remote possibility that he would never see his father again.

MAX STEPPED OUT EARLY FROM GRESSCOMBE PLACE ON Sunday morning to post a letter in the box at the end of the drive. He had written to Sam, explaining that he would be out of the country for a few days, but that they should be able to complete the purchase of the aircraft they had their eyes on as soon as he returned. He said nothing in the letter about the possibility that the land for their flying school might no longer be available. There was nothing to be gained by worrying Sam at this stage.

Why he did not simply leave the letter for one of the servants to post he would have been hard-pressed to explain. But the war had taught him to bestow his trust sparingly. Self-reliance was his unspoken watchword.

Max's progress back up the drive was observed by Lydia from her bedroom window, as she sat brushing her hair at the dressing-table. There he was, that strange brother-in-law of hers she had never understood nor greatly liked. She could not help reflecting how much more convenient it would have been if he had died in the war. Lydia would have been happy to pay tribute to him then. James valiantly deceased would have earned her fond praises. James stubbornly and inconsiderately alive was a beast of quite a different stripe.

She turned at the sound of the door opening behind her. Ashley, shaved and washed, had returned from the bathroom, ready for his early start for Paris – *their* early start, that was, his and James's.

'Your brother's already been out,' she said, signalling with a twitch of her eyebrows her bemusement at the doings and purposes of James Maxted. 'I've just seen him coming back – from a walk, presumably.'

'Perhaps he couldn't sleep,' said Ashley. 'I didn't have a restful night myself.'

'Are you worried, darling?'

'I wouldn't be, if Mother had had the good sense to send me alone.'

'What is she thinking of by involving James?'

'What is she *ever* thinking of?' Ashley sighed and patted Lydia's shoulder. 'I wish I knew.'

'You must keep James on a tight rein in Paris, darling. We don't want him . . . stirring anything up.'

'Indeed we don't. But I believe I have the means to ensure he doesn't.'

'You're not seriously considering letting him proceed with this flying school nonsense?'

'Good God, no. Pa should never have agreed to such a half-baked proposal. I haven't the least intention of allowing James to turn good agricultural land into an aerodrome. But nor do I intend to tell him that – just yet.'

'After the funeral, perhaps?'

'Yes. That's exactly what I was thinking. After we've brought Pa home and buried him. That'll be the time to tell James how matters stand. Until then, I'm hopeful he'll be on his . . . best behaviour.'

'You are clever, darling.'

'Not clever, my dear. Merely . . . practical.'

As Max crossed the hall, bound for the dining-room, where he supposed breakfast would be waiting for him, he noticed that the door to the library was open. His mother stepped out through it to greet him.

'Good morning, James,' she said quietly. 'Do you have a moment?'

'Of course, Mother.'

He followed her into the library. The room faced east and was normally one of the darkest in the house. Only at this hour was sunlight, albeit of a watery variety, flooding through the high bay window at the far end. Lady Maxted walked towards it and came to a halt by the massive floor-standing globe that was one of the more memorable fixtures of Gresscombe Place.

'When you were a child, the globe was always at this angle,' she said, laying her hand on a gleaming curve of the north-western Pacific Ocean.

'Really?' Max joined her beside it and realized that it was true. He had regularly turned the globe and peered at the islands of the Japanese archipelago and wondered what his birthplace was like. He shrugged. 'Well, it's strange to have been born somewhere one has no memory or knowledge of.'

'We lived in Japan for two years. I assure you I had little more knowledge of the country at the end of that time than I had at the beginning.'

'But you remember it.'

'Increasingly, my memories seem like recollected dreams. Spring blossom so bright it hurt my eyes. A deafening chorus of frogs after heavy rain. Junks bobbing on the water. Winking cages of fireflies on a market stall. Ghost-moths thumping against the window-screens on hot summer nights. Really, what does any of that amount to? Impressions, nothing more. And even they are fading.'

'I should like to go there one day.'

'Then I'm sure you will. You do as you please, James. You always have.'

'Are you praising me or rebuking me, Mother?'

'Neither. I am quite reconciled to the fact that you have never been what might be termed an obedient son.'

'Perhaps Ashley does enough obeying for both of us.'

'Perhaps he does. I know I can rely on him to protect your father's memory at all costs. Whereas you . . .'

'Whereas I?'

'Will go in search of the truth . . . wherever it is to be found.'

'Would you prefer me not to?'

'No one should act against their nature. I'm confident you won't. All I ask is this: if you discover your father was the victim of something other than an accident and if you discover what that something other was . . .'

'Yes?'

'I should like to hear of it before you proclaim it to the world.'

Max felt the full force of his mother's gaze as he stood before her. He had supposed she wanted him to support his brother loyally in suppressing any scandal they came across in Paris. But it appeared she did not believe him capable of fulfilling such a role. Nor did she want him to. She had something altogether more subversive in mind. 'I suspect Ashley would be more than a little alarmed by this conversation,' he said.

'Then don't mention it to him. I certainly won't.'

'Very well.'

'Do I have your word?'

'That I will tell you the truth – if I uncover it – before I tell anyone else?'

'Precisely.'

It was a safe enough bargain, Max thought. He could follow Ashley's lead and assure his mother there was no sinister explanation for Sir Henry's death. He had ample room for manoeuvre. Troublingly, though, he was beginning to believe he would need all of it. 'You have my word, Mother.'

She stepped forward and kissed him on the cheek. 'Thank you, James. I know you will keep it. Tread carefully in Paris, won't you?'

'But not *too* carefully?'

She smiled at him. 'There is no danger of you doing that.'

An hour later, after hurried breakfasts and equally hurried farewells, Max and his brother set off.

MAX SURPRISED HIMSELF BY MAINTAINING AN EVEN TEMPER and a flow of uncontroversial conversation as the journey proceeded. His brother Ashley – *Sir* Ashley now, as Max felt sure he would not be allowed to forget – expatiated, with no apparent sense of irony, on the challenges of managing the military supply chain in time of war. Aldershot sounded positively perilous in his version of events.

He had never been as near the Front as he was now going, however. The devastation to be seen from the train near Amiens, stretching around them, had a noticeable effect on him. Perhaps, Max thought, he could dimly imagine the horror buried not so deep beneath the mangled earth. It shamed him, though he hid the emotion as best he could. Ashley was not about to admit that Max had been one of those braving the hazards his crocked knee had spared him.

Ashley had cabled Fradgley at the embassy in Paris telling him of their travel plans. A note from him was waiting for them at the Hotel Mazarin on Lion-&-Unicorn-crested paper.

March 23, 1919

Dear Sir Ashley,

Thank you for your cable. I hope it will be convenient if I call at your hotel at 9.30 on Monday morning to discuss with you and your brother the circumstances of your father's regrettable demise and the procedures it is necessary to follow in order to repatriate the body. I will be accompanied by Mr Appleby of the security detail to the British delegation to the peace conference. I trust this will be satisfactory.

Respectfully yours,

W. H. Fradgley

'It's dated today,' was Ashley's first reaction.

'What of it?' Max asked, feeling vaguely curious about his brother's thought processes.

'A civil servant bestirring himself on a Sunday suggests our visit is being taken seriously. It's an indication that they mean to show us every consideration. As they should.'

A more sinister possibility had occurred to Max. The attention they were receiving suggested to him that Sir Henry's death was a problem the likes of Fradgley wanted to solve as quickly and easily as possible. And that did not necessarily involve establishing the truth of what had happened to him. 'How very reassuring.'

Ashley nodded in agreement, apparently believing Max meant what he had said. 'It is, isn't it?'

A desolate Sunday evening stretched ahead. Max had no intention of spending it dining with Ashley and enduring another outbreak of Aldershotian reminiscence. He said he was in need of an early night and went up to his room; then, as soon as the coast was clear, he took himself off in search of entertainment.

The ringing of the telephone roused him the following morning. Being jolted awake always had the same effect on him. He believed for a moment that he was back with his squadron and his first thought was the thought that greeted him unfailingly in those wartime dawns. *I'm damned if this will be the day I die.*

Then the gloomy furnishings of his hotel room came into focus around him. He fumbled for the telephone.

'James?' It was his brother. And he did not sound happy.

'Yes . . . Ashley.' Max covered the receiver and cleared his throat. 'Good morning.'

'Fradgley and Appleby will be here in fifteen minutes. I thought I ought to check with you that you'll be ready.'

'Oh, yes, yes. I'll, er . . . be down directly.'

'Did I wake you?'

'No, no. Of course not.'

'Mmm. I'll see you shortly, then.'

Max was no stranger to washing and shaving against the clock. He reached the lobby with one of the fifteen minutes remaining and spotted Ashley grumpily perusing a newspaper in the writing-room.

'How goes the world?' Max ventured by way of greeting.

'Badly.' Ashley folded up his newspaper in an explosion of rustling. 'The Reds are running amok in Budapest.'

'I had no idea.'

'Don't you follow the news?'

'Would it benefit me if I did?'

Ashley frowned at him, uncertain, as so often, whether to take Max's remarks seriously. 'That early night doesn't seem to have done you a lot of good.'

'Sometimes you can have too much sleep.'

'Symptoms of which are bags under the eyes and a deathly pallor, I assume.'

'The lighting in here isn't catching me at my best.'

'Flippancy isn't likely to serve us well today, James.' Ashley tossed the newspaper aside and stood up. 'I believe our visitors have arrived.' He nodded towards the lobby.

It was easy for Max to tell which of the two was Fradgley and which was Appleby. He took the short, thin, pale-faced man with a tight little mouth to be Fradgley, every inch the self-effacing minor diplomat, and his bulky, balding, jowly companion of the far-seeing gaze and self-possessed smile was surely Appleby.

Introductions swiftly confirmed Max's surmise. Appleby, he noted, was plain Mr Appleby, though an admission to high police rank would have been no surprise. He had the cautious, watchful demeanour of some kind of detective, combined with an air of authority.

He and Fradgley expressed brisk condolences before explaining what assistance they could offer. 'Your father's body was removed to the mortuary of the military hospital at Port-Royal,' he said. 'I assume you'd like to satisfy yourselves as to his identity.'

Ashley appeared taken aback by the possibility that it could be in doubt. 'Surely you've established that.'

'Of course, Sir Ashley,' said Fradgley, suddenly all of a flutter. 'It's merely a formality.'

'We would like to view the body,' said Max.

'Naturally.' Appleby eyed Max as if it was now obvious to him which of the brothers he should pay attention to. 'And then the address where the fall occurred?'

'Yes.'

'Then let's proceed. We have a car waiting.'

They were driven across the Seine by the Pont de l'Alma, then along the quais as far as the National Assembly, before heading south towards Montparnasse. Fradgley set out in exhaustive detail the procedures that would have to be followed to permit the removal of Sir Henry's body from France, assuring them throughout that he would personally attend to such matters and that he hoped to complete them within twenty-four hours. His purpose seemed to be to emphasize just how hard he was working on their behalf, though Max wondered if all this bureaucratic bustle was actually on someone else's account.

Fradgley was sandwiched between Max and Ashley on the rear seat, while Appleby sat beside the driver, puffing at a pipe and casting occasional glances at Max over his shoulder. *Let the silly little man talk himself dry*, his wary half-smile seemed to communicate. *Then you and I can get down to business.* All he actually said in the course of the journey, though, was a remark on the weather, after rain had begun to pelt the windscreen. 'Paris in the spring can be rather overrated, you'll find.'

*

L'Hôpital Militaire, Boulevard de Port-Royal, was an echoing warren of a place, the air tinged with dis-infectant, the corridors peopled by sombre nurses and amputees from the war learning to walk with only one leg – or none at all. The mortuary was in a distant, largely silent wing, where no nurses were to be seen, only overalled functionaries apparently immune to the prevailing chill.

Sir Henry's body was waiting for them on a trolley in a cold, windowless room. There was a taint of decay in the icy air, Max noticed. If anyone else noticed it, they did not say. But Fradgley lingered in the doorway behind them, as if reluctant to come too close.

An attendant raised the sheet covering Sir Henry's face. The right side of his head was covered by a bandage, but there was no doubt it was him, altered though he was by death: the eyes closed, the mouth unsmiling, the spirit gone.

'He suffered a severe brain injury in the fall,' said Appleby. 'Death would have been instantaneous.'

There were various cuts and scrapes around the visible part of Sir Henry's face, bruising and swelling around his eye and rucklings of the flesh at the edge of the bandage that hinted at the damage beneath.

'Were there other injuries?' Max asked.

'Most of the bones in his body were probably broken,' Appleby replied. 'It was a long drop.'

'I think we've seen enough,' said Ashley, his voice cracking as he spoke. 'It's certainly our father.'

'We should retrieve his signet ring,' said Max. 'Mother will want to have it.'

'It'll already have been removed,' said Appleby. 'Commissioner Zamaron of the Paris police has his personal effects. We're due to collect them later from the *préfecture.*'

'Could we just check, in case it's been overlooked?'

'I'm sure Appleby knows what he's talking about, James,' said Ashley.

'Even so . . .'

Appleby shrugged and said to the attendant, '*La main gauche, s'il vous plaît.*'

The sheet was folded further back to expose Sir Henry's naked torso, a patchwork of bruises, angrily dark against his chalk-white skin. Ashley started back. 'Good God,' he exclaimed. Max took some bitter pleasure from knowing how poorly prepared his brother was for encounters with the physical consequences of violent death, whereas he had seen much worse than this all too many times.

'As you see,' said Appleby, 'the ring's gone.'

So it was. But looking down at Sir Henry's lifeless hand, Max noticed something else. The fingernails had been cut severely short and none too carefully at that. Sir Henry had always taken pains about his appearance. Such clumsy trimming was not his work. Someone else had done it. Though whether before or after his death . . .

'Have you seen enough, Mr Maxted?' Appleby asked.

Max nodded. 'Yes. Quite enough, thank you.'

Appleby signalled to the attendant, who drew the sheet back over Sir Henry's face. Max bade his father a silent farewell, then turned away.

'We can go now.'

I**T WAS ONLY A SHORT DRIVE TO CARREFOUR VAVIN, WHERE THEY** emerged from the car into the heart of Montparnasse. But the neighbourhood's artistic reputation was belied by a scene of workaday ordinariness. The weather was dank and cold, the shoppers and passers-by had no time to pause for intellectual banter and the café terraces were empty.

Fradgley had had much less to say for himself since visiting the mortuary and glum introspection had claimed Ashley. It was left to Appleby to direct proceedings and to Max to ask the questions that needed to be asked.

Appleby led them away from the junction, where Boulevard du Montparnasse met Boulevard Raspail, along Rue du Verger, a quieter side-street, to the entrance to an apartment building, where Appleby stopped by the door. Max noticed, rather before his brother, the brownish-red stain on the pavement.

'Is this where he fell?' he asked Appleby directly. Coyness on the point was futile.

'Yes. I'm afraid it'll take some time for all the traces to disappear.'

Max looked up. He counted seven storeys, including

the parapeted attic windows set in the mansard roof. A fall from such a height could only ever be fatal. Appleby gave the doorbell a hefty yank.

'The concierge doesn't speak a word of English. But she's expecting us, so . . .'

Expectant or not, she was in no hurry. There was time for Max to light a cigarette and another for Ashley, who then paced around tensely with his for what felt like an age before the door was opened by a small, spry, elderly woman with a pronounced stoop, who eyed them as if they might be a pack of burglars.

Fradgley addressed her in fluent French and she gave ground. They were admitted to a vast and gloomy stair-well. Appleby demanded *'la clé pour le grenier'*, which she surrendered with some reluctance and much rattling of a key-chain. 'Shall we take the lift, gentlemen?' Appleby asked.

No one answered, so by default they squeezed aboard and, after a struggle with the inner door, rose through a wire shaft between the flights of stairs. Nothing was said during the ascent. Max could have asked if either Appleby or Fradgley knew what had brought Sir Henry to this place. So could Ashley. Neither did. But reticence, Max felt sure, would carry them only so far. Eventually, some facts, however unpalatable, would have to be faced.

They exited at the top, on the mansard level, and headed along the landing towards the nearest door, which Appleby unlocked with the key the concierge had given him.

'The information I can supply comes from Commissioner Zamaron. You can ask him to confirm it if you want to, when we see him later. He speaks good English. This attic room is used by the tenants to store possessions they have no space for in their apartments. They all have a key. It's supposed to be kept locked, but it was found to be unlocked when the police came here following your father's fatal fall. He had no key on his person and none was discovered in the attic. So, we must assume someone had simply neglected to lock the door, allowing him to enter unimpeded.'

Appleby pushed the door open and they followed him in. Four dormer windows facing the street lit a long, dust-moted chamber crammed with old furniture, packing-boxes and trunks. Most of the articles were stacked along the inner wall, where the ceiling was highest, allowing easy access to the windows. Appleby closed the door carefully behind them and crossed to one of the windows. He opened it, startling a pigeon outside, which took off in a burst of flapping wings that caused Fradgley to jump. He for one was not at ease. That was painfully clear.

'This window corresponds to the position on the pavement where Sir Henry was found,' said Appleby. 'There's also an accumulation of sludge and mud in the gutter behind the parapet in which the police discovered a boot print matching Sir Henry's footwear. So, there's no doubt it was from here that he fell.'

'Perhaps I could take a look,' said Max, sensing that Ashley was in no hurry to. Appleby stepped aside for him. Max hooked the window open as wide as it would go and leant out. The tiled roof sloped down from the window, as Appleby had described, to a leaded gutter behind a low brick parapet. There appeared to be numerous different boot prints in the silt clogging the gutter, mostly filled with rainwater.

'I'm afraid French policemen are no lighter-footed than their British counterparts, Mr Maxted,' said Appleby. 'There's also been quite a lot of rain since Friday night. But Zamaron tells me a good plaster cast of Sir Henry's boot print was obtained. The actual print, alas, is no longer visible.'

That was either convenient or inconvenient, Max supposed, depending on your point of view. 'How does Zamaron suggest my father climbed through the window? It would have been quite a scramble.'

'There was a chair in front of the window. One of those, I believe.' Appleby pointed to a stack of plain deal chairs. 'He could simply have stepped out.'

'Then I believe I'll do the same.'

'Would you fetch him a chair, Mr Fradgley?' Appleby asked, apparently unsurprised.

Carrying furniture, for however short a distance, did not appear to agree with Fradgley. But he did as he had been asked.

'Is this really necessary?' Ashley put in. 'It seems clear enough how Pa got on to the roof, James.'

'But not why.'

Ashley's expression signalled strongly that he was not sure he wanted to know why. But his own diffidence embarrassed him. It was a legitimate question.

Apparently taking pity on him, Appleby said, 'Commissioner Zamaron is in possession of information that may point to an explanation, Sir Ashley.'

'The information is not altogether edifying,' said Fradgley.

'I think we'd better hear it, even so,' Max responded, drawing a reluctant nod of approval from his brother.

'Very well.' Appleby smiled grimly. 'We're all men of the world, I trust. I'm obliged to speak plainly. According to the concierge, Sir Henry regularly visited a war widow, one Madame Dombreux, who occupies an apartment on the third floor. Madame Dombreux told the concierge she was giving Sir Henry French lessons.'

'French lessons?' Ashley spluttered. 'But . . .'

'How old is Madame Dombreux?' Max enquired calmly.

'Like many war widows, Mr Maxted, she is not old at all. I haven't met her myself. Zamaron described her as . . . *très jolie*.'

'Good God,' murmured Ashley.

'Also like many war widows, Madame Dombreux must support herself as best she can. She has a poorly paid job in the ticket office at Montparnasse station. It wouldn't be surprising if she sought to . . . supplement her income.'

'By giving French lessons.'

'Exactly so.'

'In the evening, no doubt.'

'No doubt.'

'This is disgusting,' Ashley grumbled.

'It may not be, Sir Ashley,' said Fradgley. 'It could all be entirely above board.'

'So it could,' Appleby agreed. 'The fact is that Sir Henry called here frequently. That much we know for certain.'

'But I don't imagine he frequently went on to the roof,' said Max. 'Does Zamaron have an explanation for that?'

Appleby sighed. 'He does.'

'Which we aren't going to find palatable either?'

'I'm afraid not. Zamaron's responsible for overseeing foreign residents in Paris. Hence his involvement in this matter. He happens to know that the attic room in the building opposite is the studio of an Italian artist named Spataro. Zamaron knows a lot of artists. He seems to fancy himself as something of a connoisseur, as you'll see later. He believes Madame Dombreux sometimes models for Spataro. Make of that what you will. What he makes of it is that Sir Henry may have suspected she did rather more than pose for Spataro and that he went on to the roof on Friday night in order to spy on them, then . . . slipped.'

Ashley groaned and gave ground. 'We certainly can't relay such a story to our mother, Mr Appleby. It would be . . . impossible.'

'Then I suggest you invent a more acceptable alternative.'

'The commissioner's lurid speculations will form no part of any official conclusion on the circumstances of your father's death, Sir Ashley,' said Fradgley. 'You may rest assured of that.'

'Is Madame Dombreux likely to be at home at this hour, gentlemen?' Max enquired.

'Most likely not,' Appleby replied. 'And, frankly, I'm not sure what you'd gain by speaking to her.'

'We don't want to speak to her,' Ashley declared, apparently believing it was for him to declare their wishes in such matters.

Max had already decided he would speak to the woman with or without Appleby's assistance. He did not bother to contradict his brother, but turned back to the window.

He could see at a glance that the parapet blocked the view of the attic of the building opposite. Out on the roof it would be a different matter, of course. To that extent, Zamaron's theory was sound enough. 'I believe I'll take that look outside even so,' he announced in a deliberately nonchalant tone. 'Since we're here.'

He stepped up on to the chair and out through the open window. It was quite a stretch down to the gutter. It was not difficult to imagine his father taking a fatal misstep out there at night.

Max steadied himself against the roof and stood upright. Paris stretched grey and smoke-wreathed around him. There was the Eiffel Tower away to his right. Below, a tram was clattering round a curve in the tracks in Carrefour Vavin. And directly opposite were the windows of the attic Sir Henry had supposedly climbed out there to see into. Max could not make out much of the interior. The windows were uncurtained but dirty. Something that might have been an easel draped in a sheet stood at one end of the room. Rectangular, stacked shapes that could have been paintings were also visible. Beyond that . . . nothing.

If Spataro fulfilled the archetype of a Montparnasse artist, he was probably asleep. At night, with lights burning within, it could have been very different. Had his father seen what he had feared he would see? Or worse than he had feared? Shock could have played its part in the disaster that overtook him. If so, it was a pitiful end.

The cooing of a pigeon close by drew Max's attention

to the chimney-stack behind him. He turned and glanced up at the bird, perched by one of the pots. The stack formed part of a wall supporting it and chimneys of the next building. Max noticed there were skylights set in the roof just below the apex, serving a second attic above the one he had just emerged from.

At that moment, a pale glimmer of sunlight pierced the prevailing gloom and was reflected off the rain-slicked roof. Something sparkled in Max's field of view and he realized there were fragments of broken glass scattered across the tiles immediately below the nearest skylight. Then he saw that one of the panes in the sky-light was broken. How had that come about? he wondered. How – and when?

Grasping the wooden finial above the window, he hauled himself up past the dormer roof.

'Where are you going, Mr Maxted?' Appleby called, leaning out to follow his progress.

'There's a broken window up here.'

'One of the policemen probably put his boot through it. They're a clumsy lot. Watch your step, now.'

'I will, I will.'

Max doubted if any of the police had climbed up to the sky-light. It was an awkward scramble, with little available in the way of foot- or hand-holds. One wrong move and Max could conceivably go the way of his father. A glance behind him was hardly reassuring.

But flying over the battlefields of Flanders in wire-and-canvas biplanes had immunized him against vertigo. He made it to the skylight with nothing worse than a few short slips to show for it. A hole had certainly been punched in one of the panes. A piece of wood had been nailed beneath the remnants of the pane to keep the weather out. It was obvious no policeman's boot was responsible for the damage, however. The fragments of glass on the roof proved the skylight had been broken from inside, not outside. It was puzzling – very puzzling.

He peered down through the undamaged pane into a cramped roof space. The boarded floor he could see below was thick with dust, pierced in places by assorted footprints. The footprints themselves were entirely free of dust. They had clearly been made recently – probably no longer ago than Friday.

A fatal accident in the circumstances envisaged by Commissioner Zamaron was plausible, he could not deny. But there were enough oddities and inconsistencies to suggest that something else might have happened, though what that might be he could not yet imagine. He needed to learn more. And he would, whatever Ashley said.

He slithered back down to the attic window and cast another glance towards Spataro's studio. There was still no movement there. It struck Max that if anyone had seen what happened to Sir Henry, it could only be Spataro. He would have had a perfect view – if he had been looking.

'Seen enough, Mr Maxted?' Appleby called.

'Quite enough, thank you.' Max clambered back in through the window and brushed himself down.

'Satisfied?' Ashley asked sharply, frowning at him ominously.

'I believe I am, yes.'

'Then perhaps we should be going.'

*

They left the attic, Appleby locking up carefully behind them, and headed for the lift. As they reached it, Ashley said suddenly, 'No sense our cramming in there again like sardines. You go ahead, gentlemen. My brother and I will walk down.'

Ashley brushed aside Fradgley's offer to give up his place in the lift. Appleby made no such offer. The expression on his face suggested he knew, as did Max, that Ashley had decided a quiet word between brothers was now in order.

The lift groaned and clanked arthritically down its wire shaft as Ashley and Max began a slow descent of the stairs. Max lit a cigarette and waited for Ashley to declare his position. He did not have to wait long.

'I was afraid it would be something like this, you know. Falling to his death while spying on some tart he'd become besotted with. I mean to say, it's pathetic.'

'You seem to be assuming it's true.'

'Of course it's true. How else do you explain a man of Pa's age prancing around on a roof in the middle of the night?'

'I don't. Yet. But perhaps we should speak to Madame Dombreux before we make our minds up.'

'Absolutely not. Give her the slightest encouragement and she'll be trying to blackmail us.'

'With what?'

'I don't know. *Billets doux* Pa was stupid enough to send her, perhaps.'

'But—'

'Listen to me very carefully, James. I don't want any word of this – any breath – to reach Mother.'

'Neither do I, if Zamaron's version of events is correct.'

'It's obviously correct. Fortunately, no one has any interest in bringing those events to public attention. Appleby and Fradgley are trying to avoid embarrassing our delegation here. And it sounds as if this fellow Zamaron has been told to help them do that. So, we must do everything we can to cooperate with them. Don't ask any challenging questions. And don't look down your nose in that way you have that implies you don't believe a single thing you're being told.'

'Look down my nose? I never—'

'If you want to make yourself useful, think of something we can tell Mother that will go some way towards accounting for what happened to Pa without mentioning this Dombreux woman.'

'I'll do my best.'

'You'd better. Pa's left us a truly horrible mess to clear up. It can be done. But only if we stick together. I need your support, James. Your loyalty to our family.' Ashley looked round at him as he traversed the next landing. 'Can I be assured of it?'

'Of course you can.'

'Good. I'm glad to hear it.'

No doubt he was. But Max was aware that their definitions of family loyalty did not necessarily coincide. In the end, Max would abide faithfully by his definition, not Ashley's. He understood himself well enough to know that it could be no other way.

POLICE HEADQUARTERS ON THE ÎLE DE LA CITÉ WAS A massive old mansarded building facing Notre-Dame. It was so noisy and crowded that it was hard to tell who among the gabbling, form-flapping throng might be police officers, complainants or suspected criminals. Max for one was glad of a guide through the maze of narrow corridors and echoing stairways. It was clearly not Appleby's first visit to the premises. The several greetings he exchanged along the way suggested he was a regular caller.

This was confirmed when they reached the relative haven of Commissioner Zamaron's office. He was a small, wiry, moustachioed man, with a mop of suspiciously dark hair and a policemanly combination of affability and perceptiveness. Disarmingly, he and Appleby were on first-name terms – *'Bonjour, Horace,'* and 'Good morning, Léon,' no less.

Appleby had alerted them to Zamaron's supposed connoisseurship and it was immediately apparent. Paintings covered the walls – landscapes, still lifes and portraits in contrasting styles. Were they payments in kind for favours done? Max wondered. He could not resist whispering to Ashley, 'I expect he keeps the nudes at home.' Ashley pretended not to hear him.

There had been a telephone call for Fradgley from the Embassy, Zamaron reported in his very passable English. Fradgley took himself off to return the call.

That left Zamaron to offer Max and Ashley coffee, condolences and his personal assurances of discretion and dutifulness. 'Horace has told you what I believe occurred, *messieurs*? *Très bien*. We do not need to speak more of it. A tragic accident is a tragic accident. Everything is arranged. The, er . . . *travail administratif* . . . has been dealt with.'

'He means the paperwork's in place, gentlemen,' said Appleby. 'When will they be able to take Sir Henry's body back to England, Léon?'

'Whenever you wish. Tomorrow?'

'That would suit us very well,' said Ashley. 'We're very grateful for your . . . expeditiousness.'

'Think nothing of it.'

'The paperwork,' Ashley pressed, 'will include a death certificate, I take it?'

'But of course. One has already been sent from the Mairie to the Embassy. No doubt Monsieur Fradgley is being told of this by his office.'

'And what does it state as the cause of death?'

'The cause of death?'

'French death certificates don't necessarily specify one, Sir Ashley,' said Appleby with a smile.

'Really?' Max put in.

Appleby's smile broadened. 'Really.'

'Sir Henry's possessions – those found on him – I have here.' Zamaron opened a drawer in his desk and took out a bulging manilla envelope. 'You will want to have them.'

'Indeed,' said Ashley gravely.

'I regret I must ask you to sign a receipt.'

Zamaron's doleful expression implied his regret was genuine. Max could not but admire the man's delicacy. It was only marginally sullied by the impression that he was enjoying himself rather a lot.

Zamaron handed the receipt to Ashley, who held it out for Max to see. It was printed in French, naturally. Their father's possessions had been listed in abominable handwriting, also in French. *Un portefeuille. Une montre. Un mouchoir. Une paire de boutons de manchette. Une épingle à cravate. Un peigne. Une chevalière. 41fr.*

'You should check it's all there, *messieurs,*' said Zamaron, when neither showed any inclination to do so.

Max sat forward and slid the contents of the envelope out on to the desk. There they were, each item instantly familiar: the leather wallet, the silver pocket-watch, the monogrammed handkerchief and cufflinks, the tie-pin, the humble comb, the signet ring. They were Sir Henry Maxted's props and accessories that he had carried around the world.

'All present and correct,' said Max quietly.

'Count the money, if you would be so good, *monsieur.*'

Max sighed and counted. Forty-one francs there were. He turned to Ashley. 'Will you sign for it or shall I?'

'I'll do it,' said Ashley. He had reddened slightly and his eyes had moistened, as if the sight of his father's effects, arranged on a police-station desk, had moved

76

him more deeply than viewing the old man's corpse on a mortuary slab. There was something in that, Max would have agreed. He could not really have explained why.

Ashley signed on the dotted line and Max loaded the items back into the envelope. An awkward silence loomed. Zamaron looked at Appleby and Appleby looked at Max. Ashley blew his nose. Zamaron made a meal of folding the receipt. And Max decided to put a toe into some untested waters. 'You collect art, commissioner?'

'I do, Monsieur Maxted, I do.' Zamaron sounded pleased by the question and allowed himself a self-satisfied glance around his walls.

'Is there any of Spataro's work here?'

Ashley stiffened, but remained silent. Zamaron, meanwhile, appeared blithely undismayed. He was on first-name terms with his favourite artists as well, it soon transpired. 'I cannot show Raffaele's paintings here. They are too—'

'Explicit?'

'Non, non. They are too big. Raffaele, he . . . paints on a grand scale.'

'But he does paints nudes, doesn't he?'

'Er, sometimes. Not always. He is . . . versatile.'

'And something of a ladies' man?'

Zamaron leant back in his chair and gazed studiously at Max. 'He is Italian, Monsieur Maxted. He has a reputation, like many of his countrymen. But it was my understanding that you and Sir Ashley did not wish to enquire deeply into—'

'We don't, commissioner,' Ashley interrupted, with a

glare at Max. 'We don't require any more information than we already have. Isn't that so, James?'

Max shrugged. 'Yes. Of course. I was just—'

The door rattled open and Fradgley came in, sparing Max the need to complete his sentence. 'I'm pleased to say that all the documentation we require to facilitate the collection of Sir Henry's body from the hospital is now to hand, gentlemen,' Fradgley announced, looking every bit as pleased as he claimed to be. 'There is a reliable firm of undertakers we customarily use in such situations as this. They can arrange everything and deliver the deceased to the Gare du Nord to be carried on the train you elect to travel home on.'

'They're thinking of tomorrow, Fradgley,' said Appleby.

'That should present no difficulty. The documents are waiting at the Embassy and the undertakers will be available at your convenience.'

'Excellent,' said Ashley.

So it was, in its way, thought Max. The Paris police and the British Embassy were surpassing themselves in the cause of a speedy resolution to the awkward matter of Sir Henry Maxted's fatal fall. It was hard not to be impressed. And it was equally difficult not to ponder what chances the truth had of making itself heard amidst all this speed and efficiency.

'Is there anything else I can do for you, *messieurs*?' Zamaron enquired, in a tone that presumed the answer would be no.

'One point does occur to me,' said Max in the same instant that Ashley opened his mouth to speak.

Ashley rounded on him. 'What?'

'It's simply that there's no key among our father's possessions, commissioner.'

'No key?' Zamaron frowned in puzzlement.

'Well, I'm merely wondering how our father gained entry to the apartment building on Friday night. I assume it's locked at night.'

'For heaven's sake, James,' spluttered Ashley, 'haven't we—'

'*Non, non*,' Zamaron cut in. 'Monsieur Maxted asks a good question. The building is locked at night, *oui*. The concierge, Madame Mesnet, assures me of this. But she is forgetful. She likes to take a drink. She may have forgotten to lock the door. Or else Sir Henry had a key, given to him by Madame Dombreux, which slipped from his pocket when he fell and was . . . not noticed on the pavement.'

'Yes,' Max conceded. 'I suppose one of those explanations must be correct.'

'You're satisfied on the point, then?' Ashley asked, glaring at him.

'Yes. As far as one can be.'

'Good. Well, I'm sure Commissioner Zamaron is a busy man. I think we've taken up enough of his time, don't you?'

ASHLEY WAS CLEARLY SEETHING WITH IRRITATION AT MAX – ALL the more because he could not express it – when they left Police Headquarters and travelled to the British Embassy. There the atmosphere was calm and orderly, hushed, it struck Max, almost ecclesiastical.

Fradgley had Sir Henry's passport and his travel-hardened leather suitcase, packed with his belongings from his room at the Hotel Majestic, waiting in his office for them to collect. More crucially, he had a tranche of documents – permits of one kind or another, some in duplicate, some in triplicate, and the terse but essential death certificate. From an administrative view-point, nothing now stood in the way of Sir Henry's posthumous repatriation to his homeland.

Fradgley suggested they should repair promptly to the undertaker he recommended in order to arrange the next stage in the process. To this they readily agreed. Appleby explained he would not be accompanying them. 'I don't think there's anything more I can do for you, gentlemen.' They did not argue.

As he left, Appleby said, looking at Max as he spoke, 'If you do find you need me, I can be contacted via the security office at the Majestic.'

Ashley hardly seemed to be listening. But Max was.

Their business at the undertaker's was handled with sombre efficiency. Monsieur Prettre, *entrepreneur de pompes funèbres* of the fourth generation (with the daguerreotyped likeness of his great-grandfather casting a faded gaze over his shoulder) assured them of his best and swiftest attention. He saw no reason why they could not take their father home on Tuesday's noon train. He suggested they telephone him later to confirm everything was in order.

Through gritted teeth (it seemed to Max) Fradgley offered them lunch 'at the Embassy's expense' after they had left the undertaker's. If this was intended as an acknowledgement of the service Sir Henry had rendered his country over the years, Max reckoned it erred on the side of paltriness.

The conversation over lunch was as dull as the food. Handshakes afterwards on the pavement outside the restaurant marked, Max assumed, the end of their dealings with Fradgley, but it transpired he was assuming too much.

'I'll be at the Gare du Nord tomorrow to see you off, gentlemen,' the wretched man announced. 'And to ensure there aren't any last-minute hitches. You can't take any chances with the French.'

Ashley interpreted this as a further indication of the lengths the Embassy was going to in order to smooth their path. If anyone's path was being smoothed, Max thought it more likely to be Fradgley's. But much of

Ashley's anger at him for asking unhelpful questions at unhelpful times had dissipated, so he chose not to offer this interpretation.

A somewhat testier version of the discussion they had had on their way out of 8 Rue du Verger ensued as they walked back to the Mazarin through the dank grey afternoon. But Max was well aware it would have been testier still a few hours earlier.

'You don't seem to appreciate, James, just how helpful these people are being.'

'Oh, I do, Ashley, believe me.'

'Then why must you keep provoking them?'

'I thought they might think it odd if one of us didn't query a few things.'

'What is there to query apart from Pa's sanity? How he can have put himself in such a situation is beyond me.'

'*La femme fatale.* I believe it's an old story.'

'Well, it's not a story we can allow Mother to hear.'

'I agree.'

'Then act as if you agree. And apply your mind to the problem of what we're going to tell her.'

'I will.'

'Good. Because we don't have long to think of something.'

They assuredly did not. Max claimed, accurately enough, that a walk would help clear his mind on the subject. He left Ashley at the door of the Mazarin with a tentative agreement to dine together later. Ashley had telegrams to send, to the undertaker in Epsom their family used and to their mother, alerting her to the imminence of their return. There was plenty to keep him busy.

There was plenty to occupy Max too, though it was not exactly what he had led his brother to suppose. As soon as he was out of sight of the Mazarin, he headed for the river. He was going back to Montparnasse.

William Fradgley would not have been pleased to know this. Fortunately for his peace of mind, he believed Sir Ashley Maxted had his brother's inquisitiveness well under control. He was in the process of telling Appleby so even as Max was striding across the Pont de l'Alma.

'They'll be gone tomorrow, Appleby, and the problem of Sir Henry with them.'

'You think so?' Appleby's rumbling voice was turned into a growl by the crackly telephone line from the Majestic.

'Of course. Why not?'

'The younger brother. James. He worries me.'

'You worry too much.'

'That's my job, Fradgley. To worry. The last thing we want during the conference is a scandal.'

'It's also the last thing Sir Henry's family wants.'

'But there's more than one kind of scandal. And Sir Henry tupping a young widow is far from the worst.'

'What a coarse turn of phrase you people do have.'

'It must arise from the sort of fixes we have to get *you* people out of.'

'I don't know what—'

'Have you heard anything from *le Deuxième Bureau*?'

'No. Should I have?'

'They may have been keeping an eye on Madame Dombreux.'

'Surely whatever her husband was up to was buried with him in Russia.'

'Perhaps. Perhaps not. Certainty's hard to come by in my line of business.'

Fradgley sighed. 'I'll put the Maxted brothers on the train tomorrow, Appleby. Along with their late father. As far as I'm concerned, my involvement in this matter ends there.'

'I wish I could believe mine will too.'

'Well, I must get on.'

'Yes, yes. I'm sure there are memos you need to write. Good afternoon to you.'

Max had set himself a brisk pace and was at the Gare Montparnasse within half an hour. He had no way of knowing whether Madame Dombreux would be on duty, but was happy to take his chances. If she had already gone, he would simply have to press on to 8 Rue du Verger.

He could not see the cashiers clearly behind their grilled windows, but, after annoying several people by dodging from one queue to another, he found the one he was looking for.

The cashier was a young woman, dressed in an un-flattering grey uniform. But, as Max drew closer, it became ever more obvious that she was really quite beautiful.

Her dark hair was gathered beneath her uniform cap. Her face was pale and heart-shaped and only a cast of weariness in her looks disguised her attractiveness. She kept her cool green eyes trained on the tickets and the money in front of her. Her expression was grave, her exchanges with passengers minimally polite. Max would have guessed, even without knowing, that she was someone only misfortune and adverse circumstances had reduced to issuing train tickets for a living. She had been bred for better.

He reached the head of the queue and drew her gaze by the simple means of saying nothing.

'*Oui, monsieur?*' she prompted, her voice soft and serious.

'Madame Dombreux?'

She frowned and looked at him more intently. Then she covered her mouth in surprise. He heard her sharp intake of breath. Somehow, she knew who he was.

'I'm James Maxted.'

'Of course. You have Henry's eyes.'

Her direct, unflinching reference to his father and the perfection of her English, in which an accent was barely detectable, took him aback. For a moment, he merely stared at her.

'I'm sorry,' she said. 'I did not mean to—'

'I need to speak to you.'

'—' She nodded. 'And I to you. But we cannot speak here. Meet me in the Café du Dôme at a quarter to seven. It is on Carrefour Vavin.'

WITH TIME TO KILL, MAX WENT INTO A CAFÉ OPPOSITE THE station, where he drank two coffees and smoked several cigarettes. The light outside started to fail and the streets became slowly busier as workers began their homeward journeys. Well-filled trams rattled by at intervals. He pondered the enigma of Madame Dombreux and her relationship with his father. *You have Henry's eyes.* The phrase lingered in his thoughts, along with the manner in which she had spoken it. Whatever she had been to Sir Henry, it surely amounted to more than he had been led to believe.

It was a short walk along Boulevard du Montparnasse to Carrefour Vavin. He diverted to Rue du Verger and paused to stare up at the roof of number 8. It was growing dark now. Lamplight gleamed from some of the windows. It was easy to convince himself Madame Mesnet was peering out at him from one of them. He headed on.

There were several cafés spaced around the junction. The Café du Dôme appeared to be the busiest, with one or two hardy souls braving the terrace. Inside, most of the tables were occupied. There was laughter and shoulder-clapping banter and a miasma of cigarette smoke. Max could hear the click of billiard balls from an inner room. He found a perch on one of the banquettes close to the entrance and ordered a beer. He looked at his watch and wondered what he would say when she arrived.

A quarter of an hour slowly passed. Then a large, bulky figure entered the café, colliding with Max's table as he did so. He uttered no apology, probably because he had not noticed. He was a huge man, made to look huger still by a flapping, frayed tweed suit and wild head of hair, complete with bushy beard. He headed straight for the bar, waving his hand in acknowledgement as some-one shouted his name. *'Eh, Raffaele!'*

Several of those standing at the bar greeted him familiarly. And his response clinched his identity. *'Buonasera . . . mes amis.'* A brandy was downed in mid-sentence and another promptly ordered.

It was both an opportunity not to be missed and one fraught with difficulties. For all his bonhomie, Spataro looked every bit as volatile as an Italian artist might be expected to. Perhaps the shrewdest course of action would be to wait and see how he reacted to Madame Dombreux's arrival.

But shrewdness sat ill with Max's impatience to learn as much as he could before he was obliged to leave Paris. He stood up and threaded his way to the bar.

'Raffaele Spataro?' There was no response until Max had added a tap on the arm – an arm that felt like a solid mass of muscle. 'Raffaele Spataro?'

'Si.' Spataro swung round and looked at him. *'C'est moi.'*

'I'm James Maxted.'

'You are English.'

'Yes. Could I have a word with you?'

'Ah. Words. That is all the English have.'

'I don't think the Germans would agree with you there.'

The remark seemed to make Spataro take stock of Max for the first time. 'Do you want to buy me a drink, *mio amico*?'

'I'd be happy to.'

Spataro laughed. 'Then I leave you to pay for my brandy.' He drained his second glass and smacked it down on the bar. '*Grazie mille*. I must go.'

'Wait.' Max laid a restraining hand on Spataro's elbow. 'I'd like to ask you a few questions about the death in Rue du Verger on Friday night.'

'What is that to you?'

'The man who died was my father. Sir Henry Maxted.'

'Then I am sorry for you. But I know nothing.'

'Your studio faces the roof he supposedly fell from.'

'Supposedly? What is "supposedly"? He fell.'

'Did you see it happen?'

Spataro shook Max off and gave him a glare in which there was just a hint of fear beneath the menace. 'I saw nothing.'

'You're sure?'

'*Si*. I am sure.'

'You don't look it.'

Spataro's eyes widened. Suddenly, he grabbed Max by the tie and collar. Max felt his feet being raised from the floor. He smiled, which seemed to baffle the Italian. 'What is funny?'

'You are, Raffaele. It's a good thing you're an artist, because you'd make a rotten actor.'

Spataro's face darkened and his grip on Max tightened. Then there was a shout from behind the bar. The *patron* intervened in a reproving volley of Franco-Italian that seemed to register with Spataro as something he was bound to take note of. He scowled and ground his teeth, then released Max and held up his hands in a placatory fashion. But it was the management of a favourite watering hole he was placating, not Max. 'Leave me alone,' he growled. Then he spun on his heel and stalked out.

Max rather expected the *patron* to give him his marching orders too. But he was positively sympathetic, refusing to let Max pay for Spataro's brandies and referring to '*les artistes*' with an expressive roll of the eyes.

One of the other customers massed at the bar spoke reasonable English and claimed to know someone who knew one of those who had found Sir Henry's body. 'A terrible thing, *monsieur*. Have the police found out what happened?' Max assured him they had not. '*Naturellement*,' came the cynical response.

Max decided to finish his beer outside. It was growing cold, but that hardly mattered. He wanted to be able to suggest to Madame Dombreux that they go elsewhere for their talk. After his encounter with Spataro, he felt too conspicuous for comfort at the Dôme.

He was not kept waiting long, but her arrival surprised him nonetheless. He was expecting her to approach from the direction of the station and to be recognizable by her uniform. Instead, she appeared suddenly beside him, dressed in her own clothes: skirt, coat and cloche hat. She had evidently gone home first.

'Why are you out here?' she asked at once.

'I met your friend Spataro. He got a little . . . loud.'

'Raffaele Spataro?'

'The very same.'

'He's no friend of mine.'

'That's not what Commissioner Zamaron says.'

She frowned at him and shook her head, as if surpassingly sorry that he should believe whatever Zamaron had told him. 'Why are you here, James?' Her freedom with his first name was disarming in its effect.

'I want to know why my father died.'

'You do?'

'Yes.'

'Well, so do I.' Her eyes brimmed with tears. 'I am sorry. I loved him. His death like that . . . was so awful.' She dabbed away some of her tears with a handkerchief.

'I didn't mean to upset you, *madame*.'

'But you want the truth.'

'Yes.'

'And your brother? Madame Mesnet told me of your visit. I notice he isn't with you. Does he want the truth?'

Max shrugged. 'I can't speak for him.'

'Will you buy me a brandy, James? I feel a little . . .'

'Of course. Is there somewhere else we can go? We'll attract a lot of attention here.'

'Yes. The Parnasse. Next door. It's quieter.'

THE CAFÉ PARNASSE WAS, AS SHE HAD PROMISED, QUIETER than the Dôme: fewer customers, less badinage, calmer altogether. Max watched her sip her brandy and went on watching her as he flicked his lighter for her cigarette. She was older than he by a few years. And some of those years had been hard ones, costing her much of the bloom she must once have had. She was beautiful, but no longer flawless. The cuff of her blouse beneath her check jacket was ever-so-slightly frayed. There was weariness in her looks and sadness in her eyes.

'Call me Corinne,' she said softly.

'In that case, you'd better call me Max. I'm only James to my family.'

'Max it is. The name suits you. Henry said you flew in the war.'

'I did.'

'Do you miss it?'

'The war? Or the flying?'

'Both. Or either.'

'I haven't flown a plane since I was shot down in April of 'seventeen. That's nearly two years. I missed it dreadfully at first. Now . . . it's not so bad.'

'And you'll be flying again soon, won't you?'

'Ah. Pa told you about that, did he?'

She did not answer. But Sir Henry had told her everything, of course. Max felt strangely certain of that. He was damned if he would embarrass himself or Corinne Dombreux by asking her to admit she and his father – her senior by at least thirty years – had been lovers. She had said she loved him and that was enough. Nor was it hard to understand what might have attracted Sir Henry to her. She had an air of mystery and a hint of fragility likely to attract many men – including Max, come to that.

'You speak very good English, Corinne. I'd hardly know you were French.'

'My mother was English. And I went to school there. Both my parents wanted me to be the perfect English lady.'

'You say that as if you disappointed them.'

'Living here, as I do, isn't what they had in mind for me. It's not what I had in mind for myself.'

'How did it come about?'

'I married the wrong man, Max. I am the widow of the infamous Pierre Dombreux.'

'I've never heard of him.'

'I wish no one had.'

'What did he do to earn his infamy?'

'He betrayed his country . . . so they say.'

'How?'

'He was a diplomat, like Henry. My parents were very pleased when I married him. So was I. I loved him. I thought he loved me. He was posted to the embassy in St Petersburg. I went with him.'

'And that's where you met my father?'

'Yes. There was nothing between us at first, except friendship, which flourished despite the difference in our ages. And a friendship is what it would have remained if Pierre had been faithful to me. But he was not. And he did little to hide it. Henry was a source of strength when I most needed it. He was the only friend I had in the whole of St Petersburg – Petrograd, as it was by then. When Pierre learnt of our closeness – which was entirely innocent at that point, though precious to me nonetheless – he sent me home to Paris in disgrace.

'My parents believed every lie he told them. They disowned me. This was in the autumn of 1917, just before the Bolsheviks seized power in Russia. The war was going badly. I had our apartment to live in, but no money. I found work as a seamstress. It was hard. I received a second schooling: in what the world is like for a woman with no place in society. And there was worse to come. In March last year, when the Bolsheviks made peace with Germany, Pierre was accused of prompting them to do so by revealing secret plans the French government had supposedly approved for Japan to seize Vladivostok.

'The first I knew of it was when the papers named him as a traitor. He had gone missing, it was reported. A few days later, I had a telegram from the embassy in Petrograd. His body had been pulled out of the Griboedov canal. He'd been shot through the head.'

'Good God. That must have been a terrible shock for you.'

'I'm not asking for sympathy.' There was a flash of anger in her eyes. Her pride in herself had been dented by misfortune. But it had not been destroyed.

'I'll be sure not to offer any.'

Corinne frowned at him. 'You're a lot like your father, you know.'

'My mother's forever complaining of how *un*like him I am.'

'Henry always said she misunderstood him.'

'They'd grown apart, Corinne. You must know that.'

'Yes. Of course. I can only speak of the Henry I knew. We wrote to each other after I left Petrograd. And he came to see me after he left himself, early last year.' (Was that when their relationship had moved beyond the platonic? Max wondered. Or had his father waited until she was a widow?) 'When he saw how I was living, he began sending me money, which I'm ashamed to say I accepted. I was evicted from Pierre's apartment after his death. That's when I moved here. I took the job at the station to try to make myself independent. I took other jobs as well.'

'Including modelling?'

'Yes. Do you want to know how many artists I posed for in the nude, Max? Is that it?'

'The only artist I'm interested in is Raffaele Spataro.'

'He was one of them,' she acknowledged with a sigh.

'Did it stop at posing?'

'He'd have liked to take it further. I didn't let him. I know what you've been told: that Henry fell from the roof because he was spying on Spataro to see if I was with him. It's nonsense. I wasn't there. I haven't done any modelling since Henry came to Paris. And I only modelled for Raffaele Spataro once. He's a lecher and a liar. He probably encouraged Zamaron to believe I spent the night with him to burnish his reputation as

94

the Casanova of Montparnasse.' She shook her head. 'It would be laughable if it weren't so serious. Please don't entertain the notion that I betrayed your father. It's the last thing I'd have done.'

'Why was he there that night, Corinne?'

She took a sip of brandy and looked Max in the eye. 'He was there every night. I surely don't have to spell it out.'

'How did he get into the building?'

'He had a key.'

'None was found on him.'

'He left it in my apartment. I found it when I returned.'

'Returned from where?'

'Nantes. My sister lives there. I received a telegram at the station just as I was about to go off duty saying she was dangerously ill. I travelled to Nantes at once, but the journey took hours, of course. I knew Henry would be waiting for me, but there was nothing I could do. When I arrived, I discovered the telegram was a hoax. My sister wasn't ill at all. And she wasn't pleased to see me. I'd missed the last train back by then, so, somewhat reluctantly, she let me stay overnight. I think she suspected I was making a clumsy attempt to effect a reconciliation. Little good it would have done me. I took the first train back in the morning. And when I reached home . . .'

'You think someone lured you away?'

'It didn't occur to me at the time, but my sister had no way of knowing where I worked. Yet the telegram was sent from Nantes. Someone went to great lengths to arrange my absence that night.'

'Knowing my father would then be there alone.'

'Yes. Exactly.'

'You realize what you're suggesting?'

'He was murdered, Max. I haven't a doubt of that.'

So, she had come out and said what he had already begun to suspect himself. It was murder. And murder changed everything. If it was true, it could not go unavenged. 'You must have told Zamaron where you were.'

'Naturally I told him, but he doesn't believe me. Spataro says I was with him. That's good enough for Commissioner Zamaron.'

'Surely your sister—'

'He assumes she's helping me out of a hole by saying I was in Nantes. Not that she *has* said that, as far as I know. I don't think he's actually asked her.'

'Why on earth not?'

'Because he doesn't need to. For his purposes, it's enough that Henry might have suspected I was with Raffaele Spataro. Zamaron isn't conducting a criminal inquiry. That's the beauty of his theory from his point of view. It means he doesn't have to amass evidence or test alibis. He doesn't have to do anything.'

'We'll see about that.'

'Don't waste your time with the police. They don't want to know. Zamaron's not his own master. The unexplained murder of a member of the British delegation to the peace conference could turn into a scandal. They're afraid the press – and others – will start suggesting it had something to do with the conference itself.'

'Could it have?'

'I don't know. Neither do they. So, it's safer to write it off as an accident.'

Max lit a cigarette and considered the point. 'How sure are you that he was murdered, Corinne?'

'You mean how sure can I make you?'

He smiled drily. 'I suppose I do.'

'Henry left the apartment in a hurry. He didn't lock the door behind him. He didn't take his overcoat. He was chasing something . . . someone.'

'An intruder?'

'Maybe.'

'When I went up on the roof, I noticed that one of the skylights was broken. From the inside.'

'I noticed that too.'

Max was not surprised to learn Corinne had been on the roof. What else, he wondered, had she done in pursuit of her lover's murderer?

'Did they let you see Henry's body, Max?'

'Of course.'

'They wouldn't let me. There were excuses about the severity of his injuries. When I persisted, I was told I had no right to see him because I wasn't a relative. And I won't be able to go to his funeral either, will I?'

Max shook his head sorrowfully. 'No.'

'I don't expect you to approve of our relationship. But I loved him. And now I've lost him. To a murderer no one is prepared to admit even exists.'

'I'm prepared to admit it.'

She looked at him, her eyes suddenly full of hope. 'You are?'

'Someone cut Pa's fingernails, Corinne. They made a pretty poor job of it. He certainly didn't do it himself. It must have been done after his death. Probably at the mortuary. The question is: why?'

'Do you have an answer?'

'If there was a struggle on the roof, if Pa came to grips with an assailant . . .'

'There could have been blood or skin of the assailant under his fingernails?'

Max nodded. 'That's what I'm thinking.'

She sipped her brandy and thought for a moment, then said, 'We must go to my apartment.'

'Why?'

'There's something I need to show you. I wasn't sure, but now . . .' There was a decisiveness in her gaze that had not been there before. 'Now I'm sure.'

MERCIFULLY, THE CONCIERGE DID NOT STIR WHEN THEY entered 8 Rue du Verger. They took the stairs to Corinne's apartment. 'Quieter than the lift,' she explained. That was amply proven when the sound of someone entering the building reached them as they neared the third floor. It was shortly followed by the lift clanking noisily into motion. 'Monsieur Miette, second floor back,' Corinne murmured, apparently knowing all her neighbours merely by their footfalls.

Her apartment was small, though sufficient, he supposed, for a single occupier. It was neat and clean, simply but comfortably furnished, though with few personal touches. There were no photographs on display and no paintings on the walls. Corinne's domestic existence had been pared down to essentials.

One item that was clearly inessential swiftly attracted his attention, however: a box of Cuban cigars on the mantelpiece. It could only have been left there by his father.

'He would often wait for me here,' Corinne said quietly, following the direction of Max's gaze. 'He knew the times of my shifts. He'd sit there' – she pointed to a buttoned-leather armchair beneath a standard lamp – 'and smoke a cigar and read a newspaper while he waited. I could smell the cigar from the stairs. I'd know by its aroma that I'd see him smiling at me as I opened the door.'

Ashley would be scandalized by such revelations of their father's secret life, of course. Max might have been himself. Instead, he found them curiously touching. Sir Henry the old romantic was a novel but endearing figure to him.

'There was still a trace of the aroma when I returned here on Saturday,' Corinne continued in a wistful tone. 'But it's gone now.'

'What did you want to show me?' Max asked, as eager to know as he was to change the subject.

'This.' She took a piece of paper from her handbag and passed it to him.

He frowned at her. 'I thought it was something here, in the apartment.'

'I couldn't risk showing it to you in the café, in case we were being watched.'

'Watched?'

'The apartment was searched while I was at work yesterday. I wasn't supposed to notice. But they weren't careful enough. Fortunately, I didn't leave that piece of paper here.'

'What is it?'

'See for yourself. I found it on the table by Henry's—' She broke off. 'On the table by the armchair. You'll recognize the handwriting.'

It was his father's, unmistakably: a list of some kind. Corinne lit the lamp for Max to read it by.

It was written in pencil and seemed to represent a rough financial calculation:

Capital	4,000
Mortgage	3,000
Seals	3,000
Trust	c 5,000
Chinese box	c 5,000
Contingencies Memo	c 5,000
F.L.	c 5,000
	c 30,000

'Do you know what this is about?' Max asked, turning to Corinne.

'No. I don't think he intended me or anyone else to read it. He'd probably have destroyed it if he hadn't been interrupted.'

'By whoever killed him?'

'That's how I see it.'

'Thirty thousand pounds is a hell of a lot of money.'

'I know.'

'Did he say anything to you that implied he was trying to raise a sum like this?'

'No.'

Max looked at the list again. *Capital*. Sir Henry might have had savings of £4,000. It was certainly possible. *Mortgage*. He had nothing to mortgage apart from Gresscombe Place. Surely he would not have done that without telling Lady Maxted; Ashley would know if he had. *Seals*. What that might refer to Max could not guess. Likewise *Trust*, unless there was some family fund no one had ever mentioned to him, which was not inconceivable. *Chinese box* was a Chinese puzzle in its own right, as were *Contingencies Memo* and *F.L.* The first three figures were definite amounts, the next four estimates.

'Do you mind if I copy this?'

'Go ahead.'

Max fished a piece of paper from his wallet and jotted down the details. 'I'll show the list to my brother. It might mean something to him.'

'I'd rather you didn't.'

'Why not?'

'It's difficult to explain, but . . .'

'What?'

She looked down. 'Henry said Ashley wasn't to be trusted.'

'He said that? When?'

'I don't know. Some time back, I asked him about the two of you . . . and how you got on. I . . .' She shook her head. 'I'm sorry. You must think I had no business discussing you with your father. And you're right, of course.'

'What did he say, Corinne? Just tell me.'

She hesitated a moment longer, then answered him. 'I've already told you. Ashley wasn't to be trusted.'

'Is that all?'

'No. He also said he thought you were made of the right stuff.' She glanced directly at Max. 'I'm very much hoping he was right. You're the only person I've shown that to. It's the only clue I have as to why Henry may have been murdered. You should weigh the risks very carefully before you share the information with anyone else. As you said, thirty thousand pounds is a lot of money.'

'What would he have wanted it for?'

'I don't know. But something happened about a month ago. It changed Henry. Not towards me, but

102

inside himself. His thoughts were often elsewhere. As if he was turning a problem over in his mind. He said the delegation was working him hard, but that wasn't it. Something else was going on. Something else altogether. He went to London the week after your visit and—'

'He went to London?'

'Yes. He was away three nights. He said he'd been recalled to the Foreign Office for consultations.'

'That can't be right. He wouldn't have gone back to England without seeing my mother. And as I understand it most of the Foreign Office is here in Paris. He didn't need to go to London to consult his lords and masters.'

'It's what he told me, Max. And I believed him. But now . . . I'm not so sure.'

'When was this exactly?'

'He left . . . two weeks ago today.'

Max pulled out his pocket-diary. 'That would have been . . . Monday the tenth.'

'Yes.'

'I saw him here in Paris on Thursday the sixth. He said nothing about it then.'

'He can't have wanted you to know.'

'But why not?'

The only reply Corinne could manage was a shake of the head. Then she frowned and said, 'Your diary.'

'What about it?'

'Henry had a pocket-diary too. With a coat of arms on the front.'

'Official issue of some kind, I imagine.'

'It had a little pencil in the spine.'

'What of it?'

'He didn't carry any other pencil.'

'Corinne, I—'

'Did the police give you everything they found on him, Max?'

'Yes. They did.'

'Was there a pocket-diary?'

'No.'

'There should have been. He didn't leave it here. And he wouldn't have left it at the Majestic. Besides, I'm sure he used the pencil to write this list.'

Max felt sure she was right. Sir Henry's pocket-diary had been removed. But who had taken it? And why?

'The French police didn't know what they were looking for. If they had, the list would probably have gone too. It took a while for someone to arrange a thorough search of this apartment. By then it was too late.'

'Damn them all,' Max declared, his mind suddenly made up. 'I'm not going to let them get away with this.'

'But who are "they"?'

'That's what I mean to find out. Did you ever see any of the diary entries?'

'As far as I know, Henry only used it to record appointments in connection with his duties for the delegation.'

'Do you remember him mentioning any of the names of the people he met?'

'Well, there was a Brazilian delegate he saw quite a bit of called Ribeiro. They knew one another from Henry's time in Rio. And he often referred to a man called Norris whom he reported to in the British delegation. There was a Japanese delegate he was acquainted with as well, though I can't recall his name, I'm afraid.'

'What about Ireton? Did he ever talk about him? An American. Travis Ireton.'

There was a gleam of recognition in Corinne's gaze. 'Yes. Ireton. I remember. We met him at the races at St-Cloud. A strange sort of fellow, with a lopsided stance . . . and a scar on his face.'

'That's him.'

'How do you know him?'

'He was at the Ritz the evening I dined there with Pa. We had a brief word. He was in the company of some Rumanians.'

'Really? The people he was at St-Cloud with were fellow Americans, I think.'

'I asked him if he was attached to the American delegation and got a pretty evasive answer. I had the impression he was some kind of . . . fixer.'

'What does that mean?'

Max smiled. 'I'm not sure. Next time, I'll press him to be more specific about what he does.'

'I may be able to tell you how to contact him.'

Max looked at her in surprise. 'How?'

'He's a womanizer. A girl can always tell. Clumsy flirtation usually confirms it, as it did at St-Cloud. He slipped me his card. "In case you want to call round" was how he put it.'

'And you still have it?'

'I believe I do.'

Corinne crossed to the bureau in the corner of the room, delved in a flower-patterned china pot and returned, smiling triumphantly. It was the first time Max had seen her smile and a surpassingly lovely sight it was.

He had a glimpse then of the pleasure his father must have taken from her company.

'Here it is.' She handed the card to him.

Travis R. Ireton
For all your needs in post-war Paris:
une cité des possibilités

Ireton Associates
33 Rue des Pyramides, Paris
Telegrams: Trireton, Paris
Telephone: Central 48-99

' "A city of possibilities",' Max mused as he slipped the card into his wallet. 'I wonder what he means by that.'

'You'll have to ask him.'

'I intend to.'

'I'd like to be there when you do.'

'It'll be better if I handle this on my own: man to man.' And safer for Corinne, he reflected. If Sir Henry really had been murdered, seeking out the reason was likely to be dangerous.

She knew that, of course. 'Are you trying to protect me, Max?' she asked. 'I don't want you to, you know.'

'I'm sure you don't. But if I'm to pursue this, I must do it alone.'

'Are you worried I'll get in your way?'

'I'm more worried that the irregular nature of your relationship with my father could put me in a difficult position.'

She flinched. The words had hurt her, as Max had

intended. If the cost of keeping her out of harm's way was to have her think him a prude, so be it.

'I'm sorry, Corinne, but I can't allow my family to think you and I have become allies.'

'No.' She composed herself. 'I suppose you can't.'

'I'm grateful for the information you've given me. I'll make the best use of it I can. And I'll let you know what I learn.'

'That would be kind of you.'

'Now I think I should be going, don't you?'

She nodded. In her expression there was realism as well as disappointment. It seemed he had succeeded in lowering her opinion of him. 'Yes. Of course.'

Max found Ashley consuming a solitary meal in the restaurant of the Mazarin and looking none too happy about it.

'Where have you been till this time?' Ashley growled. Fortunately he launched into a summary of how arrangements for the funeral stood without requiring Max to answer that question.

Max ordered fish and let Ashley talk himself out on the subjects of their father's extraordinary lack of judgement ('No fool like an old fool'), the cooperativeness of the French authorities ('Surprisingly obliging lot') and the thorny issue of what they were to tell their mother ('We have to think of something, damn it').

Then, as the meal drew towards a close, Max broached the subject that had been on his mind all along.

'I need to have a word with you in private, Ashley.'

His brother was instantly suspicious. 'What about?'

'This is no place to discuss it.'

'I don't want you creating difficulties, Max.'

'I know you don't.'

'But you're going to create some anyway. Is that it?'

'Shall we go to my room or yours?'

Ashley flung his napkin down tetchily on the table. 'Mine.'

There was a predictable explosion of fury from Ashley when he realized Max had been to see Corinne Dombreux. Eventually and reluctantly, however, he agreed to hear what Max had to say.

It seemed to Max as he spoke that the evidence of foul play was irrefutable, or at the very least far stronger than the evidence that Sir Henry had died accidentally. The shorn fingernails; the missing diary; the broken skylight; the hoax telegram; the searching of Corinne's apartment; the mysterious list: they all told the same story.

But it was not a story Ashley had any intention of believing. His sullen silence as Max laid the facts before him suggested as much. And, when Max had finished, he wasted no time in making his position clear.

'I don't understand the way your mind works, James, I truly don't. We agreed it was in the family's best interests to ensure no scandal attached itself to Pa's death. Now here you are doing your damnedest to sabotage that effort. Perhaps the Dombreux woman has dazzled you just as she dazzled Pa. Well, I don't propose to entertain her lies for a moment. She persuaded her sister to provide her with an alibi for her liaison with this Italian painter and you swallow it hook, line and sinker. Thank the lord Zamaron isn't so credulous. You have only her word for it that her apartment's been searched, but what if it has? As the widow of a known traitor I should think she bears careful watching. A broken skylight is a broken skylight and nothing more.

You don't know when it was broken or by whom. As for Pa's fingernails, I never noticed they were badly or clumsily trimmed.'

'That's because you didn't look at them,' Max cut in.

'I didn't need to. It's ridiculous to suggest the state of his fingernails can have any bearing on this.'

'You know it isn't ridiculous. He was always fastidious about such things.'

'It's a pity he wasn't fastidious about his choice of female company.'

'What about his diary, Ashley? How do you account for it being removed?'

'It wasn't among the items the police handed over because it wasn't found on him. It is as simple as that.'

'Then where is it?'

'We don't know it ever existed. I don't recall him using one when he was at Gresscombe. The Dombreux woman may have invented it, just as she's invented Pa's trip to England two weeks ago. Or . . .' A thought struck him. 'It could be in there, of course.' He pointed to Sir Henry's suitcase, standing in the corner of the room.

'Have you looked inside?'

'No.' Ashley's expression implied there had clearly been no good reason to.

'Well, perhaps we better had.'

Max opened the case and laid it on the floor. He had no expectation of finding anything of interest. Appleby had already had ample opportunity to examine the contents of Sir Henry's room at the Majestic and remove anything significant. His expectation was duly fulfilled. The case held only clothes and toiletries. He delved into every corner and into every pocket of the jackets and trousers. There was nothing else.

'No diary,' he said, closing the case.

'Then she made it up,' came Ashley's fatuous response.

'And the list? Did she make that up? The original's in Pa's handwriting. I saw it for myself.'

'There's no mortgage on Gresscombe Place, James. And no secret family trust. It's balderdash.'

'You think Pa wrote the list for no reason?'

'I think we can't hope to know the reason. A man's bound to leave a few minor mysteries behind him when he dies as suddenly and unexpectedly as Pa did.'

'So, you refuse to accept he may have been murdered?'

'The suggestion's preposterous. Why would anyone want to murder him?'

'That's what I mean to find out.'

'Fortunately, there's no time for you to make a nuisance of yourself by trying. We leave on the noon train tomorrow.'

'That won't be possible, I'm afraid.'

'What?' Ashley stared at him incredulously, though why he should be so surprised Max did not understand. The logic of what he had said was obvious and it did not involve leaving Paris in the near future.

'I believe Pa may well have been murdered, Ashley. That doesn't appear to bother you or the police or the Foreign Office. But it does bother me. And I intend to do everything in my power to establish the truth of what happened to him.'

Ashley reddened ominously. 'I had your word – your

111

solemn word – that you'd help me protect our family's good name.'

'I am protecting it. By seeking justice for a member of it.'

'You'll be on that train tomorrow.'

'I will not.'

'Mother expects us *both* to take Pa home.'

'She'll understand why I've stayed.'

'She most certainly won't.'

'I'm not leaving, Ashley. You may as well face it.'

'I'm warning you, James.' Ashley jabbed a forefinger threateningly in Max's direction. 'Defy me in this and there'll be consequences. You need my agreement to open your damned flying school, remember.'

'I felt sure you wouldn't allow me to forget it.'

'Stay here and you *can* forget it.'

So, it had come to that, as Max had feared it would. 'I can't trust someone who's willing to let his father's probable murder be brushed under the carpet, Ashley. You scuttle back to England and spread whatever lies you like about me. I'll stay here. And do my duty.'

MAX FELT AS IF A HEAVY AND IRKSOME BURDEN HAD BEEN lifted from his shoulders following his altercation with Ashley. It was no longer necessary to pretend they were acting in concert. The use of Gresscombe land for a flying school had ceased to be a carrot dangling in front of his nose. He had always been one to chafe at limitations on his freedom. Now he need chafe no more.

He was aware that the effort of planning for the future, something he had not needed to do during the war, had oppressed him of late. It was not his forte. He was a man of action and of instinct. The RFC had found him valuable on that account, but there had seemed no call for his particular strengths in the peacetime world. His father's murder – he did not seriously doubt it *was* murder – had changed all that. He was about to revert to what he did best.

He rose early next morning and fired off a couple of telegrams. The first was to Sam. He did not want to break the bad news to him by cable, so contented himself with a holding message. *Delayed in Paris for indefinite period.* The second telegram was to his mother, worded to alert her to what he was trying to accomplish.

Will remain in Paris until possible to report true version of events. He was confident she would see through whatever misrepresentations Ashley attempted. He was only doing what she had assured him she expected him to do. He breakfasted at a nearby café, having no wish to risk a frosty encounter with Ashley at the hotel. There he considered his position. He was tempted to proceed directly to the offices of Ireton Associates, but thinking fondly of Sam, as he had that morning, reminded him of the value of thoroughness. It could be, he knew, the difference between life and death.

A hot afternoon in the summer of 1916, waiting to go on patrol, had exhausted even Max's capacity for dozing and lazing. Hearing that Sergeant Twentyman was still working on his plane, he had gone to find out why.

Sam was alone in the maintenance hangar, fiddling with the control wires for the elevator and rudder on Max's Sopwith Camel. 'Haven't you finished with her yet, Twentyman?' Max demanded.

'Not quite, sir,' Sam replied, without turning round.

'Why are you so much slower than the other riggers?'

'I'm not, sir. I just do more than they do.'

'More of what, damn it?'

'Checking, sir.' Sam did turn round now, his smile flashing through a face darkened by oil and sunburn. 'It's surprising what you find.'

'And what have you found?'

'Nothing you need to worry about, sir. Now I've checked, she won't let you down.'

'But if you hadn't she would have?'

'Might've, sir. Easily might've. And I'd never have

114

forgiven myself if she had. There's not much I can do about the Hun. But at least I can check everything for you, can't I?'

Whether Max would be able to carry out the check he wanted to remained to be seen. He could only trust to luck. But it was still early enough to hope he would catch the staff of the Majestic on the hop.

The detective on the door looked promisingly bleary-eyed. Max confidently asserted that 'Mr Appleby' had approved his visit. This seemed to impress the detective, who, after scrutinizing Max's passport, took him in to the reception desk.

By chance, the clerk on duty was the same man Max had met there before. He recognized Max and offered his respectful condolences. He also confirmed that Sir Henry's room had not yet been reallocated.

'So,' said Max, 'there can be no objection to my taking a look at it.' He deliberately phrased this as a statement rather than a question.

'What are you looking *for*, sir?' the detective asked.

'I simply wish to satisfy myself that all my late father's effects have been removed. My mother would never forgive me if anything of sentimental value was left behind.'

The detective mulled this over for a moment, then gave his reluctant consent. There was a delay while a colleague of his was summoned to escort Max. 'Can't have you wandering around the hotel on your own, sir. You might get lost.' The clerk supplied the key and they set off.

*

The colleague was younger and friendlier and considerably tubbier. He introduced himself in the course of a lengthy tramp up two separate flights of stairs and along various winding corridors as Sergeant Benson, drafted in from the Suffolk constabulary, who was enjoying himself in Paris – 'as far as they'll let me, sir, if you catch my drift'. He was considerably out of breath by the time they reached Sir Henry's room.

It was at the back of the hotel, with a view of chimney-stacks and little else, smaller than Max had expected and poorly lit. Sir Henry's relative unimportance in the British delegation was depressingly obvious.

'Looks pretty empty . . . to me, sir,' Benson panted.

'I'll just make sure.' Max embarked on a careful inspection of the desk, wardrobe, chest of drawers and bedside cabinet. It revealed nothing. He crouched down for a view under the bed and saw only dust and what might have been mouse droppings. He did not know what he was looking for, of course, nor if there was anything to be looked for. But he knew his father to be cautious, if not secretive, by nature, despite the ample evidence of his recent recklessness. It would not have surprised Max to discover that the old man had hidden something there. It was becoming clear he had hidden a great deal about his life of late.

Max was himself no stranger to hiding things. It had been a valuable skill in the camp. Rising to his feet, he remembered the role of bunk-posts in concealing material from the guards. Surreptitiously sawing off the top of the posts supporting the prisoners' bunks and hollowing out their interiors created a space in which all manner of articles could be stashed. Max recalled mentioning this when recounting some of his POW experiences to his father during their dinner at the Ritz.

The bed in Sir Henry's room had stout brass posts topped with umbrella-shaped finials. Max was standing close to one of the posts at the head of the bed. He grasped the finial and gave it a speculative twist. There was brief resistance, then it began to unscrew.

'You certainly do believe in making sure, sir,' said Benson.

'May as well, while I'm here.' Max completed the unscrewing and lifted the finial off. He peered into the hollow post and saw nothing, though it was too dark to be sure. 'You don't have a torch, do you?' he asked.

'Not on me, sir. I'd have to go back downstairs to fetch one.'

'Would it be too much trouble?'

Benson gave a put-upon sigh. 'I suppose not. You'd better come with me.'

'If you insist.'

Benson frowned. 'Oh well, perhaps it'd be all right if you just waited here. I'll be as quick as I can.'

'Thanks.'

Benson set off and Max tossed the finial down on the bed. He lit a cigarette and wondered how long the sergeant would be. He strongly suspected he had sent him on a pointless journey. There was surely nothing to be found. He sat down on the bed.

The depression of the mattress caused the finial to roll off the coverlet and fall to the floor with a clunk. Max bent forward to pick it up. Then he stopped.

Lying next to the toppled finial was a small brass key. It had been dislodged from some crevice inside the finial by the impact. Max seized it at once and glanced guiltily round at the open doorway. But there was no one watching him.

The warding on the bit of the key suggested it fitted a Yale lock or similar. It was surprisingly heavy as it rested in Max's hand. It did not rest there for long.

Benson found Max sitting on the bed, smoking a second cigarette, when he returned, his arrival announced from some way off by his heavy tread and heavier breathing. Max thanked him for putting himself out. Armed with the torch Benson had brought, he took a look inside all four bedposts. They were all empty.

Max added further thanks as they headed downstairs. He had no wish to linger now. He had got what he had come for. True, a key was of little use if you did not know where the lock was that it fitted. But Max backed himself to find that out, one way or another, sooner or later. If there was a key, there was a lock. If there was a lock, there was something worth locking away. And he was on the trail of it.

But leaving the Majestic was not to prove as straight-forward as entering it. On the last half-landing before the lobby, they nearly collided with a bulky figure hurrying up the stairs. It was Appleby.

'I gather you've been taking my name in vain, Mr Maxted.' Appleby's basilisk stare revealed a colder, harder side to the man than he had chosen to display the day before. 'Did you find what you were looking for?'

'I didn't find anything.'

'That's right, sir,' said Benson.

Appleby ignored the sergeant's intervention and went on staring at Max. 'I think you and I need to have a word.'

APPLEBY HAD A SMALL OFFICE IN THE BASEMENT OF THE HOTEL, guarded by a gorgonian secretary. He appeared to have bolted a breakfast in order to intercept Max: an egg-smeared plate and a half-drunk cup of tea stood beside two telephones on his desk. A large map of Paris, sporting a patchy forest of red-headed drawing-pins, dominated one wall. Sallow light seeped in through frosted windows set near the ceiling, along with blurred impressions of the feet and legs of passing pedestrians in the street outside.

Benson had been sent on his way with a flea in his ear, leaving Max to plead his case for himself. Appleby had left him to stew while he spoke to his secretary, then he had returned, closing the door of the office firmly behind him.

'I'll ask you again, Mr Maxted,' Appleby began, slumping down in his chair. 'Did you find what you were looking for?'

'As I've already told you,' Max replied, smiling casually at Appleby across his desk, 'I didn't find anything.'

'Using my name to gain access to your father's room suggests to me you had a compelling reason for going there.'

'I wanted to establish nothing belonging to my father had been left behind.'

'Did you have any reason to think it had?'

'No.'

'Then why the subterfuge?'

'I didn't want to bother you. I felt sure you'd have agreed to my request if I'd put it to you.'

'You didn't want to bother me? How very considerate. It won't do, Mr Maxted, it really won't. You tricked Sergeant Benson into leaving you alone, presumably in order to remove whatever it was you knew to be hidden in the room without being observed.'

'It was no trick. I asked him to fetch a torch so I could look inside the bedposts.'

'And he, credulous idiot that he is, trotted off in search of one. Bedposts, my aunt Fanny. It was obviously a blind.'

How ironic, Max thought, that he should be credited with such deviousness, when the bedpost was indeed where the key had been concealed. 'If you're right, Appleby, I have this . . . hidden object . . . somewhere on my person. Do you want to search me?' He felt secure in the bluff. He could reasonably claim personal ownership of the key. Appleby would know no better.

'That won't be necessary.' Appleby took out his pipe and laboriously filled it, while looking at Max with fixed studiousness. 'What's this all about, Mr Maxted?' he enquired at last.

'Are you a police officer, Appleby? Nobody ever seems to mention your rank.'

'I'm not a Scotland Yard man, if that's what you mean. I have no official rank. Why do you ask?'

'I'd just like to know who's interrogating me.'

'No one is,' Appleby sighed. 'This is a conversation. Believe me, if it were an interrogation, you'd notice the difference. Now, are you going to tell me why you came here this morning?'

'Are you going to tell me why you're making no effort to find my father's murderer?'

Max had expected the question to ruffle Appleby. But it had no discernible effect. 'What makes you think he was murdered, Mr Maxted?'

'The same things that make you think it, I should imagine. It was the blood beneath his fingernails that first caught my attention.'

'There was no blood.'

'Yes, there was. Why else would the nails be so severely cut? Then I noticed the broken skylight at eight Rue du Verger. Broken from the inside. I'm not sure what that means, but it doesn't fit Zamaron's theory and I'm not surprised. A few words with Spataro convinced me he's lying. As I'm sure you know, Madame Dombreux was lured away the night my father died. That alone proves there was a plot of some kind.'

Appleby puffed thoughtfully at his pipe. 'I believe we only have Madame Dombreux's word for her visit to Nantes.'

'And her sister's, if you cared to ask.'

'Blood's thicker than water. You know how it is.'

'I know how you seem determined to make it appear. It won't wash. Not with me.'

'But with your brother?'

'Ashley wants no breath of scandal. To me the

122

scandal is allowing our father's murder to be written off as an accident.'

'A laudable attitude. But consider the national interest for a moment, as I'm sure your father would have done. The peace conference is at a delicate stage. Progress towards a treaty is far too slow. And bad news keeps coming in. This revolution in Hungary, for instance. God knows what the implications are. The Prime Minister is trying to speed things along as best he can, but to do that he has to win over both the French and the Americans. No easy task. And it certainly won't be helped by publicity being given to Sir Henry's relationship with Madame Dombreux. You're aware she's viewed with suspicion by the French authorities?'

'Because of her late husband's activities in Russia? Yes. I'm aware of it.'

'Ah. You two had a regular heart-to-heart, then. There's nothing more deceptive than candour, of course. You should bear that in mind.'

'I will.'

'An attractive woman, Madame Dombreux. There's no denying it. Eyes you could drown in. I imagine a good few men have besides your father and her late husband.'

'Do you really know anything about her?'

'I know my French colleagues believe she may have been a party to Dombreux's dealings with the Bolsheviks.'

'How could she have been? She was living here in Paris at the time. They'd separated.'

'Ah, but how long had Dombreux been working for the Reds? That's the question. And might the Dombreux' marital problems merely have been a ploy

123

to garner the Cheka a spy in Paris to add to the one they already had in Petrograd?'

'That's absurd.'

'Maybe, maybe not. Either way, it makes Madame Dombreux a spectacularly poor choice of mistress for a British diplomat. Some might go so far as to suggest it calls his own loyalties into question.'

Before Max could fashion a retort, there was a knock at the door. Appleby barked out a 'Come in' and Max turned to see a thin, grey-suited man of apologetic demeanour enter the room. Bespectacled, with centre-parted hair and a complexion matching his suit, he was so lacking in presence as to be almost absent.

'Mr Norris,' Appleby greeted him. 'Meet Mr Maxted.'

'My condolences in respect of your father,' said Norris, offering Max a limp hand. 'I, er, had the privilege of knowing him.'

'Mr Norris oversaw Sir Henry's work for the delegation,' Appleby explained – unnecessarily, as it happened. 'I thought his contribution to our discussion might be useful.'

Ye Gods, thought Max, how could his father have tolerated answering to this wet week of a man?

'I'm not exactly sure what I can tell you,' Norris said hesitantly.

'Tell him what Sir Henry did, man,' growled Appleby.

'Of course, of course. Well, his role here was invaluable, I can assure you, although perhaps . . . by some yardsticks . . . peripheral. That's by no means unusual. We've assembled a wealth of knowledge and expertise here for the Prime Minister and his senior advisers to call upon. Inevitably, some of that . . .

knowledge and expertise . . . is required only rarely . . . though crucial when the need arises.'

'You're saying my father spent most of his time twiddling his thumbs?'

'No, no, not at all.' Norris appeared disconcerted by Max's directness. 'He was in regular contact with the Brazilian delegation.'

'In particular a Senhor Ribeiro?'

'Yes. Ribeiro. How did—'

'My father mentioned him. They knew each another from Rio.'

'Ah, yes. Sir Henry . . . spent some years in Brazil. Hence his selection . . . as a special adviser.'

'What's the Brazilians' biggest bone of contention, Mr Norris?' Appleby asked in a tone that suggested he knew the answer and found it paltry, but felt it needed spelling out nonetheless.

'Well, the principal difficulty in which we have an interest revolves around settling the fate of forty-three German merchant ships detained in Brazilian ports when Brazil declared war on Germany in . . . October 1917. Actually, they were detained earlier than that, but . . . the timing isn't strictly relevant.'

'Indeed not,' murmured Appleby.

'Well,' Norris bumbled on, 'the Brazilians claim ownership of the vessels, thirty of which they've since leased to France, but we feel, as do the French, that they should ultimately be allocated amongst the allies in proportion to the amount of merchant shipping each ally lost during the war, a calculation which would leave Brazil with far fewer than forty-three. A complication is that by leasing some of the vessels France could be deemed to have acknowledged that they belong to Brazil, something we obviously don't accept.'

'And what was Sir Henry doing about this?' Appleby asked wearily.

'Essentially, his task was to monitor the strength of Brazilian feeling on the issue and the success or otherwise of their efforts to win support for their cause, while seeking to persuade them to accept a compromise that would prevent the problem becoming an obstacle to the conclusion of an overall peace treaty. Seeking to formulate such a compromise involved him in discussions with the French, obviously, as well as the Americans, who see themselves to some degree as champions of their continental neighbours. They've already sided with them, for instance, over the question of the exchange rate to be applied to payments owing to various Brazilian coffee producers for consignments of coffee trapped in German-controlled ports in August 1914. The German mark has depreciated drastically since then, of course, hence—'

'Thank you, Mr Norris,' Appleby cut in. 'We'll leave the coffee question for another day. I can't stand the stuff, so I've no sympathy for anyone involved in the trade. Would it be true to say, in conclusion, that Sir Henry's work for the delegation, though important in the narrow context you've described, was routine, normal and uncontroversial?'

'Why . . . yes. Of course.'

'I trust that's clear, Mr Maxted?'

Max nodded. 'Yes.' So it was. Which proved nothing as far as he was concerned.

'The Brazilian delegation is based at the Plaza Athénée

in Avenue Montaigne,' said Norris. 'I'm sure Senhor Ribeiro . . . as an old friend of your father's . . . would be pleased to make your acquaintance, Mr Maxted.'

'A kind thought,' said Appleby, 'but Mr Maxted isn't staying in Paris long enough to act on it, I'm afraid.'

'That isn't necessarily true,' said Max.

'I understood you and your brother were catching the noon train to London.'

'I'm staying here. *Pro tem.*'

'You are?'

'I can't leave with so much unresolved, Appleby. Surely you can see that.'

Appleby ground the stem of his pipe between his teeth and stared hard at Max for a moment, then said, 'Thank you for your time, Mr Norris. We need detain you no longer.'

He went on staring at Max while Norris took his leave, a procedure prolonged and complicated by a collision with the hat-stand and an apologetic retrieval of Appleby's trilby from the floor. Eventually, he was gone.

'Won't you be attending your father's funeral, Mr Maxted?' Appleby asked, still chewing at his pipe.

'The funeral won't be for a couple of days at least.'

'And what can you accomplish here in a couple of days?'

'That remains to be seen.'

'You'd be better advised to leave this kind of thing to the professionals, you really would.'

'Meaning you and the local police?'

'Precisely.'

'Who propose to treat my father's murder as a bizarre and undignified accident.'

'I've explained to you why that's in everyone's best interests. You were assured Zamaron's theory about what took Sir Henry on to the roof of that building will never figure in any official verdict, an assurance with which your brother seemed, I have to say, quite content. And he is now, I need hardly point out, the head of your family.'

'He must follow the dictates of his conscience, as must I.'

'So, this is an issue of conscience for you, is it?'

'I intend to leave no stone unturned in my search for my father's murderer. You may take that as a definitive statement of my position. And now . . .'

Max started from his chair, but was halted by Appleby raising his hand and by a slight but significant change in the man's expression. He looked suddenly solicitous.

'As a pilot, you were fortunate to survive the war, Mr Maxted. I'd urge you to make the most of your good fortune. You have a life to enjoy. Don't waste it.'

'What are you trying to say, Appleby?'

'I can't guarantee your safety if you stay here.'

'I'm not asking you to.'

'Paris is full of thieves, vagrants, beggars, con men, crooks and desperadoes. Go looking for trouble and you'll be sure to find it.'

'It's the truth I'm after, not trouble.'

'They're often the same thing, in my experience. Let me give you some advice, as one who's seen more of the world than you have. Give this up. Go home, bury your father and forget whatever folly led him to his death. It's good advice, believe me.' Appleby sighed. 'But entirely futile, of course.'

'Yes.' Max smiled. 'It is.'

MAX WAS IN A HURRY NOW, EMBOLDENED BY THE RESULT of his visit to the Majestic. He took the Métro – which impressed him no more favourably than the London Underground – from Etoile to the Tuileries and walked up Rue des Pyramides to number 33.

The offices of Ireton Associates were on the first floor of a handsome building near the junction with Avenue de l'Opéra. Max hardly knew what to expect. What he found was a small and apparently lethargic operation in the charge of a polite but unsmiling American secretary. She was middle-aged and schoolmarmish, chestnut hair helmeted to her head, eyes gleaming behind alarmingly winged horn-rimmed glasses. Her posture hinted at tight corsetry beneath the thick layers of tweed.

'Mr Ireton isn't here at present, sir,' she explained. 'And he sees no one without an appointment.'

'Perhaps I could make one.'

'May I ask what this is in connection with?'

'It concerns my late father, Sir Henry Maxted.'

'You're his son?'

'I am. James Maxted.'

'My condolences, Mr Maxted. I heard of your father's death. Such a sad thing.'

'Indeed. I—'

Max broke off and looked round. A flicker in the secretary's gaze had alerted him to a movement behind him. A large, not to say enormous, man in a dark hat and overcoat was standing in the corridor that led from neighbouring rooms to the main door. He might have moved on castors, given how noiselessly he had arrived there, which was all the more surprising considering the vastness of his build. He had craggy, weather-beaten features and a sorrowful expression. His nose looked as if it had been broken, possibly more than once. Max felt eerily certain it had not been broken in a sporting endeavour.

'Is there anything you need, Mr Morahan?' the secretary asked, sounding genuinely anxious on the point.

'Nothing,' came the softly growled reply. (Morahan was clearly also American.) 'But you might like to call Travis.' A faint nod in Max's direction implied he was the reason for the suggestion.

'Just what I was thinking.'

'I'll see you later.' With that, and a touch of his hat, Morahan glided out.

'Bear with me, Mr Maxted,' the secretary said, returning her attention to Max. 'I'll see if I can reach Mr Ireton.'

She spoke to the operator in fluent French, too fluently for Max to follow. As she waited to be connected, he glanced out through the window beside her desk. He saw Morahan emerge from the building on to the pavement, towering over other pedestrians in his long black coat. He paused to light a cigarette, then strode across the road and vanished down the steps leading to the Pyramides Métro station.

The secretary began speaking, presumably to Ireton, though she did not use his name. 'I have a Mr James Maxted here ... That's correct ... Yes ... Sure.' She offered Max the phone without further explanation. He took it.

'Travis Ireton?'

'The same. You're the son I met at the Ritz?'

'I am.'

'Terrible shame about your father.'

'Yes. It is.'

'You want to meet?'

'I was hoping to. I—'

'We should, I agree. But I'm spread thin today. Can you come to the office at ... six thirty?'

'I can, yes.'

'We'll talk then. Put Malory back on, would you?'

Whether Malory was the secretary's Christian name or surname was unclear. Max handed the phone to her and she began taking notes on a pad, contributing little more than 'Yes' and 'Uh-huh' as the conversation proceeded.

It took Max a minute or so to realize that she regarded him as a matter satisfactorily dealt with. His farewell nod was barely acknowledged.

Appleby's mood had not improved following Max's departure from the Majestic. His conviction that the young man had stolen a march on him was only one reason. The other was the telegram he had received shortly afterwards. He had not anticipated a peremptory summons to the godhead in London and was annoyed with himself on that account alone. He should have foreseen such a development. The Maxted affair, he concluded over a contemplative pipe, was going to require a greater share of his attention than he had so far devoted to it.

A knock at his door heralded the arrival of Lamb, the most intelligent and reliable of his operatives. He was young and moon-faced, with the mild demeanour of a bank clerk. But a keen brain ticked away inside his head. He was perfect for this line of work, taking quiet pleasure from the invisibility of his achievements and requiring little in the way of overt praise.

'Is there a flap on, sir?' Lamb disingenuously enquired.

'I have to go to London. A flying visit, I hope. I want some surveillance put in hand in my absence. This fellow.' Appleby slid a photograph culled from RFC records across his desk. 'James Maxted. Younger son of the late Sir Henry Maxted.'

'Ah. The faller.'

'As the mighty can sometimes become. We have to pick up the pieces. Maxted's staying at the Mazarin in Rue Coligny. Tail him from there. Stick with him wherever he goes, but stay out of sight. I'll want as much detail as possible.'

'You'll have it, sir.'

'If he gets into any trouble . . .'

'Yes, sir?'

Appleby deliberated for a moment, then replied. 'Don't intervene.'

With time on his hands, Max decided to see his father off at the Gare du Nord. He did so in his own way, having no wish for a further exchange of angry words with Ashley. There was a side-entrance to the station for goods and mail. And it was there that he witnessed the arrival of a hearse bearing the name *Prettre et fils, pompes funèbres*. It was discreetly managed, with a full half hour to spare before the departure of the noon train to London. Monsieur Prettre had been as good as his word.

After seeing the coffin unloaded and wheeled into the station, suitably draped, on a trolley, Max went round to the front of the building. He had spied out a café on the other side of the street, from where he could watch taxis come and go.

He did not have to wait long for one to discharge Ashley. He was accompanied by Fradgley, who looked flustered and fretful. Max amused himself by attributing Fradgley's distracted appearance to the fact that only one of the Maxted brothers was with him. But he was aware that his amusement would rebound on him if he accomplished nothing by remaining in Paris.

He watched the station clock move slowly towards noon, calculating that Fradgley's reappearance would tell him when the train had left.

Then, to his surprise, he recognized someone else clambering out of a taxi: Appleby. And the fellow was carrying a travelling bag, as if intent on taking the train to London himself.

Max could scarcely credit that such was Appleby's intention. But noon passed and the train left. He knew that because Fradgley emerged on to the forecourt at five past the hour – alone. There was no sign of Appleby.

*

133

After Fradgley had boarded a cab and vanished, Max left the café and set off southwards on foot, turning over in his mind the mystery of Appleby's sudden departure. It was far from reassuring to know that Ashley would have Appleby's company for the next seven hours. In his efforts to persuade Ashley that their father really had been murdered, Max had revealed more than he wanted Appleby to know. He could not rely on his brother to keep such information to himself. But there was absolutely nothing he could do about it now.

IRETON WAS WAITING FOR MAX WHEN HE ARRIVED AT 33 RUE des Pyramides that evening – waiting, indeed, at the head of the stairs, with a glass of whisky in his hand and a broad smile on his face. He breezily conferred first-name terms on their acquaintance while ushering Max into his offices.

'Malory's a wondrous manageress of my affairs,' Ireton explained as he poured Max a Scotch and persuaded him to sample an American cigarette, 'but she can be a little stern, especially in the a.m., if you know what I mean.'

'It's good of you to see me.'

'Not at all. Your father's death was a terrible waste. I want you to know most particularly how sorry I am.'

'Thank you.'

'We could have done this at the Ritz or the Crillon.' Ireton led Max through to an inner office, where a fire was blazing. There were armchairs arranged around it. 'But I thought you'd value some privacy.'

'That was considerate of you.'

'Do the police have a theory to account for what happened?'

'Nothing I'd dignify with the word "theory".'

'That so?' They sat down and Ireton went on smiling, but was frowning slightly now as well, as if unsure quite what to make of Max. 'Well, it was a damn shame, however it came about. Do you have any ideas yourself?'

'I believe my father was murdered, Travis.'

'You do?' The frown deepened.

'Yes.'

'I see. Well, that's . . .' Then the frown lifted. He spread a hand expressively. 'That's what I surmised, Max. Henry wasn't an accident-prone man. I wouldn't have mentioned it if you were set on buying the police's cockamamie version of events, but since you're not . . .'

'You know what their version of events is?'

'I do.'

'You're well-informed, I must say.'

'I make it my business to be. Matter of fact, it *is* my business to be.'

' "All your needs in post-war Paris". It's a broad remit.'

Ireton chuckled. 'As broad as it's long. What do you need, Max?'

'Evidence of who murdered my father and why.'

'Which you think I can supply?'

'I don't know. But then I don't know what dealings you had with him.'

'No. I guess not.' Ireton took a long draw on his cigarette. 'What I do is a little hard to define. You could say I trade in the commodity that most of the delegates and journalists and speculators and hangers-on who've gathered here spend most of their time trying to lay their hands on. Information. *Timely* information. By which I mean they hear it from me before it becomes common knowledge. For that advantage they're willing to pay. That, simply put, is my business. Your prime minister took himself and his senior advisers off to Fontainebleau last weekend to thrash out a new policy on the peace treaty. A lot of people who weren't there wanted to know what they'd settled on before it was made public. They turned to me. And suffice to say they weren't disappointed.'

'How did you pull that off?'

'It's what I do, Max. It's my living. Has been for a good many years. I go wherever information is most in demand. Just now that's Paris, luckily for me.' He broke off to tong some coal on to the fire. 'Though I'd be grateful for more springlike weather. *Paris au printemps*, hey? This isn't what I had in mind, let me tell you.'

'Isn't there a shortage of coal in the city? My hotel's cold as charity.'

'Oh, yes, there's a shortage.' Ireton grinned blithely. 'But I think better when I'm warm, so scrimping's out of the question. So it should be for you. I bet you dreamt of creature comforts like a roaring fire when you were a POW. I bet you reckoned you were owed them for laying your life on the line for your country.'

Max did not deny it, though the truth was that he had volunteered less for patriotic reasons than for the chance it had given him of flying on a daily basis. He had missed that in the camp rather more keenly than a glowing hearth.

'I saw some action in Cuba in 'ninety-eight,' Ireton went on. 'I realized then that I had no gift for self-denial. My talents lie elsewhere.' He pitched the butt of his cigarette into the fire and lit another. 'And I believe we should all make the most of our talents.'

'About my father, Travis . . .' Max engaged Ireton eye

to eye as he accepted a second cigarette. The time for sparring was over. 'What exactly were your dealings with him?'

'OK.' Ireton relaxed into his chair. 'Cards on the table. Naturally, I buy information as well as sell it. I'm a broker. People come to me because I enable them to trade anonymously. The governments or organizations they work for wouldn't necessarily approve of what they're doing. It isn't illegal, but it could be regarded as unethical, even disloyal. My discretion is one of the things I charge for. It's one the things I'm *known* for. My clients rely on it. You understand? It's not a trivial matter.'

'Was my father a client of yours?'

'He might have been.'

'As a buyer or a seller?'

'How would you feel if I said Henry was active in the information market?'

'Incredulous. He would never have betrayed his country.'

'Betrayal's a strong word. Most of the material I deal in falls well short of earth-shattering. Henry was in regular contact with the Brazilian delegation. The other South American delegations – Bolivia, Ecuador, Peru, Uruguay – would all like to know more about Brazil's negotiating tactics. And vice versa, of course. The outcome of this conference isn't going to be affected in the slightest way by trading small amounts of such information.'

'Are you saying that's what my father did?'

'Would it be so terrible if he had?'

Could it be true? Max was aware that his incredulity

138

was founded on his knowledge of his father's character. But he could not help wondering if his knowledge amounted to anything more than a set of conventional – and quite possibly false – assumptions. 'It would be terrible if it led to his death.'

'Nothing Henry worked on was important enough to get him murdered, Max, it truly wasn't.'

'What was, then?'

'I'm not sure. But . . .'

'But what?'

Ireton fell silent for a long, thoughtful moment, then said, 'To share my suspicions with you involves letting you know more about my activities than is frankly wise, considering you and I are barely acquainted. I'd like to help you, largely because I liked and admired Henry and reckon he'd probably want me to help you. But I can't allow myself to be swayed by sentiment.'

'What *would* sway you?' There had to be something, Max reckoned. Otherwise why would Ireton have agreed to meet him in the first place?

'A demonstration of your trustworthiness, Max.' Ireton nodded for emphasis. 'That's what I need.'

'What did you have in mind?'

'A small service I'd repay with my confidence in you. I'm always happier if both sides have a bargain to honour.'

'And this service is?'

'The collection of an item from a man I'd prefer not to meet face to face. A simple matter. It shouldn't cause you any difficulty.'

Words were cheap, of course. Max was not blind to the possibility that he was being led on. Ireton might have nothing of value to disclose and see this as a way of solving a bothersome problem. 'Why not send one of your associates? Morahan, for instance.'

'Ah, yes, you met Schools earlier, didn't you? Well, I could send him, but that wouldn't tell me whether you're the sort of person I can rely on, now would it? Look at this from my point of view, Max. It's a question of establishing your *bona fides*. I have to be sure of you. I can't proceed unless I am. You'll be taking a risk, of course. You only have my word for it that I can help you discover who may have murdered Henry. But you're not a stranger to risks and I don't believe for a moment you mean to shy away from this one. So, shall I tell you the name of the man I want you to meet and where and when I want you to meet him – or not?'

Sɪʀ Hᴇɴʀʏ Mᴀxᴛᴇᴅ ʜᴀᴅ ᴄᴏᴍᴇ ʜᴏᴍᴇ. Hᴇ ʀᴇᴘᴏsᴇᴅ ᴛʜᴀᴛ night in the library at Gresscombe Place. The delivery of his body in a stout oak coffin had been efficiently managed by the local undertaker. It had taken place late in the evening, at the conclusion of a lengthy journey from Paris that had left Ashley exhausted and fit only for bed.

Lydia was by contrast feeling far from sleepy. Her curiosity about her brother-in-law's reasons for remaining in Paris had thus far been held in check. Now, in the privacy of their bedroom, she proceeded to bombard her heavy-lidded husband with questions.

'Surely he understands there will be a price to pay for defying you in this manner, darling?'

'Oh, he understands. He just doesn't seem to care.'

'Doesn't he care about the good name of his own family? Or his father's reputation?'

Ashley's answering sigh converted itself into an irrepressible yawn. He had informed Lydia earlier, during a snatched quarter of an hour alone together, of the French police's theory concerning Sir Henry's death. To his mother he had offered only their official bafflement, having despaired of inventing any plausible alternative. 'James has convinced himself Pa was murdered. He says he means to bring the murderer to justice.'

'He wasn't murdered, though, was he?'

'I don't think so. But, if he was, it will have been for some scandalous reason we're all better off not knowing about. Pa made a prize fool of himself in Paris and suffered for it.'

'That doesn't mean *we* have to suffer for it as well, darling. Think of your poor mother.' Lydia was not in fact thinking of her mother-in-law at all, but even to Ashley she did not care to reveal the full extent of her callousness.

'James said he was determined to uncover the truth at all costs.'

'How typically perverse of him. As if the truth were all that mattered.'

'I felt sure my say-so regarding those fields he needs for his flying school would suffice to keep him in line.'

'You left him in no doubt that he'd forfeit the land if he went on with this?'

'I made it very clear to him. It had no effect.'

'How can he be so indifferent to his own best interests?'

'I don't know. I'd blame the war, but he's always been the same.'

'Do you think he'll come back for the funeral?'

'The day after tomorrow? I doubt it. I shall cable him with the details in the morning and leave it to him.'

'His absence will be so embarrassing, darling. How will we explain it?'

'We'll say he's ill. What other excuse can we offer? Cutting his own father's funeral is a damn poor show.'

'And raising a stink in Paris will only make matters worse. What can we do to bring him to heel?'

'Nothing. But don't worry unduly. I'm assured by those who know that his enquiries will hit a brick wall. Eventually, he'll be forced to admit defeat.'

'And then?'

'Then?' Ashley ineffectually stifled another yawn. 'He'll come home, I suppose. With his tail between his legs.'

In the few minutes between turning off the light and his descent into slumber, Ashley was visited by a frisson of doubt concerning his professed certainty that James would fail in his quest for the truth. The fellow was too stubborn and resourceful to be written off. Appleby, who had travelled with Ashley from Paris to London, had pooh-poohed the grounds for suspicion James had presented to Ashley. ('This list sounds like something and nothing to me, Sir Ashley. Your brother is wasting his time.') But, upon reflection, Appleby had perhaps overdone the pooh-poohing. And the reason he had given for being on the train – a 'family emergency' – was rather too pat for comfort. Should Ashley have been more guarded in what he said? It was a worrying question, since he found it difficult now to recall just what he had said. Damn Appleby *and* James, he thought. And with that he plunged into a deep sleep.

At that moment Lady Maxted was standing beside the trestle-mounted coffin in the library, gazing down at the death-masked face of her late husband. Part of his head was concealed by a thick white veil, to spare her the sight of his fatal brain injury. What remained visible were recognizably the features of Sir Henry Maxted, but Henry the man was gone, lost to her entirely.

She had displayed as much disappointment at the news that James had remained in Paris as she had judged Ashley and Lydia would expect. And she had allowed Ashley to give an obviously inadequate account of what he had accomplished there. Altogether, she had played the part of the meek and pliant widow quite shamelessly.

From the pocket of her dress she took the telegram James had sent her that morning. She unfolded it and reread the message. *Will remain in Paris until possible to report true version of events.* Then her gaze returned to the never-again-to-open eyes of Sir Henry Maxted. 'He has pledged himself for you, Henry,' she murmured. 'He will not let you down.'

At the same moment, glumly installed with a pint of Bass in a smoky corner of the public bar of the Rose and Crown, Walthamstow, Sam Twentyman pulled from his pocket the telegram he had also received from Max earlier that day. He reread the message for the umpteenth time. *Delayed in Paris for indefinite period.* No address was supplied for a reply.

'You're trying to let me down lightly, aren't you, sir?' Sam murmured as he put the telegram away again. He sensed the flying school he had set his sights on slipping fast from his future. And without it that future looked bleak. Ill-advisedly, as he now saw, he had paid

Miller a deposit on the planes he had persuaded Max they should buy and would forfeit it if they did not conclude the purchase within ten days. It was money he could not afford to spend. But that was not the worst of it, not by a long way. If Max abandoned his plans for a flying school, Sam would be condemned to a lick-spittle role in his father's bakery business. The prospect appalled him. To avoid it he found it hard to imagine what he would not be willing to do.

And that was not his only concern. *Delayed in Paris for indefinite period* was a message that said more than it was intended to. It sounded to him as if Max was in trouble – or soon would be. He needed Sam's help whether he knew it or not. That had often been the case in the war. Apparently, it still was.

'Flying solo's no good without a mechanic you can rely on, sir,' Sam mused. 'You should know that.'

Also at the same moment, two hundred miles away, in Paris, Corinne Dombreux was walking along Rue du Verger, on her way home from an evening shift at the ticket office at the Gare Montparnasse. She was tired and in low spirits. The shock of Henry's death had faded, but the grief of losing him was an ache she could not ease. She was relying on Max to discover who had murdered his father and why, but she did not know when she would next hear from him or whether he would be able to achieve anything. It might only make her life more difficult if he did. The authorities regarded her with acute suspicion. They could move against her at any time. Nothing about her existence was secure. Pierre had bequeathed her only adversity and notoriety.

And she did not know how much longer she could face both of them down.

As she approached number 8, a massive figure suddenly detached itself from the deep shadow of a doorway opposite and lurched across the street towards her. 'Corinne,' Spataro called. '*Attends un peu.*'

'I have nothing to say to you,' she responded, quickening her pace.

But he was too fast for her. To her surprise, she realized that he was, for once, stone-cold sober. He did not sway as he blocked her path. There was no brandy on his breath. And he did not slur his words.

'*Ecoutes-moi, Corinne.* I beg you.'

'Why should I?'

'What I have done. It gives me . . . a bad conscience.'

'So it should.'

'I want to put it right.' He grasped her by the arm. '*Tu capisci?* I want to put it right.'

THE MEETING HAD BEEN ARRANGED AT SHORT NOTICE AND AT an hour the expressions of several people round the table suggested was unreasonably early. Appleby was not one of them. The older he grew, the less sleep he needed. He suspected the same was true of C, who surveyed the select gathering from the head of the table. He had the advantage of living on the premises, of course. Secret Service Headquarters was C's home as well as his place of work. Appleby was far from sure he envied him such an arrangement, difficult though the journey to Whitehall Court had been from his sister's home in Eltham.

The war – and the work rate it had committed him to – had taken its toll on C, who looked frailer and older than when Appleby had last seen him. Rumour had it that he had never recovered from the death of his son. It might be so, Appleby conceded. He too had lost a son in the conflict and did not delude himself that he was unmarked by the tragedy. But neither he nor C was the sort of man to dwell on such matters. Stoicism was their philosophy of choice.

'Be so good as to remind everyone of the evidence that Lemmer may be in Paris, would you, Appleby?' C prompted, fixing a beady eye on him over the rim of his teacup.

'Certainly, sir.' He risked a glance at the grim-set faces of the others: four of them, of varying degrees of seniority, representing the Military, Aviation, Naval and Political sections. None appeared either overtly hostile or supportive. But that counted for little in a service where overtness was actively discouraged. The search for Fritz Lemmer, fugitive head of the German Secret Service's spy network, had involved them all at various stages since the end of the war. They were likely to resent the credit for tracking him down devolving upon Appleby – if indeed he had tracked him down. 'The evidence stems from material relating to the late Sir Henry Maxted. Murdered, we believe, though officially his death's to be treated as an accident.'

'The PM won't want to hear that a member of our delegation has been murdered,' remarked Political.

'Which is why he won't hear it,' Appleby continued. 'But there's no doubt in my mind Sir Henry was murdered.'

'We'll take that as read,' said C. 'Proceed with the Lemmer dimension.'

'Very good, sir. The first point to bear in mind is that Sir Henry knew Lemmer from his time in Japan. He was a second secretary in Tokyo while Lemmer was a naval attaché at the German Embassy. It's certain they'd have met at receptions and the like. Lemmer cut his teeth in Tokyo, of course, with the attempted assassination of the Tsarevich. I've been able to examine Sir Henry's pocket-diary for the period he spent in Paris. Most of the entries are routine appointments. But on the nineteenth of February there's a circled set of initials: F.L.'

'Could mean anything,' growled Naval.

'Or it could mean Fritz Lemmer.'

'Thin. Very thin.'

'Rather like the air the fellow disappeared into last November,' remarked Aviation.

'Exactly,' said Appleby. 'He has to have gone somewhere. Why not Paris?'

'Never mind why not,' said C. '*Why?*'

'In my submission, sir,' Appleby replied, 'because that's where the people he recruited are.'

'What can they do for him now?'

'Who can say? I think we'd all agree Lemmer's a master strategist.'

'Oh, yes,' groaned Military.

'But the show's over,' said Naval. 'The government he worked for has ceased to exist.'

'They lost the war, but maybe Lemmer thinks they can still win the peace.'

'What exactly do you mean?' asked C.

'I'm not sure, sir. But I am sure Sir Henry Maxted's murder is crucial. The initials F.L. also crop up on a list he made, apparently of sources of money. He valued F.L. at five thousand pounds.'

Naval scowled. 'Could Maxted have been one of Lemmer's people?'

'It's possible. But—'

'You made no mention of this list in your report,' C cut in.

'No, sir. I only learnt of it yesterday, from Sir Ashley Maxted, Sir Henry's eldest son.'

'What else was on the list?'

'The Trust.'

There was a quiver of disquiet round the table. 'The Tsarists *and* Lemmer?' Political winced. 'A toxic mixture.'

'Sir Henry's last posting was in Petrograd.'

'And you say the woman he was involved with is the widow of the French turncoat, Dombreux?' C shook his head. 'This is potentially very serious.'

'I can only agree, sir. Whether Sir Henry was receiving payments from Lemmer *and* the Trust, or hoping to profit from them in some other way, is unclear.' Even less clear to Appleby were the meaning and significance of other items on the list. He was reluctant to mention them for fear of being drawn into unwise conjecture. Fortunately, no one seemed inclined to press him on the point.

'What view is the *Deuxième Bureau* taking of Maxted's death?' enquired Military.

'A cautious one. They'd prefer to believe it wasn't murder. Even to admit the possibility would raise unwelcome questions about the security and integrity of the conference.'

'Show the Frogs a sand dune and they'll stick their heads in it,' complained Aviation.

'Aren't you confusing frogs with ostriches?' Political asked, smiling faintly.

But Aviation was not smiling. 'Shouldn't your section have forewarned us of this? There must have been rumours about Lemmer's whereabouts.'

'None pointing to Paris.'

'Where, then?'

'Switzerland, since you ask.'

'Never mind that for now,' said C firmly. 'We will proceed on the assumption that Lemmer is in Paris. He's not a man I want on the loose any longer than I can help it. His detention is a high priority, not least because of the rotten apples he may enable us to identify. We cannot be seen to be turning Paris upside down in search of him, however. I want nothing to be done that will bring our inquiries to the attention of the French, or, worse still, the Americans. Nor do I wish to trouble the PM with this, until we know we're on firm ground. Everything we do must be discreet and deniable.'

'A tall order,' said Political.

'Indeed. But Appleby has a suggestion.'

All eyes turned on Appleby. He did not flinch. 'Sir Henry's younger son, James Maxted. Twenty-seven-year-old former pilot. Cool-headed and courageous, according to his RFC CO. Served two years on the Western Front and spent a year in a POW camp after being shot down. I've met him and I'd rate him A for nerve and pluck. He believes his father was murdered and left me in no doubt he means to bring the murderer to justice.'

Political looked askance. 'You're proposing to use an amateur?'

'*Use* is the operative word. We steer him towards Lemmer and see what he turns up. If he lands himself in trouble with the French authorities, we disown him.'

'He's more likely to end up dead in a back alley,' said Military.

'Then disowning him won't be difficult. He's going to try his damnedest to uncover the truth, regardless of the consequences. I've tried warning him off. It had no effect. I conclude our best course of action is to give him a scent to follow and see where it leads.'

'Riskier for him than for us,' said Naval.

'Keeping track of him will be the trickiest part,' observed Political.

'I will need a few extra men,' Appleby admitted. 'Purely for surveillance.'

'An important point,' said C. 'You can have your extra men, but it must be an exclusively eyes-and-ears operation – apart from yourself – unless and until we have a confirmed sighting of Lemmer.'

'Understood, sir.'

'I rather think this is the best we can do in the circumstances, gentlemen.' C glanced round the table. 'Any suggestions, reservations or objections?'

There were none. Appleby was not surprised. This was an assignment he could either make a success of, in which case it would be taken over by others, along with the credit, or a howling flop of, in which case the blame would be his to wallow in. Such were the rules he was bound to play by.

'Very well,' C declared. 'You have conditional approval, Appleby.'

'Thank you, sir.' Though whether he had anything to be grateful for, Appleby was far from sure.

OVER A SOLITARY BREAKFAST IN THE GLOOMY DINING-ROOM of the Mazarin, Max contemplated what he had achieved so far in his search for the truth. It did not amount to much. He had a conditional promise of illuminating information from Travis Ireton, but the condition was the running of an errand that evening that might prove less straightforward than Ireton had claimed. Max had held back from contacting Sir Henry's Brazilian acquaintance, Ribeiro, in case Ireton told him something he should know before speaking to the man, but he was not prepared to let another day slip by without doing so. As for Sir Henry's Japanese acquaintance, Max had hoped Ireton would be able to identify him. Frustrating though it was, he reckoned he should wait on that possibility.

He had just lit a cigarette to accompany his coffee and begun to consider the question of how early he could reasonably present himself at the Brazilians' hotel when a waistcoated porter entered the dining-room and steered a direct course to his table.

He inclined himself by Max's elbow for a discreet word. 'Monsieur Maxted, there is a lady wishing to see you. She says the matter is urgent.'

'Her name?'

The porter's voice sank to a whisper, as if he well knew whose widow the lady was. 'Madame Dombreux.'

She was waiting for him in the lobby, anonymously dressed, eyes downcast, doing her best to attract as little attention as possible. Max suggested they step outside and she agreed with no more than a nod.

The morning was cold and bright, the slanting sunlight blurred by traffic fumes. They walked slowly away from the hotel, until they had covered enough distance to speak freely.

'Have you found anything out yet, Max?'

'No. You'd have heard from me if I had.'

'What about Ireton?'

'I'm in the process of winning his confidence.' He did not think she needed to know how that was to be done.

'Perhaps you don't need to.'

'What do you mean?'

'I may have some good news.'

'Really?'

'Yes. Really.'

'Why don't we step in here?' Max indicated the café they were passing. Custom looked to be thin enough to afford them some privacy and he was feeling cold without his coat.

They went in and settled at a table near the door. 'So,' he prompted her. 'The good news is?'

'Spataro says he will recant.'

Max knew he must have looked as he felt: surprised and dubious in equal measures. 'When did he say this?'

'Last night. He stopped me on my way home and told

me his conscience wouldn't allow him to continue lying about me.'

'I didn't know he had a conscience.'

'Neither did I. But apparently he does, buried under all that bombast, vanity and drunkenness. He seemed genuinely ashamed of himself.'

'This is—' Max broke off at the approach of the waiter. They ordered coffee. 'This is unexpected, to put it mildly.'

Corinne smiled and looked more relaxed than Max had so far seen her. The loveliness that had drawn his father to her blossomed before him. 'You see what this means, Max? The police will have to accept Henry didn't go on to the roof to spy on me. Which means they'll have to accept he was murdered.'

Max was not confident the police would be willing to go that far. But without Spataro's evidence they might eventually be forced to. 'When will he tell them he's changing his story?'

'Today. He promised me he'll see Zamaron as soon as possible.'

'And how will he explain himself?'

'He was blackmailed into claiming I was with him. He wouldn't reveal what grubby secret from his past had caught up with him. I imagine there are quite a few. He wouldn't name his blackmailer either. He said it would be dangerous for me to know.'

'So it might. But we have to find out who it was, Corinne. The police will certainly press him on the point.'

'They won't welcome his change of heart, will they?'

'No. They won't.' Their coffees arrived. Max stared down at his pensively.

'I thought you'd be pleased.'

He saw in her eyes the disappointment with his reaction. She wanted him to share her optimism. And he would have liked to be able to. But he did not trust Spataro *or* the police. 'I'll be pleased when Spataro formally withdraws his statement and Zamaron admits he's dealing with a murder.'

'I honestly think we can rely on Spataro, Max. I've never known him to be as . . . well, as earnest as he was last night.'

'Maybe I should go and make sure his earnestness is still intact.'

'Don't do that.' She touched his hand. 'You'll offend him even if you don't mean to. Absurd as it might seem, he regards himself as a man of honour. I'm confident he'll do as he promised. But it must be on his own terms.'

'I suppose you're right.' On balance, he supposed she was. Let Spataro make his grand gesture of contrition. Then, when it was safely on the record, would be the time to demand more from him.

'You won't go to see him, then?'

'You have my word.' He patted her forearm. The reassurance he intended to convey was met by something profoundly disquieting: a sense also of his susceptibility. His father's ghost hovered benignly behind her. 'I'll leave well alone.'

'Good.' Corinne moved her arm away from him in order to drink her coffee. Max wondered whether that was the only reason. She glanced up at the clock over the counter. 'I must go,' she said, draining her cup.

'Duty calls?'

156

'I'm afraid so.'

'How will you get to Montparnasse?'

'Métro. There's a *Ligne Cinq* station just round the corner.'

'I'll walk you there.'

They were at Boissière station within minutes, delayed only by a mendicant not-so-old soldier into whose feebly clutched biscuit-tin Corinne dropped several coins. The act reminded Max how swiftly he had come to ignore the human flotsam of the war washed up on the city's streets.

'Every time I see a man like that I realize how trifling my troubles really are,' said Corinne as they moved on. 'It must strike you too: how easily you could have been killed in the war.'

'It struck me every day I returned from a mission in one piece. One of my squadron leaders, Fred Collins, used to say to me, "You're lucky to be alive, Maxted. Make it count." '

'It's a good philosophy.'

'I try to live by it.'

'We all should. What does Mr Collins do now?'

Max remembered then, in all its clarity, the day Collins had died. But he had no wish to speak of it. 'I don't know. Something he enjoys, I hope.'

They had crossed Avenue Kléber and were standing at the head of the stairs leading down into the Métro station. Corinne turned and looked at him. 'Zamaron will be in no hurry to tell me I've been vindicated. I suspect you'll hear from him before I do.'

'I'll let you know as soon as I hear anything.'

'I'll either be at work or at home.'

'Don't worry. I'll find you.'

'I'll be waiting.'

To his surprise, she kissed him lightly on the cheek, then hurried down the stairs, glancing back at him and raising a hand as she turned a corner and vanished from sight.

A TELEGRAM FROM ASHLEY WAS WAITING FOR MAX BACK AT the Mazarin. He read it with some dread, though it contained nothing he could not have foreseen. *Funeral fixed for noon tomorrow St Martins. Your presence hoped for.* He could reply, explaining why he would not be there. But Ashley already knew the reason and so did their mother. It would have to go unanswered.

Whatever Spataro said to Zamaron and whenever he said it, Max did not propose simply to wait on events. He went up to his room to fetch his hat and coat, intending to proceed directly to the Hotel Plaza Athénée in search of Ribeiro. But Ribeiro, it transpired, was already in search of him. A letter on Plaza Athénée notepaper had arrived for Max during his brief trip upstairs. It was handwritten, in a sprawling script.

26 March 1919

Dear Mr Maxted,
I had the honour to be a friend of your late
father over many years. I was greatly saddened to
learn of his death. Mr Norris has told me you are
to be in Paris for a few more days at least. I should

like to speak to you. I hope it is convenient for you
to join me for luncheon at my hotel at one
this afternoon. Please let me know if it is
not. Please accept also my heartfelt condolences.
Sincerely yours,
Baltazar Ribeiro

Max sent back a note, accepting Ribeiro's invitation,
then wandered out into the city, the morning empty
before him. As yet, he had only a glut of questions
about his father and a dearth of answers. He walked to
the Eiffel Tower and took the lift to the top. From there
he could see the whole city. But to see was not enough.
He needed to understand. And he was as far as ever
from doing so. But he had some reason to hope that
might change before the day was out.

Baltazar Ribeiro was a stout, white-haired, extravagantly
moustachioed man of about Sir Henry Maxted's age,
impeccably dressed in a dove-grey suit with wing-collar
and pearl tie-pin. He greeted Max with elaborate
courtesy in grammatically perfect but heavily accented
English and repeated his written condolences with every
sign that they were genuine, tears brimming in his eyes
as he spoke of his old friend.

'I first met your father more than twenty years ago,
when he arrived at the embassy in Rio. I was new to the
city myself. You could say we discovered Rio together.'
Ribeiro smiled as he spoke, something the lines around
his eyes and mouth suggested he did often. 'It seemed
such a happy chance when I learnt that he too was in
Paris for the peace conference. I am more sorry than I

can say for this terrible accident. When is the funeral to be? I should like to attend if I can.'

'The funeral's tomorrow,' Max replied. 'In Surrey.'

Ribeiro was struck briefly silent. And in the panelled quietude of the Plaza Athénée's restaurant, where there were more waiters than customers, his silence was almost tangible.

'If it is tomorrow, in Surrey,' he resumed eventually, in a puzzled tone, 'why are you still in Paris?'

'I'm not going to be there.'

Ribeiro's puzzlement only deepened. 'Why not?'

'Because my father's death wasn't an accident, *senhor*. He was murdered. And it's more important that I stay here to find his murderer than I please my family by going home to see him buried.'

Ribeiro's smile had become a deep frown. 'I do not understand. Mr Norris said nothing of murder.'

'Mr Norris said what he'd been told to say. I imagine he's built his career on doing that.'

'But why should he have been told to say what is not true?'

'The unsolved murder of a member of one of the principal delegations to the peace conference would ruffle too many feathers. The authorities have agreed it should be regarded as an accident.'

'If this is so—'

'It is so, *senhor*. Would you like me to explain how I can be sure of that?'

Ribeiro nodded solemnly. 'I would.'

Max set out the evidence calmly and logically. He made no bones about his father's relationship with Corinne, though he did not name her. The revelation did not appear to surprise Ribeiro, who listened patiently, sipping his wine and picking at his food distractedly. Max said nothing of the list Sir Henry had left behind, nor of the key concealed in his room at the Majestic. The facts he could swear to would have to speak for themselves. Old friend of Sir Henry's or not, Ribeiro was still an unknown quantity.

'This is scandalous,' he said when Max had finished. 'They propose to regard Henry's death as a . . . stupid fall . . . when actually he was murdered?'

'That's the size of it.'

'I knew of Henry's . . . *caso amoroso*. He spoke of it to me a few times, though I could have guessed from how happy he was. She felt genuinely for him, you say?'

'She did.'

'Then I am very sorry for her. How is she?'

'She's coping bravely. And she's as determined as I am to establish the truth.'

'But what could that be? Why would anyone want to murder Henry? He had no enemies.'

'Are you sure?'

Ribeiro shrugged. 'If he did, he was careful to ensure I knew nothing of them. He made none in Brazil, I'm certain. He was a popular figure in the diplomatic community. I enrolled him in the Jockey Club. Everyone liked him. And everyone who knew him will be sorry to hear of his death.'

'He had more troublesome postings than Rio.'

'It is true. St Petersburg in the middle of a revolution must have been grim. And dangerous. He told me it was often unsafe to walk the streets. Ah!' A thought had struck Ribeiro. 'You know many Tsarists fled to Paris after the Bolsheviks took over?'

'Yes.'

'They live in the streets around the Orthodox Cathedral in Rue Daru. There are so many of them the area is called Little Russia. Henry told me this. I went to see for myself and it is true. Now I think about it, he said to me once that they had caused him some embarrassment.'

'How?'

'There is a bookshop run by a man called . . . I cannot remember his name. It begins with a B . . . I think. He asked Henry for help. There is an organization the bookseller is a member of, dedicated to restoring the monarchy. It is called the Trust.'

'The *what*?'

'The Trust. You have heard of it?'

Yes. Max had heard of it, though until this moment he was unaware of the fact. The Trust had been worth £5,000 to Sir Henry. But how? And why? 'I know nothing about such an organization, *senhor*,' Max said, adroitly avoiding the need to lie. 'What help did they want from my father?'

'They hoped he would speak to Lloyd George and Balfour on their behalf. This man B had known Henry slightly in St Petersburg. Henry could do nothing for him, of course, even if he had wanted to. He joked that they thought he was far more important than he actually was. But, still, perhaps they felt . . . insulted . . . by his refusal.'

'To the extent of murdering him?'

'It is unlikely, I agree.'

But it was not so unlikely if Sir Henry's dealings with the Trust had gone further than a polite refusal to lobby the Prime Minister and the Foreign Secretary for them. What exactly did £5,000 buy? 'Are you sure you can't remember the bookseller's name, *senhor*?'

'It is gone. But it does not matter. His name is over the door of the shop. In Russian, obviously.'

'I'll find him.'

'Be careful.'

Max smiled. 'I can't afford to be *too* careful.'

'The Russians.' Ribeiro sighed. 'We had an emperor in Brazil. We let him go into exile when the republic was created. We did not feel the need to slaughter the entire royal family. The Russians are . . . an extreme people.'

'Do you know who my father was acquainted with in the Japanese delegation, *senhor*?'

'Kuroda.' Ribeiro nodded. 'I had forgotten him. Yes. Henry knew him from his time at the embassy in Tokyo. You were born there, of course.'

'I was, yes.'

'I have not met Kuroda. I have not met any of the Japanese. They keep to themselves. And Kuroda is not a politician.'

'What, then?'

'A policeman, I think.' Ribeiro snapped his fingers. 'And there is a Russian connection.'

'There is?'

'Yes. When the Tsar the Russians killed last year was crown prince – Tsarevich – he visited Japan. There was an attempt on his life. Henry was in Tokyo at the time. He gave this policeman – Kuroda – some small assistance with the investigation of the crime.'

'What sort of assistance?'

'He did not say. And I did not ask. It seemed, as he talked of it, unimportant. It was very long ago. You will speak to Kuroda?'

'I'll speak to anyone in Paris who knew my father.'

'There will not be many who knew him well.'

'As one of those who did . . .' Max grimaced. 'I have an awkward question to ask.'

Ribeiro spread his arms wide. 'Ask it.'

'Was my father short of money?'

'Money? Your father? No. He . . . spent . . . freely when we were together.'

'He had no need to . . . raise funds?'

For the first time in their conversation, Max sensed disquiet on his host's part. Ribeiro smiled, but not quite as easily or genuinely as before. Until this moment, he had been candid and open. Now there was the slightest tinge of circumspection in his eyes and his voice. 'I cannot think of any reason for Henry to raise funds, as you put it. You have some reason?'

'Nothing definite.'

'Then . . .'

'I mean to follow every clue, however faint.'

'You should.' Ribeiro sounded fatalistic, as if he knew, as perhaps he did, that it would be futile to seek to discourage Max. 'Henry was a good friend and a good man. If he was murdered . . .'

'He was murdered.'

Ribeiro's expression had become solemn and serious. 'Then, as his son, you must seek to avenge him. And as his friend . . . I shall help you if I can.'

NUMEROUS BRANDIES HAD CONCLUDED MAX'S LUNCH WITH Baltazar Ribeiro. Disappointed that he would not be able to attend his old friend's funeral, Ribeiro had insisted they toast his memory countless times as he called to mind various incidents from their friendship. Racecourse mishaps and nightclub escapades Max could hardly associate with his father had flowed from Ribeiro's alcohol-loosened tongue. 'We both left it late in life to sow our wild oats, Max.' (Max had persuaded Ribeiro to address him by his nickname, though the Brazilian's accent made it sound like Mags.) 'I lived in Manaus until I was forty, deep in Amazonia. My father made his fortune from rubber and paid for me to become a lawyer. I married another rubber baron's daughter and led a respectable, hard-working life. Then I was selected to replace one of the province's congress-men who had died and off I went to Rio, two thousand kilometres away. I had never been to the capital before. My family stayed behind in Manaus. It was a little the same for Henry. We became a pair of middle-aged play-boys. We had a lot of fun, Max, more than our fair share. Oh, yes, they were great days. I miss them. And I miss my friend, your father.'

*

Max was aware, when he left the Plaza Athénée, that he was drunk and not necessarily the best judge of his own actions. He realized that proceeding directly to Little Russia in search of bookseller B was unwise and impetuous. But he went anyway, reckoning the walk there through the chill afternoon air would sober him up.

The chill afternoon air in fact made little impression. He reached the neighbourhood of the multi-domed St-Alexandre-Nevsky Orthodox Cathedral under no illusion as to his condition. But he was not going to turn back now.

Many of the shops and cafés in the area sported signs in the Russian alphabet. He heard more Russian spoken by passers-by than French. In a side-street off Rue Daru, he came upon a bookseller's premises and used the Ancient Greek he remembered from his schooldays to make a rough transliteration of the proprietor's name: Bukayev. He was in the right place. But Bukayev was not. The shop was closed.

No opening hours were displayed. The interior looked dusty and barely businesslike. Bukayev probably came and went much as he pleased, Max surmised. This was confirmed by a grizzled old man in a heavy overcoat and fur hat who stopped at the sight of Max peering through the shop window. After a futile foray in Russian, he switched to French.

'*Le magasin est quelquefois ouvert, quelquefois fermé, monsieur.*'

'*Vous connaissez Bukayev, monsieur?*' Max asked.

'*Un peu.*' A little was not a lot. But it was better than nothing.

167

'*Où habite-t-il?*'

'*Là.*' The man gestured to the windows above the shop.

That was something. Bukayev lived on the premises. He would have to return eventually. But Max could not wait. He too would have to return.

It was probably for the best, Max concluded as he headed for the Mazarin. He needed to sleep off the brandies Ribeiro had plied him with before addressing himself to the task Ireton had set him. And he half-hoped good news might be waiting for him at the hotel in the form of a message from Zamaron. Bukayev would keep.

As James Maxted, late of the Royal Flying Corps, was striding a touch unsteadily along the eighth arrondissement streets of Paris, another youthful RFC veteran, Sam Twentyman, was walking up the drive of Gresscombe Place, in Surrey. Any unsteadiness he displayed was due to nervousness rather than alcohol. Only force of circumstance had led him to travel there from Walthamstow. He knew Max would not want him to visit his family, but the telegram he had received had left him with little choice in the matter.

A maid answered the door. Sam asked if he could speak to Sir Ashley Maxted on an urgent matter concerning his brother and she admitted him to a darkened hallway. The house was quiet, oppressively so, as he waited. He knew, of course, that the family would be in mourning. He reminded himself to bear that fact in mind.

Eventually, the maid returned and reported that Sir

Ashley was busy in his study, but could spare Sam a few moments of his time. She escorted him to a room towards the back of the house.

Sir Ashley was walking up and down by a window overlooking rain-prinked lawns and shrubbery. There were enough papers scattered on his desk to suggest he really was busy. His greeting was barely polite. Sam's condolences were brusquely acknowledged. A handshake was out of the question.

'You're Twentyman?'

'Yes, Sir Ashley. I was in the RFC with your—'

'Yes, yes, I know that. James has mentioned you to me. What can I do for you?'

'I wonder, has Lieutenant Maxted also mentioned our . . . business plans?'

The question raised a scowl on Sir Ashley's face. 'He may have.'

'I'm worried about how our plans . . . stand at present.'

'Are you really?'

'I understand Lieutenant Maxted—'

'You can drop the "Lieutenant",' Sir Ashley cut in testily. 'My brother's a civilian these days.'

'Yes. Of course. I, er . . .'

'What exactly do you want, Twentyman?'

'I understand . . . Mr Maxted . . . is in Paris. I had a telegram from him suggesting he . . . might be there for some time.'

Sir Ashley's face darkened ominously. The scowl rearranged itself, but remained a scowl. 'Indeed,' was all he said, though it was evident he might have liked to say more.

'Can you tell me where in Paris I could find him?'

'You're thinking of going there?'

'Yes. I am.'

'I shouldn't if I were you.'

'No?'

Sir Ashley shook his head. 'No.'

'Why not?'

'The land my brother needs for this flying school you and he had hopes of establishing . . . is unlikely to be available.'

'Oh.'

'You have a trade you can turn your hand to, Twentyman?'

'Not exactly, Sir Ashley, no.'

'Well, I should advise you to find one.'

Sam could think of nothing to say to that. He shifted awkwardly from one foot to the other. He badly wanted not to believe that his hopes for the future were to be dashed.

'If there's nothing else I can do for you . . .' Sir Ashley glanced dismissively towards the door.

Sam steeled himself. 'Mr Maxted's address . . . in Paris?'

'You still want it?'

'If . . . If you don't mind.'

'Why should I mind?' Sir Ashley stalked to his desk, ripped a sheet of paper from a pad and wrote on it, then handed it to Sam. 'There you are.'

'Thank you. I'm . . . much obliged.'

'Is that all?'

'Well, I was just wondering . . . if you could tell me . . . what's keeping Mr Maxted . . . in Paris.'

'What's keeping him there?'

'Er . . . yes.'

'If you want to find that out, Twentyman, I suggest you waste some money I suspect you don't have by going to Paris and asking him.'

'Right.' Sam swallowed a tart riposte. 'I see.'

'Do you? I doubt it. Now, you really must excuse me. I have my father's funeral to arrange.'

For a second, when the alarm clock woke him, Max thought it was early morning rather than early evening. The twilight falling greyly through the windows of his hotel room could have denoted either. Then where and when and why took urgent hold of his mind and he leapt up from the bed. The time had come to do what he had agreed to do for Ireton. He set aside caution and apprehensiveness as he had done every day of his war service. In his experience, they only slowed a man's reactions. And speedy reactions could be the difference between life and death. Nothing as elemental as that, he felt certain, awaited him in Auteuil. In all likelihood, it would be as simple an errand as Ireton had predicted. At all events, he would soon find out.

He fastened his shoes decisively, donned his hat and coat and set out.

It was not until the train from Epsom reached Waterloo and Sam stepped out on to the platform that he decided to go through with it. Even then, absolute certainty only descended on him as he threaded his way through the surging mass of homebound commuters filling the concourse. He retrieved the bag he had deposited earlier in the day at the left-luggage office and knew beyond a shadow of a doubt that he had not packed it in vain. He would head for Westminster Bridge when he left the station and reach Victoria in time for a bite to eat before the Paris sleeper was due to depart. 'In for a penny, in for a pound, Sam,' he murmured to himself as he went on his way. 'You're better off chewing croissants than baking buns.' Already, he felt better for knowing that he was not going home.

Just as it had for the bustling commuters at Waterloo, so the working day had ended for Corinne Dombreux. She was confident Spataro had spoken to Zamaron by now, but until she had some confirmation of that she would remain anxious and fretful. Urging calm upon herself, she walked slowly home by her normal route.

The black Citroën parked by the kerb outside 8 Rue du Verger had no police markings, but was familiar to her as a model used by the higher echelons of the *préfecture*. This, it seemed to her, could only indicate that Spataro had indeed said his piece.

As she neared the car, the passenger door opened and Commissioner Zamaron stepped out. He looked sombre and serious, as well he might, considering the coach and horses Spataro's change of heart had driven through his absurd explanation for Sir Henry's death. Corinne lengthened her stride and looked hopefully towards him.

MAX TRIED HIS LEVEL BEST NOT TO LOOK AT THE CLOCK TOO often as he waited for Monsieur Buisson in the Café Sans Souci. The establishment was only a short walk from Gare d'Auteuil. Many of its customers were on their way home from wherever they worked. There was a high degree of coming and going. By lingering as long as he already had over his coffee and hair-of-the-dog cognac, Max felt he had made himself more conspicuous than was wise. And his perusal of the copy of *Le Figaro* he had brought with him for camouflage was beginning to feel unsustainable.

Every time the door of the café opened – which was frequently – Max glanced across at the newcomer. Ireton had told him Buisson would be carrying a cardboard map-tube. He would join Max at his table long enough to down a coffee, then leave – without the tube. A few minutes later, Max would also leave – with the tube. It really was exceedingly simple. All Max had to say to Buisson was '*Monsieur Ireton vous prie d'accepter ses excuses*'. Buisson, in all likelihood, would say nothing.

But the clock told Max, when he succumbed to temptation and looked at it, that Buisson was nearly a quarter of an hour late. Much longer and the delay would assume ominous proportions. Max sighed and decided to light another cigarette.

Just as he took out his cigarette-case, the door hinge gave a now familiar squeak. He glanced across the café. And there was Buisson, a portly, middle-aged man with flushed jowls and small eyes peering anxiously from beneath the brim of his hat. He held a briefcase and furled umbrella in one hand. The map-tube was thrust under his other arm like a swollen swagger-stick. Max rubbed his brow with his left hand, the signal Ireton had instructed him to use. Buisson nodded and moved in his direction.

He sat down with a sigh reminiscent of a slowly deflating bicycle tyre and laid the map-tube on the vacant chair between them. '*Bonsoir,*' he murmured, slipping off his hat to reveal a head of pomaded hair. Max noticed two symmetrical rivulets of sweat working their way down his temples. The sight was neither edifying nor reassuring.

'*Bonsoir,*' said Max. '*Monsieur Ireton vous prie d'accepter ses excuses.*'

'*Ses excuses,*' echoed Buisson. He took out a handkerchief and dabbed his moist upper lip. '*Bien entendu.*' He cast Max a skittering, panicky glance. Then, suddenly, without waiting to order the coffee that would have given his presence in the café a semblance of normality, he stood up, grabbed his hat, briefcase and umbrella and made for the door.

A second later, he was through it and gone. The waiter who had been bearing down on their table shrugged and retreated. Max went ahead and lit his cigarette with studied calmness. He glanced down at the map-tube.

There it was, left as agreed. But Buisson's discomposure could hardly have been less in keeping with the supposed simplicity of its delivery. Something was wrong, something to which the pointer, he sensed, was Buisson's reaction to Ireton's absence: *'Bien entendu.'* He understood, apparently. But Max did not.

He finished his cigarette, inspected the bill and laid down enough coins to cover it. Then, taking the map-tube with him, he rose and walked casually across to the coat hooks at the rear of the café. He balanced the tube on one of the hooks while he put on his coat and hat, then retrieved it. He was ready to leave.

But Max had no intention of leaving by the front door. He had already reconnoitred an emergency exit and, though he could not be sure whether the emergency was real or imagined, he had decided to use it.

He slipped through the door leading to the toilets, but ignored the steps leading down to them and pressed on through another door marked DEFENSE D'ENTRER into a decrepit storage room and out of that via a dank and dripping stairwell into a rear courtyard.

There was no lighting. He trod cautiously on the slimy cobbles and reached the corner of the building where an alley led to the street. No one was visible. A car drove slowly past as he watched, the engine labouring. He saw no cause for alarm and moved into the alley.

As he did so, a caped and uniformed policeman stepped into the mouth of the alley and looked straight at him. *'Ici,'* he shouted.

Max turned and ran. He heard the shrill blast of the policeman's whistle behind him and a percussion of footfalls. The rendezvous at the café had been a trap. He had not walked directly into it, but he was scarcely out of it either.

There was a glimmer of light ahead on the far side of the courtyard. A street lamp he could not see dimly illuminated the exposed flank of a half-demolished building. There was a scalable wall ahead of him and a void beyond it that promised escape. He ran towards it, unable to see what might be in his path, and collided blindly with a cart stowed in the corner of the yard.

Ignoring the sharp pain in his knee where he had struck the cart, he glanced back and saw several milling figures in the alley. He had only seconds to elude his pursuers. He stuffed the map-tube inside his coat, jumped up on to the cart and launched himself at the top of the wall.

It was all that remained of an originally higher wall. The surface was jagged and crumbling. Max found a clawing hand-and-foot-hold and virtually fell over it, descending into a rubble-strewn demolition site. His hat fell off in the process. He could not see it in the darkness and had no time to look for it. He hobbled through an invisible chaos of toppled bricks and other debris to a narrow street where there was at least some light, chanced his arm on a right turn and broke into a jog, suppressing the desire to run headlong for fear of the noise his shoes would make on the cobbles. There were shouts behind him that sounded promisingly confused, but no sound of actual pursuit. He jogged on, favouring the more shadowy side of the street.

He could see a junction with a wider street about fifty yards further on, but fifty yards was a long way. Sure enough, the police had negotiated the wall and the demolition site before he had covered the distance. There were loud shouts behind him. Torch beams flashed. Whistles shrieked. They had spotted him.

As he reached the junction, a dark saloon car appeared, bursting out of the night from nowhere, headlamps blazing. It swerved across the road and skidded to a halt at the kerbside next to him. Through an open window, a familiar voice addressed him. 'Get in.' It was Schools Morahan.

For a second, Max hesitated, then wrenched the rear door of the car open and threw himself in.

The car started away with a squeal of tyres and a surge of acceleration, pushing Max back against the seat.

'Where . . . where did you come from?' he panted.

'The right place at the right time. There's nothing I could have done for you if you'd walked out the front door of the café. You're smarter than you look. And I see you got the package.'

The map-tube was protruding from Max's coat. He pulled it out and dropped it on to the seat beside him, then nearly fell on to it when Morahan took a sharp left, followed shortly by a right and another right along quiet, poorly lit side-streets.

'What's in the tube?' Max demanded.

'Couldn't tell you. Ask Travis.'

'Did he know he was sending me into a trap?'

'He had doubts about Buisson's reliability. Seems he was right.'

'So, to hell with me?'

'Not quite. I came to get you, didn't I?'

'They could easily have caught me.'

'But they didn't.'

Another abrupt left turn took them on to a broad road running alongside a railway viaduct. Morahan seemed to relax. The road was straight and clear ahead, but he slowed slightly and blithely lit a cigarette.

'No one's following us. The *flics* who were chasing you were on foot and they won't have been able to get a car on our tail. You can relax.'

'Thanks so much.'

'Don't mention it.'

'Are you taking me to meet Travis?'

'No. I reckon back to your hotel's best. See Travis in the morning. You won't feel so hard done by then.'

'You want to bet?'

'If you like.'

It was hard to sustain the anger Max felt for the way he had been manipulated in the face of Morahan's cool-nerved off-handedness. And, though he would not have admitted as much, he had actually rather enjoyed himself. It was good to be back in action – albeit a very different kind of action from his days in the RFC. He sighed and rubbed his throbbing knee. 'Who is Buisson?'

'Something middle-ranking at the conference printing works.'

'What does he supply – secret documents?'

'Ask Travis.'

'Maybe I'll just keep the tube and see for myself what it contains.'

'I can't let you do that.' Morahan glanced at Max over his shoulder, the shadows inside the car rendering his expression indecipherable. 'And we don't want the evening going sour on you, do we?'

MAX WAS ROUSED THE FOLLOWING MORNING NOT BY THE alarm clock but by the telephone. Looking at the clock, he saw it was only just gone seven. The merest trickle of daylight was edging round the curtains. After the evening he had had, it was an awakening he would have preferred to be postponed indefinitely. But the hope instantly seized him that the call related to Spataro, news of whose recantation was overdue. He grabbed the receiver.

'Hello?'

'Is that you, sir?'

'What?'

'It's Sam here, sir.'

Good God, it was Sam Twentyman. Max sought in vain for a plausible explanation. Surely he could not be calling from London. 'What? Where are you?'

'Downstairs.'

'You're here? In Paris?'

'Yes, sir. Arrived on the sleeper a couple of hours ago. Not too early for you, am I?'

Max stumbled down to the lobby with his thoughts whirling. He was still bemusingly exhilarated by his close shave in Auteuil, but he was well aware that the incident illustrated just how duplicitous Ireton could be. He was also troubled by the continuing silence where Spataro was concerned. Sam's sudden appearance was a complication he would have preferred to avoid. He had not expected his friend to run him to earth, though he knew why he had. The sad truth was that Sam would soon discover he had had a wasted journey. Max supposed he should have spared him that.

There was a surprise in store for Max, however. He realized when he reached the lobby and caught sight of Sam, travel-weary and tousled but smiling the same old dependable Twentyman smile, that he was damnably pleased to see him. He piloted him out to the café he had taken Corinne to the previous morning and stood him a breakfast he looked in sore need of.

Max contented himself with coffee and cigarettes and listened with mounting concern to Sam's account of the difficult, not to say expensive, week he had had. In Sam's mind, the flying school was clearly still a viable proposition, notwithstanding Ashley's ominous utterances. Max had not appreciated just how heavily he was relying on it. Allowing him to continue relying on it was unconscionable.

'I'm sorry, Sam,' he said at last. 'You should understand that Surrey Wings is almost certainly a non-starter.'

'A *non-starter*?' It was obvious from his tone that Sam did not want to believe it. 'Why?'

And so Max set out the reasons. They hinged on the whole question of his father's death. Another surprising realization came to him as he explained why he was certain Sir Henry had been murdered and how he had so antagonized Ashley by maintaining as much that there was no possibility of Gresscombe land being used for their flying school. The realization was not a new one. Max had simply forgotten the bond of trust that he had established with Sam during the war. The plain fact was that Sam Twentyman had probably saved his life a dozen times in a dozen different ways by his assiduousness and ingenuity. He had never once let Max down. And there was no one else of whom that was true.

'I have to stay in Paris until I get to the bottom of this, Sam. You can see that, can't you?'

Sam nodded. 'I see it, right enough. That brother of yours, sir, if you don't mind me saying, is—'

'A first-class shit. I know. But he's cock of the walk now. And you were lucky. You didn't meet my sister-in-law. She pulls the strings. And she doesn't like me one little bit.'

'Sisters-in-law can be like that.'

'I'm afraid we're going to have to abandon our plans. I'm sorry, but there it is.'

'I was hoping you wouldn't say that, sir.'

'I know. Look, Sam, why don't you stay at the Mazarin tonight and see a bit of gay Paree before you head back? We can paint the town red tonight. I'll pay for your accommodation and you'll be home in time to reclaim the deposit on those blessed planes.'

'Ah, home.' Sam looked wistful. 'Not sure I've properly got one of those any more.'

'Maybe there's some other pilot you served with who'd be interested in starting a flying school.'

'None I'd trust further than they could fly without an engine.'

'It's a bugger, Sam, I know.' Max spread his hand sorrowfully. 'There's nothing I can do.'

'I appreciate that, sir. And I appreciate the offer of a night in Paris. It's handsome of you. I'll take you up on it.'

'Capital. Let's get you booked in, then I must run.'

'This Ireton, sir . . .'

'You're going to tell me he sounds like a wrong 'un.'

'Well, if the scrape you got into last night is anything to go by . . .'

'I'll be on my guard, don't worry. I won't let him pull a stunt like that again.'

'Seems to me you need as much looking after here as you did at the Front.'

'Possibly. But, fortunately for you, looking after me is no longer your job. Whatever trouble I may get into, I'll have to get myself out of it.'

After securing Sam a room at the Mazarin, and wishing him a pleasant day's sightseeing, Max took a cab to 33 Rue des Pyramides, where Malory, dressed this morning in a fractionally lighter shade of tweed, informed him that he was expected (as well he might be, Max thought) and should go straight into Ireton's office.

'Morning, Max.' Ireton greeted him with a broad smile and an expansive gesture that raised loose lassos of smoke from his cigarette. 'How are you feeling?'

'I think sore would capture it in your vernacular.'

'Ah. Schools said you seemed to be limping when he left you last night. But you've bounded in here in sprightly fashion, so I guess you're nursing nothing worse than a few bruises.'

'No thanks to you.'

'That's hardly fair. I chose a meeting-place with a rear exit, didn't I?'

'But you didn't tell me I'd need to use it.'

'Call it an initiative test.'

'I call it being set up like a decoy duck.'

'You sound angrier than you look. More fun than you'd have expected, was it, Max? Maybe it stirred a few happy memories of dogfights over no man's land.'

'You lied to me, Travis.'

'Not at all. It should and could have gone as simply as I said. But obviously they rumbled Buisson and he told them everything.'

'And what's everything?'

'I've been paying him to supply me with copies of the proofs of Supreme Council minutes and consultative papers so that my clients can have advance notice of how the great and not necessarily good plan to carve up their nations. It's his word against mine as far as that goes, of course, since I didn't walk obligingly into the trap last night and the person who did got clean away. So, all's well that ends well. Or as well as it can be, considering the documents Buisson gave you are certain to be fakes and now I have to recruit someone to replace him, which won't be easy. Rumour has it they're going to limit the decision-making from here on to a new Council of Four – Clemenceau, Lloyd George, Orlando, Wilson – because there have been too many leaks.' Ireton grinned. 'You could say I'm a victim of my own success.'

'My heart bleeds for you.'

'Don't take it like that. Sit down, Max. I'm a man of my word. You deliver for me; I deliver for you.'

With a show of reluctance, Max sat down. 'Do you know who killed my father?'

'No. But I might know *why* he was killed. Ever heard of Fritz Lemmer?'

'No.'

'I'm not surprised. Lemmer would be disappointed if you had. He was the Kaiser's spymaster. Well, maybe he still is, in a sense. A former naval officer turned intelligence-gatherer. A shadowy figure, by choice and need. Thirty years in the game, apparently.'

'What game?'

'Spying. Sabotage. Assassinations. You name it, he's had a finger in it. So they say.'

'What's he to do with my father?'

'Well, the thing is this. Cigarette, by the way?' Ireton proffered his case.

'I prefer my own brand.' Max studiously took out one of his Wills and lit it. 'The thing is?' he prompted.

'Delicate, Max, delicate. Like I told you the other day, Henry's put a few pieces of information my way since this conference began. Nothing treasonable, I assure you, just . . . titbits.'

'And like *I* told *you*, I don't believe it.'

'You're going to have to if you want to find out who killed him. The fact is, Henry was eager to raise money. I don't know why. Maybe to set up Corinne Dombreux in the manner to which he thought she should become accustomed. He wasn't typical of my sources of information, far from it, and the information he supplied was minor stuff. Then, just last week, he offered me something in an altogether different league. Or, rather, he offered me some*one*. Lemmer.'

'What do you mean?'

'Lemmer vanished last November, around the time the Kaiser decamped to Holland. Since then his where-abouts have preyed on a lot of people's minds. The word is that he recruited spies for Germany in every European government. He probably didn't stop at Europe either. Nobody except Lemmer knows who they were and they're mostly still in place, presumably hop-ing and praying their well-paid work for the Kaiser never comes to light. The question is . . .'

'Where is Lemmer?'

'Exactly. Where is he? And what's he up to? Maybe he's still in touch with his agents, many of whom could be here in Paris, negotiating on their countries' behalf. You see how significant that could be? Whose interests are they really serving? Maybe Lemmer's trying to soften the peace terms for Germany, or sow discord among the Allies. There's no way to tell. The Americans, the British, the French and all the others would like to lay hands on Lemmer and sweat the truth out of him. But they can't find him. Which means his whereabouts constitute a very valuable commodity. Off-hand, I can't think of a more valuable one.'

'And that's what my father was offering you.'

'In a nutshell, yes.'

'But how would he know where Lemmer was?'

'It seems improbable, I grant you. But not when you think about it. Lemmer is notoriously elusive, not to mention camera-shy. There are precious few people who know what he looks like. Henry happens to have been one.'

'How?'

'Lemmer was a naval attaché at the German Embassy in Tokyo in the early nineties. He hadn't perfected his knack for invisibility then. Henry met him several times, apparently. So, when he told me he'd seen Lemmer here, in Paris, I was inclined to believe him. And happy to agree to act as his broker.'

'Pa said he knew where Lemmer was? An actual address?'

'Not quite. He said he was in a position to lure Lemmer to a meeting. That would have been enough.'

'What could he lure Lemmer with?'

'He didn't say. But he assured me it could be done. For a fee.'

'How big a fee?'

'I never got the chance to find out how high an interested party might have been prepared to go. Before I could open negotiations, Henry was killed. It would have been some auction, though. Remember, Lemmer could tell a government not only who the traitors are in their own ranks but who they are in other governments' ranks. And with the right persuasion a traitor in one cause can be recruited to a different cause. Lemmer would be quite a catch.'

'Do you think he killed my father?'

'It's possible. Not personally, of course. He hires people to do that kind of thing for him. Alternatively, word of what Henry was trying to sell might have reached one of Lemmer's agents, who had good cause to fear exposure.'

'How would word have reached them?'

'I made some inquiries, as Henry asked me to.' Ireton shrugged. 'I'd be sorry to think that action on my part led to his death, but I warned him of the risks he was running and he insisted on going ahead.'

'Who did you make these inquiries with?'

'I spoke to them in strictest confidence. It wouldn't be fair to identify them.'

'Who are they?'

'Like I say, I can't—'

'Who the hell are they?' Max jumped up and leant across the desk. 'I want their names.'

Ireton did not flinch, though he frowned slightly as he looked up at Max. 'I think I've told you as much as I agreed to. More from me requires more from you. We share an interest in Fritz Lemmer, Max. I don't delude myself that you've told me everything you've found out about your father's activities. You'd have been a fool to. By the same token, I can't be expected to disclose everything I know or suspect at this stage. We have to learn to trust one another, you and I. We have to pool our resources. We have to collaborate.' The frown faded, to be replaced by the scar-distorted smile. 'Now, how does that sound to you?'

MAX WAS UNDER NO ILLUSIONS ABOUT THE BARGAIN HE struck with Ireton. 'You want me to find Lemmer for you, don't you, Travis? Then you can sell his whereabouts to the highest bidder. I take all the risks. You take all the rewards.'

'Not at all.' Ireton looked shocked by the suggestion. 'I'd be happy to split the proceeds fifty-fifty. If that's what you want.'

'I'm not interested in turning a profit. I'm interested in finding my father's murderer.'

'I know. But you may as well take your share. If only to deprive me of it. I'm sure you wouldn't class me as a good cause. Now, let's get down to it, shall we? I sounded out three people about Henry's proposition. I didn't name Henry. It was all done on a hypothetical basis. But if one of them – or an associate they confided in – knew of my links with Henry and Henry's knowledge of Lemmer, they might have figured out who my source was. That seems to me the likeliest explanation for Henry's murder. But if you confront these people and start throwing accusations around they'll know I pointed you in their direction. Given what happened to Henry, that could have unhealthy consequences for me. You follow?'

'I could say I found their names along with Lemmer's on a list I came across amongst my father's possessions.'

'That's good. You appear to have a real talent for this kind of thing, Max. A list. I like that.'

'So, who were the three?'

'Not so fast. I need to be sure you don't drop me in it. I also need to know what, if anything, you learn from them about Lemmer.'

'I won't mention you. And I'll tell you whatever I find out.'

'I have your word on that?'

'Of course.'

Ireton smiled, as if genuinely amused. 'Sadly, in this serpent-pit of a world we inhabit, the word of an English gentleman is no longer sufficient to quell all doubts in such matters. Schools will go with you when you meet them. He occasionally works freelance as a bodyguard, so the arrangement shouldn't arouse any suspicion.'

'If you think that's necessary . . .'

'Oh, I do.'

Max had no choice, as Ireton must have known, but to agree. 'All right, then.'

'Fine. We have a deal.' To Max's surprise, Ireton offered him his hand. They shook. 'OK. We'll take them in the original order. Kuroda, at the Japanese delegation.'

'*Kuroda?*' Max was genuinely surprised, but also disappointed. The first name he had been given was one he already knew.

'You've heard of him?'

'Corinne told me my father knew him.'

'Did she? Well, that's interesting.'

Max had the distinct impression his acquaintance with Corinne was well known to Ireton, though for some reason he did not want to admit it. 'I guess it's no surprise. Kuroda's certainly old enough to have met Henry when he was in Japan.'

'Why did you go to him?'

'Because there's a persistent rumour Lemmer was behind a plot to assassinate the then Tsarevich when he visited Japan in 1891. His visit was supposed to smooth Russo-Jap relations, but the assassination attempt scotched that mighty effectively. A big feather in Lemmer's cap and an even bigger grudge for the Japs to bear. So, I thought they might be willing to pay over the odds for a chance to grab him.'

'And were they?'

'Hard to tell. Kuroda's the epitome of the inscrutable Oriental. But he didn't deny they'd be interested. He wasn't going to ignore the matter, that was clear. You need to establish what he did – who else he consulted, for instance. Play on your role as the loyal son seeking justice for his dead father. The Japs have a soft spot for that kind of thing.'

'It's not a role,' Max snapped.

Ireton was unabashed. 'All the better, then. I suggest you and Schools call on him at the delegation's hotel this evening.'

'*This evening?* What's wrong with this morning?'

'Schools is tied up all day. I won't get a chance to brief him until later.'

'I can't wait that long.'

'Sorry, but you'll have to. That's the deal.'

'Who are the other two you sounded out?'

Ireton looked almost pained. 'Come on, Max. I wasn't born yesterday. Neither were you, though a lot closer to yesterday than I was, I grant you. If I tell you who the others are now, there's nothing to stop you approaching them on your own. No, no. We see how you get on with Kuroda. And we take it from there. One step at a time.'

Max gave brief but serious consideration to grabbing Ireton by the throat and trying to force the other names out of him. He felt certain the American was stringing him along for devious reasons of his own. But he could not afford to yield to temptation. There was too much at stake. 'Very well,' he said through gritted teeth.

'Meet Schools here at six.' Ireton beamed. 'OK?'

Max left Ireton's offices burning with impatience. His search for the truth seemed to be diverted or delayed at every turn.

His first thought was to return to the Mazarin and find out whether any message had reached him from Zamaron regarding Spataro. But a second thought saw him divert to Little Russia. Perhaps the morning would find Bukayev manning his bookshop.

The bookshop was open, but Bukayev was nowhere to be seen. The jingling of the bell as Max entered brought a sombre, heavy-featured young woman scurrying out of an office to the rear. She had raven-black hair, tied back severely, and was dressed mostly in black as well.

She addressed him in Russian, understandably enough, since the books filling the ceiling-high shelves all had titles printed in the Cyrillic alphabet.

191

'I am looking for Mr Bukayev,' he said, slowly and distinctly.

To his relief, she switched to English in response. 'Ah. He is not here.'

'Do you know when he'll be back?'

'A few days, maybe. He is out of Paris.'

'Damn it all to hell!' The strength of his reaction surprised her. She took a step back. He raised a hand apologetically. 'I'm sorry. I badly wanted to talk to him.'

'What about?'

'It concerns my late father, Sir Henry Maxted.'

'You are Sir Henry Maxted's son?'

'Yes. I—'

The jingling of the doorbell and the warning look he caught in her eyes cut him off. A bulky, bull-necked man in a tightly belted raincoat and pork-pie hat entered the shop. *'Dobroe utro,'* he growled.

The young woman returned the greeting in half-hearted fashion and watched the man as he began a slow prowl of the shelves. Then she looked at Max and spoke to him quietly, to his bemusement, in French. *'Un instant, s'il vous plaît.'* Her expression and the change of language combined to urge caution on him.

She hurried into the office and returned a moment later, carrying a pencil and a notepad. She offered them to Max, her glance shifting to monitor the movements of the newcomer. *'Votre nom et votre adresse, monsieur?'* she prompted.

'D'accord,' he mustered, taking the pencil and pad. He wrote the information down and handed them back.

'Merci, monsieur,' she said, smiling briskly. And that, her smile conveyed, was all she had to say – for now.

A brisk walk took Max back to the Mazarin. The morning was wearing on and soon, he knew, the mourners would be gathering in Epsom for his father's funeral. There would be many muttered questions about his absence and no one would have an adequate answer. Many would assume the worst. He wished it could be otherwise. But it could not. He had chosen his course. And he would steer it.

Vindication of a sort was waiting for him at the hotel. There was, at last, a message. *Please telephone Mr Appleby as soon as possible.* Max was only half surprised Appleby had been left to convey the news to him. Zamaron was probably too embarrassed, given his explanation for Sir Henry's death would now be in tatters. Max hurried up to his room and put a call through to the Majestic straight away.

The switchboard left him hanging for a moment, then he was connected. 'Mr Maxted?' came Appleby's gravelly greeting.

'Yes. It's me. I didn't know you were back in Paris.'

'Ah. I suppose your brother mentioned my trip to London. I returned on the sleeper last night.'

'And heard of an unexpected development?'

'Yes. I did. You already know?'

'I was forewarned that Spataro was going to withdraw his claim about Corinne spending the night with him.'

'Who told you that?'

'Corinne.'

'Really?' Appleby sounded genuinely puzzled.

'That is why you called me, isn't it?'

'No. No, I'm afraid it isn't. Spataro hasn't withdrawn his claim. And he isn't going to now.'

'What do you mean?'

'He's dead, Mr Maxted. Murdered, in his apartment, the night before last. His body was discovered yesterday.'

'*Murdered?*'

'Yes. And the police have arrested Madame Dombreux.'

'I THOUGHT YOU MIGHT LIKE TO ACCOMPANY ME WHEN I take a look at the murder scene, Mr Maxted,' Appleby went on, his tone of voice sounding bizarrely normal to Max in the light of what he had just said. 'You won't get in there on your own and I know you'll have lots of questions, so do you want to come with me? It's now or never, I'm afraid. I'm operating on a tight schedule.'

'Yes,' Max murmured. 'I'll come.'

'What?'

'*I'll come with you.*'

'Good. I'll pick you up in . . . a quarter of an hour?'

'All right. A quarter of an hour.'

'See you shortly, then. Sorry, by the way, if this was a bit of a facer. I was surprised myself.'

Surprised? Yes, Max thought as he stared at the receiver before hanging up. He was that too. Surprised and shocked and horrified. Corinne had not murdered Spataro. He was surer of that than of most things. Good God, the man was already dead when she came to report his change of heart. He was already dead and she had not known it. A trap had been closing around her.

And she had not known that either. But she knew it now. And so did Max.

'Are you still there, Lamb?' Appleby asked, returning his attention to the other telephone on his desk.

'Yes, sir.'

'I think I can give you a few hours off. You deserve it after the shoe leather you've expended over the last couple of days. I'm taking Maxted to Montparnasse.'

'Righto, sir.'

'Pick up his trail later at Ireton's. I think we can safely assume he'll find his way back there.'

'I should say so, sir.'

'Good work so far, Lamb. Well done.'

'Thank you, sir.'

The hearse drew away from Gresscombe Place under a pewter sky through flecks of snow blown on an icy wind. No words passed between the passengers in the limousine that followed it. The two Ladies Maxted, Winifred and Lydia, occupied the rear seat. They were veiled and enveloped in black. The middle seat, behind the driver, was shared by Sir Ashley and Winifred's brother, George, black-suited and sombre, although in George's case sombreness did not extend to sobriety. Ashley could smell the whisky on his uncle's breath quite clearly. There had evidently been more than the one stiffener he had admitted to.

Ashley, though he would never have confessed as much, would have quite liked to join George in a glass, not merely to render the funeral service and the committal of his father's body to the Surrey earth less harrowing, but also to quench some of the anxiety his earlier telephone conversation with the family's lawyer had left him with.

He should never have made the call, of course. Lydia had chivvied him into it. 'Stir the fellow up, darling, or we'll be waiting for ever to settle your father's estate.' It had been apparent from Mellish's tone that he did not consider the discussion of such issues before the funeral to be entirely seemly. 'I was going to suggest that I call at the house tomorrow morning, Sir Ashley, when I can set out the testamentary position in full.' It had hardly been possible to argue with that. But Ashley had pressed for an assurance that everything would be straight-forward – and had not received one. 'I would prefer to say nothing further about the provisions of Sir Henry's will until tomorrow.'

Damn the fellow. Why did he have to be so tight-lipped? Ashley knew the terms of the will as well as he did. At least, he supposed he did. But now, watching the hearse move slowly along the drive ahead of them, he was not as certain on the point as he would have wanted to be.

Max made his view of the matter known to Appleby while they were still standing in the lobby of the Hotel Mazarin. 'I don't believe for a moment that Corinne murdered Raffaele Spataro, Appleby. The very idea is absurd.'

'Sometimes facts force us to believe what we can't imagine,' Appleby countered in his irritatingly sym-pathetic manner. 'That's why I suggested we go and inspect the scene of the crime for ourselves.'

'Nothing's going to change my mind.'

'Don't be too sure. We seldom know others as well as we think we do. I've often been surprised by what people are capable of *in extremis*.'

'Corinne had no reason to kill Spataro. He was about to confirm her version of events the night my father died, for God's sake.'

'We only have her word for that.'

'You think she killed the man, then calmly came here and told me he was about to retract his statement?'

'I'll tell you what I think on the way there. We're wasting time, Mr Maxted.'

They walked out to the car and started away. Appleby closed the glass screen between them and the driver and painstakingly lit his pipe while Max waited impatiently for him to explain.

'Zamaron told me of Madame Dombreux's claim that Spataro meant to change his story,' Appleby said eventually, 'though she doesn't seem to have mentioned discussing it with you, which is odd. The fact is that she has to account for being the last person seen with Spataro before he was found shot dead—'

'*Shot?*'

'Yes. With a revolver he owned. The poor sap supplied his own murder weapon.'

'You're seriously suggesting Corinne talked her way into Spataro's apartment, grabbed his gun – knowing, presumably, where he kept it and that he kept it loaded – then . . . what?'

Appleby sighed. 'I'm not suggesting anything, Mr Maxted. Do you want to hear me out?'

Max also sighed. 'Yes, yes. Go ahead.'

'Thank you. Now, this is the sequence of events as I understand them. Three passers-by who know Spataro by sight saw him entering his apartment building at seven Rue du Verger at about ten o'clock Tuesday evening. He was in the company of a woman matching Madame Dombreux's description. She doesn't deny meeting him at that time, although she says they parted in the vestibule of the building and she does deny going up to his apartment.

'Spataro was a notoriously inconsiderate neighbour. He often played loud music on his gramophone late into the night. Jazz, usually. Zamaron's theory is that the fatal shots were fired while the gramophone was operating and hence not heard, although they may have been heard and . . . simply ignored. Bumps and thumps on the ceiling went with living below him, apparently. Everyone knew about the gun, by the way. There were complaints about him taking pot-shots at pigeons from his window. Zamaron gave him a ticking-off, but allowed him a good deal of artistic licence.

'Noise was one thing, but the tenant of the apartment below Spataro's wasn't prepared to overlook a brownish-red stain that appeared on his ceiling overnight. He thought it looked like blood and he was right. He got no answer when he knocked on Spataro's door. He went off to work, asking the concierge to investigate in his absence. After several failed efforts to raise Spataro, she used her pass key to enter the apartment. She found him lying dead on the floor. He'd been shot three times in the chest and stomach, causing extensive bleeding, and once in the head. Not a pretty sight, I imagine.

'The gun was lying by his right hand and first thoughts were that he'd killed himself. But it was soon realized the shots had been fired from a distance of several feet at least. It was clearly murder, unconvincingly disguised as suicide. The murderer had worn gloves, in order to avoid leaving fingerprints on the gun.'

'How can the police know that?' Max cut in.

'Because the murderer threw the gloves on the fire before leaving the apartment. Gunpowder residue could have been detected on them if they hadn't been burnt. As it happens, the fire died too quickly to destroy them completely. They're a pair of fine-leather ladies' gloves, in Madame Dombreux's size.'

'Is that the only evidence they have against her?'

'She was seen going into the building with Spataro shortly before the murder was committed. She was known to be angry with him for telling the police they were lovers. By claiming he meant to withdraw that statement, she might have hoped to persuade us that someone else killed him in order to prevent him doing so.'

'And mightn't they have done?'

'The someone in question being another woman, presumably, with the same glove size as Madame Dombreux?'

'The police can't know the gloves were actually worn by the murderer, Appleby. They may have been left there to incriminate Corinne.'

'They may have, it's true, but only as part of an elaborate conspiracy for the existence of which there's not a scrap of evidence. The police aren't looking for any other suspects. As far as they're concerned, they've caught Spataro's killer.'

'They're wrong.'

'See if you're as sure about that after we've taken a look at the apartment. From what Zamaron tells me, you may not be.'

Number 7 Rue du Verger was in many respects a mirror image of 8 Rue du Verger, though somewhat smarter in its common parts, gleaming brass and glowing marble attesting to more assiduous housekeeping. The concierge was younger and friendlier, though understandably downcast. '*C'était épouvantable à voir, messieurs,*' she averred as she escorted them to the lift. A terrible thing to see? Max felt sure it had been.

The entrance to Spataro's apartment was on the sixth floor. A notice from the *préfecture* had been pinned to the door, forbidding entry. But Appleby had the key and official permission. They went straight in.

What they entered was the world of Raffaele Spataro. Bright colours were everywhere, in rugs and upholstery and tapestries, not to mention the numerous huge and gaudy paintings. Leopard- and tiger-skins had been draped and strewn around as well. The man had lived in a jungle of strident shapes and tones. The paintings were a mixture of still lifes and nudes, the fruits ripe, the men muscular, the women broad-hipped and big-breasted.

'I think we can safely say Spataro wasn't keen on self-restraint,' Appleby remarked. He stopped at the foot of a staircase that led up to a large hatch in the ceiling. 'This communicates with his studio on the floor above. We'll take a look up there later.'

Appleby led the way into the drawing-room. There was no relief from the kaleidoscopic excess of Spataro's taste in furnishings and decoration. Tableloads of liquor and disorderly piles of newspapers and magazines compounded the chaos. What were surely several years' worth of party invitations filled the mantelpiece, with the overflow tucked into the frame of the gigantic mirror above it.

In the centre of the room a clearance had been made, exposing floorboards darkly stained with blood. The extent of the stain took Max aback. It was at least six feet across. 'He was a big fellow,' said Appleby. 'A lot of blood will have come out of him.'

'So I see.'

'I gather there was a rug it soaked through that they took away for evidence. Oh, and there's the famous gramophone.'

The machine stood on a sideboard, flanked by a stack of records. There was one already on the turntable. Appleby lifted it off and peered at the label.

'Proof the Devil doesn't always have the best tunes,' he said, dropping it back into place.

'Where do the police think he was shot from?' Max asked.

'From just about where you are now.'

Max looked down at his feet, though what he expected to see he could not have said. Corinne had not killed Spataro, but someone had. Someone had stood where Max was standing and gunned Spataro down in cold blood. And then the hot blood had flowed.

'I imagine she stepped closer after he'd fallen and finished him off with the shot to the head. While this' – Appleby nodded back to the gramophone – 'was cater-wauling away.'

'Corinne didn't do it, Appleby.'

'So you keep saying. The police say otherwise.'

'Does she have a lawyer to defend her?'

'Not yet, as far as I know. Under wartime regulations, I believe they can hold her without charge, let alone legal representation, for as long as they like.'

'But the war's over.'

'Not legally. Until there's a treaty, we're all still theoretically at war.'

'Can I see her?'

'That would be up to Zamaron. And what good would it do? She'll protest her innocence. And you'll believe her.'

'I already believe her. First my father, now Spataro. It's the work of the same man. Surely that's obvious.'

'Let's go upstairs. I'm told it's well worth a look.'

They went back out into the hall. The hatch leading to the studio was operated by a pulley fitted to the wall at the foot of the stairs. Appleby wound the handle and the hatch slowly rose until it engaged with a hook vertically above them. Then he gestured for Max to go on up.

The studio was lower-ceilinged than the apartment owing to the angle of the mansard roof, and the windows were smaller, but it seemed larger and airier on account of its bareness. The walls were white and furnishings were few. Spataro's paintings, on the other hand, were many.

They were propped and stacked around the studio, the route between them leading in a series of diagonals to a far corner lit by windows from both sides of the building, where an easel was set up on a dais, next to a chair and a low table supporting a spinney of paint-brushes sprouting from old jam jars.

'Looks like he painted many more than he sold,' Appleby remarked as he followed Max in the direction of the easel. There was a clunk as his foot struck an empty wine bottle, one of many dotted around the room.

Max stepped up on to the dais and looked through the street-facing window. There, on the other side of Rue du Verger, was the mansarded top floor of number 8, from which Sir Henry had fallen to his death. Spataro would have had a clear view of the event, if he had happened to be looking.

'Zamaron advised me to pay particular attention to the paintings behind the easel,' said Appleby. 'The stack there.'

There were a dozen or so leaning against the wall, covered in a paint-spattered sheet. Max moved across to them and tugged the sheet away.

And there was Corinne. Max recognized her at once, despite the distortions and exaggerations of Spataro's technique. She was depicted sitting on a chair, a coat draped loosely around her shoulders. She was otherwise naked, apart from a pair of shoes. Her legs were crossed to preserve a hint of modesty, but her breasts were fully exposed.

She had not denied modelling for Spataro, but confronting the proof of it was still a shock for Max. He told himself to accept what he saw as an artwork and nothing more. But acceptance did not obligingly follow.

'She's all woman, isn't she?' murmured Appleby.

'Why don't you—' Whirling round to be met by Appleby's confoundedly bland gaze, Max fell suddenly silent. Losing his temper now would help no one, Corinne least of all.

'Shall we take a look at the others, Mr Maxted?'

Max moved the first picture aside, bracing himself for more of the same. But on the second canvas there was only a faint pencil sketch of a woman who might have become a likeness of Corinne in a finished painting but was now only a series of suggestive lines: a nude, naturally, reclining on a couch.

The third canvas was another sketch of another nude, crouching on all fours on the low table. And the remaining canvases were blank.

'Work in progress, you think?' Appleby asked.

'She only modelled for him once,' Max said stubbornly, leaning the canvases back against the wall and replacing the sheet.

'Once, twice or umpteen times, it's proof she knew Spataro . . . how shall we put it? . . . on terms a man who loved her might resent.'

'There are lots of artists in Montparnasse, Appleby, and lots of artists' models.'

'I wouldn't like it. And I bet Sir Henry didn't like it either.'

'There was nothing between Corinne and Spataro.'

'That's the problem, isn't it?' Appleby pointed with

the stem of his pipe at the shrouded paintings. 'There may have been *literally* nothing between them.'

Max broke away and stared disconsolately through the window. Less than a week ago, on the rooftop opposite, the drama that had led him to this place had been set in motion. He had resolved to avenge his father's murder, but all that had happened so far was a second murder – and a second injustice. He wanted an enemy he could engage with, a target to fix in his sights before he pressed his triggers. But the sky was empty. There was no foe to be seen.

'Penny for them,' said Appleby, standing so close behind him that his pipe smoke drifted over Max's shoulder.

'I miss knowing who I'm supposed to be fighting.'

'You seldom see more than the shadow of your opponent in my game, Mr Maxted.'

'And what is your game, Appleby?'

'I'm here to protect the British delegation to the peace conference from any threat that may present itself.'

'What are you – Secret Service?'

'If I were, I wouldn't admit it.'

'And you're not admitting it, I notice.'

'It'll be the guillotine for Madame Dombreux if she's convicted of murdering Spataro.'

'She's innocent. You know that, don't you?'

'I know my first duty is to our delegation. And for that reason – not because I find it hard to believe a beautiful young woman is capable of murder – I have to consider the possibility . . . that you're right.'

Max turned and stated at Appleby in amazement. 'What?'

Appleby allowed himself a tentative smile. 'There are suspicious aspects to Sir Henry's death, as you pointed out. And this business with the gloves does have a contrived look about it. Also . . .' He frowned. 'I had an interesting chat with your brother on the train on Tuesday. It must have occurred to you that Sir Ashley would mention the list you found. I can't help noticing you haven't mentioned it to me.'

'All right. So you know about the list.'

'In Sir Henry's handwriting?'

'Yes.'

'Mind if I see it?'

'What makes you think I carry it around with me?'

'I doubt you'd leave it in your hotel room. I doubt you'd leave it anywhere.' Appleby held out his hand. 'I'd be very grateful if you showed it to me, Mr Maxted.'

Max hesitated, then reached into his pocket. He took out the list and passed it to Appleby. 'It's only a copy. Corinne has the original.'

'*Had*, you mean. The police have probably got it now. Unless they've sent it on to *le Deuxième Bureau*.'

'Who?'

'The French Secret Service.' Appleby ran his eye down the list. 'It's a worrying possibility, since this is considerably more enlightening than the entries in Sir Henry's diary.'

For all that the admission was casually made, Max did not doubt it was carefully calculated. 'So, you admit you removed the diary from his personal effects before they were delivered to us?'

'It was a potential source of vital information. It was always my intention to return it once I'd had an opportunity to evaluate the entries.' Appleby delved inside his coat and pulled out the diary: pocket-sized, bound in blue leather, with a lion-and-unicorn crest on the front and a small pencil in the spine. 'Routine appointments only, I'm afraid. Nothing significant.' He passed it to Max as he spoke. But he held on to the list. 'This, on the other hand, could be very significant.'

'Did you tell my brother that?'

'Certainly not. It would only have confused him. And I assume you don't really want him interfering.' Appleby returned the list. 'Made any progress interpreting those items?'

'Some.'

'Really?'

'Enough to know you must understand at least a couple of them yourself.'

'Must I?'

'The Trust, for example.'

Appleby nodded. 'A Russian monarchist organization based here in Paris.'

'And F.L.?'

'They're the initials of the man who ran the Kaiser's spy network.'

'Fritz Lemmer.'

'The very same. Not a commonly known name, of course. How did you come by it?'

'I asked around.'

'Around thirty-three Rue des Pyramides, perhaps?'

Max held a poker face. 'Why there?'

'Because your father recorded a few appointments at that address, with one Travis Ireton, proprietor of Ireton Associates, known to us as a broker of illicitly obtained information. According to your brother, you met Ireton when you visited your father earlier this month.' (Max silently and expressionlessly cursed Ashley's inability to keep his mouth shut.) 'I assume you've been to see him since. He'd know who Lemmer is. I should warn you that Ireton's the sort who likes other people to do his dirty work. I suppose that's why the French authorities have failed so far to pin anything on him. Zamaron told me they had particularly high hopes of catching him last night in the act of taking delivery of proofs smuggled out of the conference printing works down in Auteuil. But he sent someone in his place and, as it happens, that someone managed to give the police the slip. They think he was an Englishman.'

'Really?'

'Yes. He lost his hat climbing over a wall. There was a London hatter's label inside the crown.' (How fortunate it was, Max reflected, that he had not bought the hat in Epsom.) Appleby shuddered theatrically. 'Cold today, isn't it?'

'I hadn't noticed.'

'That'll be why you came out without your hat, I suppose.'

'Do you know what the Contingencies Memo is?' Max asked, eager to revert to the subject of the list.

'No.'

'Or the Chinese box?'

'Not for certain. But if I had to hazard a guess . . .'

'Why don't you?'

Appleby smiled faintly. 'All right. The head of the Chinese delegation, Lou Tseng-Tsiang, visited Tokyo on his way here for talks with the Japanese government.

While he was in Tokyo, a box of secret documents he was carrying went missing. Stolen by the Japanese, presumably. But who knows? There are so many thieves in this world. And so many secret documents. Your father served a couple of years at the embassy in Tokyo, of course. He'd have known how things work there.'

'What exactly are you suggesting?'

'Nothing. It's all too vague to base a suggestion on. But Sir Henry was swimming in uncharted waters. That much is clear, I think. And any involvement with Fritz Lemmer would have been highly dangerous.'

'I might have to involve myself with him if I'm to get to the bottom of this.'

'Which I advised you against attempting to do. I suppose Madame Dombreux's arrest makes it certain you'll go on with it, though.'

'It was already certain. It's just more urgent now.'

'There are a lot of people looking for Lemmer, Mr Maxted, and a lot of people who don't want him found.'

'Which camp are you in?'

'The former, of course.'

'Then help me track him down.'

'Most of the people looking for Lemmer are better qualified for the task than you are, so I'd say your chances of success are negligible. Besides, there's not much I can do in the way of help. I've received no firm indication that Lemmer's in Paris, though that's only to be expected where such a slippery fellow's concerned. A firm indication of his whereabouts would probably be a false trail. He was in Tokyo at the same time as Sir Henry, as I expect you're aware. Their acquaintance may have given Sir Henry an advantage of some kind, but as to what kind . . . I don't know.'

'Who might know?'

'If I were you, I'd start with Masataka Kuroda at the Japanese delegation.'

Of course. Kuroda. All roads seemed to lead to him. 'I already know about Kuroda, Appleby. He knew my father. And he blames Lemmer for an assassination attempt against the late Tsar when he visited Japan in 1891.'

'Good. No need for me to fill you in, then.'

'If you think he's such a promising source . . .'

'Why haven't I sounded him out about Lemmer myself? It's a fair question. The truth is there are limits to what I can do here in Paris. The French are a touchy lot and Downing Street doesn't want anything done that might put their backs up. Openly mounting inquiries about Lemmer would soon have me treading on *le Deuxième Bureau*'s toes, I'm afraid.'

So, that was it. First Ireton. Now Appleby. They both wanted Lemmer. And they both wanted Max to do the finding.

'There's another issue,' Appleby went on. 'Kuroda plays his cards close to his chest. He'd tell me nothing, however nicely I asked. But you're the son of Sir Henry Maxted, a man he admired and respected. As a matter of honour, he might be more forthcoming with you. If he proves to be, I could give you my expert advice on how to use any information you glean.'

'You seem to be doing what you accused Ireton of, Appleby: arranging for someone else to do your dirty work.'

212

'Ah, but, unlike Ireton, it's because circumstances oblige me to.'

'All right. I'll see Kuroda. And I'll report back to you. But I also want to see Corinne. Think you can arrange that for me?'

Appleby took a reflective puff on his pipe, then said, 'I think I probably can, yes.' His gaze drifted round the studio before returning to Max. 'One thing.'

'What?'

'Go carefully, won't you? I don't want to have to escort Sir Ashley round the scene of your murder.'

'No need to worry on that score. Ashley will think it's suicide.'

To any neutral observer, along with almost all of the mourners, the funeral of Sir Henry Maxted would have appeared to pass as a textbook example of such ceremonies: dignified, orderly and respectful. The hymns and readings were well-chosen, the graveside observances well-handled. The old diplomat was seen off as diplomatically as he might have wished, with no mention of the circumstances of his death beyond their sudden and tragic nature.

Appearances, however, as so often, were deceptive. The presence of one of those attending gave George Clissold, as soon as he saw him, a sobering jolt. He communicated the news to his sister as they followed Sir Henry's coffin out of the church at the end of the service.

'Brigham's here, Win,' he whispered.

'What?'

'Brigham. He's among the mourners.' George did not warn her against looking around to confirm the point. He knew she would never betray herself in such a way.

A nod of acknowledgement and a frown of puzzlement were the only visible reactions Lady Maxted allowed herself. But George was aware that she would be displeased, if not alarmed, by the turn of events. And already she would be considering how to deal with it.

Lionel Brigham remained, in his sixtieth year, a handsome figure of a man, perhaps, in fact, more handsome than he had ever been. Greying hair and heavier smile lines suited his rugged features. He had not run to fat in middle age, thanks to indulging in a range of energetic pursuits when not pacing the corridors of power in Whitehall. Fencing, swimming and real tennis were three of those. Rumour would have added womanizing as a fourth. He had never married nor seemed inclined to. He was not the marrying kind.

He was acquainted with many of those attending the funeral, drawn as they mostly were from the retired ranks of the diplomatic service. He told them he had been sent from Paris to represent the F.O. and would be hurrying back to attend to his duties at the peace conference. He was a busy and important man. No one could have doubted that. He was not the retiring kind.

He had been four years ahead of George at Eton and George marvelled that what the fellow had been then he essentially still was: arrogant and easy to admire. George would ordinarily have enjoyed the company of such a man. But he was a protective brother for all his other faults. He did not intend to allow Brigham to upset Winifred any more than she was bound to be upset on such a day. He found a moment as the mourners moved away from the graveside after the committal to have a quick and quiet word with him.

'Surprised to see you here, Brigham.'

'Sorry I didn't cable. Rather a last-minute decision as to who would come over.'

'Odd you should be chosen, though.'

'We go where we're sent in the service, George. We're not our own master.'

'Strange. That's exactly what I thought you were: your own master.'

'How's Winifred bearing up?'

'As you'd expect.'

'I'd like to speak to her before I return to Paris.'

'You'll see her at the house.'

'I meant alone.'

'That won't—'

'Tell her, George, there's a good fellow.' Brigham eyed him from close range. 'And tell her it's important.'

Max sat in a café in the Rue de Rivoli, his newly purchased fedora hanging with his coat on the nearby hat-stand, the knowledge heavy in his heart that at that very moment his father's funeral was drawing to its sombre close in Surrey.

He sipped his coffee and drew on his cigarette as he worked his way carefully through the pages of his father's diary. Appleby was right, damn him. It was merely a record of appointments which on their own revealed little. Corinne's name appeared nowhere. The commonest entries related to meetings with either Ribeiro or Norris. Sir Henry had apparently met Ireton just twice. He had recorded and circled the tantalizing initials F.L. on Wednesday, 19th February, but nothing else that day to explain why. There might have been other meetings, of course – and with other people – he had not recorded. Many days were blank, especially in recent weeks. There was no clue as to what he had done in London earlier in the month, nor even confirmation that it was London he had gone to. With an irritated sigh, Max closed the diary and thrust it into his pocket. No wonder Appleby had been willing to return it.

He drained his coffee, stubbed out his cigarette, flung down some coins and went to fetch his coat and his brand-new hat. There was nothing he could do before the evening, when he and Morahan were due to pay an unannounced call on Kuroda, so hurrying was pointless. But he hurried nonetheless. Walking was better than sitting and thinking to no effect.

When he reached Place de la Concorde, he paused, waiting for a gap in the traffic before he crossed to the island in the middle of the square where the Egyptian obelisk stood. He became suddenly aware of a twitching at his sleeve and turned to find a young dark-skinned man dressed in various unmatching items of military uniform smiling at him and holding out his hand importunately.

Max guessed the man – hardly more than a boy, really, to judge by his build and complexion – was an Arab of some kind, most likely Algerian. He had seen more than a few like him begging on the streets, the residue of France's colonial army. This one was different, though: less downcast, less beaten. His smile was not so much ingratiating as interrogative.

It was cold and Max had no wish to linger. He doled out a few coins and moved on, receiving no thanks beyond a faint and somehow condescending inclination of the young man's head.

Had he looked back, which he did not, he would have seen that the young man continued to watch him as he made his way to the far side of the square. And the ingratiating smile faded slowly from his face as he did so.

Halfway along the Champs-Elysées towards the Rond Point, Max tugged down the brim of his hat and turned up the collar of his coat to ward off the chill wind. As he thrust his hands into his pockets, he felt an unfamiliar object in one of them. He stopped, took off his glove and fished it out. It was a piece of paper wrapped around a small pebble. He had no knowledge of how it had got there, but immediately suspected the young Arab. He moved to the side of the pavement and carefully flattened it out.

When it lay open in his palm, he saw the message that someone had written on it in pencilled capitals: LEAVE PARIS OR DIE.

Max raced back to the Place de la Concorde, but the young Arab was nowhere to be seen. He scoured the square and the terrace of the Jardin des Tuileries in vain. The messenger had gone. But his message remained.

WINIFRED, LADY MAXTED, SELDOM HAD OCCASION TO visit the billiard-room at Gresscombe Place. It was reserved for gentlemen's after-dinner entertainment, of which there had been little since before the war. Lionel Brigham had contested a few frames there in the days when he had been a frequent visitor to the house and perhaps it was for old times' sake that he had suggested it as a rendezvous.

Most of the mourners still sipping sherry and swapping memories of Sir Henry Maxted in the drawing-room charitably assumed Lady Maxted had slipped away in order to compose herself after the stress and strain of the funeral. This was certainly what George led Ashley and Lydia to believe. 'Give her ten minutes and she'll be right as rain,' he assured them, before heading off in search of some whisky. And he fervently hoped it would be so.

But George, of course, had no idea what Brigham wanted to discuss with Winifred in private. Neither did Winifred, though various disturbing possibilities did occur to her as she made her way along the corridor that led to the billiard-room. She regarded his presence at the funeral as both suspicious and insensitive, which

219

sadly did not conflict with what she knew of his character.

He was leaning over the table with his long, supple fingers steadying the cue for some ambitious snooker shot when she entered the room. As he pulled away and stood upright to greet her, she was reminded of all the reasons she had been drawn to him in the first place. He was a handsome devil and was well aware of it. He was the kind of man women were attracted to, in part because they knew they could not trust him.

'Winifred,' he said, bestowing upon her his rakish smile. 'It's good of you to spare me a little of your time.'

'Why are you here, Lionel?'

'To tender the Foreign Secretary's official condolences on the passing of a distinguished diplomat. Along with my personal condolences, of course. Henry's death must have been a shock for you.'

'A letter would have sufficed.'

'That would have seemed cold and unfeeling in view of our . . .' his eyes twinkled beneath his bushy eyebrows as he selected a suitable phrase '. . . old association.'

'It would have seemed appropriate to me.'

'Then I'm sorry to have disappointed you.'

'Really? I find it hard to believe you've ever been truly sorry for anything.'

'A word of advice, Winifred, now you've embarked on widowhood. Don't burden yourself with regrets.'

He laid the cue on the table and took a few steps towards her. She stiffened, though she did not retreat. She could recall only too well the thrill of his touch – the electric tremor that had coursed through her body when he had folded her in his arms. But there were other sensations to recall as well. And ultimately they were stronger.

'Do you remember that day—'

'I remember every day,' she cut in. 'From the beginning to the end.'

'Ah, but perhaps we haven't yet reached the end.'

'What do you want, Lionel?'

'A word . . . about James.'

'He couldn't be with us today.'

'For his father's funeral? That's shabby by any standards. Someone said he was ill. I didn't disabuse them of the notion, which I thought was good of me. Considering I know he's in Paris, digging into the circumstances of Henry's death.'

'If you know where he is, why did you ask?'

'I didn't.' Brigham treated her to a superior smile. 'What I said was that I wanted to talk to you about him.'

Winifred gave him a look that spoke of her impatience and her distaste in equal measure. 'Please come to the point, Lionel. I must rejoin the mourning party soon or it will look odd.'

'And we can't have that, can we? Very well. I'm concerned James may blunder into danger while he goes looking for a murderer who doesn't exist. Word has it Henry kept sinister company in Paris. The sort of people who don't take kindly to being cross-questioned.'

'What do you want me to do?'

'Call him off. In his own best interests.'

'You surely don't think he'd come home at my bidding? He risked his life every day in the Royal Flying Corps. I honestly believe he enjoyed it. The more perilous a situation is, the more he seems to relish it.'

'James isn't up against the likes of the Red Baron in Paris, Winifred. These people don't play by gentlemanly rules of combat.'

'You speak as if you're personally acquainted with them.'

'I keep my ear to the ground. It's what I'm paid to do.'

'You're not paid to be concerned for James's welfare, though. So, why are you?'

'You know why.'

The old scandalous whisperings were almost audible in Winifred's ears. Brigham had always seemed indifferent as to whether they were accurate. He had left it late – far too late, she was tempted to say – to confront the issue. 'You are not James's father, Lionel.'

'Is that so? My arithmetic must be defective, then. But I don't think it is. I took the trouble to check his date of birth in RFC records, you see. The fifth of May, 1891. He must have been conceived in late July or early August, 1890. Henry was in Tokyo all summer. But you—'

'I know where I was.'

'Yes. And I know where I was too.'

'You're not his father.'

'There was no one else, Winifred. You didn't have the spirit for that kind of game.'

'You make that sound like an insult.'

'The only insult here is to my intelligence. I'd hoped for better from you than a blank and illogical denial, I must admit.'

'Why would it matter to you even if it were true? I doubt you've ever faced a responsibility in your life unless you were forced to. Certainly not a paternal one.'

He took another step closer. She did not drop her gaze. 'You don't think very highly of me, do you?'

'Why would I? I assume you don't think very highly of yourself.'

'If you're expecting me to apologize for—'

'I assure you I'm not expecting that. Merely a better explanation than you've so far given of why you're here.'

'Isn't it obvious?'

'Not to me.'

'As a man grows older, he's bound to take stock of his life and to wonder what he has to show for the years he's spent on this Earth. To know I have a son—'

'You don't have one by me.'

'It's a miracle he came through the war in one piece. Don't let him throw his life away trying to avenge a murder that never happened.'

'How can you be sure it never happened?'

Brigham lowered his voice. 'The truth is known, Winifred. And a damned discreditable truth it is too. Ashley's in possession of the facts. Squeeze them out of him, if you must. But tell James to leave Paris. Now.'

'You don't seem to understand, Lionel. He won't take any notice of me.'

'But you're not even going to try, are you?'

'No. I'm not.'

'If you won't, perhaps I'll have to.'

'How do you propose to influence him?'

'By pointing out that Henry wasn't his natural father.'

'And that you are?'

'You leave me no choice in the matter.'

'Oh dear.' Winifred sighed, more, it seemed, in disappointment than sorrow. 'Need I remind you that we weren't always as discreet as we should have been? James was a perceptive boy. I'm fairly certain he drew his own conclusion long ago – the same entirely false conclusion you've drawn. But evidently he still regards Henry as his father in every important sense. He'll probably laugh in your face. I'd do the same myself if I were less governed by my upbringing.'

'My God.' Brigham stared at her as if glimpsing her true character for the first time. 'You're a hard woman.'

'If I am, who made me so?'

'Whoever his father may have been, you're his mother. Don't you care what happens to him?'

'Of course I do. But he'll do as he sees fit. He always has and he always will. I'm proud of him for that. He has my full confidence. In everything he does.' She looked Brigham in the eye. 'Is that plain enough for you?'

S AM HAD NOT RETURNED FROM HIS SIGHTSEEING WHEN MAX set off to meet Morahan. Max slipped a note under his door explaining that the night on the town he had suggested might not be possible after all. Sam would understand. He was an understanding fellow.

The evening was colder than the day. There were flecks of snow in the flurries of rain that fell from the moonless sky. Max set a stiff pace to Rue des Pyramides to warm himself, trying not to wonder what it was like to face a second night in a police cell with no certain way of knowing that anyone in the outside world knew of your plight. Such was Corinne's dire situation. He had her to seek justice for now, as well as his father.

Morahan was waiting for him at Ireton's offices, as agreed, but Ireton himself was nowhere to be seen. Malory was on station, however. She and Morahan were drinking cocoa in an atmosphere bordering, somewhat bewilderingly, on the cosily convivial.

Malory's secretarial role extended, it soon became apparent, to a keen appreciation of all the business of Ireton Associates. The smile with which she accompanied her favourable comment on Max's new hat was unmistakably mischievous. 'It makes you look like a real *gentilhomme*, Mr Maxted,' she said.

'We weren't the only ones expecting to see you,' Morahan observed, with a glance through the window.

'What do you mean?'

'You have a friend. He's in a doorway on the other side of the street.'

'What?' Max moved towards the window to see for himself, but Morahan signalled for him to stay where he was.

'No sense in letting him see you're on to him. He's probably been with you for a couple of days.'

'That's ridiculous. I—'

'What's ridiculous is how easy I expect you've made it for him. The question is: what do we do about it? He looks English to me.'

'How can you possibly tell that?'

'The shoes. And the way he stands. Leaning without slouching. One of Appleby's men, I'd guess. I assumed we'd walk to the Bristol. It's in the Place Vendôme. But I can fetch the car and take a detour if you think we need to lose him.'

Max sighed. 'There's no point. Appleby knows I'm going to see Kuroda. He actually advised me to.'

'Ah. Take the shadow along, then.'

'Yes. I suppose so.'

'You know what they say, Mr Maxted,' trilled Malory. 'You can be sure you're going in the right direction when people follow you.'

It was easier for Max to obey Morahan's instruction not to look behind him for a glimpse of Appleby's man thanks to the pace he had to walk at in order to keep up with the giant American's loping stride. Morahan was a reassuring presence, with his vast build, his air of confidence and a voice that rumbled within him like a ship's engine. Max had taken him for an underling of Ireton's, but now, as they talked, he was not so sure. Perhaps theirs was more in the way of a partnership.

'Has Travis explained Kuroda's background to you, Schools?'

'I wouldn't work with Travis if he didn't tell me what I needed to know.'

'And how long have you worked with him?'

'Long enough.'

'Where did your paths first cross – Cuba?'

'Good guess.'

'You know him well, then?'

'Better than most.'

'Can I trust him?'

Morahan chuckled. 'I trust him.'

'That's not quite what I asked.'

'It's the best I can do.'

'Tell me, did you ever meet my father?'

'Yuh, I met him.'

'What did you think of him?'

'I thought he had the look.'

'The look?'

'A lot of guys his age fold their hand and leave the table. Quit while they're ahead, is how they'd put it. Something dies in them then. A light goes out. You can see it gone from their eyes. It never comes back. But Henry still had it. He hadn't left the table. He was still in the game.'

227

'That's good, is it?'

'It's the only way to be.'

The hushed and somnolent atmosphere of the Hotel Bristol hardly suggested it was serving as the headquarters of one of the peace conference's most important delegations. According to the newspapers Max had forced himself to read, Japan had been eased to the sidelines by the recent establishment of the Council of Four. It no longer had any say in the really important decisions, which were taken by Wilson, Clemenceau, Lloyd George and Orlando behind closed doors. The reaction to this of the leader of the Japanese delegation, Marquis Saionji, was unknown. He eschewed all public utterances.

If Masataka Kuroda proved equally tight-lipped, Max and Morahan were likely to have had a wasted journey. But unannounced or not, they were courteously received by a tiny hand-wringing functionary. He explained that Commissioner Kuroda (the title suggested he was indeed a police officer) was 'elsewhere'. Mention of Sir Henry's name and Max's relationship to him prompted a telephone call to the elsewhere in question. The functionary reported that Kuroda could not leave where he was – but they were welcome to join him there.

It was a large neo-classical house near Parc Monceau. The hefty bodyguards on the door suggested to Max that this was where Marquis Saionji was resting his venerable bones while in Paris, although no one said as much and they were not encouraged to ask.

Kuroda received them in the library, surrounded by shelf-loads of leather-bound tomes lit by one oil lamp and the flickering glow of a well-banked fire. He was unusually tall for his race, thin to the point of emaciation and impeccably dressed, more like a courtier than a policeman. He could have been any age between fifty-five and seventy with his narrow face, solemn eyes, close-cropped grey hair and incipient stoop. He was standing when they entered and made no move to sit down. Nor did he invite them to do so. Max had the impression the library was not his customary domain in the house. Perhaps he was not expected to receive visitors there at all.

He offered Max his condolences in a stiff and formal fashion, without any hint that he knew Sir Henry personally. He and Morahan had clearly met before, something the American had omitted to mention, although Max suspected he would have justified that on the simple grounds that he had not been asked. Kuroda enquired after Ireton – his pronunciation rendering Morahan as Mohan and Ireton as Iton – as well as a Miss Hollander, whom Max belatedly identified as Malory. Kuroda was particularly insistent that his good wishes should be passed on to her. Morahan explained that Ireton had recommended him to Max as a bodyguard, though whether Kuroda was entirely convinced by the explanation was unclear.

'You are Sir Henry's younger son, Mr Maxted?' he asked, the effect of his attention being suddenly turned on Max rather like that of a torch being shone in his eyes. 'You were a pilot in the war?'

'Yes. I was.'

'To soar above the ground of the enemy. This must be a wonderful thing.'

'It would be more wonderful if the enemy weren't also soaring.'

To Max's surprise, Kuroda laughed. 'Ah. Good. Yes. You are right. And you are here to discuss ... a soaring enemy?'

'In a sense. I found your name on a list in my father's handwriting. I wondered if he'd discussed anything important with you.'

Kuroda frowned. 'Not directly. But a certain matter was broached through an intermediary.'

'Can you tell me who that intermediary was?'

Kuroda glanced at Morahan, who gave a nod of consent. 'It was Mr Ireton. Though he did not say he was speaking to me on Sir Henry's behalf. I deduced it from the subject Mr Ireton raised with me and from the fact that I heard no more from him about it following Sir Henry's death.'

'Was the subject ... Fritz Lemmer?'

'Ah.' Kuroda sounded rather more surprised than he looked. 'You know about Lemmer.' (He was Lemma to him, of course.)

'I do.'

Kuroda nodded. 'He was the subject, yes.' Another glance at Morahan seemed to draw a favourable response. 'Mr Ireton said he represented someone willing to sell information that would enable the buyer to locate Lemmer. Sir Henry, I concluded, was the seller.'

'I believe he may have been murdered to silence him about Lemmer, Mr Kuroda.'

'This is as I surmised. You blame Lemmer himself?'

'Maybe.'

Kuroda nodded thoughtfully. 'An invisible opponent is

230

the hardest to judge. Is he cleverer than we think or not as clever as we fear? It has taken me nearly thirty years to measure the cleverness of Fritz Lemmer.'

'And how do you rate him?'

'Dangerous, Mr Maxted. Very dangerous. He lays traps for the unwary. Those who pursue him become his prisoners.'

'Was my father his prisoner?'

'I do not think so.'

'Could he have been responsible for my father's murder?'

'Of course. But in general he kills no one unless their death serves a purpose. And I see no purpose in Sir Henry's death.'

'If he knew Lemmer's whereabouts . . .'

'Then it would be simpler for Lemmer to alter his location. And I have reached the conclusion that the secret of his success is not the complexity we see . . . but the simplicity he sees.'

'You were presumably keen to acquire the information Travis offered you.'

'Oh, yes. I assured him I would outbid all other interested parties.'

'You blame Lemmer for an assassination attempt against the Tsarevich in Tokyo in 1891?'

'It was not in Tokyo, Mr Maxted. The Tsarevich was in Kyoto at the time. He was due in Tokyo the following day. But he never visited the capital. After the attack, which he was lucky to survive, he returned directly to Russia. The visit was a chance for Japan and Russia to settle their differences. Instead, it only deepened them. Without that attempt on his life, there might have been no war between Japan and Russia in 1904. Then no humiliating defeat for Russia, no revolution simmering in her cities, no Bolshevik takeover, no massacre of the Tsar and his family. Lemmer rears consequences as others rear canaries. He enjoys their plumage. Yes, I blame him for that. For all of that. Others think I am mistaken. They believe the assassination attempt was organized by Japanese reactionaries. And it was. But Lemmer was behind it. One of those reactionaries worked for him. I know which one, though I cannot prove it. I hope to, one day. But I have been hoping for a long time.'

'And Lemmer's been a thorn in your side ever since then?'

'He has been a thorn in the side of many.'

'Have you ever met him?'

'No. He left Tokyo before I obtained any evidence to suggest he had organized the assassination attempt. Sir Henry knew him, of course. They were fellow diplomats. He told me what he could about him. But it was not much. Lemmer is a highly secretive man.'

'Did you see anything of my father while you were both here in Paris?'

'I met him once only. I wish now I had seen more of him. But my duties for the delegation are quite demanding.' Kuroda smiled thinly. 'You would be surprised at the trouble young men of high rank can get themselves into when sent abroad to represent their nation.'

'Then there's the added burden of a seventy-year-old head of delegation who brings his twenty-year-old mistress with him,' Morahan remarked.

Kuroda's smile grew thinner still. 'You are misinformed, Mr Morahan. My lord Saionji does not

232

celebrate his seventieth birthday until later this year.'

'When you met my father,' Max pressed on, 'did he mention Lemmer?'

'No. If he had . . . I would have advised him to be very careful.'

'And did you discuss Travis Ireton's offer of information with anyone?' This was the crux of the issue. And Max did not doubt Kuroda would know it was.

'I have no way of knowing how many spies Lemmer has who still work for him, Mr Maxted. I cannot be certain who may be such a spy or who may not. The Emperor has sent more than fifty people here to negotiate for him. If you ask me is a spy of Lemmer among them, I answer yes. If you ask me how many there may be, I say I do not know. A man who reveals a secret to someone he cannot trust is a fool. I am responsible for the security of the Emperor's delegation. I cannot afford to trust anyone.'

'That sounds like a no,' said Morahan.

Kuroda nodded. 'It was intended to.' He looked at Max. 'You suspect someone heard of Mr Ireton's offer of information, calculated that Sir Henry was the source and determined to silence him?'

'Yes.'

Another nod. 'I agree. You should suspect anyone Mr Ireton discussed the matter with. Including me. Unless, of course, you trust me. Then and then only can you believe me.' He smiled. 'Have you any more questions, Mr Maxted?'

'Just one. When you met my father, did he mention the box of secret documents stolen from the head of the Chinese delegation while he was in Tokyo?'

A slight narrowing of his gaze was the only hint of surprise on Kuroda's part. And it might not have been surprise at all. 'No. He did not.'

'Between ourselves, Masataka,' said Morahan, 'did your people steal that box?'

'If we had, we would not admit it. If we had not, we would know that our denial would not be believed.'

'That sounds like a yes-no-maybe.'

Kuroda nodded. 'It was intended to.'

IT WOULD HAVE BEEN EASY FOR MAX TO DISMISS THE MEETING with Kuroda as pointless. Certainly, he had learnt little he did not already know. But the strangest thing had nonetheless happened. He found he believed every word Kuroda had said. No responsibility for Sir Henry's death could be laid at his door.

Morahan seemed to feel the same. 'For a man who speaks mostly in riddles, he makes himself remarkably plain.'

'He told no one. I'm sure of it.'

'Me too.'

'Who's next?'

'Ask Travis. I'm to report to him tomorrow morning at nine. You should join us.'

'But you know already, don't you?'

'It's Travis's show. You'll have to let him run it. Your shadow's still with us, by the way.' They were walking south-west along Rue de Monceau. The night was cold and quiet. The wind had dropped. There were few other pedestrians. Glancing back, Max saw only splashes of lamplight and dark shapes between. 'If you want something done about him, let me know.'

'What sort of something?'

'Nothing fatal.'

'Glad to hear it. I'll bear your offer in mind.'

'You do that.'

Morahan took to the Métro at Alma station, leaving Max – and his shadow – to carry on to the Mazarin without him. Irritated by the assumption Appleby and Morahan seemed to share that he was ill-equipped to deal with such surveillance, Max headed along Rue de Bassano, turned left at the first opportunity and covered thirty yards or so, then spun on his heel and marched smartly back. There was a man, damn it, moving towards him, who adroitly crossed the street and melted into the darkness as Max approached.

'Going my way?' Max called after him. 'Maybe we can walk together.'

There was no response. And there was nothing to see. Max went after him, but all the doorways he checked were empty. The fellow was smart, no question.

Max made his way back to the corner of Rue de Bassano, where he stopped, lit a cigarette and waited for him to reappear. He did not. There was a sound far off that could have been a footfall, then another, resembling a stumble of some kind. Even shadows evidently had to watch their step in the dark. But he did not show himself.

'Hello?' Max called, walking slowly towards the sound.

Again, there was no response. Nothing stirred. There were no more footfalls.

Then a door opened a short distance ahead of Max. In a brief spill of light, a portly, heavily clad man

236

emerged, trailing a tiny dog on a lead. The door closed behind them and they pottered off in the direction the sounds had come from.

As Max watched, they proceeded along the street, the man emitting occasional squeaks that were presumably comprehensible to the dog, the dog snuffling occasionally in response. They paused at a lamp-post for the dog to urinate, then moved on. If they passed anyone lurking in a doorway, they did not appear to notice.

'To hell with this,' Max muttered, throwing down his cigarette. He headed back once again to Rue de Bassano. And he did not look over his shoulder.

There were two messages waiting for Max at the Mazarin, which was two more than he was expecting. Both surprised him in their different ways. The first he opened was addressed to him in handwriting he recognized as Sam's.

Sir,
I'm going with someone who's anxious to meet you to a nightclub called Le Sagittaire. We'll wait for you there. The hotel can direct you.
Sam

According to the reception clerk, Sam had left about an hour before, accompanied by a woman he described under questioning as 'Slavic'. It had to be the young woman from Bukayev's bookshop. There were simply no other candidates, though how Sam had fallen in with her he could not imagine.

The second message had been telephoned in. It was

from Kuroda. The time recorded on it by the clerk suggested he had made the call very shortly after they had parted.

M. Kuroda asks you to meet him in Parc Monceau
– near the west entrance – at 11.15 tomorrow
morning.

Max put to the back of his mind the mystery of why Kuroda wanted to meet him again and headed straight out, armed with directions from the clerk, who permitted himself a meaningful twitch of one eyebrow when he described Le Sagittaire as *très animé*.

It was a basement establishment close to the Champs-Elysées, full of noise, smoke and couples of varying ages and races. A band was playing music Appleby would definitely not have approved of, though those dancing to it definitely did. Sagittarius himself was depicted in a vast mural, reflected in an equally vast mirror on the wall facing it. There was a palpable air of permissiveness about the place. Black men were wrapped around white women, white men around black women. Some of the men were old enough to be their partners' grandfathers. And some of the women, it struck Max, were probably not women at all. Ashley, he felt sure, would have been appalled.

On the far side of the dance floor from the jazz band was a bar and a gathering of tables. Sam waved to Max as he approached. Sam was red-faced and grinning and clearly far from sober. His companion was, as Max had surmised, the young woman from the bookshop, looking much more glamorous and indeed much more Russian with her black hair flowing over her shoulders. Her skin was even paler than Max remembered, almost white in the lamplight, so much so that the red bow on her black dress looked like a splash of blood.

'Ah, there you are, sir,' Sam slurred. 'Just in time. I'm running out of stories to entertain Nadia with.'

'Nadia Bukayeva,' the young woman said, extending a hand she appeared to expect Max to kiss. He was happy to oblige. 'I could not tell you earlier. Igor Bukayev is my uncle.'

'Delighted to make your acquaintance.' Max sat down, lit a cigarette and engaged Sam in interrogative eye contact.

'Drop of wine, sir? There's plenty.'

'You've certainly had plenty, by the look of you.'

'He is not your batman now, Max,' said Nadia, reprovingly but genially.

'He never was, actually.'

'He says you were a very daring pilot.'

'Poppycock. I was as cautious as they come. I wouldn't still be alive otherwise.'

'That is English modesty, yes?'

'That's what it is, right enough,' said Sam.

A waiter hove to and Max ordered a whisky. 'Are you a regular here, *mademoiselle*?' he asked Nadia.

'Nadia, please. We have become very informal, Sam and I.' She squeezed Sam's knee, inducing a blush that was visible even through the flush of wine.

'Nadia was asking after you when I got back to the hotel, sir. I didn't think you'd want me to let her just wander off.'

'So we came here to wait for you,' said Nadia. 'And, no, I am not a regular. More . . . an occasional.'

'Is it always like this?'

'Usually livelier.'

'Really?' Max glanced around. 'Livelier than this, eh?'

'They know how to have fun, don't they, sir?' said Sam. 'There are some sights here I never thought to see.'

'And in some cases you're not exactly sure what it is you're seeing.'

'Exactly, sir.'

The whisky arrived. 'Cheers.'

'Cheers.' Sam gulped down a mouthful of wine. 'It's been quite a day.'

'I bet it has.'

''Scuse me, sir – Nadia.' Sam rose unsteadily to his feet and stifled a belch. 'I've got to point Willy at the wall.' He stumbled off.

'Who is Willy?' asked Nadia.

'No one you know,' Max murmured, watching Sam navigate his meandering way towards a door beyond the bar.

'We need to talk, Max.' Nadia's voice was suddenly so close to Max's ear that he jumped in surprise.

He turned to find her staring at him intently. She was more serious now – more like the earnest bookshop assistant he had met earlier. 'This is hardly the place for a quiet chat, Nadia,' he pointed out.

'Can you hear what I'm saying?' Her lips were nearly touching his ear lobe. She was speaking at normal volume, but the noise around them reduced her words to a whisper that was nonetheless clearly audible.

He nodded. 'Of course I can hear you.'

'Then this is the place. No one else will hear. And anyone who sees us will think I am trying to talk you into bed.'

'But you're not, are you?'

'Do you want me to?'

Max smiled, unable to decide whether she was flirting with him or rebuking him. Maybe Sam had had the same problem. 'I want you to tell me why you came to the hotel to see me.'

'Because my uncle disappeared last Saturday, Max. Just a few hours after he heard your father was dead. I do not know where he is. I am very worried about him.'

'You've no idea where he might be?'

'No. I do not even know if he is still alive. But when the news came to him of Sir Henry's death, he was full of fear. I know that much.'

'What did he have to be frightened of?'

'My uncle is a leading member of a secret organization dedicated to the overthrow of the Bolsheviks and the restoration of royalty in Russia.'

'The Trust.'

'You have heard of it?'

'It doesn't seem to be that big a secret.'

'No. Probably it is not. Russians talk. It is one of our vices. Sir Henry had information about the Trust that he offered to sell to my uncle. Did you know this?'

Max still found it hard to believe his father had been engaged in such activities, but it seemed he was going to have to accustom himself to the idea. 'What sort of information?'

'There is a traitor inside the Trust. The Cheka know our plans before we know them ourselves. We are being destroyed from within. Sir Henry told my uncle he knew who the traitor was. He was given the name by Pierre Dombreux.'

'But Dombreux was working for the Bolsheviks.'

'Maybe he was. Maybe he wasn't. Maybe he was playing a double game. It is a dangerous thing to do.'

'So it seems.'

'We must know who the traitor is, Max. Did Sir Henry leave any sort of . . . record?'

'Nothing that will help you.'

'But will you help us, Max? If you discover the name . . .'

'I'll tell you. And you won't have to pay me for it.'

'Thank you.' She bowed her head and rested it on his shoulder. She murmured something into the muffling cloth of his jacket. For a moment, he thought she was crying.

'Don't upset yourself.' He raised her chin gently.

She looked at him with her large, dark soulful eyes. 'I am afraid, Max. And you also should be afraid.'

Max thought of the note the young Arab had secreted in his pocket and smiled. 'You're probably right. But I seem to have lost the knack.'

WHEN HE BELATEDLY REJOINED THEM, SAM MADE NO effort to deny that he felt dead on his feet. 'It's been a long day and no mistake.'

Max insisted on settling the bill and they promptly took their leave of Le Sagittaire.

'You head back to the Mazarin, Sam,' Max said once they were outside. 'I'll escort Nadia home.'

Ordinarily, Sam would have managed some kind of knowing wink at that. But he really was exhausted. Max suspected much of what he had eaten and drunk in the course of the evening had recently left him by the emergency exit. 'Righto, sir.' With that he staggered off.

It was not far to Bukayev's bookshop. The streets were generally quiet. Snow was gently falling. In Little Russia, it was quieter still and the snow heavier.

'It is a little like St Petersburg here tonight,' said Nadia as they approached the shop.

'You grew up in St Petersburg?'

'Yes. And I miss it every day.'

'Do you have any family apart from your uncle?'

'No. My father and my two brothers were killed in the

war. My mother died of a broken heart. Uncle Igor is all I have left.'

'I hope you'll hear from him soon.'

'I hope also. I do not enjoy being alone.'

They stopped at the door of the shop. There was an appeal – an invitation – in Nadia's gaze Max could have chosen to pretend he had not noticed. But the warmth and softness of her body were easy to imagine. And he wanted in that instant to do more than imagine them.

'Will you come in?'

He hesitated, then nodded. And she turned and unlocked the door.

Max was aware that the man Appleby had instructed to tail him had almost certainly followed him from the Mazarin to Le Sagittaire and on to the bookshop. Staying with Nadia was in part an act of defiance: a statement that he did not care what they knew or thought they knew about him. The rest was a simple surrender to the sensuality of the moment. Nadia needed him and he needed her. And the need was urgent.

He left as dawn was breaking. Nadia lay in bed, watching him dress. Neither spoke. Words, after their urgent couplings, seemed wholly redundant. He did not even kiss her goodbye. But in the looks that passed between them they exchanged a fitting farewell.

The snow had stopped overnight and most of it had dissolved into slush. The streets were deserted and Max wondered if his shadow was still with him. He would have had a bone-chilling vigil outside the bookshop if he was. There was no sign of him that Max could detect. But that, he well knew, was hardly decisive.

Back at the Mazarin, Max took a bath and was still towelling himself down when there was a knock at the door. He opened it to find Sam outside in charge of a breakfast trolley.

'I ordered enough for both of us, sir,' he said, sounding unwontedly chirpy. 'There's nothing like bacon and eggs after a night on the tiles.'

'It's you who overdid it, Sam, not me.'

'If you say so, sir.'

'But I am confoundedly hungry. And that bacon smells good. Wheel it in.'

Sam obliged. Max flung on his dressing-gown and they set to.

'I've something to tell you, sir,' Sam swiftly announced, munching on a sausage. 'I'd have told you last night, but I wasn't firing on all cylinders.'

'So I noticed.'

'Fact is, I may have found myself a job.'

'You mean here – in Paris?'

'Yeah.'

'But how? What sort of job?'

'Well, I thought rather than go gawping at the sights yesterday I'd do something a bit more . . . constructive.'

'Which was?'

'Like you'll know, I'm sure, a lot of the meetings to do with the peace conference are held at the French Foreign Office on the Key Dorsey. I went down there and had a chat with some of the chauffeurs. They hang around most of the day, apparently. Got myself into a card game

245

with the British drivers and helped one of them out with a distributor problem he was having. Turns out the chief mechanic they brought over from London's gone and died of the Spanish flu and they're desperate to find someone to replace him.'

'So you volunteered?'

'I'm to meet the bloke who hires and fires this morning. The pay's not bad and room and board at the Majestic's thrown in.' Sam grinned. 'Seems like you might be stuck with me, sir.'

'What about the deposit on those planes?'

'I'll cable Miller cancelling the order. I reckon I can trust him to pay me back when I get home.'

'You've got it all worked out, I see.'

'Cars are child's play compared with planes, sir. It'll be money for old rope. I should be able to spare some time to help you out. If you need me to.'

'It's a kind offer, Sam.' It had struck Max, in fact, that having a trusted ally lodging at the British delegation hotel might prove invaluable. 'But everything's much more complicated than it was this time yesterday.'

Max told Sam then about Spataro's murder and Corinne's arrest. Sam was clearly shocked by the developments. It hardly required a genius to deduce that investigating Sir Henry's death was a riskier enterprise than Max had originally supposed. And that was before the death threat delivered to him by the young Arab was taken into consideration. He showed Sam the note.

'It gets straight to the point, doesn't it?'

'But I notice you're still here, sir.'

'I've never been one to walk away from a scrap.'

'Or fly away, as I recall.'

'I don't really want to drag you into this, Sam.'

'But you reckon Kaiser Bill's spymaster is behind it all, don't you, sir?'

'Well, I—'

'Which makes it my patriotic duty to lend a hand. If I can. And I haven't given up on the flying school yet. You'll be no use to me dead.'

'Nor much alive, I suspect.'

Sam frowned. 'You reckon the boy who slipped you the note was an Arab?'

'Yes. What of it?'

'It's funny, that's all. The drivers were talking about a spate of burglaries at the delegation hotels. Petty stuff, apparently. But not so petty if you're the victim, I suppose. Anyhow, the papers have given the burglar a name: the Singe.'

'The what?'

'Singe.'

'Do you mean *le Singe* – the Monkey?'

'Ah. That'll be it. He gets in through windows so high up no one thinks they need to be closed.'

'Does he now?' Max remembered standing on the roof of 8 Rue du Verger trying to understand what had led Sir Henry to his death. 'I wonder how he gets to those windows.'

'Over the roof, maybe.'

'My thoughts exactly. But where are the Arab connections?'

'A few people have caught a glimpse of the burglar – well, someone they think must be the burglar. They say he's small and dark-skinned – Arab-looking.'

'Is that so?'

'So, d'you want me to ask a few more questions about the Monkey – after I've got my feet under the table at the Majestic?'

Max smiled. 'It seems to me I'm powerless to prevent you.'

Sam nodded. 'That you are, sir. But I thought it only polite to ask.'

IRETON SEEMED MONUMENTALLY UNSURPRISED BY HOW LITTLE Max had learnt from Kuroda. It seemed to Max, indeed, that it was just as he had expected, perhaps even as he had hoped. If stringing Max along to no purpose was Ireton's objective, it had been well served. If not, it was hard to understand why the American should look so pleased with himself.

Morahan had the decency to appear at least mildly disappointed as he confirmed Max's account of their evening's work. Malory served coffee and smiled appreciatively when Max passed on Kuroda's good wishes. 'He really is a charming gentleman,' she declared, ignoring Ireton's sarcastic scowl.

What Max did not pass on, of course, was news of Kuroda's later contact with him. He reckoned it was only fair to play Ireton at his own game. For the same reason he made no mention of Spataro's murder and Corinne's arrest. He did not seriously doubt that Ireton knew of these events. But he was damned if he would give him the satisfaction of being the first to refer to them.

'Are you going to tell me the next person you approached after Kuroda?' Max asked bluntly as soon as Malory had left them to it.

'I agree Kuroda was never likely to have breathed a word to anyone,' said Ireton, answering an entirely different question. 'But we had to rule him out. You can see that, can't you, Max?'

'I can see it was convenient for you to use me to rule him out for you. Who did you approach next?'

'Like Kuroda told you, he said he'd outbid anyone else who was interested. I took him at his word. But I needed other bidders, of course, to drive up the price he'd be willing to pay.'

'*Who?*'

'Where's the money in this world, Max, since most European countries have bankrupted themselves waging the war to end war? In my homeland, of course. The good old US of A. The American delegation was the obvious place to turn in search of a big fat bid. So, that's what I did.'

Max sighed. 'You may as well give me his name.'

'No need. I've arranged to have lunch with him at the Crillon. I've told him there's someone I want him to meet. You. But he doesn't know who you are and it wouldn't be fair to put you one up on him. Be at the Crillon at one o'clock and I'll introduce you to each other. Then we'll see what you can get out of him. He's less tight-lipped and a whole lot less cautious than Kuroda.' Ireton treated Max to one of his misshapen grins. 'He could be our man. So don't be late.'

Ireton soon excused himself on the grounds of a pressing engagement elsewhere, leaving Max to finish the coffee-pot with Morahan, who seemed in no hurry to be on his way. Max was emboldened to ask him a favour.

'About my shadow, Schools?'

'You want to lose him?'

'I want to be able to lose him when I choose to.'

'There are a few simple methods. You're on foot. So is he. That makes any form of transport your friend. Hire a taxi when there are no others about. Hop on a tram just as it's leaving. Likewise the Métro. There's a good chance you can give him the slip, at least temporarily. He can pick you up again at your hotel, of course. So, what you really need to do is to put a face to him. The Métro's probably best for that. Board a train, then jump off just as the doors are closing. Either he shows himself by jumping off as well or he stays on and loses you. I shouldn't bother trying that this morning, though.'

'Why not?'

'I watched you come in. You're not being tailed today, Max. Maybe Appleby's decided it's not worth the bother.'

'You're sure?'

Morahan shrugged. 'It's possible he's put a smarter operator on your case, I suppose. Maybe more than one man, but that's a heavy investment. I can't see Appleby running to it.'

'Why would he call it off?'

'I can't say. Maybe you should ask him.'

Morahan walked Max out. Max paused on his way at the door of Malory's office to wish her a good morning.

'Are you likely to see Mr Kuroda again?' she asked.

'She has a soft spot for our Japanese friend,' said Morahan, coming unintentionally to Max's rescue.

Malory blushed slightly and pursed her lips in

251

irritation, though whether with herself or Morahan was unclear. 'I've enjoyed talking to him about his country, that's all. It brings back some happy memories.'

'You've been to Japan?' Max asked, surprised by the possibility.

Malory sighed, more sorrowfully than nostalgically. 'I may as well tell you, if only to deny Schools the pleasure of relating it.'

'I never speak about you to anyone without your permission, Malory,' said Morahan, sounding offended by the suggestion.

'No? Well, that may be so,' conceded Malory. 'In which case I apologize.'

'Apology accepted. I'll be seeing you, Max.' With that Morahan retreated in the direction of his own office.

'Oh lord,' said Malory. 'I believe I've hurt his feelings.'

'I believe you may have.'

Malory looked at Max then with a frown of concentration, as if properly assessing him for the first time. 'Travis said you were born in Tokyo.'

'He's disturbingly well-informed.'

'But it's true?'

'Yes. I have no memories of the city, though. We left when I was only a few months old. It could as easily have been Timbuktu. You've been there?'

'Tokyo? Yes. Timbuktu? No.'

They both laughed. Some of Malory Hollander's artfully concealed vivacity broke briefly from cover.

'What took you to Japan, Malory?'

'I was a Lutheran missionary. Very young and very naive. I believed it was my duty to spread the word of God. And I set about my duty with the kind of energy only the very young and very naive possess. I'm pained to recall how insensitive I was, forcing pamphlets and prayer-meetings on all those polite, restrained and contented Shintoists and Buddhists. I'm lucky no one tossed a rock at my head. I wouldn't blame them now if they had.'

'How long did you last?'

'Three years. Three wasted years. Except that I learnt how beautiful the country is and how remarkable its people are. I gained much more from the experience than they did.'

'Does that mean you know how Kuroda's mind works?'

'Goodness, no. But it does mean I know better than to try to understand how it works. The greatest honour the Japanese do us is to refrain from telling us how stupid they think we are. I told Travis that once.'

'How did he take it?'

'He said he likes it when someone thinks he's stupid. It makes it easier to outwit them.'

'I doubt he'd find it easy to outwit Kuroda.'

'I doubt that too.'

'Do you ever think of going back to Japan?'

'I will, one day.' Malory smiled brightly at him, then added, bafflingly, 'Something tells me you will too.'

Max found it hard to believe he really was no longer under surveillance, despite Morahan's confidence on the point. He went down into Pyramides Métro station, bought a ticket to Gare de l'Est and waited on the platform with a smattering of other passengers, none of whom seemed to pay him the slightest attention. He gave them a lot of his, and elicited nothing in the way of a suspicious reaction. Then the train rolled in and everyone climbed aboard.

Max stood inside the doors for a few moments, then stepped back out. There was time for anyone following him to do the same, but no one moved. The doors closed. The train rolled out. And Max was alone on the platform.

GILBERT MELLISH, SURREY SOLICITOR, POSSESSOR OF A FINELY honed professional manner, a balding dome of a head, an aldermanly paunch and an expression of practised neutrality, settled himself in the armchair to which he had been directed and pulled a bulging file from his briefcase. He gazed at his audience through thick-lensed glasses that magnified his eyes disquietingly, and cleared his throat.

The widow, brother-in-law, eldest son and daughter-in-law of his late lamented client, Sir Henry Maxted, were gathered in a semicircle around him. Of Sir Henry's younger son there was no sign and Mellish had as yet sought no clarification of Sir Ashley's statement that 'My brother can't be with us.'

Winifred, the Dowager Lady Maxted, appeared calm and composed. Her brother, George Clissold, sat beside her, regarding Mellish through heavy lids. Sir Ashley was altogether more alert, sitting upright in his chair and fiddling with his tie. He had made no reference to the somewhat testy telephone conversation he had had with Mellish two days previously, though the frown on the face of Lydia, the junior Lady Maxted, suggested she for one was well aware of it. Mellish's correctitude had evidently failed to meet with her approval.

'It's my understanding that you're all familiar with Sir Henry's wishes for the disposition of his estate,' Mellish said by way of preamble.

'Yes,' said Ashley. 'We are.'

'Gresscombe Place and the entailed farmland is yours, Sir Ashley, along with five sixths of the income it generates, one sixth being reserved for your mother.'

'Henry laid these matters before us some years ago, Mr Mellish,' said Winifred. 'There is no confusion on anyone's part.'

'Indeed not.'

'There are no other beneficiaries, then,' said Lydia.

Mellish wondered if she was thinking of herself, but was inclined to suspect she was more concerned about her absent brother-in-law. He nodded. 'There are not.'

'I have the death certificate issued by the French authorities, Mellish,' said Ashley. 'Armed with that, I assume you can set about applying for probate.'

'Ah, there a small complication arises, I'm afraid.'

Ashley frowned. 'Why?'

'My firm has not been appointed as an executor of the will.'

'A mere detail. As executor, I will—'

'Neither have you, Sir Ashley.'

There was a brief, shocked silence. Winifred stiffened. George opened his eyes. Lydia stared. And Ashley glowered. 'What the devil are you talking about?'

'You are not an executor, Sir Ashley. Only an executor can apply for probate and in due course implement the provisions of the will. I'm sorry, but there it is.'

'A moment ago you said you understood we were fully aware of Sir Henry's wishes,' said Lydia.

'For the disposition of his estate, yes. Nothing has been changed there. Only in the matter of the executorship did Sir Henry make an alteration.'

'When did he do this, Mr Mellish?' asked Winifred.

'The revised will is dated . . .' Mellish broke off to consult the document. 'The twelfth of March.'

'March this year?' Ashley snapped.

'Er, yes.'

'But that's only . . . a few weeks ago.'

'Indeed.'

'How is this possible? He'd been in Paris since early January.'

'Not all the time, self-evidently. He telephoned me from his London club on, let me see . . .' There was a rustling of papers. 'Yes. On Tuesday the eleventh. He said he wanted urgently to make an amendment to his will and would call on me the following day to do so.'

'He came to Epsom?'

'Yes.'

'But—'

'You must be mistaken,' Lydia cut in. 'He wouldn't have come to Epsom without contacting us.'

'He came, Lady Maxted, I assure you. Having the revised will typed there and then so that it could be signed and witnessed the same day placed something of a strain on my secretarial resources. I well recall the occasion.'

'Henry was in the country,' said George. 'I saw him myself.'

Ashley turned on him. '*What?*'

'In London. The eleventh, you say, Mellish?' George nodded. 'Yes, that sounds about right.'

'You *saw* him?'

'I did. At some distance. In Lombard Street. I thought I must be mistaken, but clearly I wasn't.'

'Did you know about this, Mother?'

'Yes, my dear. George told me.'

'Well, you might have told me.'

'I didn't consider it important.'

'*Not important?*'

'Who is the executor, Mellish?' George asked, ignoring Ashley. 'You may as well put us out of our misery.'

'It's James,' said Winifred quietly.

'James?' Ashley's tone had now acquired a timbre of horror.

'You are correct, Lady Maxted,' said Mellish. 'Mr James Maxted is the sole executor of Sir Henry's will.'

'Good God,' Ashley exclaimed, 'this . . . this is . . .'

'Intolerable,' said Lydia. 'That is what it is.'

'Sometimes the intolerable must be tolerated,' said Winifred.

Ashley glared at her. 'How can you take this so calmly?'

'I imagine the appointment is legally unchallenge-able,' Winifred replied.

'Indeed so,' said Mellish.

'Then to take it other than calmly would be futile.'

But calmness clearly did not commend itself to Ashley, who squirmed and grimaced helplessly. 'I assume James could renounce the executorship if he wished,' said Lydia tightly.

'He could,' Mellish responded. 'Do you know of some reason why he might wish to?'

'Well, he's currently abroad and didn't return even for his father's funeral. That hardly suggests he's a natural choice for the role.'

'Be that as it may, Lady Maxted, Sir Henry's wishes were very clear on the point. If you can furnish me with an address for your brother, Sir Ashley, I'll—'

'Much good that'll do you.'

'But you can tell me where he is?'

'Yes, yes, damn it. Hotel Mazarin, Rue Coligny, Paris. Unless he's moved on to God knows where.'

'We have no reason to doubt his presence there, Mr Mellish,' said Winifred with some emphasis.

'Then I shall communicate with him as soon as possible,' said Mellish. 'As regards his suitability or inclination, I'll certainly offer my firm's services for the settlement of the estate.'

'He'll probably plump for that,' said George. 'He won't want to bog himself down in paperwork.'

'Let's hope not,' said Ashley, stroking his forehead gloomily.

'I'll need the death certificate you mentioned, Sir Ashley,' said Mellish, smiling uneasily.

'Yes, yes, very well.' Ashley hauled himself to his feet and headed for the door.

'Tell me, Mr Mellish,' said Lydia as soon as her husband had left the room, 'if, purely for the sake of argument, James *did* renounce the executorship, who would replace him?'

'The courts would appoint an administrator, Lady Maxted.'

'And who would that be?'

'Normally, the residuary legatee. In this case, Sir Ashley.'

'And in that event, we would be much where we were, in testamentary terms, before Sir Henry made the recent alteration to his will?'

'We would be *exactly* where we were.'

'I see.' Lydia nodded thoughtfully. 'Excuse me for a moment, would you all?' With that, she rose and bustled from the room.

Winifred watched her depart, then turned back to Mellish with a smile. 'We should have offered you tea, Mr Mellish. Would you care for a cup?'

'Or a glass of something stronger?' George suggested.

Lydia caught up with Ashley in his study. He already had the death certificate in his hand and was about to leave. She closed the door behind her, clasped his arm and fixed him with a purposeful stare.

'As executor, James is likely to prove an appalling nuisance,' she said. 'It's simply not to be borne.'

'I know,' Ashley groaned. 'But what's to be done?'

'If he renounced the executorship, you'd take over, according to Mellish.'

'Why would he renounce it?'

'To secure the land he needs for his wretched flying school.'

'I've already told him that's out of the question.'

'You're going to have to change your mind, darling.' Her grip on his arm tightened. 'Or at least pretend to.'

THE PARC MONCEAU LOOKED BOTH SPRINGLIKE AND WINTRY in pallid sunshine. The snow lay in half-thawed patches between colourfully blossomed beds of flowers. The keen wind did not encourage the pram-pushing nannies to loiter and the benches flanking the path Max followed into the park were empty.

He had taken care to arrive exactly on time, suspecting Kuroda would be punctual, and was soon rewarded by the sight of the Japanese detective walking towards him. He was wearing a Homburg, gloves, scarf and heavy overcoat and was carrying an umbrella, though no rain was threatening.

'Good morning, Mr Maxted,' Kuroda said as they met.

'Good morning, Mr Kuroda. Why don't you call me Max? Everyone does.'

'Your father did not.'

'Everyone except my family.'

'Aha. Very well. Come then, Max. I had thought we would sit and talk, but we must walk if my teeth are not to chatter.'

They headed at a brisk pace towards the gate Max had entered by. 'And what should I call you? Mr Kuroda? Commissioner? Masataka?'

'I had the honour to know your father as Henry and to be known by him as Masataka. You are the son of my friend. Therefore . . .'

'Masataka it is.'

Kuroda gave a formal little nod of approval.

'I was surprised to get your message last night, Masataka.'

'Why? You must have calculated that I could not speak without constraint in the presence of Mr Morahan.'

'I wasn't sure you wanted to speak without constraint.'

'Henry would wish me to advise you candidly, Max. I do not walk with you here this morning as a loyal servant of the Emperor. I walk with you here this morning to give you my counsel.'

'I'll take it, gratefully.'

'Then first we must acknowledge the facts. Neither you nor Mr Morahan referred to the murder of Raffaele Spataro and the arrest of Corinne Dombreux. Yet those events flow from the same source as the murder of your father. You agree?'

'Yes.'

'I believe you are in considerable danger. Have you received any threats to your life?'

Max sighed. 'Yes.'

'Which you have disregarded?'

'I'm staying in Paris until I learn the truth.'

'Your resolve is commendable. It may also be fatal. But why do you suppose the threat to your life has not yet been acted upon?'

'They think I can be frightened off.'

'They hope you can. Their difficulty is that your murder would make it hard for the police to continue to pretend that Henry's death was accidental or that Madame Dombreux murdered Spataro. That is why they stay their hand – for the moment.'

'Do you know who they are?'

'You are caught in a web. And Lemmer is the spider at its centre. That is all I can be sure of.'

They reached the gate. Max paused to light a cigarette. Kuroda declined his offer of one. They turned and began to retrace their steps.

'Henry sought in his last weeks to sell valuable pieces of information he possessed to various people. The whereabouts of Fritz Lemmer was only one such piece of information. You are aware of this, I think.'

'I am. I didn't know you were.'

'My duties require me to be aware of many things. Henry's behaviour suggested desperation to me. He was a professional diplomat. This auction of secrets was a contradiction of all he stood for. Have you discovered what drove him to it?'

'No.'

'Well, perhaps it is not your most pressing problem. Do you know what else besides his knowledge of Lemmer he hoped to profit from?'

'I have a few . . . indications.'

'Do any of those indications point to a matter that might involve my delegation?'

Max nodded. 'Yes.'

'And that matter was?'

'Something he referred to as the Chinese box. Meaning, I assume, the boxload of secret documents stolen from the head of the Chinese delegation when he stopped off in Tokyo on his way here.'

'I assume that also.'

'Stolen by your lot, according to Appleby.'

'My lot?' Kuroda chuckled drily. 'There he is mistaken.'

'Who, then?'

'I greatly fear the thief, whether or not he was Japanese, acted on instructions from Lemmer.'

'Why would Lemmer want the documents?'

'To answer that question I must entrust you with a state secret, Max. I should not, of course. It is most unwise, most . . . irresponsible. But if I don't, I estimate your chances of leaving Paris alive will be close to zero.'

'It can't be that bad.'

Kuroda cast him a sidelong glance that might have been one of pity. 'I have serious doubts about the wisdom of discussing this matter with you. You could ease those doubts by assuring me that you will disclose what I am about to tell you to no one else . . . unless to do so becomes the difference between life and death.'

'You have my word.'

'Thank you. I will hold you to it. Now, the Chinese box. There is a game played in China in which a series of wooden boxes must be fitted inside each other. It can only be done in one specific sequence. The difficulty arises from the minute differences in the size and shape of each box. This is what we are doing, Max: puzzling over sizes and shapes. There is only one solution to the puzzle. And this, I believe, is that solution.

'Lemmer's calculation from the start of the war was that the only hope Germany had of winning was to outflank its enemies. He planned to do this by neutralizing some of them and turning others into allies. So, he gave the Bolsheviks secret support to bring down the Tsar and plunge Russia into chaos. And he sought to persuade Japan to change sides. Japan's entry into the war had been a strategic disaster for Germany. They lost their Pacific naval base at Tsingtao and the island colonies it protected. Lemmer understood that if and when the United States joined in, Germany was doomed, unless Japan by then was an ally. Japan could distract the Americans, by threatening Hawaii and the Philippines. So, through agents in China, which was still neutral then, he offered the Japanese government a deal: as much territory as they wanted in eastern Russia and the Pacific, including Australia and New Zealand, in return for an alliance with Germany. From some viewpoints, it was an attractive offer. And I must tell you it was seriously considered.'

'How seriously?'

'I believe the stolen box contained a copy of a letter sent by Prime Minister Juichi to the German Foreign Minister, Zimmermann, accepting the offer. If the evidence of this letter was made public, it would have a catastrophic effect on Japan's relations with the United States and Great Britain. It might even lead to Japan's expulsion from the peace conference. The consequences of that are hard to judge. But they would be extremely grave.'

'How would such a letter have ended up in the hands of the Chinese?'

'Remember that since the Last Emperor abdicated, there have been two governments in China, struggling for mastery. I believe the letter was part of the bargain struck between the Peking government and Sun Yat-sen's rival administration in Canton when they formed a joint delegation to the peace conference. Canton was the route chosen by Lemmer for secret communication with Japan because Sun was financially dependent on Germany. The letter never reached Zimmermann, in fact, because the German high command chose to launch unrestricted submarine warfare in an attempt to crush Britain. This and a clumsy attempt to draw Mexico into the conflict led inevitably to a declaration of war by the United States. I imagine Lemmer was horrified by the stupidity of the Kaiser's senior advisers. Count Juichi was also horrified. He withdrew his agreement and tried to retrieve the letter. Sun said it had been destroyed, but no one in Tokyo believed him. We are sure he used it to buy representation here. It would have won China many concessions from Japan if it had not been stolen. Sun would have gained credit for those concessions. Now he probably curses the foolishness of Lou Tseng-Tsiang for letting the Japanese rob him. And we Japanese must let Lou – and Sun – believe he was robbed by us. We are thought to be more cunning and devious than we truly are. Misfortune is a cruel flatterer.'

They had reached a crossroads in the centre of the park and now turned right, towards the distant southern exit. 'There is something I don't understand,' said Max after they had covered ten yards or so in silence. 'How could my father know about any of this?'

'Lemmer threads his agents together as if they are pearls on a string. In a time of war, communications are vital, but also fragile. I believe Lemmer's principal agent in Russia was a conduit for the overtures he made to Japan. And I believe Pierre Dombreux was that agent.'

'Dombreux?'

'There is no better camouflage than to be thought to have betrayed your country to another when in truth you have betrayed them both to a third.'

If Kuroda was right, Max realized at once, Dombreux might have known about the Trust as well as the stolen Chinese documents. 'You're suggesting Dombreux confided in my father?'

'Yes, I am. A triangle has three sides. It is a rule of geometry. Dombreux and his wife. Madame Dombreux and Henry. Henry and Dombreux. We must ask ourselves what passed between them in the months after the Bolsheviks seized power in Russia. Lemmer's Japanese plan had misfired. Maybe he blamed Dombreux. And maybe Dombreux knew the Bolsheviks doubted his loyalty. The wolves were prowling at the edge of the wood. Soon they would close in on the dwindling camp fire. He was a frightened man with much to fear. I am not sure which of his masters, if any, he was truly loyal to: Lemmer, the Bolsheviks or *la belle France*. And I am not sure if he was as heartless a husband as he appears to have been. Perhaps he sensed his doom approaching and gave Henry some of his secrets in the hope that they would enable him to protect Madame Dombreux.'

'If so, it didn't work, did it?'

'No. Henry was outmatched. As you are. There is something else I must tell you, Max. It is a hard thing to say. This matter of Count Juichi's letter and Lemmer's probable responsibility for its theft is a very serious threat to the Japanese government. An order has been given. A man has been engaged. An assassin. He is a master of his craft.'

'What has he been engaged to do?'

'Find Lemmer. Kill him. Retrieve the letter. And kill anyone else who knows what it contains.'

'I see.'

'That is why you must speak of it to no one. For there is no one you can trust absolutely. You are a blind man who has crossed the path of a tiger. And a hunting tiger makes no sound. His name is Tarn. I know nothing else about him except his reputation.'

'Which is?'

'Formidable.'

'You think he killed my father?'

'It is possible. Yet, strictly speaking, it would have been illogical, unless Henry had first told him where Lemmer was hiding. And Tarn has not found Lemmer yet. That much is certain.'

'Does he work alone?'

Kuroda glanced round at Max in surprise. 'What makes you ask?'

'That death threat I ignored was delivered to me by an Arab boy.'

'A boy? Or simply a slightly built young man?'

'Hard to say.'

'There is a rumour that Tarn employs an assistant who could be the person you describe.'

'*Le Singe*.'

'You have been reading the newspapers. Yes. *Le Singe*. It could be him. Or someone like him.'

'What would Tarn use him for?'

'Reconnaissance. Surveillance. Gaining entry to buildings.'

'But according to the papers he's an opportunist burglar.'

'Maybe he is. When Tarn does not need him.'

'Is Tarn a Frenchman?'

'I do not know.'

'Would Ireton know?'

'It is possible. He knows many things. That is why I have dealt with him from time to time. But I doubt he would be willing to help you. He would consider it dangerous to attract Tarn's attention. And he would be right.'

They were nearing the southern gate. Kuroda stopped and Max pulled up beside him. They turned and looked at each other. Max lit another cigarette. 'As my self-appointed counsellor, Masataka, what do you suggest I do?'

'Leave Paris.'

'And if I don't?'

'Confront your enemy. He has given you some time – probably not much – to acknowledge his superiority and retreat. If you do not intend to do so, then you must attack him.'

'But first I must find him.'

Kuroda nodded. 'So you must.'

'What chance do you give me?'

'A slim one. Though no slimmer than the chance that we should ever have met. We can never see the ends of the roads our choices lead us down until we reach them. I chose long ago, as a young Tokyo police officer, to volunteer for special attachment to a foreign police force. I was sent to London and spent a year at Scotland Yard. That is how I came to learn English and to love the writings of Scott and Dickens and Hardy. It is why, after I returned to Japan, I was assigned to investigate the activities of foreign residents in our country. And it is why I find myself in Paris today, standing with you here, in the cold spring sunshine. The future is not written, Max. It is a blank parchment. What I will eventually read of you on it, or you of me, cannot be known. Until the time comes.'

'And meanwhile?'

'Tread softly. But tread swiftly.' Kuroda laid a hand on Max's shoulder. 'That is your self-appointed counsellor's considered advice.'

MAX SURVEYED THE THINLY PEOPLED BREADTH OF THE Place de la Concorde, wondering if he would see the young Arab again. But he was nowhere in sight. Outside the entrance to the pillared and porticoed Hôtel de Crillon, however, Travis Ireton was very much in evidence, smoking a cigarette and gazing about him as he prowled up and down.

'You made it, then,' he said, smiling crookedly as Max approached.

'There was no danger I wouldn't.'

'I guess not, though danger's often where you don't expect to find it.'

'Shall we go in?'

'Sure. But before we do . . .'

'Yes?'

'Back me up in everything I say, won't you, Max? It's important we stick to the script.'

'And what is the script?'

'You're a smart fellow. You'll soon catch on.'

As at the Majestic, there were guards on the door of the Crillon. These were big, burly American guards. Ireton was obviously well-known to them, however. He and Max were admitted without difficulty.

The marbled splendour of the lobby was only out-done by the mirrored and frescoed ornateness of the restaurant, but the Americans had contrived to lay a heavy transatlantic hand on the hotel's Parisian elegance. The food being consumed and the largeness and loudness of those consuming it clashed rudely with the surroundings. The very smell of the place was wrong.

Walter Ennis, their host, was a tall, good-looking, middle-aged man who would have looked better still for the loss of several stones of fat which even an expertly cut suit could not disguise. He was flushed and uneasy in his manner, though superficially jovial. His shirt collar strained round a roll of pink flesh where his neck should have been and there was a disagreeable sweatiness to his handshake. Max had the impression the Martini he was drinking was not his first of the day.

They joined him in his choice of aperitif and Ireton managed some deft introductions. He and Ennis, it transpired, had been schoolfriends in Baltimore, but Ireton had not, he shamelessly lamented, followed Ennis's path to Yale and government service. Ennis himself proffered neatly phrased condolences when he realized whose son Max was.

'I met your father a couple of times at meetings of our Latin American committee. A real gentleman. I was awful sorry to hear about his death, I truly was.'

Max thanked him and kept a studiously straight face as Ireton explained that it was Max who had proposed the three of them meet. 'He was insistent, actually, Walter. But evasive about the reason, aside from the fact that it concerns his father.'

It was clear to Max that Ennis did not like the sound of that. But he smiled gamely as they ordered their meals and moved on to a second Martini (or third or fourth, in his case). Ireton piled on the agony by asking Ennis how he thought President Wilson would respond to continued French claims for the Saar coalfields. Ennis's reaction suggested he felt this was an improper question in such company. Exasperation with his old schoolfriend, fuelled by alcohol on an empty stomach, began to exhibit itself. And Max soon became an additional target.

'What *exactly* can I do for you, Max? I reckon it's time you said your piece.'

'You're right, Walter. If I've delayed explaining myself it's because the situation's a little . . . foggy.'

'Nothing like sunlight to clear fog,' said Ireton. 'We need a few shafts of it, don't we, Walter?'

'That we do,' said Ennis.

'Then let me supply them,' said Max, keeping his tone relaxed and unassertive. 'Firstly, you should know my father's death wasn't an accident, as reported in the press. He was murdered.'

'You don't mean it.'

'He does,' said Ireton. 'This part I know.'

'I'm determined to find his murderer and see him answer for his crime.'

Ennis eyed Max queasily. 'Well, I guess you would be.'

Their lunches arrived at that moment. Ennis had ordered a steak, but his expression implied regret that he had not asked for it to be well done. Blood was evidently not what he wanted to confront on his plate.

'I found a list of names in my father's handwriting,'

Max went on. 'You're both on it. I thought I'd start by asking why you thought that might be.'

'Depends what kind of list we're talking about, I imagine,' said Ireton.

'It's hard to tell. But it's one of the few clues I have to follow. There are figures on it as well. It almost looks as if you . . . owed him money.'

Ireton's eyes widened at this piece of improvisation. Ennis's complexion darkened a shade. It was closer to red now than pink. 'I didn't owe Henry any money,' he said emphatically.

'Nor me,' said Ireton.

'Maybe we could see this list.'

'I'm afraid I don't have it with me.'

'Well, that's a shame. You're not giving us a lot to go on, are you?'

'Would some of the other names he listed help?'

'They might.'

'Lemmer.'

Ennis frowned unconvincingly. 'Lemmer? I don't think . . .'

'You know who he is, Walter. You both do.'

'No sense denying it, I guess,' said Ireton, drawing a glare from Ennis.

'I wondered if you two were in some kind of negotiation with my father . . . for information about Lemmer.'

'What makes you think that?' Ennis asked levelly.

'Well, I assume the whereabouts of the Kaiser's spymaster would be of interest to a senior member of the US delegation such as yourself, Walter.'

'You do, do you?'

'My father knew Lemmer from the time when they were both in Japan in the early nineties. He was one of very few people familiar with his appearance. That may be what got him murdered.'

'That's quite a leap you're taking, Max.'

'Were you in discussion with him about Lemmer?'

Ennis glanced at Ireton, who shrugged unhelpfully. He sighed. 'Travis here suggested Henry might know where Lemmer was and asked if I'd be interested, on behalf of the State department, in buying the information.'

'Henry asked me to put out some feelers,' said Ireton. 'So I did.'

'Did you express any interest, Walter?' Max pressed.

'Of course.'

'And did you consult anyone else about it?'

'Why do you ask?'

'I'm wondering if someone tipped Lemmer off, you see.'

Ennis's eyes narrowed. 'Are you making some kind of accusation?'

'Not yet.'

'I'm not sure I like the direction this conversation is taking.'

'Sorry about that. But murder's a disagreeable business. So's spying, of course. I gather there were people at all levels of every government in Lemmer's pay.' Max could have stopped there. But he was conscious of Kuroda's warning that he did not have unlimited time to play with. 'Let me throw another name on the list at you. Tarn.'

'Tarn?' Ireton looked at him in frank surprise.

'I don't know who you're referring to,' Ennis declared.

'No?'

'No.' Ennis flung down his fork with a clatter, tossed his napkin on to the table and stood up. 'You're going to have to excuse me for a few minutes, gentlemen. Eat on without me. I'll be back directly.'

As he headed out of the restaurant, Ireton took a sip of wine and frowned at Max. 'You seem to have got under his skin.'

'I wonder why.'

'Maybe because he doesn't like being accused of treason.'

'Is that how it sounded?'

'Wasn't it meant to? And what was that about Tarn? Where'd you—'

'Excuse me, Travis.' Max rose from his chair. Speed was of the essence. It had suddenly occurred to him that he might profit from speaking to Ennis alone. 'There's something I have to attend to.'

Max guessed Ennis had gone to the toilets and emerged into the reception area wondering where they might be. But, no, Ennis was standing at the desk directly ahead of him. Max saw the clerk take a key from the pigeon-holes behind him and hand it to Ennis, who turned and hastened towards the lifts.

Max took a slow waltz round a pillar to avoid the American's eye-line. The lifts were definitely his destination. He must be going up to his room. But why?

As soon as Ennis was out of sight, Max marched confidently across to the desk. Descrying objects at a distance was a vital skill for a pilot in wartime and he was blessed with twenty-twenty vision. He knew which pigeon-hole had contained Ennis's key and noted the number on the fobs of keys dangling in the holes either side of it as he approached. A swift calculation revealed that Ennis was going up to room 221. Max pulled up as if he had just remembered something, turned and headed for the stairs.

During the early, trivial stages of their conversation, Ennis had bemoaned 'the slow as a snail elevators' in the hotel, so Max was not surprised, on reaching the second floor and following the signs, to see the American opening the door of his room and going in. He was clearly in a hurry and Max could hear his heavy, wheezy breathing.

In fact, he was in so much of a hurry that he did not check the door was closed behind him, merely pushed it to as he entered. The latch did not engage. Max lengthened his stride.

He reached the door, pushed it carefully open and stepped inside. The room was vast, white-panelled and high-ceilinged, with tall windows looking out on to the Place de la Concorde. For a second, Max could not see where Ennis was. He actually heard his voice, barking into the telephone, before he spotted him, stooping over the desk next to one of the windows.

'Yes, it's me . . . Sir Henry's boy is the problem. He's downstairs. He's been making a nuisance of himself . . . Easy for you to say. It's me who has to carry it off . . . You'd better remember my problems are your problems . . . He mentioned Tarn, damn it . . . All right . . . God damn it, I said *all right* . . . Yes, yes . . . Yes. I'll be there.'

Ennis crashed the receiver down so heavily the telephone toppled off the desk. With a curse, he bent down and hoisted it back into place. Then he turned and saw Max.

'What the—'

'Who was that you were speaking to, Walter?'

'None of your damn business.'

'I must beg to differ, since it's me you were discussing.'

'Get out of here.'

'Not until you've told me who you were speaking to.'

Ennis grabbed the telephone and rattled the switchhook. 'Ennis, room two twenty-one,' he announced to whoever had responded. 'I need a couple of guards up here to deal with an intru—'

He was cut off by Max wrenching the phone out of his hand, so violently the wire was pulled out of the wall behind the desk. Max tossed the instrument aside and stared into Ennis's eyes. The man was frightened, probably not just of Max. His face was lightly sheened with sweat and he was struggling for breath.

'Get out . . . while you still can, Maxted,' he panted. 'You're in . . . way over your head.'

'No. You're describing yourself, Walter. I know exactly what I'm doing.'

'If you did . . . you'd quit now.'

'Who were you speaking to when I came in?'

'Go to hell.'

Ennis was obviously not going to answer any questions voluntarily. Max decided to see whether a little discomfort would loosen his tongue. He punched him hard in his bulging stomach. Ennis went over like a sack of flour, sagging on to his knees with a spluttering groan.

'Who was it, Walter?' Max demanded, kneeling beside him. 'I need the name.'

Ennis's head fell forward. His face was a purplish red. He was choking and coughing. Max thought he might be about to vomit, but now was not the moment to show him any mercy.

'*Who was it?*'

'You don't . . . understand,' Ennis gasped. 'You . . . haven't got . . . a chance in hell.'

'We'll see—'

There was suddenly a noise behind him of running, booted feet. Shadows fell across them. In the next instant something blunt and heavy struck the back of Max's head with stunning force. And he went down with it, into a pool of darkness.

TRY AS HE MIGHT TO DISGUISE IT, THERE WAS NO QUESTION that Shuttleworth, i/c support services for the British delegation to the peace conference, regarded Sam as the answer to his prayers. He needed someone with the technical expertise to keep the delegation's fleet of cars on the road who was also capable of controlling a squad of junior mechanics. A former RFC NCO engineer with impeccable credentials fitted the bill perfectly. And, as Sam pointed out, he could start straight away.

'Tomorrow morning?' Shuttleworth asked.

'Yes,' Sam replied.

'The job's yours.'

'You did say there'd be accommodation, didn't you, sir?'

'Certainly. Bed *and* board.' Shuttleworth consulted a chart hanging on the wall behind his desk. 'Your predecessor shared a room with Jenkins, who's down with the flu himself, so I can't put you in there. Let's see . . .' He sucked his pen for a moment or two, then made a telephone call. 'McLeod? Shuttleworth here. I need accommodation for a new chief mechanic. Is two eight five still empty? . . . Good . . . Yes . . . Twentyman, S . . . Got that? . . . Good . . . You'll see to it, then? . . . Thank you.' He put the telephone down and smiled at Sam. 'Another dead man's making way for you, Twentyman. But don't worry. He didn't actually croak in the room. And you'll have it to yourself, which is a bonus.'

Sam's gaze strayed to the wall chart. On it were several grids of numbered boxes, with names written in them, some crossed out and substituted with others. The name in box 285 had been crossed out, but no new name had yet been entered. And the old one was still legible. *Maxted, Sir H.*

'I'm sure the room will be fine, sir,' Sam said quietly.

Sam paid a visit to the garage before he left the Majestic. The junior mechanics seemed a decent bunch. He had encountered less promising material in the RFC on numerous occasions. It wouldn't take long to knock them into shape.

He walked back to the Mazarin to collect his belongings and leave a note for Max suggesting they meet that evening. Whether they would, he had no way of knowing. It depended on what Max discovered in the course of the day – and, he supposed, on just how alluring Max found Nadia Bukayeva. Sam regretted having been too drunk to offer any kind of competition for her favours, although he did not delude himself that the result would have been different, however sober he had been. A Russian monarchist like Nadia was bound to be a snob at heart. She would always prefer an officer.

Several large men in overcoats and hats were gathered at the reception desk when Sam entered the Mazarin. The discussion they were having with the clerk was not exactly heated, but it was certainly warm. One of them, who was older than his companions and seemed to be in charge, was speaking slowly and very firmly. He sounded as if he was keeping his temper with some difficulty.

'A man's been killed, *monsieur*, and I'd ask you to bear that in mind. You say you've no idea where Mr Maxted is or when he's likely to be back?'

Mention of the name Maxted stopped Sam in his tracks. The clerk knew he was acquainted with Max and Sam was not at all sure he wanted to be drawn into the exchanges. He turned towards the door. But it was too late.

'There is Mr Maxted's friend, Mr Twentyman,' the clerk wailed. 'Perhaps he can help you.'

One of the large men cut off Sam's retreat. He turned back to be met by the stern gaze of the clerk's interrogator-in-chief. 'Mr Twentyman?'

'Er, yes. That's me.'

'I'm looking for James Maxted. It's a matter of considerable urgency.'

'Sorry. I don't know where he is.'

'But you are a friend of his?'

'Well, yes. We . . . were in the war together.'

'Were you indeed? Mr Maxted's kept very quiet about you, I must say. My name's Appleby. Perhaps you've heard of me.'

Sam had heard of him. Appleby. Secret Service bigwig. Not to be trifled with, especially not by the likes of Sam. 'Lieutenant Maxted doesn't—'

'Lieutenant, is it? I see. The bonds of war are close,

aren't they? If Maxted chose to confide in anyone, I suspect it would be you.'

'If he did, sir, I'd respect his confidence.'

Appleby gave him a narrow-eyed stare. 'So you would, I'm sure.'

Sam heard the telephone behind the desk ring. The clerk answered it. 'If you don't mind me asking, sir,' Sam ventured, 'who's been killed?'

'A young fellow I had high hopes of. Found dead this morning, not far from here. Throat cut from ear to ear. Your Mr Maxted could have been the last person to see him alive.'

'Wouldn't his murderer have been the last person to see him alive, sir?'

'You're a sharp one, aren't you, Twentyman? You're quite right, of course. But maybe Mr Maxted and the murderer are one and the same. Now, where is he?'

'I already—'

'*Mr Appleby!*' the clerk shouted. Appleby whirled round and looked at him. 'This call is for you. From the Majestic.'

Appleby leant across the counter and took the telephone. As he did so, the illogical fear formed in Sam's mind that Shuttleworth was on the other end of the line. Sam might be about to lose his job before he had even started it. But the caller was not Shuttleworth.

'Appleby here . . . Yes, Jones, what is it? . . . What? . . . At the Crillon? . . . He did what? . . . What was he thinking of? . . . No, no. I realize you don't know. . . . I'll go straight there . . . Yes. Thank you.'

Appleby thrust the phone back at the clerk and rounded on Sam. 'Your Mr Maxted's been a busy boy,

Twentyman. Caught roughing up a member of the American delegation. What have you got to say to that?'

'I expect he deserved it, sir.'

'You do, do you? Well, let's go and find out. You're coming with me.'

THE CLAUSTROPHOBIC ATMOSPHERE IN ONE OF THE BASEMENT rooms of the Hôtel de Crillon was largely due to the number of occupants. In a space appropriate to a large store cupboard, four men were seated around a shabby desk, while two more men, dressed in US military police uniforms and built like the foothills of the Rockies, were stationed outside in the corridor, either side of the doorway itself.

Max was the one holding a bag of ice against a tender spot behind his left ear. Despite this encumbrance, he was smoking a cigarette and looking strangely at ease. The same could not be said of Sam, who was also smoking, but with transparent nervousness. The haze of their smoke had been turned to a deep fug by the effluvium of Appleby's pipe. He was on the other side of the desk from them, seated next to an intimidating slab of a man with short-cropped blond hair and piercing blue eyes. He was Frank Carver, Appleby's opposite number at the American delegation. And he alone was not smoking. Instead his prognathous jaws were champing rhythmically on a stick of gum.

'You're in a tight spot, Mr Maxted,' Carver said, with no apparent irony. 'I advise full cooperation. Unless you want us to hand you over to the French police.'

'If you decide to do that,' said Max, 'I want you to remember Sam here knew nothing about my visit to Walter Ennis. He has no share in the responsibility for what happened.'

'We'll be the judge of that,' said Appleby. 'He's your alibi for when Lamb was murdered and therefore inherently suspect.'

'I'm sorry about your man, Appleby,' said Max. 'I had no idea you were having me tailed.' That was not actually true, of course, but he and Sam had had to do some judicious editing of the facts on a nod-and-a-wink basis. 'It's not just Sam's word, though, is it? If the poor fellow had his throat cut, his murderer would have been covered in blood. I'm sure the clerk at the Mazarin would have noticed that when I called there.'

'With Lamb dead, I have no independent verification of your movements since yesterday afternoon.'

'That's hardly my fault.'

'They say Paris is a hotbed of crime with this conference going on,' Sam contributed. 'Maybe Mr Lamb just happened to be in the wrong place at the wrong time.'

'No. That's you, Mr Twentyman,' said Carver. 'Keep it in mind, won't you?'

'Are you sure you chose the right man for the job, Appleby?' Max asked provocatively. 'It seems clear Lamb was out of his depth.'

Appleby's teeth ground into the stem of his pipe as he stared at Max. 'Leave me to dwell on that question when I write to his parents.'

'I am sorry. We both are, aren't we, Sam?'

'Yes, sir.'

'The war's inured us to sudden death, I'm afraid.'

'This might go easier if you explained to Mr Maxted why you were having him tailed, Horace,' said Carver.

Max smiled faintly at Appleby. They were on treacherous ground. Carver wanted to know all that lay behind Max's fight with Ennis. But Max felt sure Appleby did not want to tell him.

'I was concerned for your safety, Mr Maxted, in view of the unexplained circumstances of your father's death and that of Raffaele Spataro,' said Appleby.

'The police have Corinne Dombreux in custody for that, don't they?' queried Carver.

'I'm not convinced by the case against her.'

Carver absorbed Appleby's reply with a twitch of one eyebrow, then looked across at Max. 'Why did you come to see Ennis, Mr Maxted?'

'I found his name on a list written by my father. I wanted to know how they were acquainted.'

'Was Travis Ireton's name also on the list?'

'Yes. It was. I asked him to arrange the meeting.'

'Good of him to oblige. I'll be seeing Mr Ireton, you can be sure of that. It's unfortunate he'd already left the hotel when we went looking for him.' Unfortunate, perhaps, Max reckoned, but entirely characteristic. 'Why did you go up to Ennis's room?'

'It was clear to me from his reaction to my questions that he was hiding something. I followed him out of the restaurant to see what he might be willing to say without Ireton sitting next to him. I saw him taking the lift up to his room and I decided to catch up with him there.'

'Where there wouldn't be any witnesses.'

'I wanted to talk to him alone. I don't deny that. I caught him making a phone call. He was demanding that whoever he was speaking to get me off his back.'

'So you say.'

'Doesn't your switchboard operator have any idea who he was calling?'

'There are calls being made and received here all the time, Mr Maxted. We installed a lot of extra lines to cope with the traffic when we moved in. No one knows who Ennis called, if he called anyone, apart from the guard-room when you started threatening him, that is.'

'Have you asked him?'

'I haven't had the chance. He slipped out after you'd been taken away. When he comes back, I'll ask him for a full account of what took place.'

'Are you sure he's coming back?'

'Why wouldn't he be?'

'Because he's running scared. I might have been able to find out *who* he's scared of if I'd had longer with him.'

'One of the other people named on your father's list, maybe.' Carver stared at Max challengingly. 'Who are they, Mr Maxted?'

'Kuroda. Ribeiro. Norris. I've spoken to them. None of them reacted the way Ennis did.'

'So, what it comes down to is that you reckon Ennis was mixed up in your father's murder.'

'Maybe.'

'Have you given me the name of everyone on that list?'

'Yes.'

'Could I see it?'

'I destroyed it.'

'Why in hell would you do that?'

'I thought it might be something it was dangerous to be found in possession of.'

'Well, that's a reasonable assumption, considering danger seems to hover round you like flies round horse shit – which I'm thinking is what you're serving up here today.'

'You don't believe me?'

'I don't believe you're telling me the whole story, Mr Maxted. Not anything close to the whole story.' Carver looked round at Appleby. 'Maybe we should have a word in private, Horace.'

'Certainly.' Appleby nodded and cast Max a fleeting glance of highly provisional approbation. There was an unspoken agreement between them to keep Lemmer's name out of this for as long as they could. Max did not seriously believe Appleby suspected him of Lamb's murder. Their alliance, such as it was, remained in place.

Carver and Appleby left the room. Silence settled in the smoke-laden air. The guards swapped places either side of the door. Max and Sam had much to discuss, but were in no position to discuss it. Max sighed and discarded the ice-bag. Water oozed out on to the desk.

'You should keep that on, sir,' said Sam. 'There's nothing like ice for a bruise.'

'Thank you, matron.'

'You know I'm right, sir.'

'God damn it.' Max snatched up the ice-bag and reapplied it to his head. 'Happy?'

'Not exactly.'

'How did the job interview go?'

'I start tomorrow. Assuming I ever get out of here.'

'You will, Sam, don't worry. Leave it to Appleby.'

Rather to Sam's surprise, Max's words proved prophetic. When Appleby and Carver returned about ten minutes later, Carver announced the questioning was at an end.

'In Ennis's absence, I propose to regard your . . . scuffle . . . as a private altercation. I'll pursue the matter with him when he returns to the hotel and I'll check your account with Ireton, so don't think you've heard the last of this, Mr Maxted. Or you, Mr Twentyman.'

'I don't see where—' Sam began. But he was cut off by Appleby.

'I'll walk the two of you out. Shall we go?'

No further word was spoken until Max, Sam and Appleby were standing out on the Place de la Concorde, some distance from the entrance to the Crillon. The men who had accompanied Appleby earlier were waiting in a car at the corner of Rue Royale. Appleby made a meal of relighting his pipe and gazed pensively in the direction of the National Assembly, on the far side of the Seine.

'I really am sorry about Lamb, Appleby,' said Max. 'Believe it or not.'

'You should be. It was your fault as much as mine.'

'I don't see how I'm to blame.'

'They killed him to demonstrate their reach and capability. And to send a message. This was left in his pocket.' Appleby pulled a piece of paper from inside his coat and handed it to Max. It was folded in half, with JAMES MAXTED written in pencilled capitals on one flap. Max unfolded it to read the message inside. LEAVE PARIS OR DIE – FINAL WARNING. 'I take it from the wording that this isn't the first such threat you've received.'

'You take it correctly.'

'Blimey,' said Sam, peering at the note over Max's shoulder.

Max passed it back to Appleby. 'Did you tell Carver about this?'

'I told Carver as little as possible. But the same doesn't apply to you and Twentyman, does it?'

'You can trust Sam.'

'You mean I have to because you do.'

'We're playing for the same team, Mr Appleby,' said Sam. He sensed it would be better to enlighten Appleby about his new job before anyone else did, so on he went. 'I work for the British delegation, just like you do. Meet your new chief mechanic.'

'You?'

'They don't come better qualified.'

Appleby frowned sceptically at Sam, then turned to Max. 'Listen to me very carefully. I may not know what you've been doing since Lamb was killed, but those who killed him probably do. And this threat' – he flapped the note in Max's face – 'isn't an idle one.'

'I'm aware of that.'

'I don't want the Americans pursuing Lemmer in their size-twelve boots. I don't want the French on his trail either. I want *you* to find him. But you don't have long to pull it off.'

'I know. That's why I tried to force the pace with Ennis.'

'You think he's one of Lemmer's spies?'

'It would explain why he cut and run.'

'If you're right, I can't keep Carver in the dark indefinitely.' Appleby forced a smile. 'It wouldn't be good for Anglo-American relations.'

'How did you persuade him to let us go?'

'I said we were more likely to get to the bottom of this with you on the loose. Which is true, of course.'

'Don't put anyone else on my tail, Appleby. It's too dangerous.'

'In the circumstances, I'm forced to agree with you.'

'I'll keep you fully informed of what I learn.'

'I doubt that. But remember, you won't be able to tackle Lemmer without help from me. It would be a fatal mistake to think you can. Do you actually have any more leads to follow?'

'A few.'

'Courtesy of Ireton?'

'He's useful.'

'He probably thinks the same of you.'

'What about Corinne? Can I visit her?'

Appleby sighed heavily. 'Yes. It wasn't easy to arrange, let me tell you. But I managed to fix it with Zamaron.'

'Thank you. When?'

Appleby consulted his watch. 'There's no time like the present.'

'Fine.' Max gave a grim little smile. 'As things stand, it's probably the only time I've got.'

Leaving Sam to get on with his move from the Mazarin to the Majestic, Max set off for Police Headquarters with Appleby. Sam's parting shot was a pained comment on the rattly note of their car engine. 'I'll have 'em all running sweeter than that by next week, I guarantee it.'

'He will too,' said Max, glancing back at Sam's receding figure on the edge of the broad pavement as they accelerated away across the Place de la Concorde.

Appleby groaned. 'If I had any sense, I'd veto his appointment. Allowing you to have an informant on the delegation's payroll is plain reckless.'

'This whole thing's reckless, Appleby. And as far as I know I'm working for you *gratis*, so it seems only fair for Sam to draw a wage.'

'Well, Twentyman's employment isn't high on my agenda, Mr Maxted, so—'

'Why don't you call me Max, like everyone else?'

'All right. Max. Did Ennis give you anything to go on?'

'Not really. But I've been thinking about the circumstances of my father's fatal fall. I mean the *exact* circumstances.'

'And?'

'Could le Singe be involved?'

'Ah. You've heard about him, have you?'

'A burglar who comes and goes by rooftops and high windows. He fits the bill, doesn't he?'

'A burglar isn't generally a murderer. They're very different lines of work.'

'Are you sure?'

'Well, if you want to learn more about le Singe . . . Max . . . ask your friend Ireton. I have reason to believe he may have used le Singe to procure secret documents for him on several occasions.'

'Really? Well, I'll certainly do that.'

Max considered what he knew of Travis Ireton as the car sped east along the Quai des Tuileries. He had supposed Ireton was on no one's side but his own. Could he have misread the man, though? Ireton had certainly contrived to obstruct Max's enquiries while claiming to want to help him. Was he covering someone's tracks – perhaps his own? Max was going to have to find out. Soon.

Zamaron was not available at Police HQ, but he had left word that Max was to be allowed to visit Corinne Dombreux. His permission came with a condition attached, though – one Appleby had chosen not to mention until now.

'You can't see her on your own, Max. I have to be there as well. Apparently, Léon doesn't trust you not to engage in some form of criminal conspiracy with Madame Dombreux.'

'Are you sure this isn't your condition, Appleby? It gives you a chance to question her.'

'That's true. But, no, it was Léon's idea.'

'Or so you let him think.'

'You're getting very suspicious, aren't you?'

'I need to be suspicious.'

'Well, I won't disagree with you there.'

The room they were taken to was a small, bare chamber buried in the dank basement of the building. Chairs were arranged either side of a table nearly as wide as the room: two on one side, one on the other, closer to the door. They took the two and waited.

A few minutes slowly elapsed, then Corinne arrived, escorted by a grim-faced policewoman. Corinne was wearing a shapeless grey dress. She looked pale and anxious. The smile she gave Max was a fragile shaft of hope. He rose to greet her and the policewoman barked out, *'Ne pas toucher'*. Meekly, he sat down again.

'I'm so sorry about all of this, Corinne,' he said, looking directly at her.

'Commissioner Zamaron insisted I be here, *madame*,' said Appleby.

Corinne glanced at Appleby, then sat down in the chair facing them. She gazed soulfully at Max across the table. 'I'm glad you came, Max,' she said softly. 'But you should forget me and leave Paris. I'm beyond your help.'

'I don't accept that. And I'm going nowhere until you're free.'

'Have you been mistreated, *madame*?' Appleby asked.

She shook her head. 'Not in the sense you mean.'

'I'm getting closer to the truth all the time, Corinne,' said Max. 'If I'm successful, they'll have to release you.'

'Have charges been mentioned to you?' asked Appleby.

'No.'

'Have you seen a lawyer?'

'No.'

'Have you asked to see one?'

Corinne looked at him witheringly. 'It's been made very clear to me that under wartime regulations I have no rights, Mr Appleby. I assume *le Deuxième Bureau* are pulling the strings.'

'I think that's a sound assumption, *madame*. Your marriage to a known traitor—'

'Was he a traitor, Corinne?' Max cut in. 'Do you really believe Pierre betrayed his country?'

'It's what they told me. I'm not sure what to believe about where Pierre's loyalties truly lay.'

'For what it's worth, *madame*,' said Appleby, 'I don't think you killed Raffaele Spataro.'

'But your influence on *le Deuxième Bureau* or the Ministry of Justice is . . . what?'

'Negligible, I'm afraid.'

'Then I will remain here until they decide to charge and try me. And then . . .'

'It won't come to that,' said Max. 'I won't let it.'

'If you cause them enough trouble, Max, they'll deal with you much as they've dealt with me.'

'Commissioner Zamaron is a conscientious police officer,' said Appleby. 'He won't ignore hard evidence that serves to exonerate you.'

'But there isn't any, is there?' Strangely, Corinne seemed harder-headed than her visitors. 'Motive, means and opportunity. I believe they're what the police look

for in these matters. And I appear to have had all three.'
She looked at Max. 'You've been to the apartment?'

'Yes.'

'You saw his paintings?'

'I did.'

'Of course you did.' She looked away then. 'I'm sorry
I posed for him. If I'd known . . .'

'You have nothing to apologize for.'

'Henry really would be proud of you, you know.' Tears
glistened in her eyes. She wiped them away with the
sleeve of her dress.

Max longed to reach out and comfort her. A guilty
memory came into his mind then of his night with
Nadia Bukayeva. The guilt was multi-layered, for there
had been a moment when he had begun to call Nadia
Corinne. He had stifled the word and Nadia had been
too absorbed in her own pleasure to notice. But he
knew. He knew and he could not forget.

'Don't take any risks on my account, Max. Please. I'm
not worth it.'

'Did Pierre – or my father – ever mention a man
called Fritz Lemmer?'

'No. Who is he?'

'F.L., Corinne. The initials on the list.'

'I know about the list, *madame*,' said Appleby.

Corinne registered mild surprise at that, but did
not dwell on it. 'I've never heard the name before,'
she declared. 'Is he . . . responsible for Henry's
death?'

'He may be. But—'

'*Fini*,' the policewoman interrupted, gesturing at a
watch she had pulled out of her tunic.

'No one told me there was a time limit,' Max protested. 'Appleby?'

Appleby shrugged. 'Rules and regulations. There's nothing I can do.'

'He's right, Max,' said Corinne. 'There's nothing you can do either. Please—'

'*Le temps est épuisé*,' the policewoman announced, advancing to Corinne's shoulder.

Corinne stood up, holding Max's gaze. 'The only thing that could make this worse is if I hear you've come to harm, Max. If you won't agree to leave Paris—'

'*Allons-y*,' snapped the policewoman, leading her away by the arm.

She did not resist.

'I'll be careful,' Max called after her. But he did not intend to be careful. He never had been. And he knew he could not help Corinne by changing now.

Max could find nothing to say to Appleby after Corinne had gone. And Appleby had the decency to let him stay silent as they made their way upstairs and out into the courtyard where the car was waiting.

'I'll walk from here,' Max announced.

Appleby looked unsurprised. 'Apart from giving Madame Dombreux something to worry about – your safety – what do you reckon that visit accomplished, Max?'

'I don't judge everything I do by what it accomplishes, Appleby. Sometimes I just . . . do.'

'And what are you going to *do* next?'

'Keep pushing. Until I can see who's pushing back.'

MAX PURGED SOME OF HIS ANGER AND FRUSTRATION BY walking so fast other pedestrians on the darkening streets made way for him with alarmed looks on their faces. He suspected his expression told its own story. The time had come to demand of Travis Ireton some direct answers to some direct questions.

But at 33 Rue des Pyramides Malory Hollander had bad news for him. 'Travis said you might call by, Max,' she said, treating him to her knowing smile. 'I'm afraid he's had to leave town.'

'*What?*'

'An influential personage is arriving from New York to join the American delegation. Travis is anxious to meet him when his ship docks at Brest tomorrow morning. His train should have left' – she adjusted her glasses to study the clock – 'about forty minutes ago.'

Max shook his head morosely. 'Damn the fellow.'

'I'm sorry. It was a last-minute decision.'

'Oh, I'm sure it was.'

'Settle for a word with me, Max?' came Morahan's voice, floating into the room from the open doorway. 'We can help ourselves to some of Travis's Scotch and stoke up his fire, provided Malory swears not to split on us.'

'And I do so swear,' said Malory. 'Provided I get a nip of the Scotch too.'

Morahan delivered a small glass of the strong stuff to Malory, then ushered Max into Ireton's office, where he closed the door and poured distinctly larger measures for the two of them. Then he tonged a few knobs of coal on to the fire and pokered it back into life.

'Travis told me what happened at the Crillon,' he said, leaning back in Ireton's chair with his long legs stretched out before him. 'I guess it looks to you like he's made himself scarce to dodge having to answer any of your questions.'

'Well, hasn't he?'

'It's not just you. Carver's been here as well. You met him, right?'

'Oh, yes.'

'Travis reckons Ennis is your man, based on his behaviour when you challenged him – and his subsequent bolt. But the scene you made risks Travis's contacts with all levels of the American delegation getting more attention than he'd welcome right now. So, he thought it best to take himself out of the picture for a while.'

'Has he really gone to Brest?'

'I doubt it, since that's where he has Malory telling everyone he's gone. Deauville, maybe? Or Monte Carlo? He likes to keep his hand in at the baccarat table.'

'I need to find out as much about Walter Ennis as I can as quickly as possible, Schools. Whether he's one of Lemmer's spies or not, he's certainly up to no good.'

'I don't doubt you're right about that.'

'And Travis knows him well, doesn't he?'

Morahan nodded. 'Better than most. They go back a long way.'

'And now they've both gone to ground. What do you make of that?'

'Not what I get the feeling *you* make of it. Travis isn't in cahoots with Walter Ennis, Max. He just doesn't want Carver prying into his business and reckons being unavailable for a grilling is the best way to prevent that. He calculates Carver will lose interest in him as soon as he tracks Ennis down.'

'Maybe so. But that doesn't help me.'

'No. And I'm sorry for that. But if Ennis was responsible for your father's murder, Carver will be better placed than you to extract a confession from him.'

'So, you suggest I just sit back and wait for Ennis to be apprehended and Travis to return to Paris?'

'It might be the safest thing to do.'

'But you're assuming he will be apprehended and that he really was responsible for my father's murder. I can't afford to assume anything, Schools. That's the other thing I want to discuss with Travis, you see: who the third person was he spoke to on my father's behalf.'

Morahan drained his glass and lit a cigarette, frowning thoughtfully as he did so. 'Travis said I was to tell you he's convinced, based on what happened at the Crillon, that Ennis is the man you're looking for. That being so, he sees no merit in naming the third person he approached.'

Max sprang to his feet to expend some of his irritation. He leant on the mantelpiece, swore heartily and took a kick at the fender, dislodging a coal into the grate, where it blazed and sputtered.

Morahan rose slowly from his chair, grasped the tongs and returned the coal to the fire. He stood where he was then, one foot on the edge of the grate, and aimed his level gaze at Max. 'What do you want to know, Max?' he asked quietly.

'The name of the third person Travis spoke to.'

'I can't give you that.'

'More than your job's worth, is it?'

'Travis doesn't employ me, Max. I work *with* him, not *for* him. I think I explained that to you before.'

'With or for, it still means you keep his secrets.'

'If I promise to stay silent about something, I stay silent. As it happens, I genuinely don't have the name to give you. You have my word on that, which I hope you'll accept.'

Morahan's earnestness brooked no challenge. Max was forced to acknowledge as much. He took a deep breath. 'All right, Schools. I believe you.'

'Good.'

'Do you have any idea who he might be?'

'No. But I can tell you this. Travis said he thought Carver would be able to identify him eventually if he sought help from Appleby.'

'Appleby?'

'The implication's clear, isn't it? The man you're looking for must be a member of the British delegation.'

FATIGUE AND FURY MADE FOR STRANGE COMPANIONS. MAX left 33 Rue des Pyramides as wearied by the events of the day as he was enraged by them. At every turn he was blocked, delayed or deflected. He trusted what Kuroda and Morahan had told him. For the rest there was only a torrent of doubt. Ennis's escape and Ireton's departure stood as rebukes to his foresight. And then there were the messages from whoever had commissioned his father's murder. *Leave Paris. Final warning.* He would not allow himself to be intimidated. He would not flee the city. But, if he stayed, what could he actually accomplish?

Max's intention was to speak to Appleby as soon as possible. The phone call Ennis had made from his room at the Crillon proved he was part of a conspiracy of some kind. The member of the British delegation Ireton had contacted might also be part of it. In Ennis's absence, his was the more promising trail to follow. And Appleby was the man to guide Max along it, preferably before he did the same for Carver.

But Max was flying on little more than fumes. He needed a hot bath and a good meal. The water at the Mazarin was seldom more than lukewarm and the food indifferent, but they would have to suffice. He found a taxi in the Place Vendôme and asked to be taken straight there.

'There's a gentleman waiting for you in the writing-room, *monsieur*,' the clerk announced as he handed Max his key.

'Who is he?'

'I regret, *monsieur*, he did not give his name. He is English and known to you, he said. That is all I can tell you.'

Max was in no mood to be trifled with. He strode into the writing-room with no clear expectations of who might be waiting for him. But at the sight of his visitor he pulled up sharp.

Lionel Brigham. Of all the people Max would have preferred not to meet again, this handsome, cocksure, smooth-mannered roué was surely the one he wanted most of all to avoid. An irksomely frequent guest at Gresscombe Place during Max's youth, Brigham had been too close to Lady Maxted for too long to ignore. There was no doubt in Max's mind that they had been lovers. And he believed there was cause to suspect Brigham might actually be his father. It was a possibility he had spoken of to no one. It was a possibility, indeed, that he had done his level best to put out of his mind, though it was undeniable that it had tainted his relationship with his mother. Unvoiced resentments were ultimately, he had discovered, the most poisonous kind.

'James,' said Brigham, rising a touch stiffly to his feet and extending a hand. 'It's good to see you.'

'Brigham.' Max accepted the handshake coolly. 'What brings you here?'

'To Paris, you mean? Or to your hotel? As to the former, I'm here with the delegation.'

God rot the man, thought Max, cursing himself for his failure to anticipate that Brigham might be in Paris. He could always be relied upon to insinuate himself into a gathering of the great and the good, even though he was neither. 'I suppose I thought you'd retired,' Max said, with a hint of disparagement.

'No such luck.'

'And what are you doing for the delegation?'

'Oh, nothing very interesting.'

'To what do I owe this visit, then?'

'I wanted to offer you my condolences on Henry's death. Such a terrible thing.'

'Indeed.'

'I was surprised not to see you at the funeral.'

God rot the man twice over, thought Max. Why could he not just leave the Maxted family alone? 'I was detained here.'

'So I gather.'

'And I'm really rather busy, so—'

'We need to talk, James, you and I.'

There was a faintly menacing twinkle in Brigham's blue-grey eyes. Max ignored it as best he could. 'We do?'

'A confidential talk. I drove myself here. Would it be asking too much for you to step out to my car? I won't keep you long.'

The car was a sleek black Daimler, parked just round the corner from the Mazarin. Brigham proposed they drive down to the Seine. 'It'll be quiet by the river,' he said.

He filled the brief journey with an account of the funeral he had attended but Max had not. Irony, and something more sinister, clung to his words.

Max remembered a day he had tried hard to forget, when he had returned home from Eton one hot Saturday afternoon in the summer of 1907. The house had been filled with silence, the staff nowhere to be found. He had called a general hello in the hall. There had been no immediate response. Then Brigham had appeared at the head of the stairs, looking less well-groomed than usual, and had come down to greet him. 'Your mother's resting,' he had said. And that was all he had said. She had joined them on the terrace a short time later, her normal imperturbability mysteriously mislaid. 'You should have told us when you'd be arriving, James.' Yes. He should have. He really should. And he only wished he had.

A later remark of his father's had alerted Max to the most disturbing of all possibilities. Sir Henry had been reminiscing about life in Japan. 'Your mother found her first Japanese summer a great trial,' he had said. 'I took pity and sent her to spend the second with friends in Kashmir.' The remark had ticked away in Max's mind like a time-bomb. It only required simple arithmetic to calculate that a child born in the spring of 1891, as he was, must have been conceived in the summer of 1890 – the summer of his mother's sojourn in Kashmir.

Brigham drove to the river bank beyond the Palais du Trocadéro and stopped near the Pont d'Iéna. The Eiffel

Tower stretched up into the night sky on the opposite bank. He snapped open a cigarette-case and offered Max a smoke. Max pointedly expressed a preference for his own brand. Brigham declined the chance to take offence and they both lit up.

'Damnably cold for the time of year,' said Brigham, coughing over his first draw.

'Perhaps you're going down with flu,' said Max. 'There's a lot of it about.'

'Yes. It carried off poor old Sykes. But I don't think it'll get me. You needn't worry.'

'I shan't.'

'It's actually yourself you should worry about. I've heard what you've been up to, James. You're playing with fire.'

'Where have you heard what I've been . . . "up to"?'

'There's more gossip circulating in this city than French francs. I asked around. And learnt you too are asking around. You should let Henry rest in peace. That's the sincere advice of someone who wishes you to come to no harm.'

'Meaning you?'

'Your mother would never forgive me if I let you stray into trouble for lack of a word to the wise.'

'Did she ask you to deliver this word?'

'No, no. Though only because, I sensed when I met her, that she feared you'd ignore any pleas emanating from her.'

'And you think I'm likelier to heed a warning from you?'

'I'm concerned for your welfare, James. I always have been. You're out of your depth here. I very strongly urge you to—'

'Give it up?'

'Yes. Exactly. Give it up.'

'At whose hands do you think I might come to harm, Brigham?'

'Oh, I couldn't say. Specifically. It's just that I know you're mixed up with Appleby. And he's Secret Service. That's dirty and dangerous work. I expect he has you running all manner of risks on his account. If you got yourself killed, he could disown you just like that. As he undoubtedly would.'

Max paused long enough to encourage Brigham to believe he might be about to give ground, then said, 'Pardon me for asking, but why should that matter to you?'

'As I told you, I—'

'We're nothing to each other as far as I'm aware. You're a sometime friend of my mother's, that's all. I neither need nor desire you to be concerned about me.'

'But I am. And there it is.' Brigham looked round at Max. 'I think you know why.'

'I'd be interested in knowing why you're so anxious for me to leave Paris.'

'Because it's a hazardous place to be asking the kind of questions you're asking. Henry should never have allowed himself to become involved with Corinne Dombreux. He was courting disaster and he duly met with it. I don't want to see you make the same mistake.'

'You don't think his death was an accident, then?'

'I think it's best to say it was. For everyone's sake. Especially yours.'

'When did you last meet my father, Brigham?'

'Some weeks ago. I bumped into him at the Quai d'Orsay. I'd probably have seen him more often if I'd been staying at the Majestic, but the place is such a madhouse I've found an apartment to rent near by. We were both on our way to meetings. There was no time for more than the briefest of words. I regret that now, of course.'

'Of course.'

'I gather there was an . . . incident . . . at the Crillon earlier today. Walter Ennis has gone missing.'

'Are you acquainted with him?'

'Slightly, yes. Just as I'm acquainted with scores of members of other delegations. I'm on more committees than I can count.'

'What about Travis Ireton? Are you acquainted with him?'

'Ireton?' Brigham made a show of deliberating on the point. 'No, I don't think so. I've heard the name, but . . . I can't say we've ever met.'

'He didn't approach you a couple of weeks ago asking if you'd be interested in buying some information from him?'

'Information about what?'

'If he approached you, you'd know.'

'Quite. But he didn't.'

'Ennis is a friend of his.'

'Really?'

'Perhaps Ennis approached you. On the same subject.'

'No. He didn't.'

'If that's so . . .'

'It is, I assure you.'

'Then I'm curious. You seem to have some insight into what led to my father's murder. How did you gain

309

that, if not from him or Ennis or Ireton? Did someone else put you in the picture?'

Brigham meticulously stubbed out his cigarette and lit another. He peered through the windscreen at the caped figures of two policemen on bicycles who rode slowly round the car and turned on to the bridge. Max found himself watching them as well. One of the policemen glanced back at the car as they took the turn. 'Since that mad anarchist took a pot-shot at Clemenceau, the French have been nervous as kittens that there'll be some fearful outrage to sully their management of the conference. They're suspicious of everything. I shouldn't really be here, talking to you. It could be hard to explain, if I was called upon to do so.'

'It was your idea.'

'So it was.'

'What's the answer to my question?'

'No one put me in the picture, James. I merely made judicious enquiries. Good God, I've been in this game for nearly forty years. I know how to find things out. It requires tact, caution and connections developed and nurtured over decades. You're clearly deficient in every one of those departments. That's why you're in such danger. You're brave and determined, which is admirable. But it's not enough. In your situation, it may even be a disadvantage. Do you sail?'

'What?'

'I have a share in a villa near Cannes. I keep a boat down there, scandalously underused. A local man looks after it for me. You could go and stay in the villa, if you like. Take the boat out. Enjoy a Provençal spring. Relax. Pamper yourself. My friends would be delighted to meet you. I might even join you there, if this conference ever ends.'

Max hardly knew what to say. The man's nerve was quite something. 'I'm not going to Cannes, Brigham. Or anywhere else. I'm staying here until I find my father's killer.'

'Or until he finds you?'

'The cards must fall where they will.'

'What a fatalistic young man you are.'

'It's what I'm resolved to do.'

'As an act of filial piety?'

'If you like.'

'The statement does you credit. But it's misplaced piety, as I think you're aware. It would seem perverse in the extreme to lose your life seeking to avenge a father who isn't actually—'

'*Don't say another word.*' The force of Max's interjection succeeded in silencing Brigham. Max turned to face him, though he could see little of his expression in the dim light that reached them from the nearest street lamp. 'I promise you this, Brigham: if I learn you were responsible in any way for my father's murder, however indirectly—'

'That's preposterous. I had nothing to with Henry's death.'

'*If* I learn that, I'll kill you. Do you understand?'

'What? You can't—'

'Be serious? Oh, but I'm being deadly serious. I want you to know that. It's not an idle threat. I can't be bought off or adopted as some kind of pet. I mean to finish what I've started. I mean to punish those who brought my father down. If you're one of them, I advise you now: do your worst before I do mine.'

'James, you've completely—'

'I'll bid you goodnight, Brigham. I'll walk back to the hotel, thanks. I need some fresh air.'

With that, Max yanked the door open and hopped out of the car. He slammed the door violently behind him and strode away across the street without a backward glance. If Brigham was his enemy, he was glad of it. Proof, one way or the other, was all he needed. Proof. And then he would act.

MAX DID NOT WALK BACK TO HIS HOTEL, AS HE HAD TOLD Brigham he would. He headed for Little Russia. The explanation he advanced to himself was that he needed to confirm Nadia was safe and well. She might have news of her uncle, or of something else that would aid his search for the truth. But he would not spend the night with her. His encounter with Brigham had left him emotionally ragged. That the fellow might be his father was a sickening possibility he had long done his level best to disregard. He wanted nothing of Brigham's. He could not, would not, acknowledge any tie, least of all of blood.

The bookshop was in darkness, but a light was burning in the room above. Max rang the bell and stepped back to let Nadia see him from the window. A lace curtain twitched, though she did not show herself. But, a few moments later, he heard a movement in the shop. And then the door opened.

She looked pale and anxious. 'Max,' she said, smiling as if it was an effort to do so.

'May I come in?'

'Ah, no.' She lowered her voice. 'A friend of my uncle and his wife are here. It is . . .'

'Awkward?'

'They will ask you many questions, Max. And they are not . . . discreet people. It is better, I think, if you do not come in.'

'I understand. Is all well?'

'Nothing has changed. I wait to hear. But I hear nothing.'

'I'm sorry. If there's anything I can do . . .'

Her voice dropped to a whisper. 'Come again soon. Last night . . .' She looked deep into his eyes. 'I need you.'

'You know where to find me. I'll say goodnight.'

'*Spokoynoy nochi*, Max.' She blew him a kiss and slowly closed the door.

Max took a long detour on his way back to the Mazarin, walking himself into a state of exhaustion on the cold and empty streets of the night-time city. It was the only way he could be sure of sleeping, with so many doubts and questions swirling in his mind.

In Sir Henry Maxted's old room at the Majestic, Sam was already sound asleep. Insomnia had always been a mystery to him, a good night's rest no more complicated than a bed to climb into. It did not even have to be a particularly comfortable bed, though this one was certainly that.

He had not been surprised to hear nothing from Max that evening, concerned though he was about him. No news was in a sense good news. He did not doubt Max would be in touch when he could. The war had only served to reinforce Sam's innate pragmatism. What would be would be.

By the same token, he did not dream much, generally waking with no memory of how his sleeping mind had occupied itself. But that was not to be the case when he came to himself on Saturday morning, with a shaft of grey morning light falling across the coverlet.

He had dreamt of le Singe, or his subconscious version of le Singe: a small, spry, dark-skinned boy dressed in ragged army fatigues, standing before him, on tiptoe it seemed, ready to dodge or spring, and pointing at him with one steady forefinger, smiling as he did so, his teeth a yellow crescent across the umber of his round, simian face. There was something white in his other hand: a stick of chalk, perhaps. The sight fleetingly transformed him into one of the teachers at Sam's old school in Walthamstow. Then there was a blur of motion. Le Singe was a crouching figure in a window. And then he was gone.

Sam sat up and rubbed his face. The dream stayed with him, refusing to leave his mind. He looked at his alarm clock. There was still half an hour to go before the time he had set the alarm for and he wondered what had roused him. The chill air, perhaps. It was desperately cold in the room.

He glanced across at the window and saw that it was open. The stay was hanging free, though he felt sure he had secured it the night before. It had not fitted properly, though. It might have worked itself loose. He lumbered over and closed it, shivering in the chill. As he did so, he noticed a mark on the sill outside: a white cross. Had it been there before? He could not say for sure. He reopened the window and rubbed the cross with his finger. He was left with a smear of chalk on his skin.

Then he turned and started with astonishment. On the wall above the bed, while he had lain asleep, someone had chalked a message.

At the Mazarin, Max was woken by a telephone call from the lobby. Sam was downstairs, sounding breathless and perturbed. Could he come up? Max, his thoughts still fuddled by sleep, slurred out his consent and struggled into his dressing-gown.

He had hardly done so when Sam was knocking at the door. 'What the devil's the matter?' Max demanded as he let him in. 'And what time is it?'

'Bacon-and-egg time, sir, but there's something I have to tell you before you tuck into breakfast. Take a look at this. I copied it down off the wall of my room at the Majestic. Your father's old room, as it happens.'

'My father's room? What are you—' He broke off as Sam handed him a piece of paper and read the message written on it.

TELL HIS SON I NOT KNOW WE KILL HIM
AND GIVE HIM THIS – HX 4344

Max reread the message when Sam had finished recounting the events of the night. It seemed clear le Singe had paid him a visit. It was no dream. The chalked words on the wall and the open window proved that.

'He must be double- or triple-jointed, sir. You'd need to be able to swing from pipes and railings like a monkey from creepers in the jungle to get to the window of that room. And I reckon he's been before. That cross on the sill is his mark. It was the first night since Sir Henry's death that there was a light in the room. His first chance, as he saw it, to send you this message.'

'He seems to want to tell me he didn't know murder was part of the deal. Fine. It's his boss I'm after, anyway. But if le Singe has a conscience, it could mean he'll give us some more help. If we can only make contact with him.'

'That's what I was thinking.'

'What did you do with the writing on the wall?'

'I rubbed it out sharpish, sir. We don't want anyone else to get the benefit of it, do we?'

'No, we don't. Good work, Sam. Now, these letters and numbers. What are they supposed to mean?'

'Looks like a car registration number to me, sir. HX is the code for central London.'

'It is?'

'I thought everyone knew that.'

''Fraid not, Sam. It's an inexplicable gap in my education.'

'I checked the cars in the garage before I left. They were all brought over from London and most have HX in front of the number. But 4344 ain't among 'em.'

'And what would it mean if it were, eh?'

'I was hoping you might have some idea, sir.'

'Maybe I do.' Max tapped his front teeth thoughtfully. 'Brigham's rented an apartment, so he's not staying at the Majestic. His car wouldn't be in the hotel garage.'

'Who's Brigham, sir?'

'A senior member of the British delegation. And a nasty piece of work to boot. Our man, quite possibly. He took me for a drive last night and advised me to leave Paris in the interests of my health.'

'What was he driving, sir?'

'A Daimler. His own, I suspect.'

'Get the registration number, did you?'

Max gave Sam a pained smile. 'Incredibly, it never occurred to me.'

'Sorry, sir.'

'But it doesn't matter. Appleby can tell me where Brigham's staying. It shouldn't be difficult to find out if he's driving HX 4344. I'll go and see Appleby straight after breakfast. Do you want to join me for a bite here?'

'Kind of you, sir, but I'd better hotfoot it back to the Majestic. I have to put the mechanics through their paces this morning.'

'All right. You go. Thanks for bringing this to me so promptly, Sam.'

'Don't mention it, sir. About le Singe . . .'

'Yes?'

'He's a weird one and no mistake. I really thought I was dreaming when I saw him. And it was like he knew I'd think that. He wasn't worried a bit. He seemed . . . calm. Calm as a pail o' milk.'

'Would you know him again?'

'Oh, yes. He's a breed all to himself.'

'Maybe he'll call again.'

'If he does, I'll be ready for him.'

'Take care.'

'I will. You too, sir.'

Max grinned. 'Don't I always?'

After Sam had gone, Max bathed and shaved hurriedly, then went down to breakfast. He was halfway through a bowl of porridge and a silent rehearsal of what he was going to tell Appleby – he had already half-convinced himself Brigham's Daimler would turn out to be HX 4344 – when a clerk materialized at his elbow.

'Telephone call for you, Monsieur Maxted. A Senhor Ribeiro. Will you speak to him? He says the matter is urgent.'

Max swallowed his spoonful of porridge and stood up. 'Take me to the phone.'

'Baltazar?'

'Yes, Max. It is I. Baltazar Ribeiro. I am sorry to be calling you so early.'

'Never mind. I'm an early riser.'

'I rise early also. I sleep badly, probably because I do not take enough exercise.'

'I'm sorry to hear that. But—'

'I generally take a little walk as soon as it is light. To give me an appetite for breakfast.'

Max's lunch with Ribeiro had not left him with the impression that the Brazilian's appetite was ever likely to be deficient, but he did not dwell on the point. 'Really? Well, I—'

'As soon as I left the hotel he appeared in front of me. He must have been waiting for me. Perhaps I mentioned to him my habit of an early walk.'

'Who was waiting for you?'

'Walter Ennis. Of the American delegation.'

'*Ennis?*'

'Yes. It was him. We know each other from the confiscated-shipping committee. But that is of no importance. You know him also, I think.'

'Yes. We met yesterday.'

'He would not say what happened between you. But something bad, I assume. He looked worried and . . . not himself. He had not shaved. His clothes were creased.'

'What did he want?'

'Someone he could trust – and you could trust also – to pass a message to you from him.'

'What was the message, Baltazar?'

'He wants to meet you. This morning. He said he wants to tell you the truth. Before it is too late. His words, Max. *Before it is too late.*'

'I'll meet him. Where and when?'

'Notre-Dame, ten o'clock. Sit in the nave and wait. Go alone. If you are not alone, he will not show himself.'

'He doesn't need to worry about that. I'll be alone.'

'Max, I—'

'It's all right, Baltazar. There's nothing for you to be concerned about. There's no danger, I assure you. We'll just talk. That's all.'

'But—'

'Thanks so much for letting me know. Goodbye.' Max put the telephone down and glanced at the clock on the wall behind the reception desk, then strode towards the stairs.

Appleby was out of the office when Max called in at the Majestic. Cursing his luck and unable to spare the time to wait, Max headed for Etoile Métro station and his appointment at Notre-Dame.

When he crossed the bridge to the Ile de la Cité that cold, grey, sleety morning, he looked ahead at the white-flecked flank of the Préfecture de Police and wondered what sort of night Corinne had passed in her cell. He feared she did not believe he could accomplish anything on her behalf. But he was going to. One chink in his enemy's armour was all he needed. And Walter Ennis might be it.

Indigent ex-servicemen and assorted beggars were thick on the ground outside Notre-Dame, hoping for a coin or two from worshippers going in or out. Max ignored them, knowing that if he gave to one he would be expected to give to all. They looked at him with their gaunt, weary faces and he felt sorry for them. But he could not take their woes on to his shoulders. He hardened his heart and pressed on.

*

The interior of the cathedral was bone-numbingly chill. Max's breath frosted in the still air. The light was thin and sallow, the windows all plain glass, the stained glass having been removed for safe-keeping during the war. A few people were lighting candles, a few others praying quietly. The vast nave was filled with echoes of shuffling feet and whispering voices.

Max settled in a pew about halfway along the nave and waited. He glanced up at the high, vaulted ceiling and ahead towards the distant altar. It was possible to believe, in such a setting, that all human concerns were petty and insignificant. But Max instinctively rejected the notion. The war had not led him to reject God. But nor had God come to his aid, as far as he was aware. Flying a fragile plane into combat above the battlefields of Flanders had made him trust his own judgement and no one else's, not even the Almighty's.

Minutes ticked slowly by. Max looked at his watch. Ennis was late, assuming, of course, he had any intention of showing up at all. A cigarette would have been a welcome distraction, but he could hardly smoke in a cathedral. Max picked up the prayer-book from the shelf in front of him, then put it down again.

'You came, then.' Ennis's voice was suddenly close to Max's ear. Half-turning, he saw the American's bulky figure in the pew behind him. *'Don't look round.'* Ennis leant forward, as if to pray, resting his elbows on the back of Max's pew. 'Do you think we're safe here, Max?' he whispered. 'Do you think the people we're dealing with recognize the concept of sanctuary?'

'You tell me, Walter,' Max whispered back. 'You know them better than I do.'

'I wish to God I didn't.'

'You could have refused to take Lemmer's money, I imagine.'

'If only it had been so simple. Lemmer doesn't generally resort to anything as crude as bribery.'

'Call it what you like. You've betrayed your country.'

Ennis sighed heavily. 'That I have.'

'And you betrayed my father as well.'

'No. I swear to God I didn't. I suspected Henry was Travis's client, true enough, but I didn't tell Lemmer that.'

'What did you tell him?'

'As little as I needed to. I warned him Travis was trying to sell information concerning his whereabouts. I had to. If he'd learnt I knew that and *not* warned him . . .'

'Your neck would be on the line? Well, it's there now anyway, isn't it? You're a wanted man, Walter. That's where your treachery's got you.'

'You think I don't know that? You think I don't regret every single damn thing I've ever done for Fritz Lemmer?'

'I don't know. Maybe you do. Maybe you don't. But you did those things. And as far as I can see no one forced you to.'

'You've no idea what you're talking about. Once Lemmer has you, he has you for keeps. You can't refuse to do what he tells you to do. That's suicide.'

'You won't tell me where he's hiding, then?'

'I don't *know* where he's hiding. He wouldn't trust me anywhere near as far as that. I don't think you understand what it's like to be one of his creatures. I've only met him once, in Berlin, before the war. He operates through intermediaries. I don't even know how many intermediaries there are between him and me.'

'We can start with the one you were speaking to on the telephone from your room at the Crillon.'

'We'll *start* with what I want you to do for me. I'm risking my life just by being here.'

'Why should I do anything for you, Walter?'

'Because you want to nail the people who killed your father and I can help you do that. But I need guarantees of my safety. It's a question of trust, Max. Or the lack of it. I've no way of knowing who's one of Lemmer's men and who isn't.'

'*I'm* not one of his men.'

'Exactly. What about Appleby?'

'Nor is he.'

'Are you sure?'

'Of course I'm sure. The idea's absurd.'

'It's not so absurd. But I think you're right. Appleby's on the level. He's one of very few I feel sure about. So, let's talk to him. I'll give you the names of the people who may have killed Henry, in return for safe passage out of Europe and a new identity to go with it. Think you can arrange that?'

If feather-bedding Ennis was what it took to find Lemmer, Max was confident Appleby would agree to it. 'Yes, I think I can.'

'Nothing less will do.'

'Then nothing less will be supplied.'

'It needs to happen soon. Every day I stay in Paris is one too many.'

'Come with me now. Why delay? You don't have to tell Appleby anything if he rejects your terms.'

'You obviously have no idea how his outfit operates. You get his agreement and meet me back here in four hours. That should give you enough time. Then I'll tell you how we're going to manage things. OK?'

'OK.'

'I'm leaving now. Stay here for five minutes before you leave yourself. Understood?'

'Understood.'

'I'll see you later.'

Max nodded a final acknowledgement. The pew-back sprang slightly as Ennis pushed himself upright. Then he was gone in a tattoo of heavy, hurrying footsteps.

Max had no intention of staying where he was for the five minutes Ennis had stipulated. He risked a backward glance after less than one and saw Ennis hurrying out through the door Max had entered by. It was his cue to stand up and go after him.

He was most of the way to the door when it was opened by someone else who was leaving. At that moment, there was a sharp crack of noise from outside, a burst of flapping wings as disturbed pigeons took flight, then a cry of alarm. Max knew at once the noise had been a rifle report. He started running.

The old man who had opened the door was frozen to the spot, staring straight ahead. Max brushed past him and rushed out into the daylight.

The beggars and passers-by had scattered. A figure lay motionless about twenty yards ahead of him on the flagstoned square in front of the cathedral. It was Ennis. He was sprawled on his back and a pool of blood was spreading beneath his head. As Max ran forward, he saw that one side of his skull had been completely blasted away. He was dead. But where was his killer?

Max reached the body and stopped. He looked down at the gaping wound. It was a livid hole gouged in Ennis's brain: an instantaneously fatal, expertly aimed shot. Where had it been fired from? From beyond the square, certainly, but where was the vantage point? The only elevated position in that direction was the Préfecture de Police. Max glanced towards it.

The multi-windowed frontage of the building met his gaze. He ran his eye up and across it. Then a movement up on the roof seized his attention. A figure was lying half in and half out of an open dormer window on the mansard level, with his rifle supported by a stand on the narrow parapet in front of him.

It was only in that instant that Max realized the peril he was in. He lunged to his left even as he heard the crack and whine of the second shot. The bullet struck the flagstone where he had just been standing. But now he was running, hard and fast, towards the trees bordering the Seine.

He felt the shot hit him before he heard it, a jolting impact in his left side. There was no immediate pain and the certainty that another shot would follow carried him in a burst of energy to the shelter of the plinth supporting Charlemagne's statue, halfway to the riverside wall.

The shot came, as he had anticipated, ripping through the air beyond the statue. He was safe where he was, but for how long? If the gunman came after him, or had an accomplice, he was finished. And he did not know how serious his wound was. There was a sensation of heat now where the bullet had hit him.

He could feel blood seeping out beneath his shirt.

Then he saw the barge chugging upriver and knew it was his only chance to escape the gunman's arc of fire. He broke cover and ran towards the bridge connecting the island with the Left Bank.

The barge was passing slowly beneath the bridge as he reached the railings, its cargo covered with a tarpaulin. A bullet pinged off the railings as he clambered over them, then he was plunging towards the barge, wondering, almost neutrally, if he would make it to the vessel or fall wide and find himself in the river.

He supposed, as far as he was able, that it did not really matter much.

MAX WAS NOT DESTINED TO ESCAPE THE ILE DE LA CITÉ AFTER all. When he next became aware of his surroundings, it was early evening and he was in bed in a river-facing room of the Hôtel Dieu, the hospital that flanked the very square where Ennis had been murdered and he had narrowly avoided the same fate.

A nurse fetched a doctor, who, in stuttering English, informed him that he had knocked himself out jumping on to the barge, but the bullet that had struck him earlier had considerably steered clear of any vital organs in its passage through his body. 'You are young and 'ealthy, *monsieur*. If there is infection, you should be able to fight it. The bullet went close to, ah, your spleen, which concerns me. But . . . we will see . . . *non?*'

Max felt too weak to seek clarification. There was a policeman guarding the door to his room, but the fact that he had been shot at from the *préfecture* hardly made this reassuring. Soon enough, though, he had more visitors: Appleby, in the company of Commissioner Zamaron and a junior officer delegated to take notes.

Zamaron expressed incredulity when Max gave his account of what had happened. Max said nothing about

Lemmer, suspecting Appleby would prefer him to keep silent on the real reason for his meeting with Ennis. He said Ennis had admitted to involvement in Sir Henry's murder and agreed to volunteer the details to Appleby in return for safe passage out of Paris. It was the truth, but not the whole truth.

A rifleman operating from the roof of the *préfecture* was too much for Zamaron to swallow, however. *'Impossible*,' he said several times. But Max knew there were dozens of witnesses to the direction of the shots. The impossible was something Zamaron was going to have to accustom himself to. He was non-committal when Max suggested the incident proved Corinne innocent of Spataro's murder. 'I will consider the evidence carefully,' was all he would say. 'It is for the magistrate to decide.'

Eventually, Zamaron and his junior left, but Appleby remained. He drew up a chair beside the bed and plonked himself down in it. 'You didn't take long to get yourself shot, I must say,' he remarked. 'There are those who are going to remind me they predicted employing an amateur would end like this.'

'Nothing's ended,' Max objected. 'I'll soon be on my feet again.'

'And back in the cross-hairs of whoever killed Ennis. I'm not sure you're safe on the streets, Max.'

'Ennis was offering us Lemmer in exchange for the safe conduct I told Zamaron about. I reckoned bringing him in was worth a few risks.'

Appleby sighed. 'The likelihood is Ennis thought he was setting you up to be killed, little realizing he was a

329

target as well. As for firing at you from the *préfecture*, I imagine the choice of location was designed to warn Zamaron he'd be wise not to ask too many questions. The place is more like a railway station than a police station, anyway. There are always too many people milling about for anyone to keep track of. *Impossible* it certainly wasn't.'

'I'm not going to give up. In fact, I reckon this shows I'm making progress.'

'Towards an early grave, certainly. It's an unwelcome development, Max, and not just because it nearly cost you your life. Ennis was a senior member of the American delegation. He was very publicly murdered. The press will want to know what's going on. I'm going to try to keep your name out of it, but it won't be easy. It may not even be possible, though, as you see, I had Zamaron fix you up with your own room to give you as much privacy as possible. I can't afford to have my department's involvement widely known. There are the Americans themselves to be considered as well. Carver will certainly want to question you. I'll hold him off as long as I can. He mustn't discover we're after Lemmer. You understand?'

'Don't worry. I can handle Carver. I'll give him the same story I gave Zamaron. Meanwhile, there's a member of the *British* delegation I need you to check up on.'

'Brigham?'

'Yes. How did you know?'

'Twentyman told me. He's waiting outside, anxious to reassure himself you're not going to die. I'll send him in when I leave. I'll find out the registration number of Brigham's car, but even if it is HX 4344 that won't give

330

me any justification to do more than ask him a few gentle questions.'

'For God's sake, Appleby, it's obviously *significant*. Brigham's up to something. He tried to talk me into leaving Paris.'

'Perhaps he was concerned for your welfare. With good reason, as it turns out. I'll look into it, all right? But Brigham's well-connected. He's said to have the ear of the Foreign Secretary. I have to tread carefully.'

'Well, I don't have to.'

'No. And I'm sure you won't, once you're up and about. You can try and persuade me to give you his address then. Meanwhile, you need to rest. I'm putting one of my men on your door. Just to make sure the police do their job. Incidentally, Carver tells me Ireton's done a disappearing act.'

'Apparently so.'

'He obviously doesn't think Paris is a healthy place to be these days. And by the look of you he's right.'

'I intend to make it unhealthy for Lemmer.' Max paused, then asked, 'Can you get me a gun, Appleby?'

Appleby's eyebrows twitched in surprise. 'It's not what most people in hospital ask for.'

'I want it for when I leave. Which will be sooner than the doctor recommends, if I have my way.'

'As you no doubt will.'

'The gun?'

Appleby chewed his unlit pipe and contemplated the request for a moment. Then he said, 'It could only be for self-defence. But then . . . I suppose you may have need of quite a bit of that.'

'It seems so.'

Appleby nodded. 'I'll see what I can do.'

Sam had brought food and a few toiletries, for which Max was grateful, though whatever the doctor had prescribed to dull the pain of his wound had dulled his appetite as well. He was almost as pleased to see Sam as Sam was to see him, though he hid it rather better.

'Mr Appleby said you got off lightly in the circumstances, sir.'

'He must have a curious definition of "getting off lightly".'

'I told him about Mr Brigham.'

'I know. He mentioned it.'

'Thing is, sir, I didn't get the feeling he was going to do much about it.'

'Neither did I. Brigham has friends in high places, Sam. Appleby can't afford to tread on their toes.'

'Luckily for you you've got a friend in a low place, then. I'll scout round the streets tonight. Mr Brigham's apartment can't be far from the Majestic and it's not likely a garage goes with it. So, I may be able to find his car. If it's HX 4344 . . .'

'Yes? What then?'

Sam tapped the side of his nose. 'I've had an idea.'

Max groaned. 'Lord save us.'

'You know what they say. If Mahomet won't come to the mountain . . .'

'What's that supposed to mean?'

'Don't worry, sir. Just leave it to me.'

MAX FELL ASLEEP THAT NIGHT WATCHING SNOW FALLING OVER the Seine. Access to his room was guarded by a French policeman and a British Secret Service representative built in keeping with his name, Burley. Max felt as weak as a baby, but was confident a night's rest would revive him. The attempt to kill him he took as a back-handed compliment. They were frightened of him. And he was determined to give them good cause to be. First, though, he had to sleep.

The snow that grew heavier as the night deepened did not deter Sam, but it did complicate his tasks. There were quite a few cars parked on the streets of the eighth *arrondissement*, but the accumulation of snow meant their registration numbers were mostly illegible. Sam began his circuit from the Majestic diligently brushing the snow off every number, but his gloves were soon sodden and his fingers numb, so he abandoned that in favour of looking for Daimlers in particular and English makes in general. His ability to distinguish them at a glance from French cars was far from infallible, how-ever. His clothes were not warm enough and he cursed the Parisian spring weather with many muttered profanities as he trudged along. Despite reviving halts for coffee and brandy at various bars, HX 4344 remained frustratingly elusive.

While clasping his coffee-cup between his frozen hands in one such bar, puffing suspiciously on a French cigarette, Sam acknowledged to himself that he had bitten off more than he could chew. Many of the apartment buildings he had passed had inner courtyards, where a car could be stowed out of sight. There were stables as well, and a few garages, to be considered. Not to mention the possibility that HX 4344 was simply elsewhere that evening. It seemed likelier that he would catch pneumonia than a sight of the damned thing.

If it even existed, of course. Perhaps it was not a registration number at all. Perhaps le Singe had played a trick on him. *Cheeky monkey*, Sam thought, smiling grimly at his own play on words.

Eventually, Sam took pity on himself and suspended the search. It was as he approached the Arc de Triomphe for the third or fourth time that he decided he should quit while he was behind. But returning to the solitude of his room at the Majestic with his tail between his legs did not appeal to him. Little Russia was a shortish walk away along Avenue Hoche. He did not know precisely how matters stood between Max and Nadia Bukayeva, but he felt sure she would want to be told what had happened, although naturally Sam would claim ignorance of the events that had led to the shooting. It was not yet midnight and he did not suppose Nadia was one to be wrapped up in bed with cocoa at ten.

She was a creature of the night if he had ever met one. And she might even be pleased to see him.

It was as he turned into Rue Daru and saw the domes of the Orthodox Cathedral ahead of him through the flurrying snow that Sam heard the throaty note of a car engine behind him and was shortly afterwards splattered about the ankles with slush from the gutter as a sleek black Daimler purred past.

Sam broke into a squelching trot to keep the car in sight. The registration number was displayed on a curved plate fixed to the spare tyre on the boot, but was obscured by snow. The car slowed ahead of him and turned left into the next side-street, the very side-street, in fact, where Sam knew Bukayev's bookshop was located. He put a spurt on.

He heard a car door slam as he neared the corner and, rounding it, saw a hatted, trench-coated figure hurrying away from the Daimler, now standing at the kerbside, its engine ticking. The bookshop was halfway along the street on the opposite side and the man steered a straight course towards it. Sam stopped running and moved into the deep shadow of an unlit doorway. The car was only a few feet from him, but still he could not make out the number. Whatever the number, though, there was something about this he did not like. And he felt sure Max would like it even less.

There were lights burning in the rooms above the shop. The man reached the door and rang the bell. A curtain twitched above. Sam thought he glimpsed Nadia's face, though he could not have sworn to it. A few moments later, the door opened. There was a murmured exchange of words. Then the man stepped inside and the door closed behind him.

'You naughty girl,' Sam said under his breath. 'Not playing fair with us, are you?' He walked hastily to the rear of the Daimler and brushed the snow off the numberplate. It was HX 4344.

Sam returned to the shelter of the doorway and stood there for several minutes, considering what he should do next. His original plan had been designed to prove Brigham drove HX 4344, but he reckoned that was now clear. The question was what he should do about it. On balance, there was still a lot to be said for obliging Brigham to bring the Daimler to the Majestic for repair. It would establish his ownership as an unchallengeable fact, though quite what it would establish beyond that Sam did not know.

He looked up at the illuminated windows of the rooms above the bookshop. He had misread Nadia Bukayeva. So had Max. It would be preferable to believe she was merely indiscriminate with her favours than what Sam actually suspected: that some greater treachery altogether was afoot.

He could delay no longer. Either he went through with it or not. 'Get on with it, lad,' he told himself, with sudden decisiveness. He left the doorway and advanced to the front of the Daimler. He looked both ways along the street and was reassured. The coast was clear. He rested his hand gently on the warm bonnet of the car. For what he had in mind, it would be easier to open her up. That risked drawing the attention of anyone passing by. And if Brigham happened to glance out of the window . . . No. It was going to be a cold and wet scramble beneath the engine, but there was nothing else for it. After another glance in both directions, he crouched down on the snowy pavement and crawled gingerly into the space between the kerb and the chassis of the car.

Max woke, at what stage of the night he could not have said, aware that something had changed – for the worse. He was bathed in sweat, his heart was fluttering, his head pounding, every part of his body pulsing with heat. He was in the grip of a fever the like of which he had never known. Moving a single muscle demanded more concentration and effort than he felt capable of exerting. There was a small bell on the bedside table for him to summon help if he needed it and there was no question that he did need help. He managed to bend his neck so that he could see the bell. The next challenge was to reach out and grasp it. He stared long and hard at it, pulling together the small amount of strength he had. Then he forced himself up on one elbow and stretched out his hand. He noticed that his fingers were trembling like leaves in a breeze. They touched the bell, but he could not seem to control them enough to take hold of it. It toppled over, rolled to the edge of the table and dropped to the floor. And Max fell back against the pillow. He could do no more.

WHEN SAM WENT TO VISIT MAX THE FOLLOWING MORNING, he was horrified to learn of the deterioration in his condition. The doctor on duty was too busy to speak to him and none of the nurses spoke English. '*Une fièvre*' was mentioned, which Sam assumed meant a fever, since Max was clearly in the grip of one and too far gone to communicate. Burley, the Secret Service man Appleby had put on the door to Max's room, told Sam the doctor had said earlier that the bullet wound had led to blood poisoning and that 'the next twenty-four hours will be critical'.

Sam was still gloomily mulling this over when Carver and a couple of men built like wardrobes arrived in the hope of questioning Max. Their frustration that this would not be possible was more in evidence than any concern about the patient's prospects. Carver turned to Sam as a substitute, but was to be disappointed.

'I wasn't there, sir. I don't know what Mr Ennis may have said before he was shot. I didn't even know Mr Maxted was planning to meet him.'

'I thought you lived in the guy's hip pocket.'

'He's never told me everything that's in his mind. He probably reckons it's safer for me to be kept in the dark.'

'But what if I don't believe you *are* in the dark?'

'Then I suppose you won't believe anything I say.'

'A US diplomat has been gunned down in broad daylight, Twentyman. I need to find out why. If turning you upside down and shaking you to see what falls out is what it takes, I'll do it.'

'I'm sure you will, sir. But nothing will fall out.'

Carver closed in and prodded Sam so hard in the shoulder that he was propelled back a step. 'The dumb act's fine, Twentyman, so long as you really are dumb. If not, you're storing up a whole lot of trouble for yourself. You can trust me on that. Because I'm one of the places the trouble will be coming from.'

'I'm sure Mr Maxted can explain everything when he's well enough.'

'You are, are you? Well, for your sake I hope he's well enough pretty damn soon.'

'I hope that too, sir.'

Carver held Sam with a glare for several seconds, then broke away and led his far from merry men off down the echoing stairs from the landing where he and Sam had exchanged words.

Sam leant on the banister-rail and watched them descend in a surge of coat-tails and jutting fedoras. They reached the ground floor and vanished from sight.

He did not move away, however. He stayed where he was, gazing into the vortex of the stairwell, wondering what to do for the best.

Then, to his astonishment, Nadia Bukayeva moved into view on the next landing down. She had clearly been waiting for Carver and his crew to leave. She looked up at him and frowned, then headed up the stairs.

'Why did you not tell me what happened to Max?' she asked as she reached him. 'I went to the Mazarin to see him this morning. They gave me the news there.'

'I'm sorry,' said Sam, flustered and well aware that he probably looked it. 'I would have . . . got in touch with you today . . .'

'How is he?' she cut in, clasping his arm. She looked genuinely worried. Sam had to force himself to remember what he had seen the night before.

'The wound isn't serious. Or it wasn't. They think he's contracted blood poisoning. He has a bad fever.'

'Can I see him?'

'Well, I . . .'

'I must.'

Sam decided to let the nurses decide the issue. Nadia talked her way past them in fluent French, charming Burley along the way. Max was sleeping when they entered his room, though hardly peacefully. Nadia stroked his hand and murmured what sounded to Sam like a prayer. She left with tears in her eyes. He would not have doubted her for a moment but for knowing more of her than she had cause to suppose. She was a consummate actress. He could not deny that.

'Can we go outside and talk, Sam?' she asked, drying her eyes. 'Please tell me as much as you can about what happened. And then . . . there is something I want to tell you. It is why I went to see Max this morning. I need help.' She looked at him with an expression of utter sincerity. 'Will you help me, Sam? There is no one else I can turn to.'

'Try Brigham,' he was tempted to say. But he said no such thing.

They went out into the inner courtyard of the hospital. The sky above them was pure blue, but the air was cold and snow lay in thick carpets on the lawns. In milder weather, recovering patients might have been taking tentative strolls there with friends or relatives. As it was, they were alone.

Sam offered Nadia a cigarette, which she gladly accepted. He held the match for her, noticing how her hand trembled as she clasped the cigarette. She pulled the fur collar of her coat up around her soft, pale cheeks and looked, gazing at him through a drift of smoke, quite breathtakingly lovely.

He told her then the little he felt he should about the circumstances of the shooting, proclaiming as much ignorance to her as he had to Carver. 'He'd have explained it all to me afterwards,' he said, referring to Max's rendezvous with Ennis. 'But he hasn't been well enough to.'

'Will he live, Sam?'

'I'll back him to. He's a tough nut.'

'I will pray for him. You should pray for him also.'

'He wouldn't want me to.'

'Do it, Sam. You do not need to tell him.' She smiled encouragingly.

'All right, then. I will.' And he would – in his own way. 'This help you need, Nadia . . .'

'It is about my uncle. He has been missing for more than a week.'

'Have you had some news of him?'

'News? Maybe. I do not know what to call it. A man called Brigham—'

'Brigham?'

'Yes. Lionel Brigham. He is a member of the British delegation. You have met him?'

'No. But I've heard of him.'

'He has visited my uncle a few times. And they have met a few more times in other places. I do not know what business my uncle has with him. He has never said. But last night Brigham came to see me.'

'He did?' Sam commenced a rapid reassessment of events. Perhaps Nadia's allegiances were not to be doubted after all.

'Why are you frowning?'

'Am I? Sorry.' He made an effort to relax his features. 'Go on.'

'I do not like Brigham. There is something in his eyes. Something . . . I cannot say what it is.'

'But you don't like it.'

'Are you laughing at me, Sam?'

'No. Of course I'm not.'

'First you frown. Then you smile.'

'Sorry. Just . . . tell me what Brigham said.'

'He said he is in contact with people who know where my uncle is. He said they had asked him to give me a message. If I want to see my uncle again, I should go to the railway bridge over the Canal de l'Ourcq at Quai de la Sambre.'

'Where's that?'

'Out in the nineteenth *arrondissement*, near the city walls. I do not know exactly. But I must go there.'

'Of course. You want me to come with you?'

'That is the strange thing. Brigham advised me to take a friend. "You may need help," he said.'

'What did he mean by that?'

'He would not explain. He would not explain anything. "Go soon, my dear," he said. "You should not delay."'

'Then we shouldn't.'

'But what will we find?'

'Wondering won't help you, Nadia. Let's go.'

Nadia seemed grateful for Sam's decisiveness. As they hurried out of the hospital, they passed the main enquiries office, where misanthropic functionaries dispensed grudging directions to visitors through a small window. One such visitor was turning away from the window with a disappointed scowl when he heard Sam speaking English and scurried over to buttonhole him.

'Sounds like you and me are from the same neck of the woods, squire,' he said in a cockney accent, laying a detaining hand on Sam's elbow as he did so.

The man was small and scrawny, with skittering, inquisitive eyes. Sam did not like the look of him. 'Small world,' he mumbled, endeavouring to disengage himself.

'Been visiting someone?'

'Why else would we be here?' Nadia asked icily.

'That's what I was thinking. Expect you've heard about yesterday's shooting. Just along from here, in front of the cathedral. Like the Wild West, they say.'

'Do they?'

'Point is, rumour has it the so-called innocent bystander they brought in here with a bullet wound is English. Thought you might be friends of his.'

'Can't help you,' said Sam.

'Sure about that, squire? Caution understandable, o' course, but there could be money in it for you. I'm with the *Daily Mail*. Phelps is the name.' Sam found Phelps' card had suddenly and magically materialized in his palm. 'We're doing a Paris edition during the conference. You've probably seen it. Always on the lookout for material. Lord Northcliffe's given us a generous budget. You could be in for a slice of it if—'

'We're not interested.' Sam thrust the card back into Phelps' hand and pressed on towards the door.

'Didn't catch your name, squire,' Phelps called after them. But Sam did not respond.

'Are you really not interested, Sam?' Nadia asked once they were outside. 'He probably would pay you well.'

'Not well enough.'

'How can you be sure?'

'Because you can't put a price on self-respect.'

'Ah, no.' She looked at him with what appeared to be genuine admiration. 'You cannot, of course.'

Sam grinned. 'Specially when you haven't got too much of it to start with.'

THEY TOOK THE MÉTRO TO GARE DE L'EST, THEN ON TO THE end of *Ligne* 7 at Porte de la Villette. From there they headed along the boulevard that followed the line of the city wall south, with the railway line to their right. The sky was blue and the lying snow a dazzling white, but the east wind cut like a knife. Beyond the railway line was the city's main abattoir, inactive on a Sunday, but emanating nonetheless a sharp, fetid tang that soured the air.

They reached the Canal de l'Ourcq where it ran in from the east and turned on to Quai de la Sambre. The railway was directly ahead of them. Beyond lay the rear of the abattoir and more bridges linking it with the meat market on the other side of the canal. Several barges were moored along the bank, but the towpath was empty. It was no place for strolling and certainly not for taking the air.

'Why have we been brought here?' murmured Nadia as they approached the railway bridge.

'There's got to be a reason,' said Sam. 'Didn't Brigham even hint at what it could be?'

' "If you want to see your uncle again, go there," ' Nadia replied. 'That is all he said.'

'And here we are.'

They reached the bridge and moved into the shadow of the arch. Out of the sun, it was colder by several degrees. Water was dripping from the ironwork above them on to the path and into the canal, where a thin skin of ice had formed along the bank.

Nadia shuddered. 'There is nothing here,' she said, her breath clouding before her.

'There must be.' Sam looked ahead, then back the way they had come. There was not a soul in sight and not a vessel moving on the canal. It had all the elements of a fool's errand. But Brigham had surely been in earnest. This was where he had said they should go and this was where they were: the very spot.

'I thought someone would be waiting for us,' said Nadia. 'I even hoped Uncle Igor would be here. But there is no one.'

'They couldn't predict when we'd arrive,' Sam reasoned. 'Perhaps they've watched us approach and will show themselves now we're here.'

Nadia walked out into the sunlight on the other side of the bridge and gazed around. 'Where could they be watching from?'

Sam joined her. 'I don't know,' he admitted, surveying the desolate scene. 'We just have to wait.'

'For how long?'

'I don't know that either.' A fear he suspected might be far from irrational suddenly gripped Sam. They had been lured to this place for some reason, even if it was not the reason Brigham had given. Someone could be watching them from any number of vantage points. And that someone could be the man who had killed Ennis and wounded Max. 'Let's wait under the bridge.'

'Why? It's warmer here.'

'But it's also more exposed.' He grasped Nadia by the arm and led her back into the shadow of the arch.

'You think this is a trap?' she whispered, her voice quavering with alarm.

'I'm probably wrong. It's just—'

Sam broke off. His eye had been caught by a movement at the water's edge on the other side of the canal. A bubble, lit by a shaft of sunlight, had come to the surface and burst. As he watched, there came another. These bubbles were rising in a patch of ice-free water around a rope tied to a mooring-ring on the towpath. And the rope was taut. There was clearly something heavy on the end of it, beneath the water.

'What is it?' asked Nadia. 'What are you looking at?'

'I'm not sure. Wait here.'

Sam took off at a sprint. He wanted to reach the other side of the canal before Nadia jumped to the same conclusion he had. If it was the right conclusion, she should be spared it if at all possible.

He ran to the footbridge by the city wall, crossed it and raced back to the bridge. It took him only a few minutes to cover the distance. When he arrived, Nadia stared across at him with an anxious frown.

'What is it, Sam?' she called.

'Probably nothing,' he called back, bending by the mooring-ring and tugging at the rope. But it was not nothing. A shape stirred in the murky depths of the water. Peering down, Sam made out what looked like a large, bell-shaped sack. He could not simply pull it to the surface. It was too heavy. He heaved at it unavailingly for several seconds, then gave up.

'I am coming over,' Nadia called.

'No. Stay there.'

'I am coming over.' And, so saying, she set off.

'I hope this isn't what I think it is,' Sam muttered to himself. Looking along the towpath, he saw an iron ladder fixed to the bank just beyond the bridge. If he could drag the sack as far as that, he would be able to come to grips with it.

He untied the knot round the mooring-ring, took the weight of the sack and looped the rope around his waist so as not to lose his grip, then started walking backwards along the path.

It was slow progress and Nadia had overtaken him by the time he had reached it. She said nothing to him, her face gripped by a dawning realization she clearly could not bring herself to express. Instead, she grasped the rope and pulled along with him.

She lost her footing at one point and fell against him, but assured him through gritted teeth that she was all right. They set to again and eventually reached the ladder, where Sam tied the rope to the top of the stile.

There was nothing to be gained by delay, reluctant as he was to take the next step. It either was what he feared or it was not. Bracing himself against the chill of the water, he climbed down the ladder.

He winced as the freezing water seeped inside his boots and trousers. It was above his knees by the time he was able to reach the sack. He took out his penknife, opened it and stabbed a hole in the material, then sawed upwards to create a slit.

A large bubble of air emerged. As it reached the surface, Sam was enveloped in a foul stench. He

348

coughed and spluttered and, glancing up, saw Nadia cover her mouth and nose. Then he looked down at the sack again and saw something white and swollen flop out through the slit.

It was the head of a man.

'I'M VERY SORRY FOR YOUR LOSS, MISS BUKAYEVA,' APPLEBY said, in a gentler tone than Sam was used to from him.

'*Moi aussi, mademoiselle,*' said Commissioner Zamaron.

They were in Zamaron's office at the Préfecture de Police, surrounded by his art collection and enveloped in an atmosphere of sombre diligence. Several hours had passed since the discovery of Igor Bukayev's body in a sack weighed down with rocks, suspended in the Canal de l'Ourcq. The deceased had been taken to a mortuary, where a pathologist was attempting to determine the cause of death.

Nadia had maintained rigid control of her emotions since her initial horror at what she and Sam had found. She spoke quietly and formally and generally avoided eye contact. The only signs of her inner turmoil were the constant clasping and unclasping of her hands.

She and Sam had explained what had led them to the canal without any need of misrepresentation, although Sam had naturally omitted to mention meddling with Brigham's car. The facts appeared to speak for themselves. Lionel Brigham of the British delegation to the peace conference was implicated in the murder of Igor

Bukayev and quite possibly in the murders of Sir Henry Maxted, Raffaele Spataro and Walter Ennis.

The enormity of the allegations against Brigham was clearly a factor in the solicitous but non-committal attitudes of Appleby and Zamaron. Officially, the Paris police still regarded Sir Henry's death as an accident and Corinne Dombreux was being held by them as a suspect in the murder of Spataro. As for Ennis, they were looking for a killer who had had the audacity to strike from their own headquarters. All in all, Sam reckoned Zamaron was a man with several headaches and no aspirins.

Zamaron had an additional difficulty where Brigham was concerned, as he was at pains to explain to Nadia. 'All the officials the British have brought here have diplomatic immunity, *mademoiselle*. I could not even question Monsieur Brigham without the agreement of . . .' He turned to Appleby for clarification.

'The Permanent Under-Secretary,' Appleby dolefully specified. 'He'd need a lot of persuading.'

'And forgive me, *mademoiselle*, but it would be . . . *comment dirait-on ça?* . . . it would be your account against his for what he said when he visited you last night.'

'Assuming he admits visiting you at all,' said Appleby.

Sam said nothing. He had not told Nadia – and he did not want to – that he had been in Little Russia the night before. He would have to tell Appleby, though – as soon as possible.

'He knows the people who murdered my uncle,' said Nadia with quiet gravity. 'You must make him tell you who they are.'

'We'll try, miss,' said Appleby.

'Can *you* question him?'

'I certainly intend to. But I can't force him to answer my questions.'

'Unless the Permanent Whatsit says he must?' suggested Sam. 'Is that the size of it, Mr A?'

Appleby glowered at him. 'How succinctly you put it, Twentyman.'

'This must be dealt with at the political level, *mademoiselle*,' said Zamaron. 'I will refer the problem to my superiors, who will refer it to their superiors at the Ministère de Justice. There are the Americans to be also considered in the matter of Monsieur Ennis.'

'Any progress there, Léon?' Appleby asked in a tone that suggested he assumed there had not been.

'*Non.* How the man who shot Ennis entered and left this building is still . . . without explanation.'

'You seem to be telling me, gentlemen,' said Nadia, 'that there is nothing you can do.'

'*Non, non.* We will investigate all the circumstances of your uncle's death, *mademoiselle*. We will seek witnesses. We will search for clues. And we will provide you with protection.'

'I'll get as much as I can out of Brigham, miss,' said Appleby. 'You have my word on that.'

'If you had seen what Mr Twentyman and I saw . . . you would not tread so softly.'

'Unfortunately, we're obliged to.'

'And I will be obliged to tell my uncle's friends that his murderers may be able to hide behind . . . diplomatic immunity.'

'Not if I can help it.'

352

'But can you help it, Mr Appleby? That is the question.' With that, Nadia rose to her feet. 'I must go home now. There is much to be arranged.'

'I have a car waiting for you, *mademoiselle*,' said Zamaron, rising hurriedly himself.

'*Merci, monsieur*.' She turned to Sam. 'You will tell Max what has happened . . . when he is better?'

'Of course.'

'For all you did, Sam . . . I am grateful.'

'Don't mention it.'

'This way, *mademoiselle*,' said Zamaron, ushering her out.

For a moment, Sam found himself alone with Appleby. 'Brigham definitely visited Nadia last night, Mr A,' he said. 'I saw him park the Daimler and go in.'

'HX 4344?'

'The very same.'

'I've confirmed it's his car. Nadia doesn't know you were spying on her, I assume?'

'I wasn't exactly spying.'

'But she doesn't know?'

'No.'

'You mightn't remain the knight in shining armour in her eyes if she found out.'

'You have to squeeze the truth out of Brigham, sir. He's in this up to his neck.'

'And four people are dead.'

'That's right. There's Madame Dombreux as well. She obviously didn't kill Spataro. You should twist the commissioner's arm to get her released.'

'How kind of you to tell me my job, Twentyman.'

'I didn't mean to do that.'

'No? Well, I—'

Appleby broke off as Zamaron rejoined them, wearily rubbing his forehead. '*Mon Dieu,*' he moaned, 'what a day!'

Appleby caught his eye. 'What a *week*!'

'You will interrogate Brigham, Horace?'

'It won't amount to an interrogation, I'm afraid.'

'But . . .'

'I'll do my best.'

'You will need to. The politicians will not want to connect these killings.'

'I know.'

'Why not?' asked Sam.

'Leave Léon alone, Twentyman. He has enough problems on his plate without being cross-questioned by the likes of you. I'll tell you as much as you need to know – outside.'

They went down into the courtyard, where Appleby's car was waiting. He told the driver to take a stroll, while they sat in the back. He obviously wanted no witnesses to what he had to say, which did not strike Sam as promising.

'Murder's not uncommon in this city, Twentyman,' Appleby began, chewing on his unlit pipe. 'The French are a passionate lot. And the war's left a good many guns in the wrong hands. Sir Henry's death really could have been an accident. Madame Dombreux really could have killed Spataro. And the Russians are notorious for score-settling, so Bukayev could be a victim of something in that line. As for Ennis, well, his murder's hard to explain, I grant you, without imagining a conspiracy to be at work. But Carver will find a way round that, if he's told to.'

'And will he be told to?'

'In all likelihood, yes. To acknowledge the existence of some kind of conspiracy stemming from the presence of past or present German spies within the delegations would be to acknowledge a threat to the validity of the peace conference. It could even lead to its suspension.'

'Crikey.'

'Exactly.'

'I expect our leaders would move heaven and earth to avoid that.'

'They would. And they will.'

'What are you going to do, then?'

'Question Brigham before he has a chance to hide behind the skirts of the Permanent Under-Secretary. If I can persuade him to give himself away . . .'

'Max seems to think he's a wily operator.'

'No doubt he is. But I have a few wiles of my own.'

'I'm sure you do, sir.'

Appleby glanced sharply at Sam. 'Do you mean to be sarcastic, Twentyman, or is it just your natural tone?'

'You'd have to ask my old mum for a ruling on that, sir.'

'Since Max trusts you, I have little choice but to do the same, at least while he's *hors de combat*. Don't think that trust is any more than highly provisional, though.'

'Oh, I wouldn't dream of it, sir.'

'If Max doesn't pull through—'

'Don't say that, sir.'

Appleby paused in deference to the sincerity of Sam's interruption. He sucked on his pipe for a thoughtful moment, then said, 'I was using Max to do things I'm not free to do for fear of sparking a diplomatic incident. You understand that, don't you, Twentyman?'

'I do, sir, yes.'

'So . . .'

'Is there something you want *me* to do for you?'

Appleby sighed. 'Much against my better judgement . . . yes.'

$\mathbb{S}$ AM HAD READILY AGREED TO APPLEBY'S REQUEST, BUT WAS not entirely confident of his ability to talk his way into an audience with Baltazar Ribeiro of the Brazilian delegation. He did not lack for nerve, but his appearance and accent often encouraged his social superiors to treat him disdainfully. He would have to tread both boldly and carefully: a tricky combination, to put it mildly.

As it turned out, however, an audience was delivered to him on a plate. When he repaired to the Hôtel Dieu to see whether there had been any improvement in Max's condition, Burley surprised him with the announcement that Max had a visitor. 'Brazilian gent by the name of Ribeiro: senior member of their delegation. Not the sort of bloke you turn away.'

Sam went into the room and found a large, smartly dressed man sitting in a bedside chair that was obviously too small for him, gazing anxiously at Max, who was drifting feverishly in and out of sleep and probably unaware that there was anyone with him at all.

Ribeiro's tanned skin and thick white hair gave him a vigorous appearance, but he was breathing heavily, perhaps because he was upset by the state he had found his old friend's son in – or perhaps because he felt responsible for it. He was clad in a voluminous green overcoat and was turning a string of rosary beads fretfully in his fingers.

'Senhor Ribeiro?' Sam asked.

'*Sim.*' Ribeiro turned a pair of rheumy eyes in Sam's direction. '*O que?*'

'My name's Twentyman. I'm a friend of Max's.'

'You are?'

'I served under him in the war.'

'Ah. I understand.' Ribeiro rose and clasped Sam's hand in both of his, grinding a rosary bead into Sam's thumb in the process. 'This is very bad. I am saddened to see him so ill.'

'How did you hear about it?'

'Ah . . .' Ribeiro hesitated.

'Max told me everything, *senhor*. I know you passed him the message from Ennis.'

'Poor Ennis. To die like that, here, in the centre of Paris. You served under Max in the war, you say?'

'Yes. Perhaps . . . we could go somewhere for a quiet word, sir.'

Sam piloted Ribeiro to a cheerless and sparsely popu-lated canteen in the bowels of the building. Ribeiro revealed en route that he had heard of Ennis's demise on the conference grapevine. The murder of a delegate had a lot of people worried. 'And they will remain worried, until the authorities can assure them the crime had nothing to do with the business of the conference.'

Naturally, Ribeiro had been rather more than worried, since he it was who had told Max that Ennis would be waiting for him at Notre-Dame. Learning a so-called bystander had been wounded, he had feared the worst. And he had been right to.

'I blame myself for passing the message,' he said glumly as they reached the canteen. 'I should have refused.'

'Max was glad to get the chance to meet Ennis, *senhor*,' Sam consoled him. 'It wasn't your fault.'

Ribeiro appeared unconvinced and the coffee the canteen supplied seemed to do nothing to lift his spirits.

'I wanted to ask you exactly what Ennis said when he called round at your hotel yesterday morning, *senhor*,' Sam ventured.

'It was as I told Max. It was not a long conversation. Ennis was frightened, though he would not say what he was frightened of. He only wanted to be sure I would contact Max and—'

'You asked him what he was frightened of?'

'Yes. He only shook his head.'

'Nothing else?'

Ribeiro raised his coffee-cup, but put it down again without drinking. He frowned thoughtfully. ' "What is wrong, Walter?" I asked. Yes. That is what I said. "What is wrong?" And he shook his head. And I asked again. And he gave me such a tired look. He was weary to his core. "Contingencies, Baltazar," he said. "It's the ones you can't foresee that get you in the end." '

'Contingencies?'

'Yes. Contingencies.'

'But what did he mean?'

'I do not know. He would say no more than that. I

asked if I could help him. He shook his head again and walked away.'

Contingencies. There had been something about them on Sir Henry's list. Sam could not exactly remember what. But the word had been there all right.

'Does it mean anything to you, Mr Twentyman?'

'No, *senhor*. But it might mean something to Max.'

'Will he recover? I spoke to a doctor who came in while I was there. He shrugged his shoulders a great deal. It is a habit of the French I do not like. He gave Max *une chance sur deux*. Fifty-fifty, you would call it. Not good.'

'Not so bad either. He faced worse odds than that every day he flew in the war.'

Ribeiro raised a smile at that. 'You hearten me, Mr Twentyman. You are better for me than the doctor is for Max, I think. This coffee, incidentally, is undrinkable. Do they sell brandy here?'

'I'll ask.'

Sam went up to the counter and enquired pessimistically after cognac. To his surprise, it was forthcoming. The phrase *Contingencies Memo* sprang suddenly into his mind as he watched the serving woman dispense the liquor. Yes. That was the item on Sir Henry's list. Valuable, like every other item on it.

When Sam returned to the table with the brandy, he found Ribeiro fiddling with his rosary beads again. He looked as if the cares of the whole city were resting on his shoulders. 'Thank you,' he said, raising the glass and taking a sip. He set it down again with a heavy sigh. 'My father, God rest his soul, once told me a happy man is a man without friends. What do you think, Mr Twentyman?'

'Did your father have many friends?'

'Oh, yes. And some of them caused him great problems. He had a generous nature. When the rubber boom ended, many of his friends asked him for help. He lent them money, which some of them never repaid. But what do you do when a friend asks you for help? Turn him away? No. Of course not.'

Sam had the distinct impression Ribeiro was really talking about himself rather than his father. Who was the friend he had not turned away? And what had he asked for? 'You and Sir Henry went back a long way, isn't that right, *senhor*?'

'Yes.' Ribeiro took another sip of brandy. 'It is.'

'You tell me if I've got the wrong end of the stick, but was there something Sir Henry asked you to do that you regret doing now?'

Ribeiro stared at him in silence for a moment. He went on staring at him as he smoothed down his moustache. Then he said, 'What did you do in the RFC, Mr Twentyman?'

'I kept the planes running.'

'How did you do that?'

'I know engines, *senhor*. I could tell from the sound of them if there was something wrong before it actually went wrong. It's a knack. You've either got it or you haven't.'

'And you have it?'

'Yes.'

'I must be careful what I say to you. You have good ears. There is a difference between listening and hearing

361

and it seems you know the difference. I cannot speak to you of what passed between me and Henry. It would not be right. But I will speak to Max. After what has happened to him, I must, as soon as he is well enough, which I pray to God will be soon.'

'Can I tell him what you'll be speaking to him about?'

Ribeiro nodded solemnly. 'You can. Tell him I know why Henry was trying to raise so much money. Tell him I know what he was planning to spend it on.'

LIONEL BRIGHAM ENTERED FRADGLEY'S OFFICE AT THE BRITISH Embassy that evening with the air of one unconvinced that anything Fradgley wanted to discuss could be urgent enough to justify an interruption of his normal Sunday routine. His expression suggested he would swiftly be demanding an explanation from Fradgley for this summons 'on a matter of the utmost importance' with a distinct presumption that it was unlikely, in his judgement, to be important enough.

The few members of staff on duty at the Embassy had been unable to enlighten Brigham in the slightest degree, other than to confirm that Fradgley was on the premises. Strangely, however, upon knocking at the door and going on in without waiting for a response, Brigham was dismayed to discover that the room was empty, the chair behind the broad desk untenanted, no one's eyes but those of the King in a framed photograph on the wall trained upon him.

'Damn it all,' Brigham remarked in his bafflement. 'What the devil's the fellow playing at?'

'Ah, there you are.' Through a doorway in the far corner of the room, leading Brigham knew not where, a figure suddenly advanced, beaming in welcome. It was

Horace Appleby of the Secret Service, a man Brigham had done his best to steer well clear of. He regarded the Secret Service as an unwise and unwarranted innovation – a johnny-come-lately to the business of government which he would have preferred not to have come at all.

'There's clearly been some mistake,' said Brigham, with as much nonchalance as he could muster. 'I'm here to see Fradgley.'

'Presently indisposed,' said Appleby, clamping an unlit pipe between his teeth. 'But even if he had been here, it's you and I who'd have done most of the talking. Shall we sit down?'

'No need. I won't be staying.'

'Please, Mr Brigham. Take a seat.' Appleby subsided into the chair behind the desk and gestured towards the chair facing him.

'There's really nothing we need to discuss, Appleby. I think I'll be going.'

'As you wish. I can't force you to stay. But there are some questions you're going to have to answer sooner or later. Very serious questions. It'd be in your own interests to hear what they are.'

Appleby was still gesturing towards the vacant chair. Brigham hesitated a little longer, then shrugged and sat down. He took out a cigarette and lit it. 'I'll give you until I finish this.'

Appleby smiled, but said nothing. His only response was to fill his pipe and light it, in a leisurely routine that declared he not allow Brigham to set the terms of their exchanges. Then he smiled again.

'Perhaps I could ask you a question, Appleby,' said

Brigham. 'Your outfit's been going, what, ten years? Can you point to one single achievement of lasting value that you've chalked up in that time? We managed to rule an empire for two centuries without . . . whatever it is you people do. Extraordinary, isn't it?'

'How would you describe your dealings with Igor Bukayev, Mr Brigham?'

'What?'

'Igor Bukayev,' Appleby repeated. 'How would—'

'I heard what you said.'

'Then perhaps you'd oblige me with an answer.'

'I don't have dealings with him,' Brigham said, slowly and carefully.

'But you do know him?'

'He's a politically active member of the Russian exile community. It would be surprising if I hadn't come across him.'

'When did you last come across him?'

'I don't know. Some reception or other.'

'A long way from the Canal de l'Ourcq, I assume.'

'The Canal de l'Ourcq?'

'Yes. Out in the nineteenth *arrondissement*.'

'You've lost me, Appleby. You probably know more about canals than I do. Father a bargee, was he?'

Appleby sent up a plume of smoke and studied Brigham intently through the haze of it. 'Bukayev's body was found earlier today in a sack suspended in the Canal de l'Ourcq, Mr Brigham. Do you want to make a joke out of that?'

'Good God.' Brigham's expression switched to one of horror. 'Bukayev's dead?'

'Yes. Just like Walter Ennis.'

'I heard about Ennis. Shocking business. But . . . did he have something to do with Bukayev?'

'You tell me.'

Brigham frowned heavily. 'What are you driving at, Appleby? I'd be grateful if you simply came out and said it.'

'You've admitted an acquaintance with Igor Bukayev. What about his niece, Nadia Bukayeva?'

Brigham's expression darkened. 'His niece?'

'Do you know her, Mr Brigham? Yes or no?

'I may have met her a few times. In the company of her uncle.'

'Ever been alone with her?'

'What are you implying?'

'Have you or haven't you?'

Brigham weighed the question for a moment, then said, 'Not that I recall.'

'Really? I wouldn't have put you down as a man of fallible recollection, I must say. And last night isn't long ago, now is it?'

'Last night?'

'You were seen.'

Brigham flinched. 'You have her under surveillance?'

'What we have is independent verification of her claim that you visited her last night.'

'She told you?'

'She did. She also told us you passed on a message to her, a message that led her to the Canal de l'Ourcq this morning – and a terrible discovery.'

'*I* passed on a message?'

'Do you deny it?'

'Certainly I deny it.' The colour in Brigham's face and

the tone of his voice suggested denial was very much what he was about. 'This is preposterous. I visited her, yes. I considered it ungentlemanly to volunteer the fact to you, but in the light of her outrageous allegation I no longer feel obliged to protect her reputation. I went to see her, at her prior invitation, for reasons the tenor of that invitation made clear enough. I spent an hour or so with her. She mentioned her uncle had left Paris for a few days. She said nothing else about him. And I said nothing about him at all.'

'Let me get this straight.' Appleby removed his pipe from his mouth and pointed the stem at Brigham. 'The purpose of your visit was . . . sexual?'

'If you insist on being specific about such matters, yes.'

'You're old enough to be her father.'

'I don't believe I have to defend myself in this regard, Appleby. I'm a bachelor. I enjoy the company of women. And Nadia Bukayeva enjoyed *my* company. There's nothing else to be said.'

'Except that she tells a very different story. And someone must have passed the message about Bukayev to her. Otherwise she wouldn't have known where to go.'

'Whoever it was, it wasn't me.'

'You contend she's lying?'

'I don't contend. She simply is.'

'Why would she do that?'

'To avoid naming the person who really passed the message, presumably.'

Appleby replaced the pipe in his mouth and relit it. 'Your work for the delegation has touched on our policy towards the Bolshevik regime, I believe. A committee you sit on formulated advice to the Prime Minister concerning the strategy to be adopted by our negotiators if the proposed meeting with Russian representatives at Prinkipo had gone ahead.'

'What of it?'

'Involving yourself with the niece of a well-known Tsarist could be seen in the circumstances as compromising. Highly compromising, I'd say.'

'You can probably cause me some embarrassment, Appleby. But nothing worse. I think you'll find I have more friends than you do.'

'More highly placed friends, you mean?'

'They tell me you were a policeman before you joined the Secret Service. I can believe it. There's definitely something plodding about you. The uniform must have suited you.'

'They tell *me* you took some leave last week in order to attend Sir Henry Maxted's funeral. Is that correct?'

'It is.'

'So, you won't deny being acquainted with him?'

'Certainly not.'

'Or Walter Ennis?'

'I met the fellow at various meetings.'

'Your acquaintances are an unlucky lot, aren't they?'

'What do you mean?'

'Well, so many of them come to a sticky end.'

Brigham lit another cigarette and gave Appleby a long, contemptuous look. 'And so many more of them don't.'

'Do you know Sir Henry's son, James Maxted?'

'Of course. I'm a friend of the family.'

'Are you indeed? Then you'll have been sorry to hear of his condition.'

'His . . . condition?'

'I assume you're aware he was injured during the Ennis shooting.'

'No.' Brigham's face drained of colour. He appeared genuinely shocked. 'I was not aware of it.'

'He's in the Hôtel Dieu, fighting for his life.'

'Good God. Are you saying . . . he may not survive?'

'It was a relatively minor wound. But septicaemia's the problem now. I wouldn't like to say what his chances are.'

'Does his mother know about this?'

'He said he preferred not to worry her.'

'But . . .'

'You look upset, Mr Brigham.'

'I am upset, God damn it.' Brigham jumped up from his chair. 'I'd better go and see how he is for myself.'

'I'm afraid I can't allow that.'

'What?' Brigham glared at Appleby. 'What the devil do you mean?'

'There's good reason to suppose the man who killed Ennis hoped to kill young Maxted as well. I've placed a guard on his room at the hospital. In view of the suspicious nature of your involvement in this matter, I can't authorize you to visit him.'

'You think I might try to kill him?'

'Your loyalties are unclear, Mr Brigham. Therefore your actions are unpredictable.'

'My God, you have a nerve.' Brigham brought his fist down on the blotter in front of Appleby, setting the lids of the bottles rattling in Fradgley's inkstand but making no discernible impact on Appleby's composure. 'I shall be lodging a formal complaint about your conduct – and your damned insinuations.'

'Please do. I've already notified the Permanent Under-Secretary of my concerns about you. I await his response.'

'His response will be to tell Cumming to bring you to heel.'

Appleby puffed at his pipe and smiled up at Brigham. It was unusual to hear C referred to by his actual surname. It could be regarded as calculatedly disrespectful, as Appleby suspected it was intended to be. But he did not rise to the bait. 'As to that,' he said in an amicable tone, 'we shall see, shan't we?'

THE BREAKING OF MAX'S FEVER WAS LIKE THE PASSING OF A storm. All, in an instant, was clear and calm. He lay in his bed at the Hôtel Dieu, conscious of himself for the first time in some indeterminate period. It was dark beyond the window of his room, but which night it was he had no way of judging. He felt cool and serene, though so weak he could barely raise his hand to his brow. The sleep he fell into then was a soft, healing slumber.

He was aware of a nurse hovering over him at some point, checking his temperature and the dressing on his wound and murmuring *'Très bien'*. He opened his eyes and tried to speak to her. She smiled at him and patted his hand. *'Dormez tranquille, monsieur.'*

Max vaguely supposed a doctor would come to see him in the morning. But it was still dark outside when gentle pressure on his shoulder woke him and he became aware of a white-coated presence beside the bed.

Max did not recognize the doctor, though it was hard to make out his features, silhouetted as he was against the dim light from the doorway. There was no other light. Someone had turned off the bedside lamp. He could just discern a suit and bow-tie beneath the white coat. The man was grey-haired and bearded and wearing some distinctive, apple-scented cologne. His face was entirely in shadow.

'Doctor?' Max murmured.

'I am a doctor, yes.' The voice was low and silky, but the accent was not French. It was altogether more middle European. 'Though not of medicine.'

'I'm . . . sorry?'

'Don't apologize, Max. You've not been well, though now, I'm glad to say, you appear to be recovering. It is actually for me to apologize to you. I was not responsible for Saturday's . . . *coup de main* . . . but those who were are to some degree under my control. I regret that it occurred. There was a certain amount of panic when it was realized Ennis might tell all. He had made himself a threat to the safety of several people. Their reaction was understandable but excessive. We cannot have assassinations on the streets of Paris. It is altogether too conspicuous.'

'Who are you?'

'I think you know who I am. I was acquainted with your father. We met in Tokyo . . . thirty years ago.'

Max was seized by the conviction that the man sitting at his bedside was none other than Fritz Lemmer. He tried to push himself upright, but did not have the strength. He opened his mouth to cry out, but a hand was clamped over it.

'They would not believe you, Max. They would think you were still delirious. I am Doctor Wahlen from Strasbourg, helping out here at the request of the

Director. Nod your head if you are willing to continue our conversation without raising the alarm. It would be to your advantage to do so, I assure you.'

Max nodded and the hand was removed. He lay where he was, his chest heaving from the effort he had made to rise. He was by no means certain that he could shout for help even if he wanted to.

'I am sorry for your father's death, Max. I rather admired Henry. He was incorruptible but surprisingly imaginative. Encountering him here in Paris was the sheerest misfortune. He had no business catching a tram so early in the morning. It was simply bad luck. Even so, I would not have expected him to recognize me. I tried to ignore him, to pretend I did not know him. I sensed the attempt was in vain, but I hoped he would realize that to move against me would be extremely risky. And why should he take such a risk, after all? Patriotism surely has its limits. I stood there, in the crowded tram, ignoring his stare, refusing to engage with him eye to eye. We did not speak. There was no acknowledgement. I thought of the last time we had met. A reception at the Russian Embassy in Tokyo, shortly before the Tsarevich's visit, in the spring of 1891. I wonder if he thought of it also. I will confess to you that I would have liked to talk to him about those days. I cannot tell you how earnestly I hoped he would not pursue me. For his sake as well as mine.'

'You expect me . . . to believe that?'

'It is the truth. Of course, I did not know then that he was involved with Madame Dombreux, although naturally I was aware he had been acquainted with her late husband. Pierre Dombreux is something of a puzzle, to me as he is to others. I thought I had him in the palm of my hand. But no. It seems he served several masters, none of them loyally. If he trusted anyone, it was Henry. That was my difficulty when I encountered Henry. How much of what Dombreux knew did he know? It was the lure he planned to use to trap me. I cannot complain. The hunter must always expect to be hunted. There is no divine law that dictates the prey may not turn upon the predator. Still, it is a dangerous game, as Henry discovered, though I suspect that came as no surprise to him. Patriotism was not his motivation. Hence my miscalculation. He wanted to profit from what he knew about me. Do you know why he needed so much money? I confess I do not. He was not a mercenary man. There must have been a compelling reason. Strictly speaking, it is irrelevant, at least to me. But it would be interesting to know.'

'You . . . murdered . . . him.' Max had to force the words out.

'Agents of mine neutralized the threat he represented. They acted with my approval, at least initially. Henry's fatal accident and Spataro's death, apparently at the hands of Madame Dombreux, constituted a coherent, not to say elegant, solution to several related problems. You could say they were actions forced upon us. The attack on you and Ennis was clumsy by comparison. I did not sanction it. There will be repercussions, you may be assured, for those who instigated it. But there it is. I still have power. My resources, however, are undeniably diminished. I am the functioning arm of an empire that no longer exists. The Kaiser's realm has shrunk to a castle in the Netherlands. So, what end do I serve now? It is an important question, as much for you as for me.'

'Why should I . . . give a damn?'

'Because you impress me, Max. You are single-minded, courageous and resourceful. We would work well together. Many of my people think you are as big a threat to their survival as your father was. They will not allow such a threat to hang above them. But if you come over to us, the threat is dissolved. You enjoy my protection. You join my secret army. You become one of my lieutenants.'

'Not . . . in a million years.'

'Do not decide so hastily. Rest here and recover. And while you do so, reflect. You can trust no one except me. I speak the truth. Everyone else dissembles, one way or the other. Oh, there is your tame mechanic, of course, Twentyman. He is loyal to you, I admit. That makes him vulnerable. What would you be willing to do to guarantee his continued well-being? Think about that also. A man of principle is always compromised by his friendships. For myself, I have no friends, no lovers, no confidants. I learnt the hard way that I could afford no such entanglements.'

Max stared hard at where he judged Lemmer's eyes to be. 'Go to hell.'

'If there is one, I undoubtedly will. But there is much to be done before I confront the hereafter. To business. Your clothes are in that wardrobe over there.' Lemmer pointed his finger against the light. 'I have examined the contents of your pockets. The list is interesting, is it not? Henry was certainly budgeting for an expensive, not to say extravagant, purchase. Whatever can it have been?

The Trust and the Chinese box were to be expected. But I was surprised he had knowledge of the Contingencies Memorandum. He really was prepared to burn his boats, wasn't he? And then there is the key.'

Max groaned. There, before him, held in Lemmer's fingers, was the key Max had found in the bedpost in his father's room at the Majestic.

'Still looking for the lock it fits, are you, Max? I'll make you an offer. Find it before I do and you can have the key back. Provided I have first sight of whatever Henry locked away. Work with me. Not for, but with. You'll enjoy it, I promise, just as you enjoyed the war. I know, I know. It should have been terrible, and so it was. But still it raised you up, didn't it? It should have destroyed you. But you were forged by the fire, not consumed. I see that in you as clear as noon. It is a great asset. Don't waste it. Learn to use it. Let me teach you how to use it. I am sorry Henry had to die. I can help you make more of his death than anything simple revenge can bring you.'

'When I'm strong enough . . .'

'Yes?'

'I'll find you . . . and kill you.'

'Bravo.' Lemmer patted Max on the shoulder. 'You prove my point for me, Max. Don't worry. You'll come to see the sense of my argument, I'm sure of it. Go back to sleep. But remember what I've said. I must go now. Doctor Wahlen has other calls to make. I hope we will see each other again. The means of communicating with me will be made known to you in due course. I will kill you if you force me to. But I will not betray you. That is my pledge.'

As Lemmer stood up, Max made a feeble grab for the hand in which he held the key. But he was far too slow. He grasped only thin air and felt himself falling from the bed.

Lemmer caught him and heaved him back, panting, against the pillows. 'Rest, Max. Rest and reflect. Then you will understand. Then you will know I'm right. *Gute Nacht.*'

Sam's first fully functioning day in charge of the delegation garage, which occupied converted stables at the rear of the Majestic, was bound to be a busy and demanding one. There was no prospect of being able to visit Max until the evening. An early telephone call to the Hôtel Dieu had set Sam's mind at rest, however. Max's fever had broken. He was much improved. He was, Sam gathered, out of the woods.

Appleby had received similar tidings and had decided, in a moment of soft-heartedness, to deliver them to Sam in person. But, when he found the delegation's new chief mechanic whistling while he worked, he guessed those tidings had already reached him.

'I'll call in on him later today, Twentyman. Any message?'

'Let those nurses tend him like a babe, Mr A. That'd be my advice. I'll see him as soon as I've finished here, which won't be till late, judging by the way your drivers hammer these engines.'

'They're not *my* drivers.'

'Aren't you part of the establishment, then, sir?'

'A moot point, Twentyman. Decidedly moot.'

'What about Brigham?' Sam asked, lowering his

voice, though he hardly needed to in the general hub-bub of the maintenance bay.

'The matter's being dealt with, as I'll be sure to tell Max. I'll also tell him about Bukayev. Suffocated before he was dumped in the canal, according to the pathologist.'

'Does Miss Bukayeva know?'

'Zamaron will inform her.'

'The poor chick. Will Zamaron let Madame Dombreux go now?'

'Things don't happen that quickly, Twentyman. You'll have to be patient. And so will Max.'

Some things did happen quickly, however, as Appleby discovered when he returned to his office. A summons had arrived in his absence. The Permanent Under-Secretary wanted to see him. 'Without delay, sir,' Appleby's secretary informed him with some emphasis.

Lord Hardinge of Penshurst, His Majesty's Permanent Under-Secretary of State for Foreign Affairs, received Appleby in his first-floor office at the nearby Hôtel Astoria, where he enjoyed some respite from the toing and froing of the Majestic. He was a tall, lean, quietly spoken man of austere bearing, who wore authority like a favourite coat. He clearly regarded Appleby as a form of life he should not properly be required to engage with. But he was too polite to say so.

Appleby was aware that Hardinge had overseen the creation of the Secret Service back in 1909. C was there-fore beholden to him and he was obviously not a man to be trifled with. Whether he regretted allowing the establishment of an autonomous intelligence-gathering organization under the aegis of the Foreign Office was bemusingly unclear.

'Do you know why I agreed to C's proposal that you be sent here, Appleby?' Hardinge opened.

'My understanding was that you were anxious to avoid secret information finding its way to other delegations and interested parties, my lord.'

'Indeed. For what would such leaking of information constitute?'

'It would undermine confidence in the delegation's decision-making procedures.'

'And if it became publicly known?'

'There would be a scandal.'

'Precisely, Appleby. A scandal. The avoidance of such is, so far as I am concerned, the principal purpose your posting here was intended to serve.'

'As to—'

'I can hardly imagine a greater scandal than the implication of a senior civil servant in a multiple murder inquiry, can you?'

Appleby offered a pained grimace by way of reply.

'Well, can you?'

'No, my lord.'

'I read your memorandum concerning Brigham and the allegations of Miss Bukayeva with considerable pertur-bation. I intended to discuss the matter with you today. It did not occur to me that you would seek to question Brigham directly before we had had that discussion.'

Appleby shifted uneasily in his chair. He would have liked to light his pipe, if only to serve as a distraction. But he hardly felt he could in Hardinge's headmasterly presence.

'Brigham came to see me last night, after your meeting with him at the Embassy. He felt you had exceeded your authority by interrogating him and I'm bound to say I agree with him, as I shall make clear to C in due course. Would you care to defend yourself against the charge?'

Appleby cleared his throat. 'It's sometimes important to question a suspect before he has a chance to prepare himself.'

'A suspect in what?'

'I've yet to establish the full extent of Brigham's involvement in the recent spate of violent deaths, but I'm certain he is involved.'

'Sir Henry Maxted, Raffaele Spataro, Walter Ennis and Igor Bukayev. They are the spate you refer to?'

'Yes. Along with my late assistant, Thomas Lamb.'

'In your memorandum, you mentioned a man called Fritz Lemmer, whom you described, somewhat melodramatically, as "the Kaiser's spymaster".'

'It's hardly melodramatic, my lord, merely accurate.'

'In essence, you believe Brigham to be one of Lemmer's spies?'

'I regard it as highly probable.'

'How would you wish to proceed?'

'I'd like him placed in some form of detention, my lord, so I can question him at length and in detail.'

'But who is to detain him, here in Paris?'

'If you withdrew his immunity, the French police could—'

'Absolutely not. The precedent such a move would set is unconscionable. There will be no detention, Appleby. The evidence you have amassed against Brigham is insufficient to justify anything of the kind. His liaison with Miss Bukayeva certainly demonstrates poor judgement on his part, but there is no reason – no reason whatever – to believe her version of events over his.'

'I can't agree, my lord. The circumstances of the discovery of Bukayev's body clearly suggest Brigham acted at the very least as a messenger for whoever murdered him.'

'And that would be Lemmer, or those acting on Lemmer's behalf?'

'Yes.'

Hardinge sighed. 'If I allowed the French to take Brigham into custody, I'd be reading a *Figaro* editorial alleging our delegation was a nest of spies before the week was out. And by next week the work of the delegation would have disintegrated in the face of a *Daily Mail*-orchestrated witch-hunt. You seem to have no conception of how serious the ramifications of this matter could be.'

'I certainly don't think Brigham was Lemmer's only recruit in Whitehall, my lord.'

'No. I'm sure you don't.'

'The ramifications *are* serious.'

'They would be, if I gave you your head.'

'With respect, my lord, I—'

'Don't tell me you take your orders from C, Appleby. I'm well aware of that. I'm also well aware of the source of C's funding, for the simple reason that I control it. Brigham is an incorrigible philanderer. He has behaved very foolishly, but not, I judge, traitorously, far less treasonably. I have sent him back to London to cool his heels.'

'You've sent him to London?'

'I have. He can do no harm there, even supposing he has a mind to. I cannot say he was any happier to go than you appear to be to hear of his going. But I'm satisfied it was for the best.'

'Well, my lord, I—'

'Have grave reservations. Yes, no doubt you do. But I am bound to take a circumspect view. The Germany Brigham may or may not have spied for no longer exists. I think even you will agree Lemmer is not acting on behalf of the present government in Berlin. I am therefore satisfied that the integrity of the conference is not threatened by the tragic consequences of whatever manner of falling-out there may have been among his former acolytes.'

Appleby summoned a deep breath, and with it his courage, then said, 'I believe you ignore this matter at your peril, my lord.'

'I am not ignoring it, Appleby. I am setting it to one side. If C decides to have Brigham questioned in London, I will not stand in his way. But here I must have quietude. The business of the conference demands it. Is that clear?'

Appleby frowned heavily. 'It is, my lord.'

'Assess the situation for C's benefit as you see fit. But I want no further harassment of senior civil servants, or minor ones, come to that, without my explicit prior approval, which you can assume will not be forthcoming. Is that also clear?'

Appleby nodded grimly. 'Yes, my lord.'

'Excellent.' Hardinge permitted himself a thin smile. 'Then I'll bid you good morning.'

THE DOCTOR WHO CAME ON DUTY ON MONDAY MORNING expressed his pleasure and satisfaction at Max's emergence from his fever. 'You have strength, *monsieur*. It is not so common since the war. You will be leaving us on two feet, I think. *Très bien, très bien.*'

Max made no reference to his nocturnal visit from Dr Wahlen. He knew Lemmer was right. No one would credit such a story. Telling it might only delay Max's discharge from the hospital. And he wanted to be out of there as soon as possible.

A tentative foray as far as the door of his room proved he would not be striding out just yet, however. The nurse who helped him back into bed recommended *bouillon de boeuf* for breakfast and a lot more rest. It was not what Max wanted to hear. But he was in no position to contest the logic of it.

Burley assured Max that Appleby would be along to see him later. But his first visitor of the day turned out to be Schools Morahan. Even sitting down, he seemed to tower over the bed. Max was pleased to see him, though. And Morahan was evidently pleased to see him as well.

'I was more or less convinced you'd get yourself

384

killed, Max. I'm glad you didn't quite pull it off. Malory sends her love.'

'What about Ireton?'

'We've had a cable. He's staying away in light of what happened to you and Ennis. Especially Ennis. *Deem it wise to lie low until all blows over.*' Morahan smiled mirthlessly. 'Travis never was at his best under fire.'

'Where did he cable from?'

'Nowhere you'll want to follow him to. If Carver quizzes you, as I'm sure he will, refer him to me. I guess you don't need to know who in the British delegation Travis spoke to now, though, anyhow. It was Ennis who blabbed, right?'

'Wrong, actually. I—'

Max broke off as one of the more senior nurses entered in full sail. 'Your . . . *notaire* . . . is here, Monsieur Maxted. *Une affaire urgente.* You want to see him?'

'Found yourself a lawyer, Max?' Morahan asked.

'Apparently. Yes. Please show him in. Whoever he is.'

The nurse frowned and went to fetch him. 'I'll leave you to it,' said Morahan. 'If there's anything I can do for you when you get out of here, you be sure to let me know.'

Morahan's helpfulness continued to puzzle Max, but he had no time to consider it further. The lawyer who bustled in as Morahan left was, to his surprise, none other than the Maxteds' family solicitor, Gilbert Mellish, a long way from his normal Surrey stamping ground.

'Mr Mellish! What are you doing here?'

'They told me at the Mazarin you were in hospital following a shooting, Mr Maxted. I'm relieved to find you looking so well.'

'I was lucky. But what I meant was: what are you doing in Paris?'

Mellish, considerably breathless from rushing around the city and climbing the stairs of the Hôtel Dieu, subsided into the bedside chair, cradling a bulging briefcase on his lap. 'Does your mother know of your injury, Mr Maxted?'

'No. And I'd like to keep it that way.'

Mellish squirmed uneasily, but did not dispute the matter. 'As you please.'

'You still haven't told me why you're here.'

'Your father appointed you executor of his will, Mr Maxted. I assumed you'd attend his funeral and I planned to inform you afterwards, though obviously not quite this—'

'He appointed me executor?' Max was as astonished as he supposed he must look.

'Indeed.'

'Not Ashley?'

'No. Though that reminds me . . .' Mellish fished a letter out of his briefcase. 'Sir Ashley asked me to deliver this to you.'

Max took the letter and thumbed it open. It was in Ashley's handwriting on Gresscombe Place headed paper, dated 28th March – the day after their father's funeral and presumably the day Ashley had made the unwelcome discovery that Max, not he, was executor of Sir Henry's estate.

Dear James,
I am sorry that we parted in Paris on somewhat acrimonious terms. I have subsequently regretted

implying that I would not allow you to use any Gresscombe land for your proposed flying school. I would certainly not wish to stand in your way where that is concerned. Lydia and I both—

Max cast the letter aside, unfinished. 'How did Ashley take the news, Mr Mellish?'

'He was . . . surprised.'

'And my sister-in-law?'

'I believe she expressed some doubt about whether you would want to accept the appointment.'

'I have a choice?'

'You do.' Mellish leant forward. 'I should perhaps explain that beyond the executorship you are not mentioned in Sir Henry's will. There is no bequest to you.'

'Everything goes to Ashley?'

'Bar an allowance to your mother, yes. I have a copy for your perusal.' Mellish flourished the document. 'Shall I?' He made to place it on the bedside cabinet. Max nodded his assent. 'You can, er, study it at your leisure.'

'I expected no inheritance, Mr Mellish. My father was a firm believer in the principle of primogeniture.'

'Can I take it you'll act as executor?'

'I'm a poor choice. As I'm sure my brother and sister-in-law have already told you. Frankly, it's a baffling decision on Pa's part. He gave me no inkling of it.'

'Nor me, Mr Maxted. He revised his will to accommodate your appointment as recently as the twelfth of this month.'

'So that's why he went back to England at such short notice.'

'Ah. You knew of the visit?'

'Only that it occurred. Not the reason. Until now.'

'There may have been several reasons. I've had a letter from the curator of the county museum.' Mellish made another extraction from his briefcase. 'It appears that after visiting my office on the twelfth Sir Henry proceeded to Guildford, where he reclaimed some ancient artefacts loaned to the museum by his father. The curator wants to know if they're likely to be returned to their keeping following Sir Henry's death. That would be a matter for, er, his executor, of course.'

'Ancient artefacts, you say?'

'Sumerian cylinder-seals, to be precise.'

'Seals?'

'Yes. You've seen them?'

'No.' Max sighed. 'And I doubt the curator will again.'

'Oh?'

'I think Pa probably sold them.'

'Really?' Mellish looked pained as well as puzzled. 'Well, you may wish to tell the curator that.'

'I can't act as executor, Mr Mellish. I don't have the time. Judging by his letter, Ashley's anxious to persuade me to renounce the role, so I may as well oblige him.' A few short weeks ago, Max would have fought tooth and nail for his and Sam's flying school. Now it hardly seemed to matter. It belonged to a different world – a different life. 'Where do I sign?'

Mellish adjusted his glasses and peered at Max. 'Sign what, Mr Maxted?'

'Whatever I have to sign to give up the executorship.'

'Well, I . . .'

'You said I had a choice.'

'Indeed. I can certainly prepare a letter of renunci-
ation. You'd need to sign it in my presence, or more
appropriately in the presence of some other notary
public, so that it can be formally lodged with the
probate registry. But that may not be necessary. I can
handle all administrative matters pertaining to the
settlement of Sir Henry's estate if you instruct me to do
so. The demands on your time and attention would be
minimal.'

'Even minimal's probably more than I can manage.'

'But there is something else you have to consider, Mr
Maxted. In many respects, it's why I've travelled to Paris.
This.' Yet another document emerged from the briefcase,
clutched in Mellish's sausage-fingered hand. 'Sir Henry
did more than revise his will when he came to see me
on the twelfth. He dictated and signed quite specific
instructions relating to an item of his property not
mentioned in the will. Mentioned or not, of course, it
still forms part of Sir Ashley's inheritance, but, as
executor, it falls to you to take the steps required to
classify it as an asset of the deceased.'

Max grimaced. 'What?'

'Sir Henry lodged the item – or items – in a safe-
deposit box at a bank here in Paris. But he did so under
an assumed name, hence the procedural difficulty. The
letter he left with me overcomes that difficulty, however.
It supplies the name and address of the bank, the
number of the safe-deposit box and his pseudonym:
Farngold. That should be sufficient to gain you access.
There will have been a key also. Did you come across
one amongst his possessions that might fit such a box?'

Max's heart sank. Oh, yes, he had come across the

389

key. Hidden, discovered . . . and lost. 'I don't have it,' he said levelly.

'No matter. The will identifies you as his executor and the letter authorizes you to take charge of the contents of the box. As soon as you're fit enough to leave the hospital, I would recommend you contact' – Mellish consulted the letter – 'la Banque Ornal and claim the property, whatever it might be.'

'Pa gave no clue?'

'None. But he left me in little doubt that it was very important to him. And possibly . . .'

'Yes?'

'To you as well, Mr Maxted, if I'm to be frank.'

'He said that?'

'No. It was an impression I had. But a forceful impression, certainly. The use of a pseudonym is also indicative of . . .' Mellish cleared his throat and fell silent, unable, it seemed, to frame his idea of what such a precaution might point to.

'Where is la Banque Ornal, Mr Mellish?'

Mellish glanced at the letter. 'Rue Vivienne, second *arrondissement*.'

'Not far.'

'No? Well, once you've recovered sufficiently, I suggest—'

'Hang that, Mr Mellish.' Max pushed himself up, threw back the blankets and swung his feet to the floor. 'I'm going now. There's no time to be lost.'

TIME TO BE LOST OR NOT, MAX DID NOT ACHIEVE AN instantaneous departure from the Hôtel Dieu. The doctor who had congratulated him on riding out his fever was fetched to caution him against leaving. 'You need to rest, monsieur. Se reposer.' It did not help Max's cause that Mellish urged the same. 'Leave it until tomorrow at least, Mr Maxted. I can wait.'

But Max could not wait. And Mellish admitted that nothing short of a personal visit to the bank would suffice. Eventually, a compromise was agreed. Max would not actually discharge himself, merely travel to the bank with Mellish, then return to the hospital.

As it turned out, Burley went with them. Having failed to contact Appleby by telephone, he decided it made no sense to guard a room whose occupant had left it. Max suffered the indignity of being conveyed in a wheelchair down in the lift to the ground floor, then along the corridors to the main entrance, where a taxi was waiting.

Quitting the chair as he exited into the open air, he was relieved to discover that he could walk short distances without difficulty, despite shortness of breath and a disquieting rubberiness in his legs. He felt better just for being out of hospital, though the coldness of the weather came as a shock. They squeezed into the taxi and set off.

Burley did not accompany them into the bank, whose ornate frontage seemed to persuade him that Max would be safe enough inside. The premises were certainly imposing, with high ceilings, classical frescos, *grand siècle* furnishings and lavishly marbled acreages of space.

They were received courteously, but the response to their request, once it had been understood, was far from speedy. They were kept waiting for close to half an hour before being ushered into the office of *le directeur*. Mellish chose to interpret the delay as no more than typical French dilatoriness, but Max had begun to fear a more sinister explanation. The involvement of the bank's senior officer did nothing to reassure him.

There were elaborate introductions. The director's surname was Charretier-Ornal. He was evidently some semi-detached member of the founding family. He did not look like a man who had worked his way up through the business counting francs and cashing cheques. There was nothing remotely clerical about him. His manner was smooth and confident, with the barest undertow of discomposure.

He read English as well as he spoke it and swiftly perused the various documents Mellish presented: the will, the death certificate, the letter of authorization. He tut-tutted as if he had detected a discrepancy before returning them, prompting Mellish to ask if something was wrong.

'The documents indicate that the Monsieur Farngold who rented box number 2576 was actually Sir Henry Maxted, who died on the twenty-first of this month,' said Charretier-Ornal, speaking slowly and carefully. 'That is your contention, *messieurs*?'

'It's not a contention,' said Max. 'It's a fact.'

'*Oui*. A fact. As you say, Monsieur Maxted. My condolences to you. I read of Sir Henry's death in the newspaper. A great tragedy.'

'You realized he was the man known to your bank as Farngold?'

'*Non, non. Pas du tout*. Monsieur Farngold was a customer like any other. We did not know it was . . . *un pseudonyme*. I never met him. The transaction was . . . routine. There was no reason for us to question his identity.'

'Well,' said Mellish, 'I trust you accept that, as Sir Henry's executor, Mr Maxted is entitled to access to box 2576.'

'*Bien sûr*. I accept it. But you must understand, *messieurs*, that the conditions we agreed with Monsieur Farngold – Sir Henry – were simple as regards to access. They were our standard conditions. He would unlock the box in private using the key supplied to him when he first rented it.'

'We don't have the key,' said Max.

'But you can open the box,' said Mellish. 'There must be provision for that to be done if the key is lost.'

'*Mais oui*. There is provision. But that is not the problem.'

'What *is* the problem?' Max pressed.

Charretier-Ornal pursed his lips and frowned. A

moment passed. Then he said, 'There was access to the box earlier this morning.'

'What?'

'A man claiming to be Monsieur Farngold came here at' – he consulted a note – 'ten thirty. He gave my staff no reason to doubt he was who he said he was. His signature matched the specimen. He had the key to the box. He was given access to it. He left at' – another consultation – 'ten fifty.'

It was as Max had feared. Lemmer had got there before them. He sank his face in his hand. 'Oh God,' he murmured.

'I must emphasize that we proceeded strictly according to the conditions of use. There was no . . . *déviation. Voyez vous-même.*'

Charretier-Ornal thrust under Max's nose a form bearing a signature in the name of H. Farngold that undeniably reminded Max of his father's handwriting. Another form swiftly followed: the specimen. They were a close match. Not exact – for how could they be? – but close enough to satisfy a credulous bank clerk on a humdrum Monday morning. Max almost felt sorry for the blustering director. They had all been outclassed.

'If the man was an impostor—'

'He was either that or a ghost, *monsieur.*' Max smiled grimly at Charretier-Ornal. 'Take your pick.'

'A friend of your father, perhaps, obeying some . . . dying wish.'

'My father died in a fall from a roof, *monsieur*. He had no time for dying wishes.'

'This is all highly unsatisfactory,' said Mellish. 'You

appear to have allowed an unknown third party access to Sir Henry's property.'

Charretier-Ornal scowled at the implication of incompetence. 'Sir Henry must have given the third party, as you call him, the key – *et le pseudonyme*. We cannot be responsible.'

'As to that, it'll be for—'

'Never mind who's responsible,' Max cut in. 'Did the man claiming to be Farngold empty the box?'

Charretier-Ornal shrugged. 'I cannot say. The boxes are opened in private, as I explained to you. We do not know what they contain.'

'Can we see what this one contains now?'

Silence briefly intervened. Charretier-Ornal looked momentarily indecisive. Then he said, '*Oui*. Let us all go and see.'

Charretier-Ornal spoke to someone on his telephone – too quickly for Max to follow what was said – then they descended to the bank's vault. A clerk who had been hovering outside the director's office fell in with them to unlock various doors along the way. A second man, less smartly dressed and introduced by Charretier-Ornal as '*notre serrurier* – our locksmith' joined them en route. Charretier-Ornal set a brisk, impatient pace, before realizing that the corpulent Mellish and the ailing Max could not keep up with him.

'You do not look well, Monsieur Maxted,' he remarked.

'I feel better than I look.'

'That is good. May I repeat my condolences on your loss.'

'You can repeat them, by all means. But they won't help.'

They reached the room housing the safe-deposit boxes. Three walls were lined with numbered, lockable steel hatches of varying sizes. The clerk had a key for the hatch numbered 2576 and removed the box that was inside.

The box, also of steel, was about three feet deep, a foot wide and a foot high. The clerk laid it on the table in the centre of the room. He said something to Charretier-Ornal in French as he did so.

'What was that?' Max queried.

Charretier-Ornal grimaced. 'He said it feels light.'

'Is he the one who brought the man claiming to be Farngold down here earlier?'

'He is.'

'Can he describe him?'

There was an exchange in French. Charretier-Ornal's glum expression remained glum throughout. Then: 'A man of sixty years or about, he thinks. English, he also thinks. Not fat. Not thin. Not tall. Not short. There was nothing to remember about him. Grey hair. Beard. He spoke quietly.' The director shrugged. '*C'est tout.*'

'Do you know who he is, Mr Maxted?' Mellish asked.

Max nodded. 'I believe I do.' He looked at the locksmith. '*Ouvrez la boîte, s'il vous plaît.*'

It required a wave of the hand from Charretier-Ornal before the locksmith swung into action. Within a few minutes, he had removed the lock. The clerk prepared to raise the lid. And they all stepped forward to see what might be inside.

It was as Max had known it would be.

ACCORDING TO SAM, WHO HAD SEEN A LOT OF PILOTS COME and, sadly, go, one of Max's most valuable assets was his optimism. 'It might sound stupid to you, sir,' he had once said under a cerulean sky into which Max was about to take off, 'but I reckon those who expect to survive usually do.'

Well, Max had survived the war, true to Sam's prediction, albeit half of it in a POW camp. And he was by nature an optimist, sometimes to his own surprise. Sitting in the vault of la Banque Ornal that morning, staring at the empty safe-deposit box on the table in front of him, he wondered how long it would be before he finally abandoned the notion of bringing his father's murderers to justice. He should perhaps have despaired there and then.

He did not contribute to the increasingly tetchy discussion between Mellish and Charretier-Ornal about responsibility for allowing an impostor access to the safe-deposit box. It was a redundant debate. The fox had had his run of the hen-coop. And he had not even left a few feathers behind him.

How had Lemmer discovered the pseudonym Sir Henry had used? How had he been able to forge his

signature so convincingly? How, come to that, had he
known which bank Sir Henry had used? The questions
only illustrated the scope of Lemmer's power. He was
always at least one step ahead of his pursuers. Several
steps, in this case.

'I'm not going back to the hospital,' Max announced as
he and Mellish, the latter still grumbling pointlessly
about the bank's ineptitude, walked out to rejoin Burley.
'The doctor said all I need is rest. I can get that at the
Mazarin.'

'What?' Mellish gaped at him.

'I'm not going back to the hospital.'

'That's surely unwise,' said Mellish.

'*Definitely* unwise,' Burley contributed.

'You're right, of course.' Max drew in a lungful of
Parisian air and knew that, however short of his best he
currently was, retreating to a bed at the Hôtel Dieu was
not to be countenanced. 'But then unwise is what I
mean to be.'

Burley had not been idle during Max and Mellish's
sojourn at the bank. He had telephoned Appleby again
and this time got through to him. He made another call
when they reached the Mazarin. Appleby, he reported,
had a lot to discuss with Max, wherever he chose to rest,
and would be with him within the hour.

The hour passed swiftly, as Max gingerly took a bath,
applied a fresh bandage to his wound, and recovered as
best he could from the disproportionate effort involved.
He would have told any other man behaving as he

was that he was being a damn fool. But he could not help that. He was not going to give in, even to his own frailty.

It was hard to tell whether Appleby's downcast expression when he arrived was due to Max's appearance or the tidings he had brought. 'Do you want to know how you look?' he asked as he slumped down in the only armchair in the room and watched Max lower himself on to the edge of the bed.

Max came to rest with a wince. 'No.'

'Good. Because I've quite enough bad news to deliver as it is.'

'You'd better get on with it, then.'

So Appleby did, relating the discovery of Igor Bukayev's body in the Canal de l'Ourcq, Nadia Bukayeva's allegations against Brigham and Brigham's subsequent departure for London. 'I've been officially warned off, Max. Brigham's boss outranks my boss. My hands are tied.'

'It sounds like Sam's been busy on my behalf while I've been laid up. I must thank him. And I must proffer my condolences to Nadia as well.'

'Well, perhaps you can console each other for your misfortunes. Although I wouldn't try anything too energetic in your present condition. Burley tells me you think it was Lemmer who emptied Sir Henry's safe-deposit box. In person, would that be?'

'Maybe. I'm not sure.' Max was not ready to tell anyone, even Appleby, about his encounter with Lemmer. He was not sure Appleby would believe him. He had difficulty believing it himself. 'Without whatever the box contained, though, and with Ennis dead, Brigham's the only possible source of information about Lemmer's network. If you can't squeeze anything out of him, I'll have to.'

'How?'

'I think I can find a way under his defences.' Brigham's weakness was his belief that he was Max's father. That was what Max would play on, reluctant as he was to do so. 'Leave it to me. I'll follow him to London and give it my best shot.'

'How soon will you be fit enough to travel?'

'I'll go on tonight's sleeper.'

'Being shaken around on that won't do you much good. And then there's the Channel crossing.'

'Is there a storm forecast?'

'Not that I know of.'

'Then don't worry about me. I only need you to do a couple of things for me.'

'What?'

'Get me the gun you promised before I leave.'

'I didn't promise anything.'

Max gave Appleby a straight look. 'Just get it, OK?'

Appleby sighed. 'Very well.'

'And can you organize the ticket?'

'All right. But you'll be on your own, you know. In every sense of the word.'

'Oh, I know. But that doesn't matter. Actually, it's how I prefer it.'

Max had a meal sent up to him and planned to take a nap afterwards, before going to the Majestic to speak to Sam. In the event, he plunged into a deep sleep and was woken by Sam coming to see him at the end of his working day. It was already early evening. Anxious as he was to set off, time was slipping through his fingers like sand.

'You should still be in the hospital, sir,' Sam said, frowning at Max with obvious concern. 'Mr Appleby said you were off to London tonight. You never are, are you?'

'Needs must, Sam.'

'You're going after Brigham?'

'Someone has to.'

'But you're not well enough. It's plain to see.'

Max strode less than fluidly across to the dressing-table and peered at himself in the mirror. 'A little pale, I grant you. A steak supper will see me right. Care to join me?'

'More than happy to, sir. But there's something I have to tell you first.'

'Appleby filled me in on everything, Sam. You did well and I'm very grateful. Finding Bukayev as you did can't have been pleasant. You can tell me all about it over a stiff drink.'

'This is something Mr Appleby doesn't know about, sir.'

'It is?'

'And in the circumstances . . . I don't think it'll wait.'

As they left the Mazarin, the reception clerk presented Max with a letter that had been handed in for him. The envelope contained his ticket for the sleeper to London and a note from Appleby. *I will meet you with the other at the station tonight.*

'What's the "other", sir?' Sam asked, craning over his shoulder as they exited on to the street.

'A bath-chair, I expect. Everyone's convinced I'm an invalid.' Max suspected Sam would worry about him all the more if he knew he was going to be carrying a gun.

'But you *are* an invalid, sir, that's the trouble. Maybe I ought to go with you.'

'And walk out on your new job? I wouldn't hear of it. I'll see my doctor when I get to London. He can do any patching-up that's needed.'

'You'll have a relapse if you overdo it.'

'I'm not letting Brigham off the hook, Sam. You may as well accept it. Now, find us a cab, there's a good fellow. Ordinarily, I'd walk to the Plaza Athénée, but as it is . . .'

'I'll find one, sir. You just stay there.'

*

Baltazar Ribeiro was dressing for dinner when they were admitted to his suite at the Plaza Athénée. His delight at seeing Max up and about was considerable, although it was swiftly followed by concern. 'Sit, sit,' he said, ushering Max to a couch.

'Before he falls down, eh, *senhor*?' said Sam. 'I have tried to tell him.'

'And as I've already told Sam, I can't afford to rest. I've lost enough time lying in that hospital already.'

'Drink a little brandy,' said Ribeiro, fumbling with a bottle and some glasses. 'It gives strength when you need it.'

Max did not argue and accepted a tot. 'I expect you can guess why we're here, Baltazar,' he said, swallowing some down.

'Of course. I meant what I said to Mr Twentyman yesterday. It is time to share the secret with you, Max, and I am glad to have the chance – glad because you are well enough to be told.' Ribeiro drew up a couple of armchairs, one for himself, one for Sam, and sat down. He drank some of his brandy and gazed earnestly at Max. 'Henry was my friend. I did not feel I could tell you this when we first met because he had trusted me to tell no one. But so much has happened since then that I think now you should know. Still, it is not easy. I feel I am . . . betraying him.'

'I understand,' said Max. 'But if this information helps me bring his murderers to justice . . .'

'I do not see how it can do that. But at least you will know what was in his mind. In truth, it is a simple story. *O amor*. Love. He was planning a future for himself and Corinne Dombreux. He was not a rich man. His wealth was in the estate in England. He needed money of his own to give them a comfortable life somewhere. And I . . . suggested a way to get it.' Ribeiro frowned at his own folly – or that of Sir Henry. 'I inherited land in Amazonas from my elder brother, Francisco, land that had once made our family rich from the rubber it produced. But the business went into decline around the turn of the century because of competition from Asian plantations. Now the land is nothing except jungle. An Englishman is to blame for this, I must tell you. A man called Wickham smuggled thousands of rubber seeds out of Brazil that were used to start growing the crop in Malaya. Our monopoly was broken. Our rubber trees grow wild, you must understand. We did not plant them. We could not compete with the close-grown Asian plantations. The riches . . . evaporated.'

'Baltazar, I don't quite—'

'Wait, wait. I will explain. Francisco had a plan. He believed plantation rubber could be successfully grown in Brazil. It only required labour to clear the land and expert knowledge of how to cultivate the crop. He bought options on several neighbouring estates and sent a trusted man to Malaya to study how it was done. Then he died. And the war came. But the options stand. I inherited them from him. I have had discussions with representatives of two large American corporations who are interested in investing in Francisco's scheme. Motor cars are the transport of the future, Max. One day everyone will want to own one. And every car has four tyres made of rubber. This could make me rich again many times over. It could have made Henry rich too. If he had lived.'

'You persuaded him to put some money into this venture?'

'I offered him the opportunity, as a friend. Firestone and Ford – there now, I have told you who the American corporations are – do not want the price of rubber to be set by Britain, France and the Netherlands, the imperial powers who control the rubber-growing areas of south-east Asia. They fear a cartel, with the price going up and up. A separate source of rubber, in Brazil, controlled by them, appeals to them greatly. They will pay handsomely to secure it. But I must take up the options if I am to be the one they pay. And for that I need liquid cash. I have some, of course. But not enough. I asked Henry if he would like to be my partner. He said yes. And he said he thought he could raise the rest of the cash we would need. I did not ask how. But I swear to you I did not think he meant to risk his life to do it.'

Max contemplated the irony of his father's fate. His relationship with Corinne was a late-life chance of happiness. Naturally, he wanted to give her all the luxuries she had been denied in recent times. Then Ribeiro came to him with a proposition that must have seemed heaven-sent. All he needed was his share of the investment. And so he turned his mind to such assets as he could trade in. It was a short list – and, as it turned out, a dangerous one. 'Where did he plan to take Corinne, Baltazar?'

'He did not say. Rio, maybe. He loved the city and would have enjoyed introducing her to it. With his share of the profit, he could have bought a grand mansion in Botafogo and a villa in Petrópolis to retreat to in the summer and a private art collection and a racehorse and more fine clothes and jewellery than Madame Dombreux could ever have worn.'

'Is this really rubber you're talking about – or gold?'

'Rubber *is* gold to Henry Ford and Harvey Firestone, Max. They will pay whatever I ask.'

'Will you still go through with it?'

'If I can raise the money to buy the options, yes, I suppose I will. But I must be honest with you. There is profit and there is joy. They are not the same. Money is paper and the possessions you buy with it. Joy is in the spirit. And there is no joy for me in this now Henry is dead. Especially if I believe, as it seems I must, that he died because of my accursed scheme to make us both rich.'

'You shouldn't blame yourself. I'm sure my father wouldn't want you to.'

'No. He would not. He was a good man.'

'About Ennis, Baltazar . . .'

'*Sim?*'

'Sam tells me Ennis mentioned "contingencies".'

'Ah yes. He did. I do not know what he meant.'

'Does the phrase "Contingencies Memorandum" mean anything to you?'

Ribeiro shook his head. 'No. A document maybe. Something to do with the conference.'

'Something my father saw as a source of money, actually. But what exactly it was . . . or is . . .'

'I did not know he carried so many secrets. They did not weigh him down. I will say that. The last time I saw him, his heart was light.'

'Did he ever mention a man called Fritz Lemmer to you?'

'Lemmer?' Ribeiro frowned. 'Yes. I think he did. Not

406

recently, though. Years ago, when we first knew each other, in Rio.'

'What did he say?'

'*Meu Deus!* It is so long ago. But I do remember the name. Yes, Lemmer. What was it? What was it Henry used to say?' Ribeiro stroked his moustache as he cast his mind back. 'Somehow, I think, he was involved with an assassination attempt against the Tsarevich in Japan. Yes. Japan. That is where Henry knew Lemmer. You know him also?'

'I'm beginning to. He's a dangerous man. As Pa discovered.'

'I am sorry I did not tell you the whole truth when you first came to see me.'

'It wouldn't have made any difference, Baltazar. It wasn't your rubber venture that got my father killed. It's what he did to fund it.'

'Rio has the most beautiful racecourse in the world, you know, with the mountains and the bay and the clear, clear light.' Ribeiro shook his head in mourning for times past. 'Such days we had there, Henry and I.' He sighed. 'He always liked long odds. It was a weakness of his. I believe you may have inherited it.'

'You could be right.' Max rose slowly to his feet, gratified by the lack of pain in his side. 'I certainly wouldn't suggest you back me to win.'

'But you will run the course, even so?'

Max nodded. 'Oh yes. To the end.'

IN THE END, MAX HAD HIS STEAK AT THE GARE DU NORD. HE was tired, but oddly exhilarated. Lemmer had got the better of him so far, it was true, but Brigham was vulnerable for reasons Lemmer was almost certainly unaware of and Max was confident he could exploit the fact.

He asked Sam to tell Nadia where he was going and why. He had hoped to see her that evening, but the visit to Ribeiro had eaten into his reserves of time and energy. He also asked Sam to apologize to Mellish on his behalf for giving him no warning of his departure. Sam reiterated his opinion that a man in Max's condition should be going nowhere except the nearest hospital. But he knew Max was not going to change his mind. 'You are a stubborn so-and-so, sir, you truly are.'

Appleby arrived to see Max off with barely ten minutes to spare before the train left. Max had begun to suspect he was not going to be supplied with the promised gun, but Appleby had actually been delayed by a wrangle with Carver. 'It may be just as well you left the Hôtel Dieu when you did. He was hoping to interrogate you. Naturally, I claimed ignorance of where you'd gone.'

The revolver came with a box of ammunition. 'As far

as anyone's to know,' Appleby emphasized, 'you bought this from an ex-serviceman in a bar.'

'I'll remember that.'

'What kind of marksman are you?'

'I wasn't bad with a machine-gun mounted on a Sopwith Camel.'

'Have you ever fired a revolver?'

'No. But don't worry. The other chap won't know that.'

He boarded the train with Sam, who stowed his bag in the first-class sleeping compartment Appleby had generously paid for. They shook hands before Sam got off. No words were spoken. They had said all that needed to be said. Max lit a cigarette, his first since the shooting, and waved from the window as jauntily as he could manage when the train drew out. Appleby had already left. Only Sam remained to wave back.

Max surprised himself by sleeping well as the train wound north through the night. A pink-streaked dawn was breaking as the ferry left Calais. His Channel crossing with Ashley seemed an age ago, though in fact only a week had passed since then. Time, as he knew from the contrast between active service and confinement as a POW, was a deceptively elastic commodity.

It was mid-morning when the train reached Victoria. Max felt sore and weary, despite all the sleep he had had. He made straight for the flat. Tuesday was not one of Mrs Harrison's cleaning days, so he was safe from mothering by her. A shivering fit on the ferry had subsided as rapidly as it had come and his wound seemed to be healing well. He was still several paces slower, in thought and movement, than he was used to being. He was not quite as firmly fixed in the world as he knew he should be. It was as if he was slightly drunk when in reality he was stone-cold sober – and deadly serious.

After a soothing bath and a closer shave than he could have managed on the train, he telephoned the Foreign Office. He was put through to Brigham's secretary. She was all plummy-toned unhelpfulness at first, but, after consulting Brigham at Max's insistence, she changed her tune. 'I'll put you through, Mr Maxted.'

'James?' Brigham sounded suspicious, as well he might, but also strangely solicitous. 'I'm glad to hear from you. How are you? I've been worried about you.'

'You know about the shooting?'

'Yes. I'd have come to see you if I hadn't been, well, banished in effect, as a result of an absurd misunderstanding. Are you phoning from the hospital? It's an unusually good line.'

'No. I'm in London.'

'What? How's that?'

'I discharged myself. It wasn't a serious wound. I feel fine.'

'Really?'

'Really.'

'But what brings you to London?'

'You do, Brigham. I've been thinking about what you said when we met in Paris. I shouldn't have flown off the handle as I did.'

'Well, it's understandable that—'

'The fact is, I think I may have misjudged you.'

'You do?'

'It's an awkward situation. I'm sure you appreciate that.'

'Of course.'

'I wonder if we could meet and talk things through a little more calmly.'

'I'd be delighted to, my boy. When can you manage? How about lunch at my club? My unexpected return to London means I have an empty diary.'

'Lunch at your club would suit me very well.'

'Then I'll see you at the Athenaeum at one.'

Max donned an artificial persona as well as one of his better suits for lunch with Brigham. He would be reasonable, open-minded and receptive. He would imply that his brush with death had made him appreciate how justified – and genuine – Brigham's concern for his welfare was. As to their possible blood relationship, he would suggest it was a question they could never hope to answer conclusively; it might best be left open. They were men of the world. Not all marriages were happy. Not all adulteries were contemptible. Oh, yes, Max intended to be everything he needed to be to set Brigham at ease.

The ploy was remarkably successful. Brigham greeted him in the entrance hall of the Athenaeum warmly, if nervously. 'We got off on the wrong foot last time, James. I can't tell you how pleased I am to have this chance of setting matters right.'

411

They went into the dining-room and sat at a window table. Brigham was well-known to the staff and other members. He was in his element, which was exactly where Max wanted him. Max ventured an apology for his behaviour when they had last met. Brigham assured him it was unnecessary. They relaxed over aperitifs. Brigham referred again to the 'misunderstanding' that had led to his departure from Paris. Max did not oblige him to elaborate.

Wine began to flow, though Max made sure more of it flowed down Brigham's throat than his. He recounted his war experiences. Brigham described the life of a diplomat. They both expended a deal of delicacy in discussing Brigham's friendship with Max's mother, while refraining from specifying what it might mean they were to each other. Neither of them mentioned Walter Ennis or Igor Bukayev. Neither spoke directly of the circumstances of Sir Henry's death.

Late in the meal, Max shifted the ground of their conversation, as he had always intended to. 'I think I may have threatened to kill you when we spoke that night in Paris, Brigham.'

'I trust you're not planning to now.' Brigham's voice was slightly slurred, his face flushed, but not with anger. He was, in fact, smiling broadly.

'No. My narrow escape at Notre-Dame has made me realize how foolishly I was behaving then.'

'I did warn you.'

'Indeed you did. I should have listened.'

'Paris may not look like a snake-pit, but that's what it is while this damned conference brings half the world's rogues to its boulevards. You were lucky not to be killed.'

412

'I know. Blundering around the city accusing every third person I met of involvement in Pa's murder wasn't the wisest way to proceed.'

'Probably not.'

'I've made myself a few enemies in the process.'

'Just as well you've left Paris, then.'

'Yes. But some of them have a long reach, I fear. One in particular.' Max lowered his voice and leant across the table. 'Fritz Lemmer.'

'Lemmer?' Brigham's eyes widened in an impressive show of surprise. 'You surely haven't crossed his path.'

'You know who he is?'

'The Secret Service do brief us from time to time, albeit reluctantly. Yes, I know who Lemmer is – and what he used to be – though I've always suspected his importance was overestimated.'

'Pa posed a threat to Lemmer. I believe that's why he was killed. And I believe it's why my life is in danger.'

'You think it is? I assumed you were just . . . in the firing line . . . when Ennis was shot.'

'I need help, Brigham. *Your* help.'

'Well, if there's anything I can do . . .'

'How do I get Lemmer off my back?'

'Perhaps, if you leave him alone, he'll leave you alone.'

'I'm afraid I may have got too close to him already for him to take that line. I think I have to send him some kind of message if I'm to persuade him to call off the dogs.'

'How do you propose to do that?'

'You know a lot of people, Brigham. I remember you told me I lacked connections. And you were right. But you have connections, don't you, built up over the years?'

'A good many, yes.'

'So, could you use them to communicate with Lemmer on my behalf?'

'With *Lemmer*?'

'Yes.'

Brigham sat back in his chair and frowned. 'You know what they say he did for the Kaiser. You know how he's supposed to operate. And now, as I understand it, he's on the run. You can't seriously suppose I have any way of approaching him.'

'Not even if my life depends on it?'

The frown deepened. 'I'd have to find someone who was – or knows someone who was – one of Lemmer's spies.'

'Or still is.'

'Exactly. Which is something no one in their right mind would admit, or even encourage another to infer. Good God, it's what Appleby more or less accused me of being on the basis of that Russian girl's crazy allegations.'

'I wouldn't ask how you managed it, Brigham. I'd simply be grateful. I just want Lemmer to understand I'm not a threat to him, as I'd be prepared to demonstrate in any way he asked.'

Brigham cocked his head in a show of perplexity. 'What do you mean by that, my boy?'

'I'm not sure. You probably know how these things work better than I do. It's just that I've begun to see the wisdom of the old saying: if you can't beat 'em, join 'em.'

'You surely wouldn't want to *join* Lemmer's operation.'

'Not as such, no. But it's effectively defunct, isn't it, with the Kaiser in exile? Lemmer's in no position to damage British interests, so doing him some small service would harm no one. You catch my drift?'

'I couldn't possibly advise you to strike terms with a man like Lemmer, James. The war may be over, but he's still an enemy of this country.'

'Friends and enemies can be a little hard to tell apart in the situation I find myself in.'

'I appreciate that, but—'

'Is there really nothing you can do for me? I don't know where else to turn.'

Surely Brigham would give ground now. Surely he could not ignore such an appeal. Max gazed pleadingly into the eyes of the man who so badly wanted to believe he was his father. And something shifted in Brigham's gaze. 'I suppose there are . . . avenues I could explore.'

'You'd be willing to do that for me?'

'Yes. But this is a delicate business.' Brigham craned forward and dropped his voice to a whisper. 'If we're to discuss it further, I'd prefer we did so in a more private setting.'

There was no one within earshot. Most of the other tables had emptied long since. But Max was not about to challenge Brigham's logic. A more private setting would suit him very well. 'We could go to my place in town. It's in Mount Street.'

'I believe I may have been there.'

When and why Brigham had been there he was unlikely to say and Max had no wish to ask. The flat had originally been bought by Sir Henry as a pied-à-terre within easy reach of the Foreign Office. During his many long absences abroad, Lady Maxted had used it for visits to London to shop or see a play or . . . otherwise amuse herself. Max could have guessed that Brigham would have found his way there at some point, but he could not afford to indulge the distaste he felt at the thought.

'Listen, James, I ought to put in an appearance at the office this afternoon.' Brigham glanced at his watch. 'What's left of the afternoon, anyway. I'll call on you at the flat at, say, six o'clock. By then I'll have been able to give some thought to your problem. I want to help you, I really do. And I will if I possibly can.'

'I can't tell you what a relief it is to hear you say that.' What a consummate liar Max was becoming. He quite appalled himself.

'Don't worry, my boy. There's a way out of everything if you look hard enough.'

'I hope you're right.' And so another lie tripped from Max's lips. For there would be no way out of the trap he was setting for Brigham. He would see to that.

A SURPRISE AWAITED SAM IN THE REPAIR BAY OF THE garage at the Majestic that morning: a black Daimler, registration number HX 4344, with Hegg, one of the keener if not necessarily most proficient mechanics, at work on its clutch. Since, as far as Sam knew, Brigham had left Paris twenty-four hours earlier, the car's arrival was a puzzle he immediately set about solving.

'When did this come in, Billy?' he asked, joining Hegg by the open bonnet.

'Last night, just after you'd gone, Mr Twentyman. The gears are slippin' somethin' awful. But I'll fix that.'

'It's not one of our fleet cars.'

'No. The owner must've brought it with him from London. Decent bloke. None of that shoutin' and stampin' you get from some of—'

'You met him?'

'Yeah. Last night, like I say.'

'You *met* the owner? Here? Last night?'

Hegg scratched his bristly head. 'Yeah. Mr Norris. What's the problem?'

Sam had never heard of Norris. He spent several

minutes in the relative privacy of his cubby-hole of an office trying to decide what to make of the development. Norris, he concluded, was probably a friend Brigham had asked to take the car in for repair in his absence. He would naturally have given Hegg the impression he was the owner, probably without even meaning to. Yes. That was it. That was the only logical explanation.

After satisfying himself that there were no urgent matters requiring his attention in the garage – and with the minor mystery of Norris's stewardship of Brigham's Daimler pushed to the back of his mind – Sam slipped out to pay a call on Max's solicitor at his hotel, a short step away on the other side of the Champs-Elysées.

He found Mellish consuming breakfast in a gloomy corner of the hotel's dining-room, introduced himself and reported Max's sudden departure. 'He asked me to say how sorry he was he couldn't let you know, sir.'

'Is he really well enough to travel, Mr Twentyman?'

'He thinks he is.'

'And is he coming back here? Or should I follow him? I need to take his instructions regarding his father's estate.'

'Oh, he'll be back.'

'When?'

'Ah well, that's the question.' Sam shrugged.

And Mellish sighed. 'I see.'

Sam was tempted to press on to Little Russia and pay a call on Nadia, but he did not like to be away from his post for long. He had only just started the job, after all, and could not afford to have his reliability called into question.

As chief mechanic, however, he was blessed with a telephone. It was not difficult to find a slack moment during the morning to call Nadia at the bookshop. But there was no answer. It occurred to him then that she had probably closed the shop for a period of mourning. He would have to contact her later.

Within half an hour or so, however, he was summoned from the inspection-pit to take 'an urgent call'. Nadia was on the line.

'Max has left the Hôtel Dieu, Sam. They do not know where he is. What is happening?'

'He felt well enough to leave, so he did. He's had to go to London.'

'London? Why?'

'Could we meet later? I could explain then.'

'Yes. That would be good. You are busy until when?'

'Six o'clock or so.'

'Come to the shop then.'

'All right, I'll be there. How are you . . . bearing up?'

'It is not easy, Sam. But I must not keep you from your work. *Da—*'

'Before you go . . .'. Sam cut in.

'Yes?'

'Have you heard of a man called Norris?'

'*Norrees?*'

'Yes. A member of the British delegation. A friend of Brigham's. Norris.'

'I . . . do not think so.'

'Well, never mind. It was—'

'Why are you asking?'

'It's probably nothing.'

'But possibly something?'

'Exactly. Don't worry. I'll sort it out.'

The comings and goings of members of the British and Dominions delegations were, as Shuttleworth had warned Sam when appointing him, usually but not always predictable. Monday had gone smoothly and calmly, as had half of Tuesday. From noon onwards, however, there was a sudden surge of demand for cars to shuttle important (and some not so important) person-ages between the Majestic, the Quai d'Orsay, the Crillon, the Edward VII (headquarters of the Italians) and the Place des États-Unis (home from home of President Wilson). The Council of Four, reliable rumour had it, had resolved to despatch a peace mission to Budapest in an attempt to bring the new Bolshevik government in Hungary to heel. The emissaries were to leave that evening, so a procession of cars to the Gare de l'Est was bound to follow. Ensuring enough roadworthy vehicles would be available became Sam's sole pre-occupation for the next few hours and drove apparent trivialities such as Norris's claim to Brigham's Daimler far from his thoughts.

In London, Max had to rest on a bench in St James's Square, and another in Berkeley Square, on his way back to the flat. Lunch with Brigham, and the mental manoeuvrings his plan had committed him to, had drained his limited resources. He reckoned it was just as well he had several hours in which to prepare himself for the second round. His wound was not paining him, but he remained well below par, with all manner of disquieting symptoms to remind him of the fact. Bizarrely, he seemed to have lost his taste for tobacco, as several unsatisfactory attempts at smoking had demonstrated. But he felt certain persistence would cure that.

Entering the flat, Max was momentarily convinced someone had been there in his absence. The memory of le Singe's singular talents for covert entry prompted him to check every window. There was nothing amiss, far less ajar, yet certainty that all was well eluded him. He could not convince himself one way or the other that the doors of the various rooms were or were not as he had left them. He went down to the porter and questioned him, accomplishing nothing but to leave the poor man worried about Max's state of mind. He returned to the flat and checked the exit from the kitchen on to the service stairs. Nothing seemed wrong. Yet nothing seemed quite right either. After starting at his own reflection, glimpsed in the bathroom mirror as he walked past the open doorway of the room, he forcefully told himself enough was enough. He lay down on his bed and tried to sleep, convinced he would not be able to. But he was wrong. Sleep came soon enough, pouncing as if from nowhere.

Sam had reconciled himself to being late for his visit to Nadia. It was well past six o'clock when he finally left the garage, with most of the cars back and no problems reported. He had squeezed in a wash and brush-up earlier, so there was nothing to detain him. It was only as he was on his way out that he remembered the Norris puzzle, which he had intended to mention to Appleby. He diverted to Appleby's office in order to do so, but found it empty. He scrawled a note and propped it against the ashtray on the desk:

Mr A: I meant to tell you HX 4344 is in the garage. It was brought in last night by Mr Norris. Not important, I suppose?

Twentyman

It was a cold evening. But the thought of seeing Nadia again warmed Sam as he hurried round Place de l'Etoile and turned up Avenue Hoche. He was not worried. He did not think Mr Norris, whoever he might be, was important in any way at all.

MAX WAS WOKEN BY THE RINGING OF THE DOORBELL. HIS first reaction was surprise that he had slept so long. Squinting at the bedside clock, he saw that it was a few minutes past six. Obviously Brigham had arrived and been sent up to the flat by the porter. The doorbell rang a second time.

It was as Max pushed himself up that he realized something was wrong. A weight dragged on his right wrist. He could not at first believe what he saw when he looked towards it. He was handcuffed to the bedpost. He stared at the short stretch of chain between the cuffs in sheer astonishment. Was he dreaming? He tugged at the chain. No. He was not.

'James?' Brigham's voice carried from the hall. He was inside the flat. But how? 'James? Where are you?'

'*Brigham,*' Max shouted. 'How did you get in?'

'The door was ajar. When you didn't answer the bell . . . Where are you?'

'In the bedroom.'

'Are you unwell?' Max heard Brigham's footfalls in the passage as he hurried towards him.

'Be careful. There may be someone else here.'

'Someone else? Who?'

'I don't know. But—'

Brigham reached the open door of the bedroom and stared in, amazed. 'What the devil's going on?'

'I'm not sure.' Max rubbed his forehead with his free hand. It was true. He was not sure of anything. 'I woke . . . to find myself like this.'

Brigham entered the room and moved to the bed-post. 'I don't understand,' he said. 'What do you mean? How could this have happened?'

Max had no answer to give. But one came, nonetheless, delivered in a low, husky voice. 'I did it.'

Max looked up. Brigham turned round. A man was standing in the doorway: short, thin and dressed in the trousers and waistcoat of a black suit, with a dark shirt and a black bow-tie. He was narrow-faced and virtually chinless, with a beaked nose and a prominent brow that cast his eyes in shadow. His dark, receding hair was short and lacquered. Altogether, he should have looked unimposingly bank-clerkish, but the way he held himself and the arrogance of his stare would have created a far from unimposing impression, even without the gun he was holding.

'What the devil . . . ?' Brigham began, taking half a step forward.

'Stop,' said the newcomer, raising the gun slightly and pointing it at Brigham. Brigham stopped. 'Move when I tell you only. Or I will shoot you.' He sounded deadly serious. His accent and syntax were not English, though what his nationality was Max could not have said with any certainty. The gun looked strangely familiar, though. It was either the same model as the revolver Appleby had supplied – or the very same revolver.

424

'What do you want?' Brigham demanded.

'Information.'

'We'll, er, help you if we can.' Brigham glanced back at Max and winked, hoping, it seemed, to reassure him that they could talk their way out of this. 'Won't we?'

Max rose to his feet, sliding the handcuff up the bed-post until it was stopped by the cross-rail at the top. He looked straight at the man with the gun, determined to give him no ground. 'You're Tarn, aren't you?'

The man's reaction – or lack of it – confirmed Max was right. This was Tarn, the hired assassin, Kuroda's 'hunting tiger'. 'Sit down, Mr Maxted. Please. Or I shoot Mr Brigham. With your gun.' He was wearing fine back leather gloves, Max noticed. He would leave no fingerprints.

'The noise of a gunshot will carry though the build-ing,' Max countered. 'The police will be called.'

'Too late for Mr Brigham. And for you.' Tarn pointed the gun at Brigham's head. 'Please. Sit down.'

'Do as he asks, Max,' said Brigham. 'For God's sake.'

'All right.' Max sat down.

'What do you want to know?' Brigham asked, his voice cracking with anxiety.

'Where is Lemmer?' Tarn asked calmly.

'Who?'

'Lemmer. Please. You work for him, Mr Brigham. You know where he is. Have you told Mr Maxted?'

'No. That is, I don't work for anyone called Lemmer. I've no idea what you're talking about.'

'What will I do to make you tell me, Mr Brigham? You have an idea of that, maybe?'

'I don't work for Lemmer. I'm a British diplomat, for

heaven's sake. You have no right to threaten us like this.'
Brigham looked round at Max. 'You know this man,
Max?'

'He's the assassin, Brigham. Do I really need to tell
you? He killed my father. And Raffaele Spataro. Walter
Ennis, too.'

Tarn spat dismissively. 'Ennis was not me.'

'But the others?'

'Mr Brigham knows about the others. He hired me.'

'I did no such thing,' Brigham blustered. 'This is outrageous. I've never met you before in my life.'

'You sent your man to me. You paid the fee.'

'What "man"?'

'Where is Lemmer? You will tell me, please. The
Japonais pay bigger than you. For them I end Lemmer.
Where is he?'

'I don't work for Lemmer. I don't know where he is.'

'Tell him, Brigham,' said Max. 'He'll kill you if you
don't.'

'I can't tell him what I don't know.' Brigham stared
imploringly at Max. 'You surely don't believe I hired
this, this . . . creature . . . to kill Henry?'

Brigham was angry as well as frightened. And somewhere beneath both of those emotions, written starkly
on his face, Max glimpsed a truth he would never otherwise have credited. Brigham did not work for Lemmer.
He had not hired Tarn.

'Enough,' Tarn cut in. 'You will tell me where Lemmer
is, Mr Brigham. You will tell me everything. I will make
you tell me. Come this way.' He stepped back and
signalled with the gun for Brigham to leave the room.

'Where are you taking me?'

'Walk in front of me, please. Now.'

'He can't help you, Tarn,' said Max. 'Don't you see? He truly doesn't know.'

'He knows. And soon I will know.'

'Who approached you? Who said he was Brigham's man?'

'If you shout for help, Mr Maxted, I will kill Mr Brigham, then you. And no one probably will hear your shouts. But they will find your bodies later. Your gun, remember. Murder and suicide. That is how the police will think it was.'

'And if I stay silent?'

'I will let you live, maybe.'

'Do as he says, Max,' said Brigham, looking back at him from the passage. 'It's our only hope. If I can convince him I'm telling the truth . . .'

'Enough,' said Tarn. 'Move, Mr Brigham. Or I shoot you here.'

Brigham shook his head despairingly and started walking. Tarn followed. They could have covered only a few yards, though that was enough to take them out of Max's sight, before Tarn spoke again.

'Go into the *salle de bain*.'

They entered the bathroom. Max heard their footsteps echo against the marbled floor.

'Put this on your left wrist, Mr Brigham.' Max heard something click – another pair of handcuffs, he surmised. 'Get in.'

'In the bath?'

'Now.' There was a pause, during which, Max imagined, Brigham did as he had been told. Then: 'Put it round the pipe and fix it to your right wrist.' There was

427

another click and a rattle of metal against metal. 'Kneel down, Mr Brigham.'

'What for?'

'Kneel down. Please.'

A moment passed. Then there was a thump and a cry of pain.

'Are you all right, Brigham?' Max called.

'Tell him, Mr Brigham,' said Tarn.

'I . . . I'm all right.'

'Now tell *me*. Where is Lemmer?'

'I don't know.'

'You know.'

'As God's my witness, I don't.'

'You will tell me.'

'I can't. *I don't know*.'

There was a sudden, indecipherable sound. Then Max heard a gurgling, scrabbling noise. And Tarn's voice: *'Tell me.'*

'Leave him alone, Tarn,' Max shouted. 'He doesn't work for Lemmer.'

'Do you work for Lemmer, Mr Maxted?' Tarn responded, raising his voice above Brigham's spluttering and choking.

'What are you doing to him?' Max wrenched at the handcuffs. But they were firmly fixed. He could not move so much as a pace from the bed.

'Do you work for Lemmer?'

'No. Of course I don't. Neither does Brigham.'

'I think he does. Well, Mr Brigham?'

The choking ceased and gave way to coughing. Tarn had given Brigham a moment to recover – and to confess. But it was only a moment.

428

'Well?'

'I don't . . . know where Lemmer is. You must . . .'

'You must believe me,' Max imagined Brigham had been about to say. The irony was that now, too late to help either of them, Max did believe him. Somehow, he had got the wrong man. So had Tarn. But Tarn did not know that yet. And Max suspected it would take Brigham's death – and his too – to make him understand.

'Where is Lemmer?'

THERE WERE NO CUSTOMERS IN THE SHOP WHEN SAM entered. Nadia emerged from the rear office to greet him. She was dressed in black, as usual, but this was the sombre, unrelieved black of mourning, and she was paler than he recalled. The smile that might once have warmed her expression was missing. There was something tremulous about her – fear, he suspected, fused with grief.

'I am glad to see you, Sam,' she said, kissing him lightly on the cheek.

'Are you alone here, Nadia?'

'Yes.' She looked puzzled. 'Of course.'

'Didn't Zamaron say he was going to give you protection? I expected to see a bobby outside.'

'Bobby?'

'Policeman.'

'Ah. Yes. There were two. I sent them away.'

'Why?'

'My uncle's friends are nervous people, Sam. They do not like the police. They would doubt my loyalty if they saw I was being guarded by the French authorities.'

'They would?'

'Doubt and exile march together. Now, come upstairs. I will close the shop.'

Sam had not been in Nadia's flat before. It appeared to contain almost as many books as the shop, along with a lumber-room's worth of china, paintings and extravagantly framed mirrors.

'My uncle brought from Russia only the things he said he could not live without,' Nadia explained, following Sam's gaze. 'Now they will live without him.'

'Will you stay here, running the shop?'

'I am not sure. Tell me about Max, please. I need to understand what is happening.'

It did not take Sam long to explain that Max had gone to London in pursuit of Brigham. Nadia expressed concerns he could only echo about how fit Max was to undertake such a journey.

'I am worried for him,' she said.

'You and me both,' Sam admitted.

'Whenever I close my eyes, I see my uncle in that sack in the canal,' she said, shaking her head sadly.

'It was a horrible thing. You shouldn't have had to see it.'

'But I did.' She stroked her neck reflectively. 'Do you have a cigarette, Sam?'

He pulled out a pack and offered her one with an apologetic grimace. 'They're French. I ran out of Woodbines.'

'Woodbines?'

'Proper British fags.'

'Ah. I see. These are fine. Thank you.'

He lit the cigarette for her and one for himself.

'What did you mean about the other man – Norrees?'

'Norris. A friend of Brigham's, as far as I can tell. He brought the car in yesterday for repair.'

'What car?'

'Brigham's Daimler.' Sam remembered then that he had not told Nadia about his encounter with le Singe. Evidently, neither had Max. And something he could not quite have defined deterred him from doing so now. 'It was the registration number of the car that first put Max on to him,' he continued inaccurately.

'Why is the number important?'

'I'm . . . not sure.' Sam was floundering. 'Max didn't say.'

'Does he think this . . . Norris . . . is an accomplice of Brigham's?'

'He's got no reason to.'

'If they are friends . . .'

'Max doesn't know that yet.'

'Ah. I see. But you must tell him, of course. It may be important.'

'Oh, I will. As soon as he gets back.'

'We should take a drink for his safe return. Will you have a glass of wine with me, Sam?'

'I'd be happy to.'

'Sit down. I will bring the wine. Make yourself comfortable.'

She went into the kitchen at the rear of the flat, leaving Sam to choose a fireside armchair. He finished his cigarette and lit another, gazing up at a murky oil painting above the mantelpiece of a stern, hawk-nosed figure in the naval uniform of a bygone era.

'Relative of yours?' he asked, when Nadia returned with the wine.

'Yes. The most famous of them all. Admiral Viktor Vitalevich Bukayev. A lover of Catherine the Great, if you believe the stories that are told.'

'And do you believe them?'

'When I want to.' She handed him his glass and raised hers. 'For Max's safe return.'

They drank the toast. The wine was strong and peppery and hit some kind of spot, though Sam would very much have preferred a pint of Bass. Nadia sat down opposite him.

'Max told you about the Trust, Sam, yes?'

'Your organization? Yes, he did.'

'Not mine. My uncle's. There is a traitor in it who must be found.'

'Do you reckon your uncle rumbled who the traitor was?'

'Rumbled?'

'Worked out. Found out.'

'Ah. Yes. I think so. I think that is why he was killed.'

'Maybe Max can get the name out of Brigham.'

'Maybe. Yes. Or out of Norris.'

'Well, it's possible, I sh . . . sh . . .' Sam rubbed his eyes. 'Sorry. It's been a busy day. It must've taken more out of me than I thought. Thish wine's gone shtraight to my . . . head. I . . .'

'You look tired, Sam. Maybe you are hungry also. I can give you something to eat, if you want.'

'No, that'sh . . . that'sh . . .' Sam made to set his glass down in the grate, but tipped it over in the process. He heard it smash on the tiles, but the sound seemed to come from some more distant place. He felt queasy and woozy all at once. 'Shorree,' he managed to say in a slow,

433

slurred voice that he did not recognize as his own. He tried to push himself up from the chair. But his legs gave way beneath him.

He half-fell, half-rolled, to the floor, where he was aware of little beyond the musty smell of the rug he found himself lying on. He looked up, but could focus on nothing. The room was a blur. Nadia was nowhere to be seen.

Then he heard her speak. But she was not speaking to him. 'You can come in now. He is—'

But he heard no more.

'He is helpless,' said Nadia, turning to look towards the kitchen.

A thin, grey-suited man walked into the room. His face was pinched and narrow, his mouth pursed, his eye piscinely moist behind the lenses of his round-framed glassed. 'So I see,' he said quietly.

'What will you do with him?'

Herbert Norris stood for a moment, gazing down at Sam, who was sprawled unconscious on the floor. He tapped his lips thoughtfully and frowned.

'You should not have taken the car to the hotel garage,' said Nadia, with an edge of reproof in her tone.

Norris looked mildly at her. 'You should have told me he worked there, my dear.'

'I did not think it was important.'

'Ah, well, the things we think unimportant are often the things that catch us out, don't you find? To be honest, I had no idea they were interested in the car at all. I can't quite understand why they were. But never mind. Once Tarn has dealt with young Maxted – and we've disposed of Twentyman here – Appleby will have no reason to suspect me.'

'What about *me*?'

'You have nothing to worry about. Your performance as the grieving niece is entirely convincing. The Trust will be more of a problem for you than Appleby. I shall recommend you be allowed to leave Paris. I'm sure we can recruit another informant among your fellow exiles. They generally spend so much and earn so little that corrupting them is child's play.'

'You do not respect my people, do you?'

'I respect professionalism, my dear, wherever I find it.'

'Is that why you use Tarn?'

'I certainly wish others would take note of how thorough the man is. He'd never be associated with anything as crass as the Ennis shooting.'

'But he is outside the organization. He is not bound to us.'

'He does what we pay him to do. And he does it well. Killing Appleby's man was unnecessary, perhaps, but I can forgive him the odd surrender to vanity.'

'What if he discovers you have misled him?'

'Why should he care? His fee's generous enough to console him for any minor misrepresentation. He's altogether ideal for our purposes.' Norris sighed. 'But even Tarn can't be in two places at once. Twentyman falls to us.'

'What are you going to do with him?'

'Dobson will arrive here shortly with a large packing case. We'll stow Twentyman in it and remove him. You needn't concern yourself with what happens to him after that.'

'I would like to know.'

'Why?'

Nadia looked down at Sam. 'He is not a bad man. I do not want him to suffer.'

'If only bad men suffered in this business, my dear, it would be easier on all our consciences. But that's not how it is. As it happens, he'll have drowned long before the effect of the drug wears off, so his will be a painless quietus. He's as good as dead already.'

EXACTLY TWO MONTHS EARLIER, ALMOST TO THE HOUR, SAM was struggling with a recalcitrant carburettor on one of Twentyman & Son's bread vans in the yard behind their bakery in Walthamstow. Darkness had long since fallen. He was working with the aid of a lamp on a trailing wire suspended from an adjacent post. It was cold and damp and everyone else had gone. By rights, he should have gone himself. But Sam was in no hurry to return to the family home, where his welcome back from the war had failed to match the touching vision of loved ones' reunions relayed in the newspapers. His brother viewed him as a cuckoo in the nest, while his sister regarded him as a rival for a position in the business she had earmarked for her fiancé, a man who had braved shot and shell in the trenches while Sam, as she saw it, had lazed around airy hangars in the French countryside polishing propellers.

The truth was that Sam would have been delighted to grant his siblings' generally unspoken (but occasionally muttered) wishes and take himself off to a different job and a home of his own. But he was constrained by penury and the harsh fact that an expertise in the workings of aero-engines was a qualification for nothing bar unemployment in the brave new post-war world. The Royal Air Force (as the RFC had become in the last months of his service) had jettisoned him – and many others like him – with perfunctory thanks and little ceremony. He was on his own now. His father would say otherwise, so too his brother, but that was how it seemed to him. The loaves might rise in the bakery. But he would not.

'Buggeration,' he swore, as he gave his already bruised thumb another knock with the spanner. He sucked the joint to ease the pain and wondered if he should abandon the task. Some deliveries tomorrow would just have to be late. That was all there was to it, apart, of course, from the apportionment of blame. That would be his to bear, without question.

'Sam?'

It was a voice Sam did not immediately recognize, calling from the open wicket door in the gate that led to the street. He moved clear of the van and peered towards it. 'Who's there?'

'It's me, Sam.' A figure in a hat and overcoat stepped through the door and walked towards him. 'Max.'

'Who?'

'James Maxted, Sam.' The newcomer reached the pool of light cast by the lamp, whipped off his hat and smiled – a familiar, self-mocking, defiant smile. 'Don't you remember me?'

'Bloody hell, sir, it's you.' Sam grinned inanely. 'You're a sight for sore eyes and no mistake. I never expected to see you again.'

'I've been in a POW camp. You didn't think I was dead, did you?'

'No. We got the word you were all right. I just . . . didn't reckon our paths would ever cross again.'

'Well, here I am.'

'How'd you find me?'

'You told me often enough your family ran a bakery in Walthamstow. It wasn't difficult.'

'I'm surprised you made the effort.'

'Now I have, how about a drink to celebrate surviving the war?'

Sam's grin broadened still further. 'That sounds just the ticket, sir.'

They adjourned to the Rose and Crown, where Sam had eked out several mournful pints since his homecoming. But Max was paying and eking was not what either of them had in mind.

The first pint vanished while they did little more than laugh and joke and savour the sweetness of the moment. Comparing notes on Max's experiences as a POW and the remainder of the aerial war as seen from Sam's fly-on-the-ground point of view occupied them for most of the second. Then Max surprised Sam by reminding him of a conversation they had had a few weeks before he was shot down.

'We talked about what we might do after the war, if you recall.'

'We did that, sir, yes.' Sam had not forgotten. The miserable couple of months he had spent at the bakery had ensured he had been in no danger of doing that. 'We settled on a flying school, didn't we?'

'Yes. An attractive idea at the time. Flying without

being shot at. And being paid by others to show them how to do it.'

'I bet a good few of our old comrades had the same idea.'

'No doubt. But what have they done about it?'

'Sweet FA, I should think, sir.'

'Exactly. And why do you suppose that might be?'

'Oh, the usual reasons. No money. No land. No balls.'

'You'd need a natural flyer who's also a good communicator, backed up by a smart mechanic, a nice flat piece of land within easy reach of London and enough capital to set the operation up and see it through some lean times.'

'You've got it about right there, sir.'

'So, you'd better stop calling me "sir" and switch to "Max".'

'Why's that, then?'

'Because we're not in the RFC any more, or whatever they call it now.'

'RAF, sir.'

' "Max".'

Sam grimaced. 'I'll never get the hang of that, sir.'

'Well, try, for God's sake. We're going to be partners.'

'We are?'

'Unless you tell me your heart's in the bakery business.'

'No, sir. Too much of the wrong kind of dough.'

'I virtually was an instructor for a lot of the younger pilots.'

'You were, sir. And a damn good one.'

'You're the best mechanic the squadron ever had.'

'Well . . .

'Spare me the false modesty. I think I'll be able to twist my old dad's arm into leasing us some land near Epsom.'

'Sounds perfect.'

'And I have a little money put by.'

Sam took a deep swallow of beer and looked Max in the eye. 'I'd work my socks off, sir.'

'I know you would, Sam. I know you *will*.'

'They're practically giving planes away out at Hendon. Engines and parts too. The lot.'

'What do you say, then?'

'You really mean it?'

'Of course. You don't think I came all the way out here just for the pleasure of your company, do you? We could make a go of this, Sam. I know it. Are you game?'

'You bet I am.'

'You won't regret it.'

'Neither will you, sir.'

'I think this calls for a toast.' Max ordered Scotch for them both. They clinked glasses. 'To the future.'

'To the future,' Sam echoed.

They downed the drinks in one and smiled at each other. In that moment of blind optimism, the future they had drunk to looked long, bright and inviting.

But it was not to be.

THE WORLD TURNS ON A SIXPENCE. NOTHING CAN BE foretold. Certainty lies only in the actual.

A figure drifted gently into Max's field of vision while his attention was fixed on what was happening in the bathroom. It was only a sudden draught from the window that made him look round. Then he started in surprise.

It was le Singe: a small, agile, dark-skinned boy, wearing bits and pieces of army uniform and a cautious smile. He raised a hand and pressed his forefinger against his lips. His eyes were wide, his gaze eloquent: *'Do not speak; do not move.'* Max stared at him and frowned a question: *'What then?'*

The boy stepped past him so nimbly it was as if his feet were not touching the floor. He lowered his finger from his mouth and opened his hand. A small key was lodged in his palm. He smiled more broadly still and nodded in confirmation of Max's guess.

'Where is Lemmer?' Tarn's voice carried from the bathroom.

'I . . . don't . . . know,' came Brigham's answer in a series of strangulated gasps.

'You will tell me.'

442

The choking began again. Max looked at le Singe. The boy grasped the handcuff attached to Max's wrist, slid the key into the lock and released it, then lifted it away carefully so that it did not rattle against the post. He gave a final nod. '*I have done what I can for you*,' it seemed to declare.

Max returned the nod, then moved. There was no time to reflect or consider. He had the advantage now. And he meant to take it.

Brigham was kneeling in the bath, his arms stretched ahead of him, his wrists handcuffed to the pipe supporting the taps. Tarn was crouched over him, tightening a narrow strap round his throat. The sound coming from Brigham was a spluttering, sputtering struggle for breath, for life itself. Tarn might give him another chance to speak. But it would make no difference even if he did. Brigham could not tell him what he wanted to know.

The gun would make a difference, though. Tarn had left it on the laundry basket next to the washhand-basin. He could easily reach back and grab it if he decided to finish Brigham with a bullet. But it was not in his hand at that moment.

Max had not survived as a fighter pilot by hesitating in a crisis. He strode forward and seized the gun.

Tarn sensed some movement behind him. He swung round, flinching in alarm and amazement as he registered Max's presence in the room.

Max raised the gun as Tarn lunged at him. The barrel was pointing straight at Tarn's forehead as he pulled the trigger. He could not miss.

And he did not.

Dobson's muscularity had been as useful to Norris in the recent past as his taciturnity. He arrived as promptly as Norris had assured Nadia he would, unloaded a large, empty packing case from the back of his van and carried it into the shop and up to the flat. He said nothing, grunting some kind of greeting to Nadia and various acknowledgements of orders from Norris. They bundled the inert and unconscious Sam into the crate, nailed it shut and, with Dobson doing the lion's share of the humping and heaving, carried it back down to the van.

Norris told him to wait while he returned to the flat for a parting word with Nadia. With his cargo safely stowed, Dobson stood behind the van, lit a cigarette and, smoking it, wondered idly what the exact nature of Norris's relationship with Nadia might be and whether there would be time for a second cigarette.

His wonderings were rudely interrupted by a sharp blow with a cosh to the back of his neck, eliciting one of his limited range of grunts. He went down like a sack of coke from a coal-lorry.

Norris was in the midst of urging Nadia to remain calm in the days ahead, and patient with regard to his efforts to arrange her departure from Paris, when he heard the engine of the van cough into life. He rushed to the window, just in time to see it pull away, leaving a sprawled figure in the street behind it.

Schools Morahan was attuned to the need to act decisively when circumstances required it. He had not anticipated such circumstances would arise that evening, but he was not unduly surprised. Life, in his experience, was generally predictable – until it ceased to be. Malory had given him the name of the member of the British delegation Ireton had approached on Sir Henry's behalf because she, like Morahan, was worried about what would happen to Max when he left hospital. She had overheard a telephone conversation between Ireton and Herbert Norris that left no room for doubt in the matter. She was also acquainted with a secretary at the British delegation who had access to the addresses of delegation members not lodging at the Majestic or neighbouring hotels. This was only what Morahan would have expected. Malory Hollander was a woman of greater resourcefulness than Ireton seemed to appreciate. The fact that Norris was sharing a flat in the 16th *arrondissement* with Lionel Brigham had struck Morahan as nothing less than sinister in light of Brigham's banishment from Paris.

He went to the Hôtel Dieu to warn Max of Norris's possible role in events, only to be told Max had already left, as he had the Mazarin by the time Morahan reached it. Morahan proceeded to Norris's address in the 16th with no great hopes of accomplishing anything, but arrived just as Norris was leaving and followed him to Little Russia. He knew Nadia Bukayeva slightly because of her late uncle's dealings with Ireton and had never trusted her. Her associations with Norris only confirmed his doubts about her. He saw Sam Twentyman go into the shop and not come out. A little later, a man drove up in a van and carried a large packing case up to Nadia's flat. Then he returned, with Norris helping him to carry the case, now clearly much heavier. What was inside? Morahan reckoned he could guess. And he always backed his own guesses.

Morahan drove fast to the Avenue Hoche and pulled in under a street lamp. He climbed out, hurried round to the back of the van, yanked the doors open and clambered in beside the packing case. There was a tool-box inside the van as well. He grabbed a jemmy and levered the lid off the crate, the nails tearing loose as he let his strength tell. Tossing the lid aside, he shone a torch in on Sam and checked he was still breathing. He was, though deeply unconscious. Several slaps to his cheeks brought no response. Drugged, Morahan concluded. He would need medical attention. There was nothing for it but to drive him to the Hôtel Dieu. It was frustrating not to be able to settle matters with Norris and the treacherous Nadia, but Morahan was well aware that he could not afford to declare his loyalties too openly. There were sleeping dogs that must be left to lie, while there were others, awake and barking, that must be brought to heel. He clambered back out of the van, returned to the cab and drove away.

Weakness began to overtake Max as he coped with the aftermath of Tarn's death. He had been carried to this point on a surge of adrenalin. Now his limbs felt rubbery and his wound twinged at every move. He found the key to the other pair of handcuffs in Tarn's pocket and released Brigham, reduced by his ordeal to a stumbling, mumbling old man. Nothing coherent was said by either of them as Max helped him out of the bath and led him slowly to the bedroom, where he laid him on the bed. Le Singe was gone, as Max had known he would be. Had he stayed long enough to witness the death of his master? Max would have needed to understand the working of the boy's mind better than he did to answer that question.

There was a lot of Tarn's blood on Brigham and spatters of it on Max too. Tarn himself, his head split by the bullet Max had fired at point-blank range, was a dark, bleeding, spreadeagled form in the bathroom. Max leant against the door-jamb and gazed in at the body as he recovered his breath from the effort of moving Brigham.

He felt no satisfaction at having slain his father's murderer. He had wanted to learn the full truth of the night Sir Henry had died and feared now he never would. Tarn had snatched the chance away by forcing Max to kill him and the identity of those who had hired Tarn was more elusive than ever, now Brigham's innocence had been so starkly demonstrated. Sir Henry's assassin had covered his tracks by dying in them.

Max stumbled on along the passage to the drawing-room, where he telephoned for an ambulance – Brigham would certainly need one even if shock was the worst of what he was suffering from – and then called the police. He had shot a man dead. There would be many questions asked of him. He might even be arrested, though he felt sure he would be vindicated by what Brigham had to say, as soon as he was capable of saying it. He could not quite grasp in his mind all the ramifications of what had happened. He would simply have to await them.

He poured himself a Scotch and one for Brigham as

well, which he watered, then set off back to the bedroom with the glasses, taking a couple of gulps from his as he went.

Brigham moaned some kind of recognition as Max entered the room and set the glasses down on the beside table. 'There's an ambulance on the way,' Max said, surprised by his own hoarseness. 'They won't be long. Do you want a little whisky?'

But Brigham seemed not to have heard. He frowned and feebly raised his hand, as if trying to point.

Max turned and looked at the wall facing the bed. And there, in chalked letters, he saw le Singe's parting message.

M AX MIGHT EASILY HAVE BEEN ARRESTED, BUT HE LOOKED little better than Brigham when the police arrived. In the event, they were both packed off to St Thomas' Hospital, with constables in tow.

After a doctor had satisfied himself that Max was no worse than badly shaken, though certainly in need of bed-rest in view of his wound and recent fever, a fox-faced Scotland Yard inspector by the name of Denslow invited him to explain what had happened. Max adhered as closely as possible to the truth. Tarn was a hired assassin who would have killed them both if they had not killed him first. He made no mention of le Singe, having no wish to set the police on his saviour's trail and secure in the knowledge that Brigham had not seen the boy. He claimed Tarn had foolishly left the key to the handcuffs within reach. As for any message Brigham might later say he had seen written on the bedroom wall, Max planned to suggest, if he needed to, that it was a hallucination. He had already ensured it was no longer visible.

Max referred Denslow to Appleby for confirmation that he had been trying to track down his father's murderer in Paris and had followed Brigham to London under the misapprehension that Brigham was party to the murder. Appleby's Secret Service credentials had a satisfyingly intimidating effect on the inspector, who undertook to contact him as soon as possible.

Soon translated into an hour, which was as long as it took Denslow to return with the news that Appleby had vouched for Max and would be on his way to London to do so in person as soon as he had dealt with 'a related incident' in Paris. As to the nature of that incident, Denslow was in the dark. He clearly had no desire to become embroiled in Secret Service business and began treating Max with exaggerated respect. 'We'll just wait until you feel well enough to make a formal statement, Mr Maxted.'

A terrible conclusion formed in Max's mind as he drifted in and out of sleep that night. Brigham's innocence, amply demonstrated by his ordeal at Tarn's hands, pointed to Nadia's guilt. Brigham had told her nothing about her uncle. Nor had anyone else. She had not needed to be told. She had consented to Igor Bukayev's murder. She might even have engineered it. And she had probably implicated Brigham at the behest of whoever in the British delegation Ireton had sounded out on Sir Henry's behalf. But why in that case had le Singe given them the registration number of Brigham's car? Unless . . .

Max was feeling quite well enough the following morning to undertake a short walk along the corridor to Brigham's room. He found Brigham bruised and weary, but eager to express his gratitude.

'You saved my life, James,' he said, his voice reduced to a hoarse whisper by the damage Tarn had inflicted on him. 'I can't thank you enough.'

'I saved my own too. It was self-preservation, really.'

'That fellow . . . Tarn . . . killed Henry?'

'I believe so. He was paid to do it by those who feared they might be exposed as spies working for Fritz Lemmer.'

'But . . . Tarn was looking for Lemmer.'

'The Japanese paid better. He said so himself.'

'And you . . . thought I was one of . . . Lemmer's people?'

'Yes. I was trying to give you enough rope to hang yourself.'

'I may be many things, James, but I'm not a traitor. The idea's absurd.'

'It didn't seem so absurd at the time. Especially not when Nadia Bukayeva said her piece.'

'So, I have my . . . liking for the ladies . . . to blame for this, do I?'

'Someone in the British delegation was pulling Nadia's strings, I'm sure of it. Tell me, does anyone else drive your car?'

'My car?'

'The Daimler. HX 4344.'

'You know . . . the registration number?'

'Does anyone else drive it?'

'Well, since you ask . . .'

'Yes?'

'The chap I share the apartment with in Paris. I let him use it . . . from time to time.'

'Who is he?'

'Herbie Norris.'

'*Norris?*'

'Yes. You know him?'

Norris. So, that was it. The meek maundering Mr Norris was not at all what he had chosen to appear. 'I know him,' Max said dolefully. Though all that flowed from such knowledge was far from clear to him. Had le Singe set out to mislead them, acting on Norris's orders? Or had he been misled himself?

'Are you saying . . . Herbie Norris works for Lemmer?'

'It looks like it.'

'Good God.'

'I'll alert Appleby as soon as I can.'

Brigham shook his head in disbelief, wincing at the effect on his throat and coughing so badly Max had to fetch him a glass of water. 'Thanks . . . my boy,' he gasped, after talking a few soothing sips. 'Norris is simply the last man I'd have thought capable of . . . spying. He seemed . . . straight as a die and . . .' He smiled weakly. 'And dull as dishwater.'

'It probably suited him to have you think that.'

'Of course. And it's . . . surprisingly easy . . . to misread people, isn't it, James?' Brigham looked Max in the eye and held his smile.

'Yes.' Max nodded – a small enough gesture, but full of meaning, a meaning neither of them could mistake. 'It is.'

'I'll make the police understand . . . you had no choice but to shoot Tarn. It was . . . him or us.'

'That it was.'

'What about the writing . . . on the wall? Will you tell them about that?'

'I'd rather not.'

'It was . . . intended for you, wasn't it?'

'I think it was, yes.'

'Would you prefer me . . . not to mention it?'

'Very much.'

'I won't, then.'

'Thank you.' Max nodded his appreciation, which was more genuine than he could ever have imagined it would be of any act of Brigham's.

'You're not going to tell me what it said, are you?'

'I don't know what it said. I don't even know what language it was written in.'

'Japanese.'

'Really?'

'I think so. I can't read Japanese script, of course, but . . . I recognized it. And Tarn . . . was working for the Japanese, wasn't he?'

'So he said.'

'Now Tarn's dead, will you . . . drop this?'

'Maybe.'

'Or maybe not.' Brigham looked at Max knowingly.

'I should leave you to rest.'

Max stood up, relieved Brigham had said nothing, even indirectly, about the possibility that they were father and son. He no longer suspected Brigham of any responsibility for Sir Henry's murder. But that did not mean he was no longer suspicious of him in other ways. His view of the man had become disconcertingly complicated since their life-and-death struggle with Tarn.

'I'm glad—' Max began. Then words deserted him.

'When I'm back on my feet,' said Brigham, 'I'll

probably . . . go down to Cannes . . . for a while. They can cope in Paris without me.'

'I'm sure they can.'

'I don't suppose . . .' Brigham gazed up at Max and found the answer in his face. 'No. Of course not.'

Max returned to his room and went to the cabinet where his clothes were hung. From his jacket pocket he took the piece of wallpaper he had unceremoniously torn from the bedroom wall at the flat and looked again at what had been written on it.

ファーンゴールド

Was it really Japanese, he wondered. Brigham had seemed in little doubt. But le Singe was more likely to be fluent in Arabic than Japanese. How could he have written it? And what did it mean?

As to that, Max knew who would be able to tell him. And he would ask him, just as soon as he could.

MAX CHARMED A NURSE INTO HELPING HIM SEND A telegram to Appleby, warning him Norris was the rotten apple in the barrel. When Appleby arrived at the hospital that evening, however, Max realized he must have left Paris before the telegram had reached him. But, strangely, he already knew about Norris.

'You don't need to worry about him, Max. He no longer poses any kind of threat. I'll explain why when you've told me what happened here. Inspector Denslow seems . . . confused.'

Max did his best on that front, admitting for Appleby's benefit the role le Singe had played in events, but instinctively avoiding any mention of the message on the wall. He wanted to know what the message said before he told anyone about it.

'I'll call in at Scotland Yard tomorrow and have a word with Denslow's boss,' said Appleby when Max had finished. 'I've already spoken to him on the blower and I'm confident there'll be no charges brought against you. Killing Tarn could be regarded as a public service. You'll have to appear at the inquest, of course, along with Brigham. But that'll be a formality.'

'I want to get back to Paris as soon as possible.'

'I'm sure you do. And you'll want to hear my news, as well.'

'Is it good news?'

'Some of it is, yes. Which is probably as much as we can ever hope for in this life.'

Appleby's account began with Sam's impulsive decision – inspired, as it turned out – to sabotage Brigham's Daimler. The car's subsequent delivery to the Majestic garage for repairs, not by Brigham but by Norris, initiated a chain of events that led to Sam walking into a trap in Nadia Bukayeva's flat.

'Norris must have decided to eliminate Twentyman for fear his plan to cast suspicion on Brigham would fall apart once we discovered he had the use of the Daimler. I think le Singe was trying to tell you the driver of that car was your enemy, you see. What he didn't know was that there were two drivers. And what Norris didn't know was that Morahan had followed him to Little Russia, so was able to intervene before they could dump Twentyman in the Seine.'

'How's Sam now?'

'Recuperating at the Hôtel Dieu. The drug they used left him pretty groggy, but he'll soon be up and about. He asked me to say hello.'

'Good old Sam.'

'And good old Morahan. Why he should have bothered to involve himself I don't really understand, but I'm glad he did. Twentyman had left me a note about Norris's use of the car, but it would have been far too late for him by the time I read it. As it was, Morahan telephoned me from the hospital and put me in the picture.'

'Have you got Norris in custody? Is that what you meant about him no longer posing a threat?'

'I couldn't have taken him into custody even if I'd had the chance, Max. Nor could the French police. I'd been warned off by the Permanent Under-Secretary and Foreign Office staff enjoy diplomatic immunity, remember.'

'Nadia Bukayeva doesn't, though.'

'Good point. And one not lost on me. I hoiked Zamaron out of bed and persuaded him he should arrest her for conspiracy to murder Twentyman and probable complicity in her uncle's murder as well. Time was of the essence, of course. I was afraid she'd already have done a bunk.'

'And had she?'

'Oh, yes. It looked like she'd packed some clothes before leaving. I think we can assume she's not planning to return to Paris in the near future.'

'She must have been the traitor in the Trust Pa was offering to identify.'

'That's how I read it. But working for Lemmer rather than the Cheka. Or maybe for Lemmer as well as the Cheka.'

'Had Norris gone too?'

'Not exactly. Though gone he certainly had in one sense.'

'What do you mean?'

'We found him in Nadia's flat, Max. Him and his assistant, Dobson. Both shot dead.'

'Nadia killed them?'

'Who else? She must have ice in her veins. I imagine she opted for a scorched-earth policy once she realized

Norris's plans were miscarrying. Perhaps she calculated he'd decide to kill her rather than risk her confessing all under interrogation, improbable though it seems to me that any interrogator could get more out of her than she was willing to give. Whatever her reasons, though, she carried it off efficiently. Two clean head shots. Bang bang, they're dead.'

'And she got away?'

'Clean away, I regret to say.'

Appleby sighed and thrust his pipe, with which he had been fiddling, back into his pocket, apparently concluding that lighting it in a hospital was out of the question. But he burrowed in his bag and pulled out a bottle of whisky with a satisfied smirk that suggested he regarded it as a more than adequate substitute. A grubby tumbler also emerged, inscribed SE & CR, evidently purloined from the train. He poured himself a generous measure and sloshed some into Max's water glass.

'Your health, Max.'

'Well, despite the setting, I don't feel too bad. And being the subject of a police inquiry does get you a private room here, so I'm not complaining.' Max raised his glass and took a sip. 'Even so, I'd have discharged myself by now if I had a home to go to. Denslow put the flat out of bounds.'

'He tells me he's finished with the flat now. And you could always visit your family, of course.'

'Not a good idea. As soon as the police are off my back, I'll head for Paris. Tomorrow, I hope, if you can do your stuff at Scotland Yard.'

'You don't really need to go back to Paris, Max. You've killed the man who killed your father. The man who

458

hired the killer is also dead. And Zamaron's confident the magistrate will approve Madame Dombreux's release now it's obvious Spataro was one of Tarn's victims. You've done all that could have been expected of you – more, frankly, than I thought you were capable of.'

'But Norris was only one of many spies in Lemmer's network. And your condition for helping me, as I recall, was that I track down Lemmer for you.'

'With Norris dead and Miss Bukayeva gone with the wind, I'd put your chances of doing that at close to zero. I could and maybe I should encourage you to persist. It's what my boss would expect me to do. You might turn up some other spies and they might take us closer to Lemmer. But you've had several narrow escapes already.' Appleby paused and looked at Max thoughtfully, then went on. 'My son would be the same age as you, if he hadn't been killed at Loos, you know. He was a volunteer too.'

'You've never mentioned him before.'

'No occasion to. I shouldn't drink Scotch, really. It makes me sentimental. Oh, before I forget, you might like to know what I've found out about the Contingencies Memorandum. It's keeping Carver and a few others in the American delegation awake at night. No one will give me chapter and verse, but I gather it's a document in which President Wilson sets out variations to be made to his supposedly inviolable Fourteen Points – his much-vaunted programme for world peace – if certain contingencies arise during the peace conference. Some of those variations wouldn't paint him in an honourable light. If it reached the press, there'd be hell to pay. So, if your father got hold of an authentic copy . . .'

'It would have fetched a high price at auction, so to speak.'

'It would. And if it was in that safe-deposit box of his . . .'

'It might already be in Lemmer's possession.'

'Indeed it might.'

'Doesn't that possibility worry you?'

'Personally, no. Why should I care if he throws a spanner in the conference works? Departmentally, I should probably hope he does. American embarrassment equals British advantage.' Appleby shrugged and topped up his glass. 'Peace is almost as dirty a business as war.'

'You should drink Scotch more often, Appleby. It mellows you.'

Appleby grunted, apparently considering mellowness an accusation bordering on the insulting. 'Have you found out what your father was raising money *for* yet?'

'Corinne Dombreux and a comfortable life with her, probably in Brazil. He planned to invest the money in a business venture of Ribeiro's.'

'Ah.' Appleby looked almost disappointed. 'So that was all it was.'

Or was it? After Appleby had gone, Max turned out the light and lay watching raindrops forming at intervals on the uncurtained window of his room. The sky beyond the window was black, the rain falling from clouds he could not see. The truth, it struck him, was like that, revealing itself, if at all, only by its effect on something else. He had the sense that there was a greater, darker truth beyond all that he had so far learnt. Why had his father appointed him his executor if not to discover what that was? Had the safe-deposit box hidden the secret? Or was it hidden somewhere else, still waiting to be found? If Max gave up now, he would never know for certain, never quite be able to dismiss from his mind the fear that he had turned his back on what his father had died for. And that, he knew, he could not bear.

MAX HAD PERSUADED APPLEBY IT WOULD BE BEST IF THEY went to Scotland Yard together the following morning. The doctor who had treated him on his admission raised no more than a token objection to discharging him and conjectured that Brigham would be fit enough to leave within a few days as well. 'You should go gently, though, Mr Maxted. You have youth on your side, of course, but the body takes its own sweet time to recover from the sort of thing you've put it through lately, young or not.'

Max assured the doctor he would lead a quiet life for the next few weeks, which he had no intention of doing. He headed for the flat first, for a change of clothes, where he was intercepted by the head porter, anxious for a word about the events of the night before last. Max brushed the poor fellow off with an assurance that there would be no further visits from the police, then hurried on to Scotland Yard.

Appleby was waiting for him at the bottom of Whitehall, puffing contentedly at his pipe. He led Max into Metropolitan Police headquarters with the air of a man returning to his natural domain. Several people they passed greeted him cheerfully. Their destination was the office of Chief Superintendent Mappin, a genial fellow with a booming voice who also seemed pleased to see Appleby – and Max, to judge by his warm handshake and prompt assurance that his force were not about to cause problems for a young gentleman who had saved the life of a senior civil servant and despatched a foreign assassin into the bargain. 'Tarn, you think his name was? Well, we'll ask our French colleagues if they know him. Then the Belgians, if they don't. Then . . . Well, maybe someone will claim him, maybe they won't. I take it we can agree, Horace, that we're all better off without him?'

'Very much so, Bill. We think he was responsible for several murders in Paris. A nasty piece of work in every way.'

'And the fewer of those we have on the streets of London, the happier I am. The coroner will have the final say, of course, Mr Maxted, but we'll tell him we're satisfied you killed Tarn in self-defence. We'll need a signed statement from you before you leave and you'll be required to give evidence at the inquest in due course. Oh, and we'll have to hang on to the gun until then. Strictly speaking, you don't have a licence for it, but we'll overlook that, shall we? Forgot to hand it in when you were demobbed, I dare say, like a lot of you chaps.'

'I was certainly glad of it on Tuesday night, Chief Superintendent,' said Max.

'I'm sure you were, Mr Maxted. Glad and no mistake.'

Accommodating as Mappin was, Max was not able to leave Scotland Yard before the morning had stretched into the afternoon. The dictating, typing and signing of a statement absorbed a laborious couple of hours and he was also fingerprinted – 'for the purposes of elimination', according to Denslow.

Appleby left while Max was waiting for his statement to be typed. They exchanged parting words in a corridor.

'If you decide not to go back to Paris, Max, I'll understand.' It was as close as Appleby seemed able to come to repeating his advice of the night before.

'I'll be on tonight's sleeper,' said Max. He wanted no misunderstanding on the point.

'Then you'll be ahead of me by twenty-fours hours. As a personal favour, try not to get into any more trouble before I catch up with you.'

Max smiled. 'I will try.'

He returned to Mount Street to pack his bag, only to encounter the head porter again. Mrs Harrison had been and gone, considerably put out by the state she had found the flat in and alarmed in particular by the bloodstains in the bathroom.

But Mrs Harrison had not been the only caller. A *Daily Mail* reporter had been there, asking questions. 'We had a lot of trouble getting rid of him, Mr Maxted, I don't mind telling you. I shouldn't be surprised if he came back.' Max proffered an apology and decided to spend most of his time elsewhere before boarding the sleeper.

The reporter was not the end of it, however. 'Your solicitor's been looking for you as well.' Of course. Mellish was still expecting to be given some kind of instructions about the estate. It was predictable – though Max had failed to predict it – that he would come to London. Unfortunately, as the head porter revealed, Mellish had met Mrs Harrison. He therefore knew everything that had happened. He might easily take it into his head to inform Ashley, a complication Max could do without.

He hastened up to the flat and telephoned the solicitor's office in Epsom, hoping Mellish had returned there by now. But he had not. Max left a message, asking him to take no action until they had spoken. He could only hope that would cover it.

He went to Victoria station and bought a ticket for the eight o'clock sleeper, then took himself off to the Tate Gallery, where he spent more time in the tea-room than he did admiring the art, a commodity for which he had never had much use. Rain forced him on to a bus for the return journey to Victoria. The Londoners he was jammed in with grumbled about the weather and the coal shortage and the incompetence of the government – concerns that seemed a million miles away to Max.

The concourse at Victoria was bustling with commuters and luggage-laden Continental travellers. Max bought some cigarettes for the journey – though, oddly, he had still not quite recovered his taste for them – and headed for the departures board.

'James!'

He recognized George Clissold's voice with some surprise and turned to see his uncle approaching through the crowd. 'Uncle George? What are you doing here?'

'Looking for you, my lad, at your mother's bidding. She wants to speak to you.'

'But—'

'She's waiting for us in the station hotel. And she's already waited long enough to test her temper.'

'I have a train to catch.'

'I know. But it doesn't leave for half an hour yet. Shall we?'

Max had no choice but to walk with George in the direction of the hotel entrance. He was not ready to face his mother, but it seemed he was going to have to.

'How did you find me?' he asked as they steered as straight a course as they could contrive through the streams of arriving and departing passengers.

'Mellish alerted your mother to your latest brush with death.' *Damn the fellow*, thought Max. Why had he had to go and do that? 'He mentioned you got yourself shot in Paris as well. Win's a phlegmatic character, but it's fair to say she's worried about you. You should have kept her informed, James, you really should.'

'I was trying *not* to worry her.'

'Well, you failed, I'm afraid. She's been to Mount Street and extracted all the details from the porters. She's also visited Brigham.'

'She has?'

'Let's not pretend we don't both know about Win and that blighter. I can only hope she doesn't start seeing him again now he's done something vaguely heroic. You were the one who saved the day, though, weren't you?'

'Well, I—'

'Yet here you are, scuttling off back to Paris without a

by-your-leave. Win guessed that's what you'd do. It was her idea to come here. You're a far bigger mystery to me than you are to her. Have you found out what got Henry killed?'

'Yes. And Mother won't enjoy hearing about it. I suppose I . . .'

'Wanted to spare her the truth?'

'As long as I could, yes.'

'Well, my lad, the time's come. You're just going to have to spit it out.'

Lady Maxted was waiting, with tea set before her, in a quiet, palm-dotted lounge of the hotel. She greeted Max with a frown that blended pride at his derring-do with bafflement at his eagerness to slip back to France without telling her what he had learnt. But there was something else in her gaze as well: relief.

'You look better than I'd feared, James. Mr Mellish said you'd been *shot*.'

'That makes it sound worse than it was. I'm fine.'

'And this appalling attack you and Mr Brigham were so lucky to survive?'

'We were lucky, yes. But survive we did, with nothing worse than a few bruises to show for it.'

'You've uncovered the truth about Henry's death, haven't you?'

Denial was pointless. 'Yes, Mother, I have.'

'When you left Gresscombe Place last month, you promised to tell me what you learnt before you told anyone else.'

'I still don't know everything. I didn't want to . . .'

'Shock me?'

Max forced himself to look her in the eye. 'It's not an altogether pretty story.'

'I never thought it would be.'

'Even so . . .'

'I think I'd better hear it, James. Ashley doesn't know I'm here, by the way. I didn't alert him to Mr Mellish's call. So, I'll be free to decide whether to disclose any information you give me to him and Lydia – or not. Don't imagine I'm unappreciative of the efforts you've made and the risks you've taken. But I'm entitled, as your mother, as your father's widow, to be told what led Henry to his death. And don't worry about missing your train either. George and I will be travelling with you to Dover. That should give us all the time we need.'

PROMISING THE WHOLE TRUTH WAS EASIER THAN DELIVERING it. Even as Max recounted to his mother what he had discovered in Paris, he was aware of omitting almost as much as he revealed. Lady Maxted seemed to be aware of this as well. She did not press for information about the woman Sir Henry had planned to spend his retirement with. Nor did she ask for details of his scheme to raise money to fund their life together. It was enough, apparently, for her to know why he had been murdered and by whom – that his murderer was dead and that the man who had commissioned his murder was also dead. Justice, after a fashion, had been served. And of that she was glad in her own sombre, reflective way.

It was not as simple as that, of course. Norris was not the only agent of Lemmer's to whom Sir Henry had posed a threat. The decision to set Tarn on him must have been a collective one. There were guilty men – and women, in the case of Nadia Bukayeva – who had escaped punishment and would probably continue to do so. Lady Maxted understood that and urged her son to accept it, as she was willing to.

'These other people may still see you as a threat, James, may they not?'

'They may.'

'Then why return to Paris? Staying away would draw a line under the affair. And if what you say – and what I infer – about the sort of people they are is correct, a line must be drawn somewhere. You cannot pursue them all.'

'There are some loose ends I have to tie up.'

'So, you will come home soon?'

'I'm not sure how long it will take.'

'I can persuade Ashley to allocate the land you need for your flying school, you know. Lydia doesn't call every tune. And the executorship gives you something to bargain with, as perhaps your father foresaw.'

'I can't think about any of that now, Mother. I can't predict what I may yet learn – and where learning it may lead me.'

'At what point does bravery become foolishness, James?'

'When you overstep a mark you can't see until you've overstepped it.'

'Is that thought meant to comfort me?'

'I won't lie to you, Mother. That's probably the only comfort I can offer.'

They parted in wind and rain on the platform at Dover Marine station. George had gone to secure a taxi to take him and Lady Maxted to the Lord Warden Hotel, where they planned to stay overnight before returning to London. Max would soon have to board the steamer for Boulogne. He thought everything had been said that needed to be said. But his mother, though she trusted her brother in all matters, had one last thing she wished to say to her son – and to her son alone.

'I am aware what Lionel believes he is to you, James, and my conversation with him yesterday left me in little doubt that you are aware of it too.'

'There's no call to speak of it, Mother.'

'You thought him a traitor.'

'And he's not a traitor. I was ready to believe the worst of him. I was wrong. I admit it.'

'I am not concerned with that. A man who behaves as he does must expect to be misjudged. What concerns me is the possibility that you will credit his claim of . . . a blood relationship . . . because you now know he is not quite as bad as you thought him.'

'I really don't—'

'There is something I must tell you, James.'

Max looked at his mother, her expression veiled by the shadow of her hat and the rain-blurred glare of the station lamps. 'Are you sure?' he asked levelly.

'Absolutely. Lionel Brigham is not your father. Believe me in this if in nothing else. If I had a Bible with me, I would be willing to swear upon it. You are Henry's son. There is no margin for doubt or uncertainty. You are his son and no other man's.'

No margin for doubt or uncertainty? How could that be? Sir Henry had unwittingly revealed to Max where his mother had spent the summer of his conception. Either she was lying to him now, which he could hardly believe, or there was something he was not being told. And this possibility was only strengthened by what she said next.

'Honesty is always partial, James. No two people can or should reveal everything of themselves to each other.

I will not be interrogated about this. Nor will I interrogate you about those many things you have chosen, wisely or not, to keep from me. But you are Henry's son. That is the truth. Carry it with you – along with your mother's love – in whatever trials still await you.'

It was a rough crossing and a largely sleepless journey followed from Boulogne to Paris, as Max analysed his mother's words in search of what he took to be their hidden meaning. It still eluded him. And sleep came, perversely, just as the train was entering the Gare du Nord.

He was not required to vacate his cabin for another hour, which he dozed through, before breakfasting in the station café. He bought a copy of the Paris edition of the *Daily Mail* and forced himself to read it. There was nothing yet about Tarn, which came as a relief. The editorial was a dire warning against leniency towards Germany. Max could not help wondering if Lemmer planned to use any of the material he had removed from the safe-deposit box to win some concessions for his country. It was a worrying thought. But there was nothing he could do about it. Whatever advantage access to the box had handed to Lemmer was his to exploit.

Max went straight to the Mazarin from the station and dropped off his bag, then headed for the Majestic. He found Sam just where he had expected to find him, supervising work in the hotel's garage.

'They winkled you out of the hospital, then,' said Max, soft-footing his way to Sam through the clamour of tuning engines and then surprising him.

'It's you, sir,' Sam responded, whirling round to greet him with a broad smile. 'Alive and well, I'm relieved to see.'

'The feeling's mutual, Sam.' They shook hands warmly. 'I gather we've both been in the wars.'

'You can say that again.'

'Can you spare me a few minutes?'

''Course I can. I'll make us some tea. Come into my parlour.'

Sam fired off some parting instructions to the mechanic he had been talking to, then led the way to his tiny office, where he had rigged up a Primus stove.

'I've managed to get hold of some English tea,' he proudly announced, setting the kettle to boil and lighting a cigarette. 'Smoke, sir?'

'No, thanks. But tea will slip down a treat.'

They sat down, Max in the only chair, Sam on an upturned box, and regarded each other with smiling bemusement. 'Mr Appleby told me you'd gone and killed Tarn, sir. But not how you'd managed it.'

'I had help, Sam. From le Singe. Without it I wouldn't have survived.'

'What's his game, sir?'

'I don't know. But I'm glad he's playing it. I owe him my life. I gather you owe Morahan yours.'

'That's right, sir. We're a lucky couple of beggars.'

'I'm afraid I read Brigham wrong.'

'And we both read Nadia wrong.'

'So, we're gullible as well as lucky.'

'That's about the size of it. But better gullible than unlucky, don't you reckon?'

Max nodded. 'I do.'

473

They swapped stories of their narrow escapes as they drank tea from enamel mugs. From Sam, Max did not withhold le Singe's message. He showed him the scrap of wallpaper with the Japanese characters written on it.

'Does that really mean something, sir?' Sam asked.

'Yes. And I intend to find out what.'

'You're not dropping it, then, with Tarn and that turn-coat Norris both dead?'

'Did you think I would?'

'Not really, sir. I never expect you to take the easy course.'

'I'm sorry you had such a rough time of it in my absence, Sam. If I'd been here—'

'It mightn't have turned out as well as it did. And it wasn't that rough. I never knew my life was in danger until after it stopped being. I came to in the hospital to find my forehead being stroked by a nurse with the face of an angel, telling me I'd nearly suffocated and should take it easy. It wasn't difficult to do as she said. The worst was learning Nadia was a snake in the grass.'

'There's treachery everywhere you look, I'm afraid.'

'And salvation in strange places. I still don't under-stand why Mr Morahan stepped in. I'm just thankful he did.'

'I plan to ask him. But I don't expect to learn much. He keeps his own counsel.'

'That he does, sir. But I'd be happy to hear what he tells you – even if it doesn't amount to anything – over a glass or three this evening.'

'Good idea. We've both earnt a night on the spree.'

'See your family while you were in Blighty, did you, sir?'

'I met my mother.'

'I don't suppose the subject of those fields your dad earmarked for you cropped up, did it?'

Max offered no immediate answer. He drained his mug and set it down by the kettle, then gazed out through the glass-panelled door into the maintenance bay. 'I couldn't drag you away from all this, Sam,' he said at last. 'You're doing your country such sterling service.'

'You mean you *won't* drag me away.'

'I mean I don't know what the future holds.' Max turned to Sam and grinned. 'Apart from standing you more drinks than will be good for you this evening.'

MAX ENTERED THE OUTER OFFICE OF IRETON ASSOCIATES AT 33 Rue des Pyramides, to find Schools Morahan and Malory Hollander discussing horse-racing form, with laughter bubbling in their voices. Max had a fleeting impression, not for the first time, that they shared some secret purpose over and above their work for Travis Ireton, that they were partners in an enterprise whose significance eclipsed their everyday concerns – and of which they would never speak.

The impression was all the more fleeting because of the pleasure they took at his arrival. Malory kissed him and Morahan pumped his hand.

'I knew Tarn by reputation, Max,' said Morahan. 'I'd never have expected you to be able to outwit him.'

'I was lucky. And so was Sam.'

'He was. Sometimes, though not often enough, fortune smiles on the righteous.'

'I want to thank you for what you did.'

'I just happened to be in the right place at the right time.'

'It didn't just happen, though, did it? I gather you both decided I needed looking after and Sam was the beneficiary.'

'We were glad to be of service.'

'Would Travis have approved?'

'We didn't ask him,' said Malory. 'That's what happens when you make yourself elusive.'

'He's still lying low?'

'He is,' said Morahan. 'But he's back in Paris. Business would suffer if he stayed away any longer. You won't be seeing him here for a while, though. Carver mistakenly thinks Travis knew about Ennis's dealing with Lemmer and wants to sweat the details out of him. So Travis is keeping out of his way. I'm meeting him this afternoon at Enghien racetrack. He feels safe in a crowd. Malory's just been picking me a winner from the paper.'

'Héliad in the four o'clock,' said Malory. 'The track will suit him.'

'We'll see about that. Any message for Travis, Max?'

'None you'd care to pass on.'

Morahan smiled. 'Understood.'

'Grand as it is to see you, Max,' said Malory, 'you really shouldn't stay.'

'She's right,' Morahan sighed. 'Carver's stationed a guy in the café across the street to monitor comings and goings here. He'll report your arrival and I'd guess Carver would take a long talk with you as second best to one with Travis.'

Max had no wish to encounter Carver. At the very least the man would waste a lot of Max's time. 'I'd better make myself scarce, then.'

'Have you heard about Corinne Dombreux?'

'What?'

'Commissioner Zamaron regards me as his new-found *meilleur ami* since I helped him wrap up those several murder cases that have been cluttering his desk. Best of all from his point of view, and thanks to you as well as Nadia Bukayeva, the principal suspects are all dead. Never mind that Norris probably didn't hire Tarn on his own initiative—'

'Or that Tarn didn't shoot Ennis.'

Morahan looked surprised and curious. 'He didn't?'

Max shook his head. 'No. But what about Corinne?'

'Oh, I pointed out to my buddy Léon that she's obviously innocent and that by arranging her early release he could avoid being obliged to look for the police officers who might have dosed up the evidence against her. This very morning he telephoned me to report that the magistrate's set her free.' Morahan glanced up at the clock. 'She's probably on her way home already.'

'*Ligne Trois* from Concorde to Notre-Dame-des-Champs would be your quickest route,' said Malory.

'Give her my regards when you see her,' Morahan continued.

'You've met Corinne, Schools?' Max asked.

'Once, yes.'

'How did that come about?'

'She called by here one day hoping to see Travis. He was out. She got me instead.'

'What did she want with Travis?'

'She never actually said. I advised her to make an appointment. It was only later that I discovered she knew Henry. So, if I was guessing, I'd say she was anxious about his dealings with Travis and planned to charm Travis into telling her what those dealings were.'

'And did she make an appointment?'

'Yes,' said Malory. 'Travis told me to invite her to have lunch with him if she called again, as she duly did.' She flicked open the desk diary in front of her. 'Wednesday, March twelfth. Café Voltaire, Place de l'Odéon.'

'The twelfth?' Sir Henry had been in England that day, changing his will and reclaiming his father's Sumerian antiquities. Corinne had never mentioned lunch with Ireton. She had never mentioned meeting him after their encounter at St-Cloud. 'Did Travis say what happened?'

'Not that I recall. But then I doubt I asked.'

'Schools?'

'Nope.'

'If you want to dodge Carver, Max,' Malory said softly, 'you really should go.'

'Yes. Of course. One other thing, though. Do you speak Japanese, Malory?'

'I picked up a few of the basics.'

'What about reading it?'

'Are you kidding? Have you seen what Japanese looks like?'

Impulsively, Max took the scrap of wallpaper out of his pocket and showed her le Singe's message. 'Like this?'

Malory squinted at the markings, then nodded. 'Yes. Just like that.'

'Any idea what it means?'

'No. Except . . .'

'What?'

'Well, there are no *kanji* in it. It's mostly *katakana*, I think, so that suggests it's a foreign word translated into Japanese.'

'Really?'

'Probably.'

'Kuroda could tell you what it says,' suggested Morahan.

'Just what I was thinking. Where would I be likeliest to find him, d'you think?'

'Now?'

'Or later.'

'There's a Council of Five meeting today. It's a sop to Japan for being excluded from the Council of Four. Their delegates will be out in force. So, he'll probably be with them at the Quai d'Orsay until . . .'

'Some time after Héliad romps home in the four o'clock at Enghien,' said Malory with a superior smirk. 'Is that writing on a fragment of wallpaper, Max?'

'Yes, it is.'

'Where's the wall it came off?' asked Morahan.

Max did not answer. All he said as he strode towards the door was, 'I must go.'

'Then go well,' Morahan called after him.

'Amen to that,' murmured Malory.

As Max hurried away from 33 Rue des Pyramides in Paris, heading, as Malory had recommended, for Concorde Métro station, Appleby advanced slowly into C's office at British Secret Service Headquarters in London.

Nine days had passed since C had approved his proposal to use Max as a means of tracking down Lemmer. The plan had so far failed to achieve its desired result. It had produced other effects, however, not all of them to C's liking, as his forbidding expression and the absence of any other member of staff served to confirm. What he had to say – and what Appleby might say in response – he evidently did not judge suitable for committee consumption.

'Sit down, Appleby, sit down,' C began in a tone he may have intended to be neutral, but which somehow carried gruffness at its edges. He closed a file he had been studying. 'I've just taken a look at the minutes of last week's meeting to remind myself of the conditions upon which I approved your operation.'

'Oh, yes, sir?'

'The justification you advanced for using James Maxted as a proxy in the search for Lemmer was that we could disown him if we needed to.'

'Indeed, sir and—'

'I specifically told you to avoid drawing our inquiries to the attention of the French authorities and *at all costs* to keep the Americans out of it.'

'Yes, sir,' said Appleby glumly. The course of their discussion was set and it was not set fair.

'I must congratulate you. I cannot recall in the admittedly short history of this department an operation that has miscarried so comprehensively and so quickly. I have had Lord Hardinge bending my ear about your harassment of senior civil servants and reminding me that my budget for this year is still only provisional. I have had the commissioner of the Metropolitan Police reporting that you conferred departmental privilege on Maxted in respect of their investigation of a homicide at an address in Mayfair earlier this week. The US Department of State has been in touch with the Foreign Office seeking information they believe we may possess about Lemmer's where-abouts following the assassination of a member of the American delegation in Paris last Saturday. The *Deuxième Bureau* wants to know what we have to say about the murders of two members of *our* delegation last Tuesday. One of our own men, a promising young agent whose father I know personally, is also dead. Meanwhile, extreme measures are having to be taken to hold the press at bay. And Lemmer, I feel sure you will confirm, is as elusive now as he was when you last sat in this room.'

Silence settled over them, moderated by C's stertorous breathing. He appeared to be waiting for Appleby to mount a defence, with little expectation that it would be adequate.

'Well, sir—'

'Yes?'

'Things obviously haven't gone as I'd hoped.'

'I should perhaps add understatement to the list of your talents when I next review your personal file,' said C unsmilingly.

'There have been some valuable outcomes.'

'Pray apprise me of them.'

'We've exposed one of Lemmer's agents in our delegation.'

'But sadly he's not available for interrogation.'

'No, sir. Nor is Lemmer's agent in the American delegation. But the damage the Americans have suffered is greater than any done to us. I believe Lemmer now has information likely to prove very embarrassing to them.'

'The Contingencies Memorandum?'

'Yes. The Japanese may also be in difficulties.'

'Because of these Chinese documents you think he's procured?'

'Yes. I suggest the French can be fended off by demanding an explanation from them for the bungling at best, the sabotage at worst, of inquiries into the death of Maxted's father.'

'Sir Henry. The lovesick old fool – if I read your report correctly – who set this disastrous sequence of events in motion.'

'It may be he was that, sir. Or it may be he wanted to be thought that.'

'What are you implying?'

'I believe there's more to be discovered yet about Sir Henry and his dealings with Pierre Dombreux.'

'Who we assume was another of Lemmer's spies?'

'Yes, sir. But it is only an assumption.'

'As is your claim that Lemmer had penetrated all the leading delegations in Paris.'

'We know about Norris and Ennis, sir. There are bound to be others. If we can take one of them alive, we may find a trail that leads to Lemmer.'

'A faint hope, Appleby, considering that I imagine you'd start looking for these "others" by investigating Norris's known friends and associates. Lord Hardinge wouldn't allow that, I'm afraid. It would be more than my job's worth, never mind yours.'

'It's the obvious way to proceed, sir.'

'Then you'll have to find an *un*obvious way. Before you try, speculate for my benefit about Lemmer's motives. His network, however extensive, no longer serves any purpose. The Berlin government has no use for him, even supposing he has any use for them. And our fly on the wall at the Kaiser's court-in-exile assures us they have no contact with him at all. So, what is he trying to achieve – and for whom?'

'I don't know, sir. Frankly, that's what we should probably be most worried about. Lemmer has a plan. It's in his nature. He's plotting to some end. But what that end might be . . .'

'Why did you disobey my orders where young Maxted was concerned, Appleby?' A frown like a brewing storm had taken over C's never entirely benign features. 'You were supposed to disown him if anything went wrong, as I think we can agree it did.'

'He risked his life for us, sir, and nearly lost it – twice.'

'That's your explanation?'

'Yes, sir.' Appleby braced himself. 'It is.'

'Mmm.' The frown lightened – marginally but significantly. 'The gesture does you credit, Appleby, even if nothing else does in this sorry affair. We cannot simply wash our hands of those who help us for noble reasons, however advantageous it might be to do so. Can Maxted be of further use to us?'

'It's hard to see how, sir.'

'Yet he worsted Tarn, a seasoned killer.'

'He did, sir, though not without assistance.'

'From le Singe?'

'So he said, sir.'

'And whose side is le Singe on?'

'Difficult to judge, sir. We know almost nothing about him. He's . . . a rumour made flesh.'

'More flesh and less rumour is what we need all round, Appleby.'

'What do you want me to do, sir?'

'Return to Paris, for the time being. The situation in the Council of Four is tense, as I'm sure you're aware. It's perhaps fortunate for us that the PM's too busy wrangling with Clemenceau over the Rhineland to give any attention to our problem with Lemmer. We'll keep our heads down for a while and review the situation in a month or so. But talking of heads, I'll be candid. Yours may well have to roll.'

Appleby was unsurprised. He had taken too many chances. He had offended too many powerful people. 'I stand by my report, sir.'

'Good. Backing down won't help you. I'm not sure what would, short of a breakthrough on the Lemmer front. Think you can pull one off?'

'With my hands tied as they are, sir? No. But . . .'

'Never say die, eh?' C's gaze narrowed to a squint. 'At your age, you could opt to retire now the war's over. But I dare say you haven't a great deal to retire *to.*'

'I'd prefer to stay on, sir.'

'Yes. Of course you would. Well, we'll see.' C sighed heavily. 'That'll be all for now, Appleby. You can go.'

'Thank you, sir.'

As Appleby rose to leave, C cast him a strange, almost pitying look. He seemed about to add something, then changed his mind and flapped a dismissive hand towards the door, through which, a moment later, Appleby retreated.

IT WAS NOT CLEAR TO MAX WHETHER MADAME MESNET recognized him or not. But she admitted him to 8 Rue du Verger readily enough and confirmed, somewhat grudgingly, that Corinne was in. '*Madame Dombreux? Oui, monsieur. Elle est à la maison. Au troisième étage.*'

He climbed the stairs to her door, accompanied, it seemed to him, by his father's ghost. It was easy to imagine Sir Henry walking up with him, breathing heavily, rocking slightly in that arthritic way he had, humming to himself some old music-hall tune as they went. For an instant, Max was convinced he smelt the old man's cigar smoke drifting past him.

They reached the door. And Max was alone. He knocked.

There was no response, though he was certain he had heard a movement inside the apartment. He knocked again and called her name. 'Corinne? It's Max.'

There was an interval of silence. Then the door opened and she looked out at him. She was pale and hollow-eyed. But to see her in her own clothes rather than the grey smock she had worn while in custody was a relief. There was disbelief in her gaze and more vulnerability than there had been before. Confinement

486

had left its mark. She had not known, of course, how long she would be held. She had not known Max would be as good as his word and win her liberation.

'Can I come in?' he asked lamely.

'Of course.' Tears sprang suddenly into her eyes. 'I'm sorry. Please.' She stepped back, dabbing away the tears with a handkerchief.

He entered and closed the door. 'How are you?' he asked, horrified by his own banality.

'Oh, Max.' She hugged him then, clinging tightly to him. 'I never thought this day would come.'

'I told you it would.'

'I didn't dare believe you.' She broke away, but held him by the hands as she looked at him. 'Is it all true? The man who killed Henry is dead and the man who paid him to kill Henry is also dead?'

'Yes. It's true.'

'And you are well and safe?'

'As you see.'

'You look thinner, Max. And your colour is not so good. They tell me you were shot.'

'A flesh wound. I'm fine.' He smiled. 'Though tender when hugged.'

'I'm sorry. I didn't—'

'No, no. It's all right. You're not quite your old self yet either, Corinne. We've both been through the wringer, haven't we?'

'They said you were in London. When did you get back?'

'This morning. I came here as soon as I heard you'd been freed.' He glanced past her, his attention taken by something he could see through the open door of the

487

bedroom at the end of the passage. A suitcase was open on the bed, with clothes and other articles piled in and around it. He frowned in puzzlement. 'Are you . . . going away?'

Corinne let go of him and nodded solemnly. 'I have to. It's a condition of my release. I must leave Paris immediately and stay away for the duration of the peace conference. It was made very clear to me that if I refused they would continue to hold me.'

'But on what charge? I thought the police had admitted you were innocent.'

'Of poor Raffaele's murder, yes. But I can be accused of complicity in Pierre's alleged treason at any time they wish and detained indefinitely under emergency wartime regulations. And the war cannot officially end while the conference continues.'

'Where will you go?'

'Nantes, to begin with. My sister has agreed to take me in, probably against her better judgement. I won't stay with her for long. Though where I'll go from there . . .' She shook her head. 'I simply don't know.'

'But you'll write and tell me when you're settled?'

'If you want me to.'

'Of course I want you to.' Max wondered if, like him, Corinne had imagined a possible future in which they were not so far apart. Irony was knotted around them. But for his father, they would never have met. And but for his father, he might have spoken some of the words that had formed in his mind.

'Then I'll write. But to what address?'

'I'm not sure. My solicitor will know where to find me. Write to him.' He took Mellish's card from his wallet and handed it to her. 'You will, won't you?'

'Yes.' She smiled. 'I promise.'

'When will you set off?'

'This afternoon.'

'So soon?'

'I was advised to leave without delay. I have no choice but to comply.'

'Do you have time for lunch with me before you go?'

'Oh, Max, there's such a lot I have to sort out. Lunch would be lovely, but . . .'

'Say you'll come.' He smiled defiantly at her. 'There's so much I have to tell you.'

'Tell me now.'

'Only if you agree to lunch.'

She gave in and smiled back at him. 'All right.'

She had made coffee and there was more than enough for two. They sat drinking it by the window of the sitting-room. The window was half-open and the sounds of the city – clopping hoofs, rumbling carts, rattling trams, barking dogs, raised human voices – filtered in around them. As Max recounted his experiences of the previous ten days, he made excuses to himself for resorting to minor misrepresentations in order to avoid mentioning certain things – such as his night with Nadia Bukayeva and his wish to believe the worst of Brigham because he might be his son – on the grounds that they changed nothing materially. The truth of why Sir Henry had been killed and by whom and at whose instigation was established now, doubtful though it was that it would ever be formally acknowledged.

'Tarn wasn't simply an assassin,' Max explained. 'He

specialized in disguising his murders as accidents – or as the acts of others. I suppose Norris and his accomplices feared Pa might have confided in you, so Tarn planned to silence you as well, by having you take the blame for Spataro's murder, which also conveniently disposed of a false witness against you before he could change his story.'

'And Henry took all the risks he did so that he and I could live in luxury?'

'Apparently so. His money was tied up in the estate in Surrey and I suppose he didn't think it would be fair to the family to try to take any out. Ribeiro's scheme promised an independent source of wealth.'

'But I would have gone anywhere with him, even if he'd been penniless. He must have known that.'

'He probably did, Corinne. But he wanted you to enjoy the finer things in life after being denied them for so long.'

'Instead of which, Henry is dead and I am homeless and jobless.' She looked away, out through the window.

Max saw her chin trembling from the effort it took her not to cry. He stretched forward and took her hand. 'I'm sorry.'

She squeezed his in return, then let go. 'I had plenty of time to think while I was in custody,' she said, her voice thick with emotion. 'I suppose I always knew Henry carried secrets with him of which he would never speak. And I suppose I knew those secrets were dangerous. When he went to London, I didn't really believe he'd been recalled to the Foreign Office. I never told you before – I didn't want you to doubt my loyalty to him – but while he was away—'

'You went to see Ireton.'

'You *know*?'

'Morahan told me. Just this morning.'

'Ah, Mr Morahan.'

'He sends his regards. He said you wanted to know what dealings Pa had with Ireton.'

'Yes. I met Ireton for lunch in the hope of finding out. It was a waste of time. Mine *and* his. It soon became clear we had different expectations of each other. He said a lot. But he told me nothing. Except, of course, what I already knew: that he would steal me from Henry if he could, or even share me with him.' She shuddered. 'He is not an honourable man.'

'As his behaviour since has confirmed.'

'Henry should have known better than to do business with him.'

'There's no one else in that particular business.'

'No. I suppose there isn't. I wonder, though, if there wasn't something else Henry was trying to arrange through someone other than Ireton.'

'What makes you think so?'

'The Arab boy who saved your life. Le Singe. You said he can travel across roofs, up and down sheer walls and in and out of high windows.'

'Better than any gymnast.'

'Then it must have been le Singe Henry was chasing when he went up on to the roof. No one else could have got in here so easily. Tarn used the boy to lure Henry on to the roof and then . . .'

'Pushed him off.'

'Yes.' She shook her head, surprised by her own reactions, it seemed. 'I'm glad you killed Tarn, Max,

491

however useful he might have been alive. I'm glad he had a split second in which to understand that he was going to pay for what he'd done.'

'I don't think le Singe realized what was going to happen. He's been trying to make amends for it ever since.'

'But why did Henry go after him, Max? That's what I can't stop asking myself. *Why?*'

'I don't know.'

Max had told only Sam about the message on the wall in London. He had kept it from Corinne so far, assuring himself that he should find out what the message meant before disclosing it to her. That was not the only reason for his reticence, though. Corinne was surely right. There was a secret within the other secrets Sir Henry had borne. Max could sense it. He could almost smell it, as distinctly as the cigar smoke he had imagined on the stairs. But he could not see it. He could not touch it.

'Do you think you will ever know?' Corinne asked.

'I think I will, yes. One day.'

Before leaving, Max borrowed the key to the attic and retraced the steps his father had taken on the last night of his life, reasoning out the sequence of events as he went. The pursuit: le Singe swift and agile, Sir Henry slow and lumbering. Le Singe would have had to hold himself back, so that Sir Henry could not fail to know where he had gone. Then, as Sir Henry entered the attic, le Singe broke the skylight in the loft space above and scrambled out on to the roof. Sir Henry followed, through the window ahead of him, emerging in the gulley behind the parapet and turning to—

Tarn struck. Not cleanly, though. There was a struggle. But the younger, stronger man prevailed. Sir Henry was pushed back over the parapet. He lost his footing. He fell.

Max stood where he had stood once before on the roof, the city spread around him like an arena. He stared out and down into the air his father had fallen though.

There was nothing to see. He looked up, towards the apex of the roof, where le Singe could have crouched and watched as the deed played itself out. There was nothing to see there either. Except the blank sky. Against which the mind could paint any picture it cared to – until the true one was known.

THE COUNCIL OF FIVE MEETING HAD BROUGHT A HORDE OF functionaries to the French Foreign Ministry on the Quai d'Orsay. Max had to join a lengthy queue for a word with the portier who controlled access to the building beyond the entrance hall. Military police were guarding the stairs and corridors. No one was going any further without a good reason.

Just as Max was wondering whether he would be able to persuade the *portier* to send a message to Kuroda, he saw the representative of the Japanese delegation he and Morahan had spoken to at the Hotel Bristol descending the main staircase, wringing his hands as ever. He appeared to be on his way out of the building.

Max intercepted him as he headed across the hall. 'Excuse me. You may not remember me. We met last week, at the Bristol. I was—'

'Ah yes.' The man nodded in recognition and gazed at Max through circular steel-framed glasses. 'You were looking for Commissioner Kuroda.'

'That's right. I—'

'Your name is Maxted. You were with Mr Morahan.'

'You have a good memory.'

'It is part of my job, Mr Maxted. To remember things.'

'I'm looking for Commissioner Kuroda again. Is he here?'

'Ah, no. I am sorry. He is not here. I do not know where he is. I will see him later, though. If you want me to give him a message . . .'

'How much later is that likely to be?'

'I cannot say. He is busy with many things.'

'It's rather an urgent matter.'

'Can I help?'

Max hesitated. He contemplated having to wait another day for an answer to the question that had been burning inside him for far too long already. He could not do it. It was a simple matter of translation. It was not really important who did the translating. 'That's kind of you, Mr . . .'

'Yamanaka.' The name came with a courtly bow.

'Well, Mr Yamanaka, the thing is this.' Max took out the scrap of wallpaper and showed him the message. 'Can you tell me what this says?'

Yamanaka peered at it. 'Of course. It is written in Japanese. You cannot read it?'

'No.'

'It is a Japanese translation of an English word. An English surname, I think.'

'Really?'

'I think so, yes.'

'What is the surname?'

'Farngold.'

Max wandered out into the open expanse of the Esplanade des Invalides, thoughts whirling in his head. Farngold. Suddenly, the name had meaning –

significance. It was not – it had never been – merely the pseudonym Sir Henry had used for renting a safe-deposit box at the Banque Ornal. It was a door, opening on to a hidden world. Like a row of dominoes, the consequences of the discovery toppled in Max's mind. Sir Henry had appointed him as his executor not only because of what the box contained, but because of the name it was held under. Lemmer had guessed he would use the name because they shared the knowledge of its importance. Farngold. Written by le Singe in Japanese, a language he surely neither spoke nor wrote. But Japan was where Sir Henry and Lemmer had first met. And that was where the secret must have been spawned, nearly thirty years in the past. Farngold. It was the answer, if only he knew the question.

Max was not optimistic that Corinne would ever have heard Sir Henry mention the name Farngold, but he certainly intended to find out. They had arranged to meet for an early lunch at La Closerie des Lilas in Boulevard du Montparnasse. Max arrived shortly before 12.30 and bagged a prime table.

As he waited for Corinne, he leafed through the café's copy of *Le Figaro*. His eye was taken by an article on an inner page under the headline *Le Marquis Saionji et la maîtresse indiscrète*. As far as he could glean, Ohana, the *'très jeune'* mistress of the *'vénérable'* head of the Japanese delegation to the peace conference, was embarrassing her *'vieux protecteur'* with her lack of reticence and might be to blame for Japan's exclusion from the new all-powerful Council of Four. Max wondered if this explained Kuroda's absence from the Quai d'Orsay. If so, he was not to be envied. Silencing a loose-tongued geisha did not sound like an easy task.

Absorbed in the effort of translating the article, Max was surprised by the sudden appearance at his table of a meek, tubby, balding, placid-featured man in a tight-fitting suit that looked to have seen better days. 'Monsieur Maxted?'

'Yes.'

'My name is Miette. I am a neighbour of Madame Dombreux. I work near by.'

'You do?'

'Madame Dombreux asked me to give you this.' He handed Max a letter. 'Please excuse me.'

With that Miette was gone, leaving Max to open the envelope bearing his name and to read the letter it contained.

My dear Max,
I have set off early for Nantes. By the time
Monsieur Miette delivers this to you, my train will
have left. I am so sorry to disappoint you. I could
not bear to exchange farewells with you. I feel it is
better to go now, before the little courage I have
deserts me. You should stop looking for answers.
There must always be some that elude one in this
life. Go home. You have avenged Henry. That is
enough. Leave the past behind. Make a future for
yourself, as I will try to do for myself.
Corinne

Glancing down, Max noticed that there was something else in the envelope. He slid it out on to the table.

Mellish's card. Corinne wanted him to understand clearly that he would not hear from her again. She had made her decision and was going to live by it.

Despite what Corinne had said in the letter, Max hurried from the café to the Gare Montparnasse. He scoured the concourse and the waiting-room. There was no sign of her. And a clerk confirmed a train for Nantes had left half an hour previously. She was gone.

It took a visit to 8 Rue du Verger to convince himself of the fact, though. *'Partie, monsieur,'* Madame Mesnet insisted. *'Partie sans espoir de retour.'* She had gone. And she was not coming back.

M AX HEADED NORTH, BACK TOWARDS THE QUAI D'ORSAY. He had no particular destination in mind. What he should do next he could not decide. He forced himself to address the question: was Corinne right to draw a line under what had happened and seek a new start in life elsewhere? Quite possibly, he could not deny. The clue he was following now was faint and perhaps illusory. Farngold might be just a pseudonym after all.

But he did not believe that. And it was not in his nature to let such uncertainty rest. He might be forced to eventually. Until he was, though . . .

He crossed the river at the Pont de la Concorde, then struck west to the Plaza Athénée, reasoning that Sir Henry might have talked about Farngold to his old friend and confidant, Baltazar Ribeiro.

They informed him at the desk that Ribeiro was in the hotel, but busily engaged with a working lunch in a private room. Max prevailed upon them to send a message in, requesting a few minutes of Ribeiro's time. He said he would wait outside.

*

'Max!'

Ribeiro emerged at a half-charge into the frail spring sunshine on the Avenue Montaigne and beamed at Max as if seeing him was the best thing that had happened to him all day, as perhaps it was.

'I have been worried about you,' Ribeiro declared, breathing heavily. 'It is a relief to see you looking so well.'

'I'm sorry to call you out of a meeting, Baltazar. If the matter had been less urgent . . .'

'Does this concern Herbert Norris?'

'You've heard about him?'

'Of course. I knew him. He was the British delegation's representative on the shipping committee. It is rumoured that he was implicated in Henry's murder. Is it true?'

'I'm afraid so, yes.' Max was aware he owed Ribeiro a fuller explanation of events than he currently had the energy or inclination to supply. 'I'd like to be able to tell you everything I've learnt, Baltazar, and I will, but I simply don't have the time at present. What I wanted to ask you now was whether my father ever mentioned to you someone called Farngold.'

'Farngold?'

'F-A-R-N-G-O-L-D.'

Ribeiro frowned, then shook his head. 'No. I do not think so. It is not a name I remember.'

'You remembered Lemmer.'

'Yes, I did. But not this name. It is important, yes?'

'Very.'

'So, it has not ended with Norris?'

Max shook his head. 'No. It hasn't.'

Max headed for the Mazarin because, for the moment at least, he could think of nowhere else to go.

He was barely aware of his surroundings as he approached the hotel and as a result nearly walked into the car door that opened across his path when he was only a few yards from the entrance.

Frank Carver glared out at him from the rear seat of the vehicle. 'I'd like a word with you, Mr Maxted,' he said grimly.

Max sighed. He felt tired and dispirited and in no mood to fend off questions from Carver. But it seemed he had no choice in the matter. 'I can't help you,' he said simply.

'Let me be the judge of that. Get in and we can talk while Joe drives us around town.'

'Must I?'

'I can't force you to. But I'll keep after you if you don't, getting grouchier all the time. So, why not do us both a favour and climb aboard?'

The drive was a circular tour of the 8th *arrondissement*. Their discussion had its circularities too. Carver was convinced Max knew more than he was willing to admit about Sir Henry's involvement with Lemmer's network of spies. He also blamed Max for Lemmer's possible acquisition of a document – the Contingencies Memorandum, obviously, though he never referred to it as such. And he suspected Max of working for or with Ireton in some unspecified capacity. Max made it as clear as he could that he had only ever acted in pursuit of the truth about his father's death. He was not responsible for all that had flowed from that.

'It's over, Carver. Tarn's dead. So's Norris. I've done as much as I can for my father. And there's nothing I can do for you.'

'Why'd you come back to Paris, then? Why are you still in contact with Ireton?'

'I'm not. I went to his office this morning to thank Morahan for saving the life of my friend, Sam Twentyman. And I came back to Paris to see Sam.'

'Bull. You're up to something. The French may have decided to close the book on this, but I can't afford to. There are too many unanswered questions.'

'I agree. But I don't have any of the answers to give you.'

'Why do I find that so hard to believe?'

'I don't know. Maybe you're too cynical for your own good.'

'If I learn you're holding out on me . . .'

'You won't, because I'm not.'

'No? Well, for as long as you stay in Paris, I'll assume you are. So don't think you've seen the last of me. I'll be watching you. Waiting for that false move I bet you'll make in the end.'

Silence fell between them. The car drove on slowly along the Champs-Elysées, approaching the Rond-Point for the second time. A few moments passed. Then Max said, 'Can I get out now?'

MAX SET OFF SOUTH ALONG AVENUE D'ANTIN. HE HAD only covered twenty yards or so when a car pulled in beside him. Fearing Carver had changed his mind and wanted to ask him some more questions, he put his head down and kept on walking.

'Max!'

It was not Carver's voice and not his aggressive tone either. Max turned round to find himself looking at the overcoated and smiling figure of Masataka Kuroda, standing by the stationary vehicle.

'Can I walk with you, Max? I was waiting for you at your hotel. We have been following you.' He nodded to the car. 'Did you enjoy your tour with Mr Carver?'

'Hardly.' Max returned Kuroda's smile and shook his hand. 'It's good to see you, Masataka.'

'You also, Max. Shall we walk?'

'Yes. Let's.'

Kuroda said something to his driver in Japanese and the car started away. He and Max fell in together and carried on along the avenue.

'I assume Yamanaka told you I was looking for you earlier.'

'He did. And that you had something you wanted to be translated.'

'He did the honours.'

'Farngold.'

'That's right. Does the name mean anything to you?'

'I cannot say it does. May I see . . . the piece of paper?'

'Certainly.' Max took the scrap of wallpaper from his pocket and unfolded it for Kuroda to look at.

Kuroda squinted at the writing for a few seconds. 'Strange,' he said. 'Very strange. May I ask where it came from?'

'My flat in London.'

'Ah. Where you killed Tarn?'

'You know about that?'

'Of course. His death is a blow to those in my government who hoped he would eliminate Lemmer. It has caused consternation. They hired the finest archer, only for an arrow to sprout from his chest.'

'I was lucky, Masataka, that's all.'

'All? You should not speak so lightly of luck, Max. I am more glad than I can say that you survived. I expected to hear of *your* death, not Tarn's. Luck is a gift from the gods. You should be grateful for it.'

'I am, believe me.'

'It gives you a chance to extricate yourself from the intrigues surrounding Lemmer. Those who authorized the hiring of Tarn are shamed by his failure. Those opposed to such extreme action are therefore in the ascendant. While they remain so, you would do well to leave the fray.'

'But what if there's more to be discovered?'

'About Farngold, for instance?'

'Exactly.'

'Who wrote the name?'

'I didn't see it done.'

'Was it le Singe?'

'It seems unlikely he'd know how to write anything in Japanese.'

'Unlikely, but not impossible. There is a rumour that he has been employed to enter hotels and offices used by various delegations in order to examine documents and memorize their contents. It seems he may have what is called a photographic memory. It is even possible that the burglaries he is supposed to have committed were intended to distract attention from the real purpose of his activities. If this is true, he may be capable of reproducing a word he had seen written in Japanese without understanding what it means.'

'Who's rumoured to be his employer, Masataka?'

'No one knows. But you and I could hazard a guess.'

'Lemmer.'

'It may be so. Ultimately, that is. Presumably, Lemmer would have engaged his services through intermediaries. Tarn must have known what le Singe was doing, remember, but it did not help him find Lemmer. One may see the strings on the puppet, while the hand pulling the strings remains invisible.'

'Still, it's surely no coincidence that the word was written in the language of the country where Lemmer and my father first met.'

'You think Farngold – whoever or whatever it is – connects Henry with Lemmer?'

'I think it may.'

'And how will you find out if it does or not?'

505

'I don't know yet.'

'Maybe you will never know.'

'Maybe I won't.'

'Then consider well the wisdom of abandoning your search. You are young. Life lies before you, with all its pleasures and fulfilments. You deserve to enjoy it. Why not allow yourself to do so?'

'Because I don't like giving up before I have to.'

'No.' Kuroda patted Max on the arm, almost paternally, as if imparting some resigned reflection on Sir Henry's behalf. 'And you will not give up, of course.'

They parted at the Pont des Invalides, where Kuroda crossed the river, heading for the Quai d'Orsay. Max watched him go, a tall, thin, courtly figure, moving at his own pace though the Parisian afternoon. His advice was sound. Max had accomplished more than could reasonably have been expected of him. He had defied the odds. He had won.

But he had no sense of victory. Nadia had escaped. Lemmer was unscathed. And le Singe's message still pointed to an untold truth. He could not simply walk away.

No one was lying in wait at the Mazarin this time. But still the reception clerk had a surprise for him. 'There is a parcel for you, Monsieur Maxted.' He lifted it out from beneath the desk.

It was about the size of a shoe box, wrapped in brown paper and fastened with string. Max's name was written on it in large capitals. There was no address. It had not come through the post.

'When was this delivered?'

'A couple of hours ago, *monsieur*.'

'Who by?'

'He did not give his name. He said you would be expecting it.'

' "Expecting it". He said that?'

'*Oui, monsieur*.'

'What did he look like?'

'Er . . . *quelconque*; ordinary. He was . . . well-dressed. Not young. Grey-haired, with a beard. And glasses. He spoke quietly. You know him?'

THE PARCEL HELD MONEY: LOTS OF IT. THE BUNDLES OF banknotes spilt out on to the bed in Max's room at the Mazarin and he gazed at the heap in astonishment. It amounted to thousands of pounds, as far as he could tell, though there were more US dollars and French francs than sterling. Lemmer had told the reception clerk Max would be expecting to receive it. But he had not been, of course. He had not foreseen this, not remotely.

His first thought was that it was a crude bribe. Then it came to him. It belonged to his father. It was Sir Henry's stockpile of money from the safe-deposit box at the Banque Ornal – and now, with bizarre appropriateness, delivered to his executor. The gesture was pure Lemmer. He had not wanted the money. He had wanted the documents the box held. Now he had them, Max was welcome to the cash.

There was no explanatory note. Max sifted through the bundles in search of one, though he felt sure he would search in vain. Lemmer trusted him to understand the message. The money had been wrapped in a sheet of newspaper: Max pulled it free from beneath the bundles and cast it aside.

As he did so, he noticed that someone had ringed in bright-red ink an advertisement on what was the back page of the previous Sunday's edition of *Le Petit Journal*.

MALADIES INTIMES. Guérison rapide peu
coûteuse.
Consultations gratuites par docteurs-
spécialistes.
Discrétion absolue. Pharmacie Claverie,
24 Boulevard de Sébastopol, Paris.

The phrase *Discrétion absolue* had been underlined in red as well. It might mean nothing. A sheet of newspaper was a sheet of newspaper, a marked advertisement nothing out of the ordinary. But did anything really mean nothing in the world of Fritz Lemmer? Max doubted it. He doubted it very much.

He locked the money in his suitcase and headed out.

There was no queue at the counter of the Pharmacie Claverie. A mild-mannered man in a white coat faced Max across it with a smile that contrived to be both welcoming and discreet. *'Bonjour, monsieur. Vous desirez?'*

'Bonjour. I, er . . . *Je m'appelle Maxted.* James Maxted.'

'Ah, Monsieur Maxted.' The pharmacist seemed to know the name. *'Attendez un moment.'* He bustled off into a room behind him, reappearing a few seconds later with a small dark-brown bottle in his hand. *'Votre ordonnance.'* He passed it to Max with a broadening of his smile.

'C'est . . . pour moi?'

'Oui, monsieur.'

'*Mais . . .*'

'*C'est tout, monsieur.*' The pharmacist nodded emphatically, not to say dismissively. '*Merci beaucoup.*'

Max did not examine the bottle until he was outside, though it felt suspiciously light. Sure enough, there were no pills inside, just a plug of cotton wool and, beneath it, a tightly folded piece of paper.

It was a page torn from a railway timetable, showing services from Paris to Melun, a place he had never heard of, via numerous other places he had never heard of. The column listing the timings for one of the services – the 11.35 departure from the Gare de Lyon – had been outlined in red.

As Max set off back along the quai towards his hotel in Paris, pondering how to respond to what he did not doubt was an invitation from Lemmer, a very different kind of invitation was being considered by his mother in the drawing-room at Gresscombe Place in Surrey.

'Would you care to explain why you told us nothing about this, Mother?' Ashley asked snappishly.

'Ashley is head of the family now,' put in Lydia, quite unnecessarily, since Lady Maxted was well aware of his status.

'I'm bound to ask *when* you intended to inform us,' Ashley continued. 'But for the letter I had from Fradgley telling me the French police had changed their minds about how Pa met his death and my subsequent telephone conversation with Mellish, we might still be in ignorance of these appalling events. We were horrified to learn that James had actually killed a man –

in the London flat, of all places. Such shocks aren't good for Lydia in her present condition.'

'Have you been to the flat?' asked Lydia. 'What state is it in?'

'Is it your unborn child you're concerned about?' Lady Maxted responded. 'Or the redecoration bill?'

'What we're concerned about, Mother,' said Ashley, with heavy deliberation, 'is limiting the damage to our family's reputation that James may have caused by involving himself in such . . . mayhem.'

'He killed an intruder in self-defence. And the French police are evidently satisfied, based on what Mr Fradgley has written to you, that the intruder in question murdered Henry. I'm bound to say that we should all be grateful to James for what he has achieved. Don't forget he also saved Mr Brigham's life.'

'But to shoot a man through the head,' gasped Lydia. 'It's . . . too awful for words.'

'Then spare yourself the distress of finding any words, my dear. Many men shot other men through the head in the war. We regard them as heroes and rightly so. James has done what he swore to do. I for one am proud of him.'

'I still don't understand why you didn't tell me what had happened as soon as you heard of it from Mellish,' Ashley complained.

'I knew how you would react. It was an emergency. I needed a calm atmosphere in which to address the matter.'

'Calm atmosphere? What the—'

'And I had George to advise me.'

'This isn't good enough, Mother,' Ashley declared, in

something close to a shout, adding a slap of his hand on the arm of his chair for emphasis. 'It really isn't.'

'Where is James now?' Lydia demanded.

'He's gone back to Paris.'

'Why?'

'He said there were some loose ends he wanted to tie up.'

'Loose ends?' spluttered Ashley. 'Hasn't he caused enough trouble?'

'He seems to think not.'

'Good God Almighty. He's insufferable, completely insufferable.'

'Did he say anything about the executorship before he left?' asked Lydia.

'The executorship?' Lady Maxted affected a vagueness of tone calculated to rile her daughter-in-law.

'Yes. The executorship.'

Lady Maxted paused theatrically, then said, 'As a matter of fact . . . I don't believe we spoke of it.'

'More money than either of us has ever seen before,' said Max a few hours later, opening the suitcase in his room at the Mazarin to show Sam Sir Henry's hoard of cash.

Sam whistled in disbelief. 'And more than I'll ever see again. That's for sure.'

'Lemmer certainly has his own way of doing things.'

'I'm sorry to hear that, sir.'

'Why?'

'It means you'll go after him. Just like you always went after the Boche pilots who had the biggest reputations. It's in your blood.'

'If I go after him, it'll be to learn the truth – the whole truth – about my father.'

'Understood, sir. Still, it's a pity.'

'What is?'

'The flying school. I'm sure we could have made a success of it.'

Max smiled. 'We still can. You're wrong about never seeing this much money again, Sam. Legally, it belongs to my brother, but he can go hang. I intend to salt it away so that you and I can start that flying school eventually. Ashley's never going to give us those fields at Gresscombe, so we'll need to buy land as well as planes when the time comes.'

'Are you sure that's a good idea, sir? I mean—'

'As I recall, we were both sure it was a good idea when we talked it over at the Rose and Crown. You haven't changed your mind, have you?'

Sam looked aghast. 'Changed my mind? 'Course not. But . . . all this money. I, er . . .'

'Let me worry about the money.' Max clapped Sam on the shoulder. 'I can't predict how long it's going to take me to do what I have to do, Sam. The question is: are you willing to wait? You could always look for another partner.'

'You're joking, aren't you, sir?' Sam grinned. 'I'll never find anyone else I'd want to go into business with who'd actually be willing to go into business with me.'

'Rubbish.'

'It's the truth, sir. So, like my girl said to me before I went off to war: "I'll wait for you." But unlike her, I mean it. Anyway, I've got a job until this conference ends, haven't I? The way they're going, I reckon they could still be here come Christmas. And Paris is definitely one up on Walthamstow. The way I see it, I'm sitting pretty.'

'Good man.' Spontaneously they shook hands, confirming the renewal of their bargain. 'I doubt you'll see much of me for quite a while after tonight, Sam. You appreciate that, don't you?'

'I do, sir.' Sam knew better than to ask any questions about Max's pursuit of Lemmer. And Max liked him all the more because of it. 'You'll take care, won't you?'

'Of course. When did I ever not?'

'You don't want me to answer that, do you, sir?'

'Absolutely not. Now, to more serious matters.' Max pulled several notes out of a bundle of French francs and slipped them into his pocket, then closed the suitcase and locked it. 'It's time to go and get roaring drunk, I think, don't you?'

APPLEBY WAS SLEEPILY AWARE OF HIS TRAIN'S ARRIVAL AT THE Gare du Nord early the following morning, but he intended to doze on for an hour or so before emerging into the Parisian dawn. He distinctly recalled telling the steward so and was therefore none too pleased to be roused by a persistent knocking at the door of his cabin. 'Go away,' he bellowed. *'Va-t'en!'* But it did no good. Eventually, he hauled himself out of his bunk and opened the door.

'Good morning, Appleby,' said Max, beaming in at him. His voice may have been gravelly, but his chin had the smoothness of one who had already bathed and shaved. 'Can I buy you breakfast?'

They adjourned to the station café. Neither, it transpired, had much of an appetite. Coffee and his pipe satisfied Appleby's needs. It was coffee for Max too, supplemented by brandy. 'Hair of the dog,' he explained, without elaboration.

'Are you leaving Paris already?' Appleby asked, nodding to the suitcase Max was carrying with him.

'Maybe. I don't actually know.'

'It's too early for riddles.'

'I'll keep it plain and simple, then. How did your meeting at HQ go?'

'Not well, thanks to your exploits. My ears are still ringing from the reprimand.'

'Sorry about that.'

Appleby grunted. 'It can't be helped.'

'Ah, but perhaps it can. I have a proposition for you.'

Appleby's gaze narrowed. 'Go on.'

'Lemmer wants me to work for him.'

'*What?*'

'He came to see me while I was laid up at the Hôtel Dieu. Turned up at my bedside in the middle of the night, masquerading as a doctor.'

'Are you joking, Max?'

'No. I didn't tell anyone about it at the time because I didn't think they'd believe me. But it was him. Softly spoken, mild-mannered man. Beard and glasses. Professorial air.'

Appleby nodded slowly in amazement. 'So they say.'

'He offered me exciting and lucrative employment.'

'As a spy?'

'Something in that line. He said I'd enjoy the work.'

'And what did you say?'

'I told him to go to hell.'

'So I should hope.'

'But now . . .'

'Yes?'

'He's contacted me again since I came back to Paris. Indirectly. The offer's still open. You could even say he's made payment in advance. The suitcase contains the money he found in my father's safe-deposit box. Lemmer wanted the documents that were in it, of course, not the money. He's returned it to me as a gesture of good will. I was hoping you'd agree to bank it for me. In an account where it can be held for the duration.'

'The duration?' Appleby sat back in his chair and looked thoughtfully at Max. 'What have you got in mind?'

'There's something I haven't come to grips with yet that connects Lemmer with my father – some secret they shared, dating back to their days in Japan, I suspect. I mean to find out what it is. And I'm not going to stop until I do. Which is why I've decided to accept Lemmer's offer.'

'*Accept* his offer?'

'It's the only way I can get close enough to him to get to the heart of the mystery and maybe live to tell the tale. Don't you see, Appleby? Working for Lemmer gives me the protection I need. It gives me a chance. I have to take it.'

'All I can see is that Lemmer's an enemy of our country. And anyone who works for him is guilty of treason. Do you really want to tell me that's what you propose to engage in?'

'Of course not.' Max leant across the table and fixed Appleby with his gaze. It was vital there be no misunderstanding between them. 'I'm telling you because I can accomplish something else beyond teasing out the truth about my father. I can learn what Lemmer intends to do with his spy network now the war's over – what plans he has, what plots he's hatching. And I can learn who's in his network. This is your chance as well as mine, Appleby. I can be your man on the inside. I can bring him down for you.'

Appleby looked at Max fondly, almost sorrowfully. 'Have you any conception of how dangerous what you're suggesting would be? Lemmer's bound to be doubtful of your loyalty. He's going to require ample proof of it. And any evidence to the contrary – the faintest suggestion that you're feeding information to me – will be fatal for you. Literally fatal.'

'I'll have to tread carefully, then. And trust you to do the same.'

'You've obviously already made your mind up.'

'It's a unique opportunity, Appleby. You're not going to refuse to help me, are you?'

Appleby took a fretful chew on his pipe, then said, 'No. Of course I'm not. As a representative of the Secret Service, I should do everything in my power to encourage you. And, if it comes to it, I will. But as you and I sit here this morning, Max, I say this to you. Don't do it. One way or the other, it'll destroy you. Let your father's secrets rest with him. Walk away. While you still can.'

Max smiled softly and shook his head. 'But I can't, you see. That's the point. I *can't* walk away.'

Appleby sighed. 'Then be it on your own head.'

'So, you *will* help me?'

Another sigh. 'Yes. But what we're discussing is no job for an amateur. And that's what you are.'

'Teach me a few of your professional tricks, then.'

'I'd have to get approval from the top for an operation like this, Max. I couldn't discuss covert communication methods with you without authorization. And without some mastery of those methods you'd be sunk.'

'What are you talking about? Codes? Invisible ink?'

'That sort of thing, yes.'

'We used lemon juice at school.'

'It's no laughing matter.'

'I'm not laughing.' Max looked at his watch. 'You've got about five hours to turn me into a spy.'

'*Five hours?*'

'It's all I have, I'm afraid. Delaying my response would make Lemmer suspicious before I even started.'

'I couldn't get authorization in that time, let alone train you to any level of competence.'

'I'm a quick learner. And this is an emergency.'

'For God's sake, I've already had my knuckles rapped for letting you wreak havoc. Do you seriously expect me to go out on a limb for you again?'

'Lemmer's the target, Appleby. I'm just the arrow. How badly do you want him? How badly do your bosses want him? Playing it by the book won't work. This is our chance. Our only chance. Now. Today. What's it to be? Yes or no?'

A lengthy silence followed as they pondered each other's seriousness of purpose. Then Appleby groaned. 'Five hours, you say?'

'Yes.'

'Well, we'd better look lively, then, hadn't we?'

MAX STEPPED DOWN FROM THE TRAM IN FRONT OF THE Gare de Lyon, travelling bag in hand. He checked his watch by the station clock. It was twenty past eleven and he was neither early nor late. Warm spring sunshine fell hearteningly on his face as he walked unhurriedly towards the station entrance.

He paused in his progress by a post-box, where he took a letter out of his pocket and glanced at the name and address he had written on the envelope – *G. A. Mellish, Esq, Mellish & Co., 119a High Street, Epsom, Surrey, Angleterre* – before dropping it into the slot.

Max entered the station, made his way to the ticket office and bought a first-class single to Melun, then consulted the departures board to learn which platform his train was leaving from. Next he wandered across to a news-stand and bought a copy of *Le Figaro*. The Paris editions of several British and American newspapers were also available, but he had no wish to advertise his foreignness.

He strolled, with every appearance of casualness, to the platform where the train was waiting. It was not a popular service. There were few other passengers. He climbed aboard, glancing at his watch as he did so. In no more than a few minutes, the train would leave. He could disembark before then and walk back out of the station into the safe and secure normality of one version of the rest of his life. But he was not going to. His course was set.

He sat down. He had the compartment to himself, though, strangely, he felt as if he was being watched. He opened the newspaper, but crooked his wrist so that he could follow the ticking down of the minutes to 11.35.

11.35 came. And 11.35 went. So did 11.36. At 11.37, there was a shrill blast on a whistle and a general slamming of doors. Then, at the last moment, the door of his compartment was yanked open and a man jumped in, slamming it shut behind him. The train was already moving. Max was no longer alone.

The man was of about Max's age, lean, sallow-skinned and narrow-shouldered. He was wearing a raincoat, despite the mildness of the day, which he did not take off. He removed only his hat as he sat down, diagonally opposite Max. He had thinning, sandy-coloured hair and a pinched, raw-boned face. He was breathing heavily, presumably because he had had to run for the train, and the cigarette he immediately lit activated a phlegmy cough. He unfolded a newspaper and began reading it.

The train lumbered out of the station, past goods sidings and warehouses. Max settled back in his seat. All he could do now was wait upon events. Lemmer would show his hand when he wanted to and not before.

Perhaps he already had, in the form of Max's tardy fellow passenger. Perhaps not. Time would tell.

The train stopped at every station as it slowly lurched and wheezed its way out of the city and south through a succession of villages separated by flat, open countryside.

With the other occupant of the compartment buried in his paper, Max began to assume nothing would happen until he reached Melun. He relaxed and closed his eyes, wondering if he would be able to catch up on any of the sleep he had missed the night before. He had always been a ready catnapper.

'Excusez-moi, monsieur!'

How long Max had dozed – whether he had dozed at all, indeed – was unclear to him. His fellow passenger had tapped him on the knee with his newspaper and now, blinking across at him, Max saw that he had an unlit cigarette in his mouth and was waggling a match-box to demonstrate that it was empty.

'Pouvez-vous me donner du feu?'

Max delved in his jacket, produced a box of his own and obliged the fellow with a light.

'Merci, monsieur.' The man took a draw on the cigarette, coughed, then said, 'Next stop, Max.'

'What?'

'Next stop.'

The train was slowing, though only green fields were visible through the window. The man turned his newspaper in his hand so that Max could see the back page. He had seen it before. It was the previous Sunday's edition of *Le Petit Journal*.

'Discrétion absolue,' the man murmured.

The train slowed still further, the roof of a small station coming into view as it juddered to a halt. Max stood up, pulled his bag down from the luggage-rack and moved towards the door, only to discover that his companion had already opened it for him.

He stepped out on to the platform and looked back, thinking there might be some last signal or direction. But the man did not so much as glance at him as he slammed the door.

Max saw only one other passenger disembark – a middle-aged man wearing a tweed suit. The guard blew his whistle and the train cranked back into motion.

There were a couple of cottages next to the station. Otherwise it was surrounded by fields, though the roofs of the village it evidently served were visible in the distance. A lane marked by a line of poplars led away from the station towards them.

The noise of the train faded as Max followed the tweed-suited man along the platform to the ticket office. The man turned through a narrow gateway next to it into a small courtyard at the front of the station, lifted a bicycle out from behind a bush, attached clips to his trousers and climbed on to the machine, then pedalled slowly away along the lane, glancing back at Max as he went.

Max watched him go. Rural quietude descended. Only birdsong reached him on the gentle breeze. He lit a cigarette and smoked it through as he paced up and down, wondering if somehow this had all been a wild-goose chase.

Then he heard the thrumbling note of a car engine approaching along the lane from the direction of the village. He strode forward for a view of the vehicle.

It was a small Peugeot two-seater. And he recognized the driver.

The car pulled in beside him and stopped. 'Hello, Max,' said Nadia Bukayeva, gazing at him from beneath the brim of her fur-fringed hat. 'You are surprised to see me, yes?'

'Why are you here?'

'He sent me to collect you.'

It was futile to pretend he did not know who had sent her. But there was something he genuinely did not know. 'Why you?'

'To test you, I think. Maybe to test me also. I was shocked when he told me. Why are you coming over to us?'

Max had expected to be asked the question sooner or later. But he had not expected Nadia Bukayeva to be the one who asked it. He steeled himself. 'The offer was too good to refuse.'

'Of course. It always is. But remember: no one will trust you until you prove you can be trusted. That is how it is for all of us.'

'Did Norris trust you?'

'I did what I had to do. That is how it is also. But I am glad Sam did not die.'

Max looked her in the eye. 'You should be.'

'Because otherwise you would kill me, yes?'

Max did not reply, but went on looking at her. She did not flinch. And neither did he.

'Will you come with me now?'

'Where are we going?'

'To meet him. He is not far. He is waiting for you.'

'Very well.' Max tossed his bag into the dicky seat and climbed in beside her. 'Let's go.'

Nadia nodded, put the car into gear and started away.

As the car crossed the bridge over the railway line, a shadow detached itself from the larger shadow of the station canopy: a slightly built, dark-skinned young man, dressed in weather-stained army clothes. He briefly shaded his eyes to check the progress of the car, then he turned and moved swiftly along the platform towards the gate into the courtyard.

James 'Max' Maxted's story continues
in the second part of Robert Goddard's
THE WIDE WORLD trilogy in

THE CORNERS OF THE GLOBE

M AX COULD ONLY WISH HE HAD MADE THE CROSSING FROM Scotland in such weather: calm, cool and benign, the sea sparkling, the sky blue, with puffs of cloud herded at the horizon like well-behaved sheep. He stepped out of the Ayre Hotel into the peace of early morning, lit a cigarette and gazed around him.

The few locals already up and about would probably have identified him as a visitor even if they had not seen him leave the hotel. Tall, lean and youthfully hand-some, dressed in clothes that were just a little too well cut to have been bought from an Orcadian tailor, Max looked what he was: a man out of his element. Yet he also looked relaxed and self-assured: a man as unlikely to attract suspicion as he was condescension.

He turned towards the harbour and started walking. The staff of the Ayre had warned him that Kirkwall Bay did not normally appear as it did now: an anchorage for dozens of US minesweepers and support vessels, most of them stationary at this hour, but some with smoke drifting up from their funnels. They were there to clear the thousands of mines laid around the Orkneys during the war, a task expected to take them many months.

Max knew little of the sea war, sharing the general

prejudices of those who had engaged the enemy on the Western Front that the Royal Navy had had a cushy time of it, Jutland notwithstanding. His gale-tossed passage across the Pentland Firth had forced him to reconsider, however. He did not envy anyone who had spent the past four and more years in these waters.

Of all the places in the world where he had never expected to find himself, the Orkneys were high on the list. But he was aware that there were currently a good many people there who wished themselves elsewhere, doubtless including the crews of all those American minesweepers he could see strung out across the bay.

The same was certain to apply to the crews of the interned German High Seas Fleet, under Royal Naval guard in Scapa Flow. Until glancing at an atlas shortly before his journey north, Max had supposed Kirkwall overlooked the Flow and he would therefore have a good view from the city of the captive ships. But Kirkwall was on the northern side of Mainland, the Orkneys' principal island, albeit at its narrowest part. To the south, enclosed by Hoy, South Ronaldsay and various other smaller islands, lay the vast natural roadstead of Scapa Flow, where seventy-four German warships were corralled at anchor.

Max would see them soon enough, of course. He knew that. They were why he had travelled to Orkney. And they were why he was out so early.

But early or not, he was not proof against unlooked-for encounters. As he passed the Girnel, the old grainstore facing the west pier, he saw a woman he recognized approaching along the harbour front. It was too late to think of avoiding her. She smiled and raised a hand. He smiled too and waved back.

Susan Henty was clearly no local herself, a tall, big-boned young woman with a horsey look about her, dressed in newish tweeds. She had auburn hair and a broad, open smile. Max imagined her as an enthusiastic rider to hounds in the Leicestershire countryside she had already told him she hailed from. She was impossible to dislike, which was half the problem in itself. He could not afford to appear secretive. But neither could he afford to reveal much about himself, least of all the truth.

'An early riser too, I see, Max,' she said as they met.

'I thought I'd take the morning air.'

'Me too. I walked down to the cathedral. Rather a fine structure, actually.'

'Selwyn not up yet, then?'

'Probably still in bed, poring over a map. He's very excited about seeing the Ring of Brodgar. As you are, I trust.'

'Well, I . . .'

'Selwyn's so pleased you agreed to help him.' Most women looked up at Max. Susan Henty engaged him levelly eye to eye. She lowered her voice confidentially. 'I'm not sure he believes I'm completely reliable when it comes to surveying.'

'I'm not sure I'm completely reliable.'

'Perhaps not, but you're a man, which makes all the difference.' She smiled. 'This trip's doing Selwyn no end of good, Max. I'm more grateful than I can say for your willingness to indulge him. How's your driving, by the way?'

'My driving?'

'Yes. You know.' She mimed turning a steering-wheel.

'Ah, that. Not too hot, I'm afraid. A better pilot than a driver, to be honest.'

'Then I'll do it. One of the few blessings of the war is that it enabled women to take up things like driving without anyone disapproving. And I'm rather good behind the wheel, if I say so myself.'

'I'm sure you are.'

She affected a frown. 'Do I detect a note of sarcasm?'

'Not at all.'

'Mmm. I'll have to be on my guard with you. I can see that. Now the hotel's recommended a garage where we can hire a car. And it looks like a fine day for it. So, shall we leave around ten?'

'Suits me.'

'Good. See you later, then.'

Max tipped his hat and watched Susan Henty stride on her way, back towards the Ayre. He disliked misleading her. He disliked every aspect of the subterfuge he was obliged to practise. It was a damnable game to have to play.

He lit another cigarette and waited until Susan was out of sight. Then he walked smartly along the street fronting onto the harbour, past the Kirkwall Hotel – of altogether grander appearance than the Ayre – and out along the east pier.

It was considerably longer than the west pier, with an extension added on to the seaward curve where it enclosed the harbour. Max strolled past a warehouse and assorted stacks of cargo and on towards the far end, passing another building that sported a prominently stencilled sign: US NAVAL PERSONNEL ONLY. An American marine of considerable bulk was standing by the door. He stifled a yawn as he returned Max's 'Good morning'.

A US Navy cutter was moored on one side of the pier. Max headed for the other side, propped his foot on a bollard and tossed the butt of his cigarette into the sea as he gazed idly out towards the massed minesweepers. He glanced at this watch and checked the time. Yes. He was neither late nor early. All he had to do was wait.

And not for long.

'GOOD MORNING.'

The man was bulky and bearded, but had a sprightly look about him that owed more than a little to his mischievously twinkling eyes. He was dark-haired, thirtyish, dressed in a US Navy lieutenant's uniform. He was wearing a greatcoat, despite the mildness of the morning, and smoking a cigarette. His accent was indeterminately American. West coast or east or where in between was hard to gauge.

'Good morning,' Max said cautiously.

'I'd take you for an educated man.'

'That's gratifying.'

'And you're English, right?'

'Yes. I am.'

'Maybe you can settle an argument for me. Your prime minister before Lloyd George was Asquith?'

'He was.'

'And before him . . . Balfour?'

'No. Campbell-Bannerman.'

'Ah. I lose the argument, then . . . Max.'

Max nodded in acknowledgment that the preliminaries had been satisfactorily concluded. 'Fontana?'

'Lieutenant Grant Fontana, United States Navy. At your service.'

'What's your role here?'

'Liaison with the local merchant marine. Which is handy for you, considering I know a drifter skipper who likes to make a little money on the black market – including illicit bartering visits to the German ships in Scapa Flow.'

Max paused before responding. 'That does sound handy. Can he be trusted?'

'He can be trusted to do what he has to do to stay out of trouble. And I can land him in a whole load of trouble any time I like, as he well knows. But on the subject of trust . . .'

'Yes?'

'Who was that woman you were talking to?'

'Susan Henty. I met her and her brother on the ferry.'

'You met them?' Fontana suddenly seemed less friendly. 'You should have made it your business to meet no-one.'

'They're harmless.'

'So you say. What do they think you're doing here?'

'My brother was killed in the *Vanguard* disaster.'

'Remind me what disaster that was.'

'HMS *Vanguard* blew up while anchored in Scapa Flow on the night of 9 July 1917, with the loss of more than seven hundred souls. Probably caused by the spontaneous combustion of cordite in the magazine, though there were rumours of sabotage.'

'And one of those seven hundred was your "brother"?'

'Sub-Lieutenant David Hutton.'

'So, that makes you Max Hutton?'

'As far as the Hentys and everyone here's concerned, yes. I've come to see where it happened – to pay my respects.'

'Touching. Truly touching.' Fontana sucked a last drag out of his cigarette and flicked it away. 'Listen, I don't want to know what you're after on that German ship. I've done what the boss wanted me to do here: make it possible for you to get on board. It's not going to be easy, but Tom Wylie's the man to do it. I'll see him this evening and explain to him what's wanted and brief you on the plan straight after. Ok?'

'Ok.'

'Meet me in the back bar of the Albert at nine o'clock. Mounthoolie Lane. It's Saturday, so it'll be busy. And noisy. No-one will pay us any attention.'

'I'll be there.'

'Any questions?'

'Which ship will Wylie take me to?'

Fontana gave a mirthless little laugh. 'You'll find out when the time comes and not before. I mean to stick to the rules even if you don't. The boss doesn't like deviations.'

'But he isn't here, is he, to worry about how we get the job done?'

'Not here? Well, that depends on exactly what you mean by "here". I often feel he's looking over my shoulder watching what I do.'

'Do you feel that now?'

Fontana lit another cigarette and contemplated Max as he drew on it. 'You should feel that now. It'd be good for you. Stop you taking too many chances. This is your first big job for him, isn't it? If you want to live to do another, you need to be more careful. Guard your tongue and watch your back. That's my advice. I'll see you later.'

Fontana did not wait for a response. He turned and strode away across the pier towards the moored cutter. Max watched him from the corner of his eye as he started down a flight of steps to reach the craft.

The cutter got under way and headed out across the bay towards the minesweepers. Then Max began a slow, measured amble back along the pier.

THE FERRY FROM ABERDEEN TO KIRKWALL HAD TAKEN THE weather as it found it: foul but no fouler than was often the case, according to a member of the crew who seemed to think Max was in need of reassurance, callow Londoner straight off the sleeper from King's Cross that he obviously was. Fresh air was the only cure for sea-sickness Max knew, so he sat out the voyage on deck, with occasional descents to the saloon to warm himself by the stove.

He was striding back and forth by the rail, muffled up and clapping his arms together, when the ferry docked at Wick to pick up more passengers. That was when he caught his first sight of the Hentys. There was something in their attitude to one another, as well as a slight facial similarity, that told him they were brother and sister rather than husband and wife. And the sister's anxiety about her brother was also apparent, even as they hurried along the pontoon to board. She watched his every step with a worried frown, as if he might fall or stumble – or simply collapse.

The Hentys also shunned the salon and fell into conversation with Max as the only other passenger who preferred the open deck. Selwyn Henty, big-boned like his sister, but with thinning hair and an altogether less robust appearance, confessed at once that claustrophobia rather than sea-sickness was the problem in his case. 'I did some tunnelling in the war. Since then I don't seem to be able to tolerate sharing confined spaces with other people.'

The war had left other marks on Selwyn Henty: a gaze that never fixed itself on anything for longer than a few seconds and a tremor of the hands that the motion of the ship disguised until it came to lighting a cigarette or taking a nip from his hip-flask. He spoke with nervous rapidity as well, often jumbling his words.

Jumbled or not, however, his eloquence on the subject of ancient megaliths was undeniable. He was seeking to put the finishing touches to a theory he had devised – 'a mathematical solution', he termed it – concerning the prehistoric stone monuments of Britain. Those of northern Scotland were particularly illuminating, apparently. He and his sister had followed a fortnight in the Outer Hebrides – 'The Callanish circles must be seen to be appreciated, Mr Hutton' – with a tour of the stone rows of Caithness – 'Fascinating, quite fascinating' – and were now heading for the Ring of Brodgar on Orkney. 'You've heard of it, of course?'

Max had not. Nor did he gain any inkling of the nature of Selwyn's 'mathematical solution' from rapid-fire references to azimuths, extinction angles and the rate of decline of the obliquity of the ecliptic. Susan Henty gave him a few sympathetic grimaces during her brother's disquisition, to which she added an apologetic explanation when Selwyn descended to the heads.

'Selwyn's never told me much about his wartime

experiences, Mr Hutton, but they've taken their toll on him, as you can see. He wasn't always so intense. This research project is good for him, though. If he can see it through and publish his findings, I think he'll have been able to put some healing distance between himself and all the things that happened to him in France. Of course, he's lucky to be alive when so many of his comrades aren't, but his survival has come at a price.'

'At least he has you to help him through it,' said Max.

'I do what I can. And you? Is there anyone to help you through it?'

'Oh, the RFC was a breeze compared with the Army.'

'I don't believe that for a moment.'

'It was, I assure you. I'm ridiculously unscathed.'

The broad, confident smile Max gave Susan Henty then was much the same as the one he gave both her and Selwyn as they set out in the hired Humber from Kirkwall the following morning. He was a free agent until he met Fontana again that evening. There seemed no reason not to enjoy himself as best he could.

Susan, however, proposed that they take an indirect route to Brodgar along the southern coastal road, so they could have a view of Scapa Flow and the interned German fleet. Since this would also give them a view of the waters in which HMS *Vanguard* had been blown up in 1917, claiming the life of Sub-Lieutenant David Hutton among hundreds of others, Max was in no position to object.

He prepared himself to appear moved by a first sight of the place where his supposed brother had died and was dismayed, when the time came, by how shamelessly he performed the role.

The Flow itself was a bowl of blue sea, enclosed by the mountainous bulk of Hoy and a string of smaller, lower-lying islands. Dotted across it were the grey, recumbent warships of the German High Seas Fleet. They stopped to view the scene from the hill above Houton, where a nearly circular bay was ringed by the jetties, slipways, workshops and hangars of a seaplane base.

A seaplane was taking off as they arrived. Watching it, Max experienced a pang of nostalgia for the days when he had flown virtually daily. As it was, he had not heard the wind in the wires as he piloted a craft into the sky for two long years. Fortunately, Susan, looking round at him from the driver's seat, interpreted his doleful shake of the head as a sign of mourning for his late brother.

'Do you know where the *Vanguard* was when it happened, Max?' she asked.

'What?' His reactions snapped into gear. 'Oh yes. She was anchored off Flotta. There.' He pointed to what he judged was the correct island. 'It happened at night. There was no warning.'

'None.'

'You can be glad of that small mercy,' said Selwyn. 'At least your brother didn't know he was about to die.' Whether Susan sensed the same meaning as Max did in Selwyn's words – that he had felt certain he was about to die on numerous occasions – was hard to tell.

'There's that, yes,' Max acknowledged.

'Was his body recovered?'

'No.' It seemed safest to deny there was a grave to visit. 'But there's a memorial to all the victims at the Naval Cemetery on Hoy. I plan to go and see it.'

'A frightful thing,' said Susan. 'The death of so many – in an instant.'

'When did you hear of it?' asked Selwyn. 'You said you were a prisoner of war by then.'

'The camp commandant passed on the news. He added his condolences.'

'He did?'

'They were good about things like that.' Max recalled as much from the manner in which other prisoners had received such tidings. The tactics of misrepresentation were beginning to become instinctive, he realized.

'Perhaps you think we're being too hard on them now we've won.'

Max wondered for a moment if Selwyn was trying to pick an argument. If so, he would be disappointed. 'No, I don't. They started it.'

'Yes. And let's not forget it.'

'Well, perhaps we could forget it for the rest of the day,' Susan suggested, her voice tightening slightly.

Selwyn had little choice but to agree. 'You're right, of course. Pre-history awaits us. Drive on, sis.'

The Ring of Brodgar stood on a hill halfway along an isthmus of land separating Lochs Stenness and Harray. Only thirty-six of the original sixty stones remained, according to Selwyn, but he reckoned that was enough for his purposes. The site was breathtakingly lovely, with or without the monument. Spring flowers were scattered richly across the turf. The blue waters of the lochs mirrored the sky above. The air was cool and fragrant.

But Selwyn had no interest in the scenery. Ropes, ranging rods and a theodolite were unloaded and the survey work began. Max threw himself into the task, which consisted of measuring as precisely as they could the distances between the stones, their relative heights and the diameter of the circle they formed.

Or was it a circle? Selwyn revealed during a break back in the car for sandwiches and tea from a thermos that the ring might actually be an ellipse. 'The elliptical form lends itself more readily to the creation of Pythagorean triangles, you see,' he explained, though naturally Max did not see.

'The people who built this were familiar with Pythagoras?'

'No. They predate him. That's the wonder of it.'

'But what—'

'We'll know more when I analyse the data.'

With that Selwyn was off, theodolite under arm, striding back towards the stones.

'He doesn't have the patience to explain it properly,' sighed Susan. 'But it's all there in his head. And you've been such a sport. It goes much better with three.'

'What does he think this circle – or ellipse – was for?'

'Observation of the sun and moon for the determination of solstices and the prediction of eclipses. He's detected precise alignments for just those purposes at all the sites we've been to.'

'But building this in its original form must have been a massive undertaking. Think of the man-hours involved in quarrying and transporting the stones, let alone erecting them. It seems incredible.'

'A few thousand years from now it'll seem incredible men spent so much money killing each other on the Western Front for four years.'

Max smiled grimly. 'I don't think it'll take anything like as long as that.'

Susan sighed. 'No, it won't, will it? Now, we'd better report back for duty. Selwyn's beckoning rather petulantly.'

It took longer than Max had anticipated for the survey to be completed to Selwyn's exacting standards. It was late afternoon when they started back to Kirkwall. Half a mile or so along the road they passed four standing stones which Selwyn believed to be all that remained of another, smaller circle. He proposed to return the following day to survey it as best he could.

'We may be able to establish its relationship with Brodgar. Care to lend a hand, again, Max?'

'Do say you'll come,' Susan urged him.

But Max's availability hinged on what Fontana had arranged for him. He could not afford to make any promises. 'I'll let you know in the morning. I might wake up as stiff as a board after the hard labour you've put me to.' He had, in fact, already experienced several twinges from a month-old bullet-wound in his side, but he did not propose to mention it.

'That's the problem with you RFC johnnies,' said Selwyn. 'No stamina.'

Selwyn laughed as he spoke, for the first time Max could recall. Susan's surprised glance at her brother suggested she had not heard him laugh recently either. It seemed Max's company really was good for him. As to whether he would have the advantage of it much longer . . .

'We'll see about that,' Max said softly.

Read on . . .

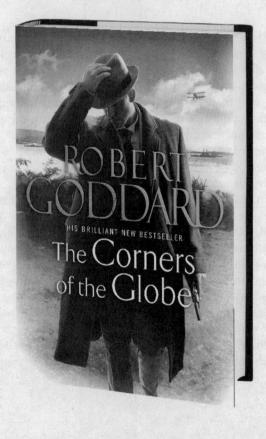

ROBERT
GODDARD

HIS BRILLIANT NEW BESTSELLER

The Corners
of the Globe